The Grand Adventures of

PERIMA

A HOUSE FAIRY

A TRUE STORY AS NARRATED TO
Daphne Charters

CONTENTS

PART III: SULIC AND I

EPILOG AND NOTES

FOREWORD
—— *By Michael Pilarski* ——

Dear Reader,

Fairies are apparently very patient. Perima's adventures have been waiting a long time to see the light of day.

We don't know the actual date that Daphne Charters transcribed Perima's stories but most likely it was 50 or 60 years ago.

Before Daphne passed in 1992, she wrote me that "I don't think the fairies had me write down all these stories for nothing. They are part of an overall plan". She asked me if I would be willing to get all her writings published. I said yes, and then proceeded to procrastinate. Not that I stopped working for the fairies, but I had a lot on my plate. In 2008 we had Volume I of Daphne's Charters Collected Manuscripts published as *Forty Years with the Fairies*. It contained the history of Daphne's work with the fairies and chronicled many amazing adventures and insights into the lives of nature fairies. Fast forward to 2024 and my good friend Douglas DeMers was inspired to take up the baton and get Volume II published. Perima is by far the longest story of Daphne's fairy works. In fact, it is an epic journey!

Let's be clear. Daphne did not write this. Daphne was so good at talking with, and listening to, fairies that she transcribed hundreds of stories that were told to her by the fairies as well as by a dozen or so discarnate humans and the Deva Marusis. Daphne was one of the top humans in the 20th century in terms of the depth of her relationships with fairies. She not only talked to them and listened to them with uncanny acuity, she worked with them and went on journeys and adventures with them in higher planes of being as well as lower planes. The stories range from experiences in what we might call hellish planes as well exalted realms of Love and Light. Perima's adventures touches on both.

Here is a story about Perima and Eileen Kilgren. Eileen Kilgren was the manager of Galway Traders in Seattle for well over twenty years. The Irish Import store had the best stock of Irish-made clothes, foods, literature and crafts in the Northwest. Eileen had deep Celtic roots and at one point started having relationships with fairies and other spirit beings.

Eileen's writings were the closest thing to Daphne' Charters writings that I have come across. The title and subtitle of her 2003 book was *"Tales from the Spirit Realm 2: Further adventures with devas and demons, fairies and faeries"*.

Eileen presented at several of our Fairy & Human Relations Congresses and we became friends. Being good at English grammar, we enlisted Eileen to help proofread *Perima: The Grand Adventures of a House Fairy*. After reading the material for a bit, Eileen decided to connect with Perima in whatever spirit realm Perima was now in. Eileen was successful in getting in touch with Perima and they became friends. I begged Eileen to have Perima dictate a new foreword for the book. Eileen agreed to do so, but never got around to it before Eileen left the physical realm in 2016.

I asked Eileen to give my apologies to Perima for taking so long to get her book out. Perima sent back a reply. "No worries, it will all happen at the right time, when it is supposed to happen."

But it just goes to show, if Eileen could connect with Perima, others can also. The veils between the realms are real but some can penetrate them. People physically alive on Earth can connect with discarnate humans, fairies and other realms of beings. We are all spirit-beings learning our capacities. Evolution to higher planes of being is one of the laws of this universe. Perima is a shining example.

Thank you Douglas DeMers for helping make this the right time.
Michael Pilarski
April 27, 2025

ACKNOWLEDGEMENTS

The body of Daphne Charters *Collected Manuscripts* works included three volumes. This is Volume II of Daphne Charters's work whose full title now has become *The Grand Adventures of Perima, a House Fairy – a True Story, as Narrated to Daphne Charters*.

Many beings contributed to bringing this volume from manuscript into print.

First and foremost is Perima, the fairy who narrated her life story to Daphne Charters.

And of course, a huge thank you to Daphne Charters.

Thanks to Daphne's devoted friends in England who typed up her handwritten notes and sent them on the United States: Philip Groom, David Nall-Cain and her niece Gay Burdett.

Our special appreciation goes to our good friend RJ Stewart who, in 2008, published Volume I as one of the first ventures of his new publishing house.

A big thank you to for OCR scanning from the typed manuscript into editable Word document and PDF files: Zite Hutton.

Thank you to Aera Spreckley for manuscript review to preserve British look and feel.

Thank you to the following people, who corrected the Word documents that had been OCR scanned: Douglas DeMers, Mahala Frye, Michael "Skeeter" Pilarski, Robin Rice, Sylvia Platt and Sandra Talt.

Thank you to Bob Paltrow for producing the amazing cover and more...

And finally a multi-colored thank you to all the fairies, devas and humans who assisted this multi-evolutionary project from behind the scenes.

How this book came about, and Notes to the Reader

—— By Douglas DeMers ——

There are to be three volumes published from Daphne Charters' collected fairy manuscripts – Volume I (*Forty Years with the Fairies*) went to press in 2008, and Volume II (this book!) and Volume III were soon to follow.

And so it goes.

Life happens; people get busy; life goes on, and fifteen years later – at the 2023 Fairy & Human Relations Congress, Skeeter asked for volunteers willing to find and correct scan-to-text errors from the original Volume II manuscript. Skeeter had divided up the 438 original manuscript pages into 8 sections of approximately 50-60 pages each. I had the time and interest to work on this, so I volunteered to work on the final section. Once I got the digital file, it still took me a couple months before I made the time to begin the process of comparing what I had on a paper copy with what the computer scan-to-text program had generated as an editable file. That work is tedious – shifting focus from paper to computer screen and back. But soon I was captivated and enthralled by Perima's story, and I finished my part, eager to see the whole work complete!

After a few months of nagging Skeeter about the progress of the Perima book, he finally acknowledged that Volume II (this book) kept taking a back seat to his numerous other projects, and he was asking for a volunteer to move the Perima book project along.

I immediately volunteered – taking on this labor of love.

I was able to track down the other folks who had volunteered to do the correcting. Some had done their sections, and I completed the remaining sections. A big "Thank you!" to Zite Hutton – who had done the scan-to-text and had digital copies of not only the .docx files, but the PDF files scanned from the original manuscripts. This made my subsequent correcting work so much easier! I could now have the .docx file I was editing on one half of my computer screen, and the corresponding PDF image of the original manuscript on the other side of the screen.

I learned a lot about Perima and her story; about fairies in general, and I marvel at the pearls of wisdom I have found in this book. There are many.

It is my hope that you will enjoy reading about Perima's life story up to the point she joined Daphne's band of fairies in England.

There are additional stories about Perima in Volume I (*Forty Years with the Fairies*) if the reader desires additional information.

Note to the Reader:

Although Daphne had learned how to communicate with fairies and other unseen beings, it is important to keep in mind that any kind of translation from multi-dimensional beings and images to words passed through Daphne – a human translator from England in the late 1940s through the late 1980s. As with all such translations or channeling, it is best that one approach this material with curiosity and an open mind, and embrace that which feels right to the reader, and set aside that which does not.

My intention was to keep this book true to the original manuscripts that Skeeter received from Daphne's friends in England after Daphne's passing.

Note to the Parents:

This unabridged story does have some content less suitable for young audiences.

British Spelling vs. American Spelling

Some words have a different spelling in British English than in American English. We have kept the British spelling.

Some words include 'ou' instead of 'o', such as clamour, colour, endeavour, glamour, honour, labour, moulded, neighbour, saviour, savour, and splendour.

Some words use 're' instead of 'er', such as centre.

Some words use double letters where in the US we would only use one, such as marvelled, travelling, and modeling. Conversely some words use single letters where in the US we would use two, such as fulfilment.

Some words use 's' instead of 'z', such as exercise, harmonise, neutralise, organise and recognise.

For a complete rundown on the differences between British and American spelling, wikipedia.org has a nice writeup on the subject.

Also, the frequent use of Capital Letters was common in Daphne's era, although Daphne often used Capital Letters to give emphasis and to denote respect or even reverence.

—— PART I ——
MY YOUTHFUL YEARS

CHAPTER 1
MY CHILDHOOD HOME

My story begins many hundreds of moons ago when, as a young fairy, I lived with my guardian. He was both loving and wise, and as my consciousness expanded he revealed as much of his knowledge as I could at that time understand. He taught me to converse with trees and the more mature flowers; indeed every plant in our garden received a personal greeting each day, and in return they bloomed with a beauty unusual even in the happy land where we lived.

The Lord of the Weather heard our invocations for warmth and moisture, and the fairies and lesser nature spirits who gave power to the plants to aid their growth, thrived under his love and gentle care.

Sheer joy of living possessed me as I watched the clouds being chased by the angels across the sky. Sometimes they sped Earthward and gathered me in their arms before resuming their work once more. Together we explored the air currents; how beautiful they were, their delicate colours interlacing with one another, some to blend, others to retain their individuality while forming intricate patterns through which the wind whirled in playful abandon, singing whistling or wailing when a dead-end was reached and it could proceed no further.

Floating down these paths was always an adventure, for I never knew who or what I might meet on the way. Carefree butterflies, their wings scattering the tinted air, dived and soared in joyous play. Seeds with Nature's parachutes rode the breeze purposefully as though they knew where they were going – and perhaps they did.

Tiny air atoms were there in their millions; so small that I could not see them until the angels loaned me their expansive vision enabling me to discern their diminutive faces, perfectly formed with the sweetest expressions. I tried to talk to these bodiless faces but they did not answer, being totally absorbed in their constant movement within the currents of air which composed their world.

We were a large family for our guardian loved all young things and each of us was given an animal to cherish. I had always loved birds and one day three small golden balls were presented to me. They were so tiny that I was almost afraid to touch them but soon they became my greatest delight; three treasures which gave me countless hours of happiness until the day came when, having reached maturity, they flew away. My tears fell but my guardian bade me weep no more.

"That is Life, little one," he said. "Young creatures are given into our keeping for a short while and then, like your birds, they become aware of the Vital Spark within them; then they leave those who have loved them in order to experience Life's woes as well as its joys. One day you too will fly away."

"Never," I sobbed as I wept afresh at so sad a thought.

"But yes, little one. You have work to do and when you are ready, you will accept your destiny, or all I have taught you will be of no value."

"But I will come back."

"And so will your little birds. They will not forget your love; indeed they will need it for a while longer, but the time will come when being with their own kind will be sufficient to sustain them during their sojourn on this plane."

My guardian's words were true and within an hour a golden streak flashed across the garden and alighted on my shoulder. The birds returned separately or together at gradually lengthening intervals, and then they came no more; but by that time I was more used to their absence, although their presence never ceased to give me joy.

A week passed and then two, and my heart became heavy; for to lose loved ones is always sad. Then my guardian called me to him and I saw on the ground at his feet three more fluffy balls, this time as green as emeralds, and once more my heart beat with happiness for the diminutive lives placed in my care.

The green birds grew and flew away too; but always there were others, of sapphire blue, violet or of brilliant pink, each more scintillating than the last or so they seemed to me; but perhaps my own growth gave them added beauty in my eyes. Birds became a symbol of life to me and they taught me many lessons.

I loved them and in return they saluted me with sweet songs, but after a while their needs changed and their desire for experience became more urgent than security and I was forsaken, each separation bringing its sadness; yet I was consoled by the knowledge that I had played a vital part in preparing and launching a fragment of life into a new phase of the Eternal Cycle.

This happens to all of us and as my guardian had warned me, this necessity for change overcame me too. At the equivalent of about sixteen years of age in a human being, a fresh trio of birds arrived. Stroking their soft heads and feeling their little beaks nibble my fingers drove away the pain of all the previous flights into the unknown. My guardian was watching me intently. As I looked at him, a tear trickled down my cheek. "When these three make their final flight, I must leave you," I said.

His expression saddened. "I have waited for these words with each new gift of birds for the past year."

"Why cannot I be content with so much happiness?"

"You are more evolved than birds. If it is not enough for them, why should it satisfy you?"

"My indecision has waxed and waned for many moons."

"I know for I have watched you with an aching heart, but I have held the silence, for when decisions are in the making, a single word can change the course of Destiny: you might have listened to my voice instead of that of The One."

"I did not hear Him speak; I was not listening for Him. It was a little voice within. I argued with it but it gave me no peace."

"Have I not told you, child, that He dwells within each of us. It was He who spoke even if you failed to recognise Him."

"I only know that I must leave you, and yet to face the outside world fills me with fear."

"It is exciting too: the great adventure for which your many years here have been preparing you. You are young but you have learned self-control and compassion for those weaker than yourself. Armed with these qualities you will succeed where others with greater courage and intellectual ability may fail.

"And remember, although our lives may now take different paths, all roads eventually meet; and where there is love between two entities, they can, in truth, never be parted."

I watched the little birds grow with increasing sadness and as they began their flights beyond the garden, I waited anxiously for their return. The time came when no flash of gold skimmed the lawn and I knew the hour of parting had come.

Feeling like stone I embraced my guardian for the last time and controlling my tears I began my journey, the garden and fields gradually fading behind me. I wandered aimlessly in my misery for a long time but eventually my youth and the need for replenishment forced me to will myself to my destination which was a Centre of Culture a hundred miles away.

CHAPTER 2
THE CENTRE OF CULTURE

My new life proved to be as different from the old as though I were living on another planet. Fairies, like humans, are not always kind, and my lack of ability to understand the teachers' thought-forms often earned me derisive laughter from my fellow students.

I was used to teasing, as any member of a family must be, but mockery and contempt for my efforts were outside my experience; and only my will prevented tears from flowing until alone in my little room I gave vent to my disillusionment and despair.

My guardian's teaching had been of the Ancient Wisdom rather than of hard facts pertaining to life in the outside world, and he had not warned me of the frailty of the potential Goodness inherent in each and everyone. He had instilled in me its capacity for growth and the limitless heights attainable through it, but I now realized that this quality in many is so outweighed by conceit, desire for applause or malicious humour that at times I found it difficult to believe in its existence at all.

If many mocked, the gentler students pitied my ignorance of the world they knew much better than I did, and through them I learned how to shield myself from the ill-will of others, firstly by mentally surrounding myself with a protective circle so their derision could not reach me. Secondly, I offered to help them in the subjects in which my knowledge was greater than theirs because of my guardian's tuition; these included religio-philosophy, music and painting.

* * *

As time passed, the absorption of all the teaching came more easily to me, until few continued to mock because I knew more than they, and eventually those who jeered were far outnumbered by others ready and willing to defend me.

About this time I came to the conclusion that my studies should now be concentrated on the subjects that one day I hoped to teach. Music and painting were a great joy to me but I was not prepared to give my life to either.

Living within a comparatively enclosed community taught me that, although still inexperienced, I was already able to help others. This is a talent which not everyone acquires early in life, and many there had not been blessed with a wise and loving guardian as I had, and therefore they found it difficult to develop love for their fellow students. I noticed too that often the most intellectually advanced were deeply defective in tolerance of the shortcomings of others.

My guardian's teaching of the Ancient Wisdom and the manners accompanying it proved of greater value to me than the figures and symbols well known to the other students. It is true that my deep obeisance to the teachers caused laughter at first because a slight nod was all that was required of the pupils, but when I received not only a bow in return but courteous consideration for my lack of worldly knowledge, some followed my example and also enjoyed increased attention and assistance.

I continued my studies in the arts and religio-philosophy but I realized that my outlook must now be broadened as well as my mind. In order to become more physically observant, I took courses in botany and mineralogy, and branching out from these I learned to heal with the essences of plants and through the elements and compounds of Earth, Water, Air and Fire. Delight grew with knowledge as the miracles of Nature were revealed to me, but where others saw in a dissected flower only its component parts, my extra-vision showed me more. At first a glowing aura became apparent round each tiny seed within the pod; later its colour told me whether a potential plant was strong and happy or sickly and sad, whether it would reach maturity, die before it attained flower-hood or fail to grow at all.

When I told my teacher what I saw and felt, he called me a dreamer, so, unable to share my newfound knowledge with others, I cherished it as a treasured secret within me.

Although I knew that auras are not composed of the same substance as thought-forms, in order to reassure myself, I decided to put my powers to a practical test. Choosing six seeds, I examined them with my extra-vision and found that two were already dead, although with normal sight they looked in every way the same as the others. Of the remaining four, one was weak but had sufficient light to enable it to push its way above the ground and unfurl a leaf or two, and three were strong enough to bring forth flower and fruit.

Preparing some soil, I mixed it well so that the six seeds should enjoy an identical chance of growth. Tenderly I planted them and placed markers of different colours beside them. The days passed and at last a tiny shoot appeared and then two more. Later the weak one pushed its way into the sun but although I continued to watch for the other two, they failed to grow. My excitement mounted as the three proudly unfurled their leaves before me but when they burst into sweet-scented flower, the fourth which had but a single leaf, withered and sank to the ground. I then began a further series of experiments, followed by others and each time my extra-vision was correct.

Armed with the immaculately kept data of my findings, I bowed low before my teacher and requested that he would do me the honour of perusing my records. This time he smiled and embraced me.

"I merely wished to make certain of your ability," he said. "Many desire the extra-vision but they are deluded into thinking that they have it when they are but making thought-forms of what they wish to see. You have proved your sensitivity to my satisfaction, and now we will perform further experiments before the rest of the class."

My heart was aglow with contentment but I merely bowed and retired to my room where I laughed joyfully with the flowers which had proved my talent.

✑ CHAPTER 3 ✑
A NEW FAMILY

During this early part of my life I learned the important truth that any knowledge received from an outside source must be submitted to my own tests, otherwise I found myself in a static state, content with the knowledge itself instead of seeking to understand both it and its purpose.

In other words facts are of little value unless they are put to their proper use and prove advantageous not only to the recipient but to his environment and those around him. This is an ideal which I still endeavour to put into practice.

When my awareness reached a point when I was ready to impart my knowledge to others, employment was found for me with a family which was desirous of furthering their education.

How happy was my life there, for a great love dwelt in the mansion, embracing not only its occupants but every fairy who lived on the estate. All forms of life thrived, from the smallest flower to the great trees which whispered to one another through the years, and from the tiny lap dog to Lunus, the leader of the group.

He had earned his beautiful home through hard work on the Earth plane where he had been in charge of a large territory of cherry trees; and now he desired to occupy his leisure period in the tranquil astral conditions by developing his own mind and those of the fairies who dwelt in his house.

His companion with whom he had worked and lived during part of his Earth span, was not as adaptable as he was and it was not easy for me to persuade her to develop her mental capacity instead of giving all her time and energy to the plants in the garden.

"Of myself, I am nothing," she said. "I am only what I do." It is praiseworthy to be self-effacing but the task entrusted to me was to impart the knowledge that, in developing oneself, one has more to give to others.

One day I was with her in the garden; a young flower was wilting and she was trying to revive it by giving it power.

"The flower is dying," I told her gently.

"It will survive if I imbue it with the will to live."

"The Soul-particle has already left its body."

"It is limp, but I have revived others as weak as this one."

"You might have saved it had you read its aura earlier."

She hesitated and I knew that she wished to chastise me for arguing with one with Earth experience, but her good manners prevented her.

The flower withered and re-entered the ground, but a few days later I found her giving power to another which looked equally dejected.

"It grows stronger every second." I smiled at her.

"It is as limp as the other," she said sadly.

"But its Life-particle is still within the body." This flower recovered and she asked me to explain to her the difference between the two.

"This one has descended to this plane many times and the other but a few. Nothing you did would have saved the first. It had not the will to live."

"Then it is not I that give them this will?"

"Your will enhances that of the plant. When the will to live dies, yours cannot replace it."

"It is strange that one so young should know so much. I have had the experience of eighty years on Earth and yet I did not know this truth, for I recognise it as such now."

"Dear lady," I said bowing low, "I am young in experience but mature in mind. My life has been spent in acquiring knowledge yet to be put to the test."

"And I have experience but little education. Perhaps we could teach each other."

"No happier prospect could come my way," I told her, "for to give is essential and to receive a joy, but when they are reciprocal, results are assured."

❁   ❁   ❁

And so, in order to help me, my lady mentally returned to the Earth of faded memory and brought it to the surface of her mind. She recalled a hurricane which ravaged the orchard and left her group with the ruin of many years' work. Another time locusts came, leaving nothing but gaunt phantoms which raised their naked arms in protest to the crackling sky.

Tears and toil had been her lot through drought and flood, but happiness too had been briefly hers when for ten years her life had been sweetened by three young ones who were placed in her care. Yet misery followed when, despite her constant striving, they died before their span had barely begun: six years for one, four for the second and the third faded away at eight.

"I did my utmost but I could not save them." She wept at the memory.

"And where are they now?"

She brightened as she replied, "They have done well and visit us when they are able."

"You gave them love and in reality they thrived even if you could not keep them. Their Earth bodies failed but they themselves were evolving because of your loving care."

Once she had started, her memory was always able to pick up the thread of her life where we had left it; and so eventually I had all the details of her Earth span.

During the telling of her tale I encouraged her to paint the marauding locusts and the anguished trees, but when her story was complete I suggested that she should try to illustrate her reactions to her misfortunes.

Angry streaks of scarlet and purple were splashed across the background. A bulbous eye stabbed through with black barbs glaring from a corner, while great tears wove a pattern of contorted shapes in despairing colours.

I had never seen such tragedy depicted. It was crude and ugly but so had been her experience, yet it manifested power and a talent greater than my own.

"It is evil," she said appalled. "It must be destroyed."

"No. No. You must let me take it to an expert. There is something here that is not in me. It is greater than I am. You have a wonderful power of expression but it must be guided along the right channels for it could do much good, but if it is checked too firmly or unleashed without control, it could do ..... yes, evil."

The expert was impressed but agreed with me that the painter of such a picture must be harbouring a great bitterness which should be brought to the surface rather than repressed.

I therefore suggested a variety of subjects for her pictures, such as flood and drought interspersed with blossom time and harvest; but whatever the theme, all depicted a savage desire for revenge against Nature. An ugly dark mass was always present and one day I asked her to tell me what it portrayed.

"The One" she said belligerently.

"Oh no," I said, horrified. "That cannot be your idea of the Lord of Nature, of the Sun behind the sun."

"But it is. Evil, vile, destructive, arrogant, unheeding of the despair He causes."

"But He does not will destruction," I said. "He is Good. It is the forces of Evil unleashed for centuries on Earth, which gain temporary control of the Elements."

She sighed. "When I am here I understand that this is so, but when I am painting I relive that ghastly time when I was without The One I really know. You told me to paint my reactions to my misfortunes, and this is how I felt about Him"

"Could you not now recognise that your disasters were caused by the forces of Evil and correct your misconception of Him even in your memory?"

She gazed at the patch of writhing murk which dominated her latest painting, and above it there appeared a ray of light, placed there by her will. "In reality He must have been present, or nothing would have survived. He sought me out for I did not seek Him. He sent Lunus to help us to salvage the few trees that were left. He saved not only them but me. One day He bore me away to heaven itself, or so it seemed to me then – to this my garden, which thrives in the sun and the gentle rain, and comes to flower and fruit at the proper time. What more could a fairy wish?"

"To find the way to the real Heaven."

"This is my heaven," she said. "This and Lunus. I am filled with happiness. I want nothing else. Teach Lunus, but leave me to my simple toil; for to achieve growth instead of death and disease is all that my heart desires."

"If that is your wish, I will respect it," I said, "but others will succeed where I have failed for no-one can stand still. We must advance or regress."

All colour left her face. "Not back to Earth to the locusts, to my shrivelled body and distraught mind."

"Oh no," I said, "Forgive me. I did not mean to frighten you, but if you do not exercise your mind as you do your will and love for the plants, they will not bloom to perfection as they should."

"But they are beautiful now," she insisted, gazing round in a kind of rapture.

"But are they beautiful to Him?" I asked gently.

Her brow puckered in doubt. "You mean that they could be dimmed in His eyes because of my lack of culture?"

"Your will has helped the flowers to become what they are. They are part of you as you are part of them; they have been instrumental in making you a different person from the one you were during the greater part of your Earth span. You and your beloved flowers are indivisible. If you broaden your mind, your flowers will benefit."

"Then teach me so that the knowledge you give me may also become part of them in some mysterious way."

I bowed and retired feeling that I had won a worthwhile victory, for apathy in the presence of knowledge is as much the enemy as is ignorance.

❊ ❊ ❊

I stayed with them for ten years, during which time I both studied and taught, joined them in their meditations and carried out many experiments with seeds and plants. By this time both had reached the degree of knowledge which needs to be put to the test by the exchange of ideas with other people; and so they decided to move, together with their house and garden to a less remote part of the country where they could join in the life of a cultured community. My work was done and with sadness in our hearts we bade one another farewell.

CHAPTER 4
THE SEMINARY

I now became a member of a Seminary for Higher Learning in order to further my studies. Having earned the right to a small dwelling of my own, I acquired a charming apartment in a quiet region of the town and here, during long periods of solitary meditation I learned about myself: who "I" was, in Whom I had my Being, and from Whom I was never separated even when apparently alone. I could feel my will soar towards Him but always it stopped on the threshold of realisation not daring to proceed.

"Have no fear," my new Teacher-guide encouraged me.

"But what if I enter Him and never return?"

"That would be the most wonderful event that could happen to you or any being," he smiled, "but you will not gain this privilege for countless years until you are All-knowing and perfect."

"Is there no further advance than the threshold?" I asked.

"My dear young pupil, of course there is. There is no sudden act such as you fear. The entry is step by step; in fact you are ever drawing nearer to Him."

❊ ❊ ❊

Through life I have learned the truth of the Teacher's words. Some steps have been small, others a leap, but each has led to joy not fear. Now when I soar and know that I have reached the bounds of my present comprehension, I do not hold back for many brinks have shown me that each is a threshold to a new and greater understanding. Sometimes instead of rising, I find myself plunging into an abyss, but not for long for Those in Whose charge I am catch me and bear me upwards again to the Entity or place which will lead me to a further Truth.

We learn our lessons, not mainly through books or the spoken word as do human beings on Earth, but through becoming. At first we experience the reality of the facts we have learned at School. As an example we are told that mountains are made of rock and that some bear vegetation and contain certain minerals. Men on Earth must as a rule believe what others have discovered, for they have not the time or the money to prove for themselves the truth of statements made by explorers or scientists. But on the Astral Plane we are able to become a mountain, a tree or a river and to analyse its component parts and its state of progress through its present thoughts. The being we enter is known as the "host."

In order to become something or someone else, it is usually necessary for personal consciousness to be vacated; otherwise we do not become the mountain, tree or river as it really is, but the host plus a part of our own consciousness, thus falsifying the issue. First we must achieve such deep relaxation that we enter a vacuum of no thought, no self. The little that still remains of our personality is drained back into the pool of awareness that we use each day. Then, without mind or body, the "I" is placed into the host, blends with his "I" and so becomes it. When the lesson has been absorbed, we must be removed by waiting guardians, for we are quite content in our mountain, tree or river being and would not leave of our own accord.

I also learned how to merge with one or more people in a group and to explore the communal mind while keeping my own, the degree of blending and the number of those participating giving many variations.

It is not permitted to enter another's consciousness without that person's consent, or harm could be caused. On the Earth plane and below, this is sometimes perpetrated by demons or by those who have recently died and are ignorant of the uses of their new astral and etheric forms. They enter the aura of the incarnate person and so share his consciousness, bringing confusion or possibly a change of personality. The worst result can be madness.

To human Earth intelligence it would seem impossible to obtain permission from a mountain to enter and become it, but only part of its consciousness is manifesting on the Astral Plane. Its higher self is quite capable of rational thought of a limited nature and any mature mountain would gladly give permission for the entry of a more developed mind than its own, both for the experience and for the enhancement of its own mental powers. Sometimes if a highly evolved entity has shared its being he might, on vacating the mountain, leave a particle of his own mind for the benefit of his host as a token of gratitude.

This blending is of even greater importance in the higher spheres. On the Astral Plane it teaches us about the mountain, tree or river that we enter, but on more ethereal levels, it is partly for the purpose of teaching them through our greater experience, thus helping them to evolve.

At this advanced school I learned not only to lose myself and become countless other entities in the Fairy Kingdom but also to open my own consciousness to receive others into it that they might share my knowledge. At first a slight fear caused me to hesitate when this next step was suggested to me by my Teacher-guide. There seemed to me to be a wide disparity between entering a mountain or a tree and allowing another person of a similar status to share my mind and form.

"You should be willing to give that which you yourself have received," he told me.

"I would be happy for any flower to enter my mind, or a tree or mountain if that is possible, but I have secrets that I do not wish to share with another person."

"Of course a young fairy has secrets. We will shut them up in a good strong container where no-one will find them," he said with a smile.

"You are teasing me."

"Indeed no. But there comes a time when some secrets should be revealed to a privileged person, and it is better that they should be found rather than through over eagerness or reluctance, they are presented as inadequate thought forms which might be misunderstood."

"They are my desires and aspirations. They are possibly my most precious possessions. I do not want to share them with anyone."

"I was not joking when I advised you to put them in a container, wrap them up well and hide them in a cloak of darkness. They will not be detected, I promise you."

"Should not blending be an act of love, when nothing is withheld?" I asked.

"Blending with love is the best and most beautiful form; indeed you cannot blend with one towards whom you do not feel at least affection; the greater the love, the more complete the immersion."

"I have become many beings in a lower grade of evolution without loving them deeply."

"Because they are not as evolved as you, their power to love is correspondingly less. Your mild form of gratitude would equal their highest form of love. Think about my suggestion because it is the next step, but you must only agree to take it when you have absorbed the idea sufficiently for it to become agreeable to you."

❖　❖　❖

Many seasons completed their cycles before I eventually fell in love. He was a serious-minded fellow student, in whom there dwelt a resolute purpose to perfect himself through knowledge. I was slightly in awe of him for he had such deep concentration that nothing outside his chosen path seemed to interest him. Females were not included in his calculations and perhaps this made him more attractive in my eyes.

It became an overruling desire to win his attention, so I lingered after most the others had left the classroom, pretending to be working on my record of the lesson. Some of the more diligent pupils also remained to continue their studies; so it was some time before we were alone together, for he always left while others were still present.

At last the day came when he was still pondering on some problem and only I remained. His head was bent in complete absorption as I watched him secretly, although I kept my eyes on my notes.

"The procedure must be correct and yet in practice it fails me," he muttered. Silence followed broken only by my pulsing heart. It was so strong I feared it would impede his reveries.

"Ten breaths inhaled, held, exhaled, then cease. Stillness invades the vehicle and the I is set free. It is clear enough and yet, in practice, I remain as though held down with metal chains. How I hate myself for being thus imprisoned when I should be soaring to the heights." He became aware of my presence and scowled. "I believed I was alone," he mumbled. "Did my thoughts reach you?"

"Yes they did,"I said, my eyes still lowered although I longed to show him my sympathy with a gentle glance. "So many breaths are not really necessary," I whispered shyly.

His eyes seemed to bore through me, as he delved into my mind to determine whether I spoke the truth or was merely boasting to attract his attention.

"Look at me," he commanded and joyfully I obeyed. For a while I lost sight of him as a whole, he became an enormous pair of eyes which probed me and found my secret. My heart battered against my breast until I felt that both must burst. He became a young male again, disturbed, surprised and disbelieving.

"Tell me about the breathing," he said, and I noticed his own was erratic.

"At first one inhales and exhales, then the power is absorbed without breathing until the will severs all bonds, and one floats away." My eyes never left his as I spoke and he slowly drew nearer in answer to my yearning.

He entered my aura enfolding me in his own, and firmly held me until I ceased to breathe. I could feel his heart swelling and contracting. "Be still," I whispered, and his will calmed his turmoil, holding it in check as though with iron bands. He became aware of my non-breathing and, again using his will, the motion of intake ceased and he absorbed the stillness with me. Our minds locked and intermingled, groping to find in one another similar thoughts to weld us together in an even firmer embrace. I found much to admire, and his ruthlessness thrilled, not appalled me. "He is male," I told myself and his egotism became, for me, a symbol of his maleness.

Slowly we parted, each thought being unravelled until we became our two selves once more, feeling both shaken and dazed.

"Why have I never seen you before?"

"Because your eyes are fixed on yourself." The reply was reluctantly torn from me.

"I must perfect myself. It is the duty of each and every one of us."

"I love your single-mindedness. It is so male. But I am female and I know that one can unfold one's self only by forgetting it and serving others."

"You illogical little darling. The idea is both fresh and charming, yet so completely nonsensical."

"It is the truth," I said, "both are right. Your knowledge of the necessity to seek perfection is correct; my understanding of the way to attain it is also accurate. That is why a female is necessary to a male so that the two concepts become one."

"The idea that a female is necessary for my attainment of perfection is new to me. I will consider it, but whatever my conclusion, it is my desire to be near you. Your beauty and your power to absorb knowledge attract me. Let us meet again that I may consider more of your ideas."

"It will be my pleasure," I replied, overjoyed at his interest in my mind.

Our companionship led to many blendings and one by one I released my secret aspirations to him.

"You are too ambitious for a female," he chided me one day. "Your desire to attain At-Oneness is ludicrous. The One is male and females are inferior to males. You can never attain malehood. How can you therefore attain Him?"

"Females are inferior only in the eyes of males who lack understanding. The One is not male. 'It' is male and female. A person of whatever sex who does not desire At-Onement does not know the meaning of Life."

"It is not necessary for females to have a reason for Life apart from their care of others of our species."

"If that were the sole purpose of our being, our consciousness could not expand."

"It is useful to develop the mind, the better to care for the young and the requirements of males. Love of The One is also good if it keeps you humble."

"His Greatness fills me with humility every time I think of Him, but it is His Concept that I should grow even as a plant grows."

"A plant grows solely to give joy to others."

"No, it grows that His Will may be done."

❋   ❋   ❋

Our arguments were endless and always led to his striding away in exasperation leaving me trembling with misery because I could not show him the Truth. Meditating on the possibility of error in my thinking, I endeavoured to gain his point of view, but could not do so; and eventually I reached the bitter conclusion that our minds could never properly blend to produce the bliss which comes into being only during a true union.

Although my studies were far from complete, I thought of leaving the Seminary, but my problem was solved by the voluntary departure of him who had caused me to grow in experience while neglecting my studies.

"Females are outside my plan of life," he told me. "You divert me from my work and you are guilty of spiritual arrogance, unsuited to your sex. I am entering an all-male establishment where the inmates strive only for release from all distraction. I shall be with others who share my ideas and aspirations."

Although his decision saved me from taking a step which would have changed my chosen path towards knowledge, my failure to open his mind to alternative roads to salvation filled me with distress. He was the first to whom I had given my mind in love and he had refused it. Controlling the tears which were trying to flow, I bowed to him and left.

❋   ❋   ❋

Oh! my poor heart, benumbed with anguish for the love which had sprung so joyously from it, only to be cursorily spurned. It felt clogged as from a surfeit and for days the pain in my breast nullified my attempts to work or even to think constructively. Our Teacher's kindly eyes searched my face for the slightest indication that I wished to share my burden but I refused to meet his gaze. It was as though I was made of cold, hard rock with a volcano about to erupt, in place of a heart. I attended classes and made notes like an automaton, but although my mind accepted the proffered knowledge, there was no satisfaction in its absorption.

"We will talk." I had reached the exit to the classroom when my further passage was barred by his will. Obediently I turned and walked towards him.

"All first loves are strong; that is why at times they are so hurtful, my little wounded dove," he said. His kindness penetrated my control and I began to weep.

"Even your symbols of sorrow are like diamonds. A jewel can produce only other gems."

"A jewel without lustre is as worthless as a piece of quartz."

"A gem can be buried by soil or enclosed in rock yet it shines in reality, even if its light is hidden from those who pass by. Your light has been hidden by grief but now a little escapes in your sad and lovely tears."

"I do not feel lovely. My beauty died when he tore my mind with his departure."

"It would have been tainted had he stayed. His is the mind of youth bent only on self-devotion, though cunningly disguised as release from self. You are young in appearance but old in wisdom. Your love is for the Universe and Him who made it. These two types of individuals can meet but they cannot blend."

"Oh! but we did blend. I knew all his mind and he mine."

"To explore is not to blend, little dove. To blend is to unite and be one. Only similar minds can blend. Thoughts which are inharmonious remain aloof, watching each other like snarling dogs, bent on each other's destruction."

In spite of my misery, a faint smile moved my lips.

"It was not like that when our minds were knit; it was later that he rebuked me for what he had found."

"Your aim was to find similar thoughts to link with yours in love veering away from those you did not like, you failed to note their destructive intent. Had you been together for a much longer period, his rude mongrels would have vanquished your gentle thoroughbreds."

He cupped one hand beneath my fallen tears and brushed them with the tip of a finger. "Diamonds are precious; we must not waste them," he said as he gently placed them on a plant by his side.

"I love him still. He rends me asunder with his absence."

"You love love. He captured you because he needs love even though he spurns it. You mistook attraction for love once you were blinded by desire. Come with me and I will lead you to a balm to heal your wounded heart."

A tiny warm glow kindled inside me as his understanding and gentle humour began to infiltrate my citadel of despair.

❊ ❊ ❊

He led me through the vast grounds attached to the Seminary. We crossed a broad highway and entered a dim, dark wood. As we penetrated the deepening gloom I realized that no herb essence or soothing rays would be dispensed by expert hands in a Centre of Healing; a subtler cure was in his mind and soon would be in mine.

We approached a clearing in the trees where several squalid dwellings stood, tumble-down and filthy from lack of love or care. The strident sounds of a quarrel burst from one of them and out flew a sobbing child who hurtled past us into the darkness of the undergrowth. Compassion plucked at my heart-strings as I thought it never would again, and I made a movement towards him.

"No," said my Teacher. So side by side we stood in the dank, clinging shadows waiting expectantly for I knew not what.

A sound leapt towards us; it was not a child's cry but the sweetest notes ever to emerge from a fairy flute.

"Very softly," he cautioned as we crept towards the music-maker. A grubby urchin, cheeks blotched with tears, squatted on the ground, his eyes seeking Heaven through the clutching branches overhead, as he skilfully coaxed the exquisite sounds from the crude pipe he held to his lips.

My heart throbbed with tenderness for the sorrowful waif as he sought for comfort in this all-wise way. We were now drawing near him, but so absorbed was he in the creation of his music that he was unaware of our presence until the last note sped from his pipe. He blinked at us, as his plain little face broke into a tremulous smile.

"It's pretty, isn't it?" he said shyly.

"It is difficult to believe that such heavenly sounds could emerge from that little pipe," I replied holding out my hands towards him.

"It isn't just a pipe," he said, placing it tenderly in my outstretched palm. "I made it. It is part of me and it is all I have in the world to love."

"Are there no other children in your home?"

"Seven, but they all hate me because I'm happy." He rubbed the tears which trickled down his cheeks with the back of his fist. "I don't look very happy now, but I am inside, even when my eyes lament their unkindness, for it hurts them more than me."

Glancing at my Teacher in wonder that so young a child should know so much, I saw that he was smiling too. The little pipe demanded my attention as it pulsed with life in my hand. Observing it with my extra-vision I saw that it was in truth not roughly hewn from wood as I had thought, but was made of silver skilfully embossed with scrolls and symbols.

"Who are you?"

"I do not know except I am not what I seem. My heart bursts with joy until the fetid air sparkles like a million jewels and the dust on the floor turns to pure gold."

"Teach me," I said, falling on my knees at his feet.

For a moment he looked startled; then from faraway I heard, "Rise, my child. You have work to do despite your troubled heart." Soon he added normally, "Play my pipe, and the music will heal you as it always does me."

Raising it to my lips, I blew a long, sad note filled with anguish for my love so lightly cast aside. The child sang as I played and the trees quivered in sympathy and added their own song to ours. Soon, instead of leading the child, he led me, and the music changed from a heartfelt lament to a paeon of exaltation, rejoicing in our gift of life.

"To be is rapture," he sang and I found myself believing in his phrase. "Rapture, pure rapture," he flung to the sky and I seemed to hear in the distance the echo, or was it an angel's reply to a brother? I know not the answer to this day, but from that moment my wounds began to heal. Often I returned to the wood to look for the child and his music, but all was silence. And yet in that silence his joyous phrase "Rapture, pure rapture" welled up inside me, but despite my endeavours, I never found him again.

∽ Chapter 5 ∼
The Student-Teacher

My studies once more continued in an even rhythm until the time came when my Teacher-guide considered me ready to accept further duties. He personally took me to my new home where many young children, who had recently descended from a higher plane, dwelt.

How sweet they were and yet at times I discerned their sadness as they gazed with astonished eyes at their surroundings, which to me appeared idyllic, as though they were striving to recall the lost light of their previous homes. Sometimes a tiny face would pucker and tears fall from tightly-closed lids as if the owner was seeking to recapture past joys by rejecting the present. A faint memory of my own similar endeavour returned to me as I enveloped the sad babe in love, singing of happiness and the rapture of being alive.

As soon as the children became used to the new conditions, smiling faces greeted me, but once more I experienced the pain which I had known when my little birds had flown away. Each one wound a tiny thread of love around me; and when it left to be placed in the care of other guardians, the thread went with it rending my heart anew. Five years passed in delight when each new gift-child came from above, and sorrow as progress claimed it for a different phase of life.

"Now you are ready for adult love," my Teacher-guide told me one day. "That which you have received from the little ones you have tended will act as a barrier of purity to ward off undesired affections. You are now to enter a world which is preponderantly male, where a female is a rarity. Do not however be deceived by desire, for one and all will desire you. Be patient. Be wise. You have a natural dignity, which will restrain the wilder elements whose need is to possess and to subdue, rather than to cherish."

"I have been buffeted enough."

"If you had not, you would not be fit to go into the wilderness where your culture is sadly needed."

"Wilderness?" I cried in dismay.

"You have lived a privileged life until now. You must take your beauty of person, experience and knowledge where it is most wanted, but the time is not yet. To prepare yourself, you will teach an all male class reserved for those who are not to be trusted to work diligently in the presence of female students."

"My knowledge of the male sex has been restricted," I said, hoping to escape this unpleasant task.

"That is the reason for this consignment; your ignorance must be rectified. Do you wish to live in a protected world for the rest of your Astral span?"

"It would be safer."

"Those who prefer safety to experience do not progress."

❧ ❧ ❧

The students who were to become my pupils were immature spiritually, though many were intellectually advanced. Dressing myself for my introduction to them in a severe dark coloured dress, and making myself as plain as I was able, I presented myself for my new teacher's inspection.

"Is this really the beautiful Perima? If I had not arranged this meeting, I would scarcely have recognised you. Perhaps you are wise though. Come, we will test your disguise and at the same time ascertain the students' powers of observation."

Our entry caused little stir among the assembled class and, having performed the required bow, the students lolled back taking no further interest in me; that is all except one whose eyes never left my face as though I appeared to him as a radiant beauty from a higher sphere. I could sense his will seeking mine as though to capture my attention for himself alone, but I did not encourage or even acknowledge him.

The teacher stayed by my side as I talked of music to my mainly listless audience, but when my fingers began to persuade soft sweet sounds from my lute, the mood changed. Flushed by this response, I began to sing, swaying gently to the rhythm.

"Sing," I urged them. "Sing with me," and to my relief all joined in, gradually drawing closer to me.

"That was excellent," I cried with delight as the last note hovered and died.

"She's beautiful" - an amazed whisper spread round the room.

"Mirror yourself Perima," the teacher said. Turning my concentration on my face and form, I saw that I now looked as I normally do, but slightly flushed at my unforeseen success. I then noticed that a fastening had fallen from my dress and the movement of my arm while plucking the lute had caused the sleeve to slip from my shoulder, exposing more of my body than is customary by a teacher before her pupils. Blushing, I hastily covered the area thus exposed.

"Beauty cannot be so easily concealed," the teacher smiled. "You are fortunate students to have both a charming and talented instructor."

"I was wrong and nervous," I said apologetically,"but if you will help me, perhaps my inexperience will be of little account. I love music and to share my slight knowledge with you will give me great joy, but I cannot give you anything that you do not wish to receive... Oh, I am expressing myself badly but if you are willing to learn all I know, our lessons could bring pleasure to all of us."

"Come in a different dress," called one.

"Some colour on your lips would make you really pretty."

"Put a sparkle in your eyes as well as your fingers."

"The first lesson is over," the teacher interrupted. "You will rise to your feet and show due deference to the youth, beauty and exceptional talent before you." Heads nearly touched the ground and my own bow was not only a return salute to the class, but a demonstration of my gratitude and humility because, despite my initial error of endeavouring to conceal that which The One had seen fit to bestow on me, I had succeeded in winning the interest of these young males, even though, at present it was directed towards my person rather than to the subject I was teaching them.

* * *

This period of my life proved to be a new experience for me. Whereas with the babes, my love was given unstintingly, now I had to curb it. Love is a force which flows from all in varying degrees but it is wayward and difficult to control. Children and plants thrive in its radiance but adolescents, particularly males, can become over-inflamed; and much harm can be done by a teacher, however well-meaning, if he or she is ignorant of its power.

Innocently I sang them love songs, in which they joined with enthusiasm, leading to undesired caresses. These I countered with sharp reprimands but nonetheless after-school fights followed.

Marches had a certain appeal for the younger students but dances, unless very vigorous, were deemed effeminate. Tales of adventure leading to a gentle blending of auras between courtly knights and shy maidens surprisingly proved popular and reasonably safe as far as my person was concerned, although dreamy eyes conveyed their message and my will was kept in constant combat with youthful yearnings.

I discovered that the student who had gazed at me so ardently before I gave my first lesson had a natural talent for music and a fine clear voice. Sometimes when I was alone in the classroom after the others had left, a wistful air would float through the window from the courtyard below.

There was something about his voice which helped to heal my still ailing heart and its purity of tone conveyed to me that I need have no fear of this lad forcing unwelcome attentions on me. When the last note rose towards me and died in mid-flight, I would go to the window to thank him for his song, but he had always gone and I was left with an unaccountable feeling of loss.

A good-humoured grin often accompanied the twinkle in his eyes when he spoke to me, but he was overcome with shyness if I tried to read a hidden message. No attempt was ever made after that first day to attract my attention or to seek my company alone. To all outward appearances, he was just one of the class and yet his face haunted me; it was somehow familiar and yet, ponder as I would, no memory of a previous meeting returned. Sometimes one of the students would sing a duet with me, the others accompanying us with instruments and background chorus.

"Sulic," I said to him of the wistful voice, "it is your turn to sing with me. Have you a preference?"

"Any subject will place an undying song in my heart," he replied. By this time the students had learned good manners, and such a reply was now a normal occurrence.

"Then we will sing of the sun and the wind in the trees."

"May the air from my throat be warmed by your inner sun," he said, bowing low. As our voices blended, a warmth indeed swept through me. The breeze soared towards the sun.

"Adored soul, my yearning for you is both pain and bliss." My fingers faltered on the strings for the words were not of the song. I looked towards my fellow singer but his eyes were closed as he sang of boisterous breezes blowing the sunbeams from their course, as they sped to kiss a flower.

✻ ✻ ✻

As the students were leaving at the end of the class, I said, "Sulic, I have worked out some variations for this song. If you would care to stay we could try them out."

"To obey your slightest wish is my delight," he replied, with lowered eyes.

The room emptied and we stood apart as befitted teacher and pupil. A shyness swept over me which held me silent.

"The variations?" he murmured vaguely, his thoughts plainly elsewhere.

"You are strangely familiar, Sulic. Tell me, have we met before?"

"My heart burst when you first entered the room in your drab dress and attempted disguise those three years, five months and fourteen days gone by."

"It was clever of you to recognise me. Did we meet as children?"

"No."

"Forgive my poor memory. Tell me where and when it was."

"It was ago."

"Ago?" I pondered. "The name means nothing to me. Where is it?"

"Long ago and through the ages."

Trembling, I felt myself recede until my extra vision showed me a different view to the one from the window. Two negro fairy children played together, grew, embraced, then they changed to brown-skinned islanders laughing as they skimmed the waves. We shivered on an ice cap, wilted in the sun and sought the shade of a cactus in which to laugh and make love. We wept at some loss, danced in ritual robes, suffered, were sick, were lost in the dark, but always we loved and laughed again.

❊ ❊ ❊

"Laugh, Perima. You never laugh now." His voice called me home, home to his arms, and I laughed as I had not done for years, because I had found my love, him who holds the key of my being, my fount of joy, without whom there is neither true delight nor reality, for without him I am only half myself.

In joy we went to my Teacher-guide to tell him how we had found each other again, but he looked grave. "Sulic lacks education, he has much to learn, not being of your industrious nature, he has fallen far behind you on the road to Wisdom."

"But I love him. I will give him all my knowledge."

"You may give, but can he receive? Knowledge and Experience walk hand in hand. Either without the other is like an ornamental cherry tree, which bears flowers but no fruit. "

"You cannot be so cruel as to part us when I have waited so long and travelled so solitary a road."

"People are parted only by their own consent."

"I do not consent. Doubt, loneliness and lack of laughter have often been my lot since I left my guardian. I need gaiety to make me grow. I realize now that for years I have been like a stunted tree striving against wind and rain to reach the sun while others with greater stature and stamina have overtaken me and bask in his beams, while I still linger in the shadows."

"All young things feel stunted when they meet others who have reached the light. They fail to understand that their tall and favoured neighbours were once struggling like themselves."

"He is right," said Sulic sadly. "Now, except in love, your mind is on a higher plane than mine. If you are a stunted sapling then I am but the grass round your roots."

Tears filled my eyes. "You too are against my desire for joy." He held me close.

"Your unhappiness is mine for we share all but wisdom. I have loved life too well. To battle with the elements in their wilder moods, to fly with the wind and rain in play, to help plants grow, to laugh and live through my senses has been enough. Now I have learned of other needs besides those of my outer form; my mind must grow too; but alas I have found this truth later than you have. During this last descent to a lower plane, you worked while I played, and now we must both pay the price. Forgive me. What a laughing jackass I have been; but now my mirth is over." Two tears left his eyes and trickled down his cheeks.

"Must we leave each other now?" I asked forlornly.

"The longer we stay together, the greater the anguish of parting."

My will searched desperately for a solution but I could find none. "Lend me your mind, my Teacher," I begged him; "you are so wise. There must be a path, however stony, that we can tread together."

"I see two roads, little dove," he said. "They run parallel but they do not meet this side of the horizon."

I felt my power drain away and consciousness left me. When it returned only my Teacher-guide was with me.

"Sulic is already treading his path", he told me gently. "You must begin your journey too, or he will reach the horizon before you."

"Why did we meet again if only to experience the pain of parting?"

"To show you the roads you each must take. Would you wish to continue rising when he must descend?"

"He is not going to Earth," I said appalled.

"Not now. That is in the future." Mentally bruised and defeated though I was, I wearily collected my scattered thoughts until some order was restored.

"Show me my road. He will need to know that I too am on my way that his burdens may be bearable."

"It lies through the wilderness of which I warned you," he said.

"And those who need me. If it leads me to Sulic, no matter what the hardships, I will succour the many."

CHAPTER 6
THE WILDERNESS

T he wilderness was a seemingly endless plain of grey- green grass, punctuated by a few scrawny trees lifting their near-naked branches to the leaden sky as though in lamentation for their plight. Droves of untamed beasts roamed its reaches free from fear for no one desired to molest or exploit them.

Wherever there are animals there are fairy people, for we understand the needs of those lower down the life scale than ourselves. The herdsmen who cared for them lived a rough and lonely life, driving them to fresh pastures, finding water for them in times of drought and tending to their simple needs.

Near the centre of the prairie was a group of tumbledown huts, to which they returned at regular intervals for rest and replenishment after their arduous work in the wasteland. This near-derelict village was to be my future home.

We too have our problems with the less-developed members of our Evolution and I was fully aware of the conditions I was likely to find. As I approached I saw a building which appeared to be some kind of recreation centre, as discordant sounds, which I presumed was music, assaulted me.

Garish lights blazed through the entrance and windows, through which I could see thought forms of scantily dressed girls in suggestive poses, covering the walls. Unkempt females sang coarse songs as they twined their limbs about the herdsmen, who competed for their favours by telling crude jokes and teasing them.

Having learned the lesson of the effect of beauty on my music pupils, this time I was looking my best; my cheeks and lips were tinted; my hair shining and immaculate. Wearing a dress of verdant green, I walked through the entrance. For a moment no-one noticed my presence so absorbed were they in their bawdy frolic; one of the girls cackled raucously, "Look 'oo's 'ere. Come ter the wrong plice, ain't yer?"

I smiled at her but my heart was beating with nervous tension, for I realised the importance of this first meeting with my new charges.

"No, I am your new Superintendent-teacher. What a cheerful, bright room you have here. But perhaps someone would be kind enough to show me my own house for I have come a long way..."

❊ ❊ ❊

A long way indeed from the heights of a new found love from the past to the depths of the parting of our ways.

No-one moved; then my eyes rested on a young male who was visibly wavering.

"I'll show you ma'am," he offered shyly and hurried past me into the burning heat outside.

"It is cooler here though the air is torrid," I said. "There is too much red inside; it magnifies the natural temperature."

"We likes de red, ma'am, after all de dark and dreary green o' de land."

"Red is a lovely colour, but it is so full of vitality that it should be used with discretion. When painting a picture for instance, too much can belittle the gentler hues."

"You paint, ma'am?" he asked, his ugly face lighting up.

"I have studied it for many years. My work is good enough to give pleasure to myself and I hope to others too."

"I draws when I's wid de beasts, but dey don' look like cattle to no-one but me."

"Perhaps they are out of perspective?"

"I don' know 'bout no pers – pers ... what you said."

"Would you show them to me sometime?" He became shy again but fumbling in his pockets he produced some crumpled leaves. I spread them out and found myself in a strange world of smiling cattle faces, horns and tails entwined in a pleasing pattern and flowers being watered by benevolent eyes.

"These are fascinating," I said. "Have you more?" He shook his head. "Dose I done today. De oder fellers steals 'em when I's sleepin'. Den dey wakes me and larf and larf and dey toss dem to de wind. I tries to pick dem up but de wind larfs too and tears dem to shreds afore I can reach dem."

"You are my first pupil," I said. "And now, where is my home?"

"It arn't much ma'am. It's de one at de end."

❊ ❊ ❊

His words were all too true; it was a ramshackle hovel, fallen into disrepair from lack of love. As I approached, I felt it tremble. Was it with fear or hope?

"Pretty house," I whispered, "I can see you beneath your neglect and dirt. You and I will be friends." My words were gentle but my thoughts were not. I swept past the bewildered youth down the street and into the recreation rooms once more, my eyes blazing.

"I have come here after a great personal tragedy. I did not expect a welcome but not even the common civility due to any stranger has been accorded to me. My house is an insult. Either it is made habitable or I leave."

An amazed silence followed for they had not been thus addressed for years. One of the girls giggled hysterically while another yelled "Go on! 'Op it. We don't want no bossy school marms 'ere."

"Oh! yus we does. I want me rights and heducation. I've 'ad to shout for 'em long enough."

Turning to find that my ally was a surly looking ruffian, I nevertheless encouraged him. "You are right to insist on an education; knowledge can overcome many of the minor problems of Life."

"You 'ad to fight for it too, ma'am?" he grinned.

"I have had to fight for many years but not with my fists. Knowledge has strengthened my will; it is with my will that I fight." Becoming bolder I said "Would anyone here like to meet me in a battle of wills?" My eyes swept over them but none accepted my challenge for they knew that my single will was stronger than all of theirs together.

"My house will take six of you until nightfall to clean and colour. Who will volunteer?" There was a wild rush through the entrance and I was left alone with seven sulky girls.

"Your appearance is a disgrace," I said. "You are dirty and unkempt, and your clothes are in the worst possible taste."

"You arn't unlucky like us. We arn't never 'ad nothin'."

"Luck has little to do with your slatternly looks and ways. Have you ever made the slightest effort to improve yourselves by hard work. I do not need to use my extra-vision to tell me the answer. I am here to teach you but I can only do this if you wish to learn. Would you be interested in face and hair improvement, or pretty clothes? I can make materials, face-tints, dyes, varnishes as well as books." Silence greeted my offer, only one pretty slut showing any interest.

"Do not any of you desire more permanent blendings than the rough onslaughts you now receive. I really can teach you how to improve your looks which could lead to gentler and more lasting relationships."

"You got a bloke?"

"Yes, but at present we must travel different roads; perhaps to enable me to help you to a better life. I do not know. It is hard to understand." Feeling my tears beginning to gather, I turned and hastily left.

*   *   *

The years that followed led to many contests of will in which I was not always the victor. The theories which had been expounded to me when I was at the Seminary by no means always had the desired results, and sometimes I despaired of making a lasting impression on these wayward entities who preferred pleasures of the senses rather than the mind.

My house was always open for any who cared to enter. At first I had few visitors, yet welcoming lights always shone from my window, revealing a charming interior with fresh flowers. These I regularly conjured up with my mind and will, for my garden failed to bear more than a few hardy herbs owing to the heat of the near barren plain.

Sometimes one or two of the girls came to seek my aid, not to improve their minds but their appearance, and with this I was glad to help them. A few had a hint of future prettiness and I was able to tell them how to enhance their best features with the application of colour and how to disguise their figure defects with the use of less flamboyant clothes.

For the others who asked for help I could, sadly, do little outwardly, for they were really ugly, but I encouraged them towards cleanliness and neatness. I also introduced them to perfumes and these seemed to give them confidence, and their usual sullen demeanour gradually changed to a more pleasant expression. However most of them had no desire to change. Grumbling seemed their only mitigation from their dreary life, and they mostly ignored me.

My one frequent visitor was the lad who loved to draw. His pictures were so original that I did not wish to spoil them by confusing him with technique, but I was able to help him with my encouragement and advice over basic materials. Leaves stuck together with cow spittle are not the ideal foundation for a picture, so I advised him to look for suitable pieces of tree bark and flat stones. I also taught him how to hide his completed work from his companions, until they came to appreciate its charm and humour of his arts. Eventually some of the thought forms of nude girls were replaced by his drawings.

*   *   *

When my work proved beyond my strength of will to continue, I retired gratefully to my house to play soft music to calm my sense of failure. One evening I thought of the child who had entered my life when I needed solace so desperately. My voice rose towards Heaven, hiding behind the dark, unfriendly sky.

"To be is rapture," I sang, and again I discovered the truth of his phrase. The song soared and bore me away from the scene of my sadness to a land that was fresh and clean. Breathing in the sparkling air, I was freed from misgivings. I had been chosen and I would prevail. To doubt was wrong. The One makes no errors and would rectify mine.

"Rapture, pure Rapture." The notes came from the distance; the music lured me away from my vision, and as the song came nearer, I realized it was mine. I was back in my house, my lute fallen from my listless hands.

"Bravo, bravo! Play again!" several voices shouted in unison from outside the open window; then their forms appeared in the doorway

"I have been away," I said dreamily. "Now I will tell you what I saw."

Retrieving the lute tenderly I plucked the strings and from me poured the story of my visit, I described how the sparkling air had revived me and I had found myself in a land scintillating with light, its beams dancing and twinkling like jewel coloured stars. I had strolled through meadows lush with flowers which were teased by soft breezes as they sang their way through petals and leaves. A waterfall spilled from invisible heights, laughing as it splashed the upturned faces of the plants below. A miniature palace had risen before me and near it clustered smaller dwellings... pink, blue, green and yellow, sparkling gaily with joyous life.

"We are yours. Take us down. Please take us with you," they pleaded. As I played and sang, thought forms like pictures illustrated the story and, as the final request reached my audience, a clear vision of their village as it ought to be appeared to all.

"Give the thought form power," I begged them. "Do not let it fade because it may not come again."

A dozen rough wills joined mine and the miniature model, though losing some of its beauty, became less ethereal and more practical.

"I'll 'ave the big 'un," said a cheerful voice.

"No, the palace is for all. Oh! what joy. Tell me you like it and will help me to build it. We will call down the waterfall too and have a flowering oasis in the wilds."

❖ ❖ ❖

There was silence as they clustered round the model of thought, hardly believing their eyes.

"It'll take years to cart the stones let alone shape 'em."

"No, no, that is not the way," I said laughing. "You are fairies. Your power is will. You have it but you do not use it. Let me help you. Take the model outside and I will explain." We placed it in an empty space opposite my home and I stood before it.

"Choose a house," I said, and a girl pointed to one in gentle green. Gathering my powers I concentrated on the front wall with its pillared entrance and wide windows, and I placed a larger version behind the model. "I need your help. Look at the wall and think green on to the outline now appearing." Some of them followed my directions and my structure became clearer in both shape and colour. Interest was rising and more joined in until a single wall stood solidly before us.

"Now for the doorway," I said as I willed a gap. A whoop of excitement greeted my success but before I had time to add the portico, they surged forward, chasing each other in and out of the opening and round the edges of the wall.

"A wall with an entrance is not of much use to anyone," I said. "Calm yourselves and help me to complete the house." Our further efforts produced a reasonable reproduction of the original, and the whole village gathered round to admire it.

"Can I 'ave yourn, now you's got this," one of the girls asked.

"It will last only a few hours. Much hard work is needed before we can build houses which will remain stable. This one is not for me but for anyone who will agree to give it power regularly, and we will build other houses for all who want them. Dear friends," I said, tears welling into my eyes, "I beg you to abandon these woebegone hovels which are held together only by base emotions. Let us together build a new village made by our joint concentration and mutual determination. Your hopes and desires will form the substance of the walls themselves, creating a happy place for the well earned rest from your labours – a place with water and flowers where males and females can form relationships both loving and lasting. Our thoughts will make the village as we want it to be, and as we live in it, it will help us to achieve a better way of life."

For several minutes they, whispered together. "Orl right, lady, when do we start?"

"This minute, for if we do not give the house a continuous stream of power, it will fade.   '

"You," I said to the male who had spoken, "you have influence in the community. Divide into groups of six or seven and will this model to live with the gift of particles of your own life-force. Do not fail or let others fail, for if we lose that which has been given to us in this wondrous way, we may not have another chance."

* * *

They worked well for several weeks but progress was slow. They wanted to go too fast for their limited ability, and I could not prevent them from beginning a new wall or even a building before the one on which they were working had been stabilized by power and will.

In vain I pleaded with them to have patience, but they had so little; and my own was not enough to counterbalance their deficiency. And so my 'vision' ended in failure and they returned to their old way of life and I was left with the part consolation that I had at least given them the seed of their potential abilities, which one day would find proper expression.

This disappointing result did not diminish me as a teacher in their eyes and all now treated me with respect. Some even made moderate progress when their desire for knowledge overcame their lethargy. Occasionally their casual unions with the opposite sex changed into more lasting relationships and they would visit me together and ask my advice on joint problems or tell me of their future plans.

* * *

However I achieved some success with the power centres which I had set up on my arrival. These I had considered necessary as many of the fairies lacked stamina and they would sometimes lose their bodies, not as an act of will, but owing to the fact that they had not the energy to sustain them.

When a centre is built for any group, all must contribute, so I called them together and told them to stand in a circle. I explained to them that they must think of the great Reservoir of Power which lay beyond their vision then they should will it down, inhale it deeply, hold it, then expel it through their solar plexus. At first the results were almost negligible, but I made them persevere until they were able to see the descending light passing through each other and we produced a small area within the circle which we replenished each day until sufficient stability was achieved for it to remain during our absence.

Later I judged that the stage had been reached when a little could be withdrawn and I asked their leader to choose six friends to sit with him in the centre of the pool of power. They began to glow as a feeling of well-being swept over them. At first this satisfied them but on later occasions they rose to their feet and danced, gambolled in friendly combat, or played simple games.

They learned that the more they gave to the centre the more they could re-inhale, leading to greater pleasure and strength. They also learned that some were greedy, and there was less or none for others, but with my help they evolved a system by which each was restricted to a set time for replenishment, and everyone enjoyed his rightful share. Thus I was able to contribute to their recreation and bodily well-being, if not to the expansion of their minds to the extent that I had hoped.

I had to accept the fact that my influence was infinitesimal and sometimes I wondered why I, with my long years of study and my intense desire to serve my fellow fairies, should have been directed to these people, when anyone with even a modest education could have done as well if not better than me.

A longing for companionship of like minds filled me, and I yearned for my love, my Sulic, whom I had found again and so quickly lost. My loneliness was greater than if I had been on a mountain-top with no other soul within reach; for those around me drained all spiritual aspiration from me, binding me to the barren earth with their frequent demands for my attention to aid them in some modest and often useless project. I loved them, for their need was so great; or perhaps it was only pity that I gave them, and that was why I failed.

❉ ❉ ❉

Yet another day dawned. It began as usual with the advent of the Sun, whom I had always worshipped, gradually forcing his searing rays through the seemingly impenetrable darkness of the menacing night. It was my waking custom to watch this wonder daily for it portrayed the Light which all my life I have accepted as the precious gift which is with me not only externally, but also growing within me as I tread my destined path.

On that memorable morning He appeared to have an even greater struggle than usual to pierce the resistant gloom, but at last one single beam fell on my waiting form. I stretched out my arms in welcome, then bowed in reverence and gratitude for He was all that I had of my other world.

When I raised my eyes once more, my heart all but leapt from my breast, for diving like lightning down the ray were three golden birds. At first I supposed them to be three of those I had loved and brought to maturity many years ago, but as they came nearer I recognised them as the golden hawks of the Sun God. I trembled for these are manifestations of The God Himself.

I heard a voice. "You have done well, my child." Tears streamed from my eyes. "Lord I have failed, but a cruel lesson has been learned. I was so certain that my desire to serve, backed with the will to succeed, would overcome all obstacles, but not only have I failed to help these people, but I have lost the desire and the will to do so."

"You have not lost them; they have been taken from you. It is time for you to leave this place that another may have the chance to serve them. The young judge success and failure by results. We do not. Success lies in trying to overcome the insuperable, and this you have diligently practised for many years. Look towards the horizon."

I obeyed and, through my tears, I saw a swirl of dust in the distance. "There comes your successor. Leave all, mount the back of the largest hawk; he will carry you swiftly to your destination."

And so the majestic bird, escorted by his two brothers, bore me through the already burning heat into the clear sweet air above, and once again I inhaled the unpolluted Breath of Life which sustains us all. Although my steed was a hawk, to me he was the Phoenix, rising from the ashes – a recurring resurrection, not through death to Life, but from one phase of Life to another.

CHAPTER 7

ANOTHER DOOR OPENS

I enjoyed a period of rest, alone in beautiful surroundings, filling myself with the power of which I had long been deprived, for so little had filtered through the barriers of lust and ignorance by which I had been imprisoned. How sweet was the song of the birds, who seemed to sense my sadness as they chirruped to cheer me from dawn to dusk. The perfume of the canopies of flowers intoxicated me, and the beams of light flashing through the air comforted but failed to rouse me.

I remained in this state of inertia for many weeks until one day a note I knew infiltrated my dream-world, an unmistakable sound I had not heard since leaving my guardian's house. I trembled with joy for I was certain he was coming to take me back to my childhood home. Standing before me he regarded me seriously for a moment, then he enfolded me in his loving arms and the remnants of my sense of failure dropped away like a dirty garment.

"My little one. My own dear little one," he repeated as he pushed me gently to arm's length and regarded me tenderly. "How beautiful you are."

"I have been so ugly. Am I really pretty again?"

"I said beautiful. You used to be pretty but now you shine with achievement; your light holds me in a glowing embrace."

"When can we go?" I asked, sighing with happiness.

"Are you weary of your lovely refuge?" I gazed gratefully at the land that had succoured and cleansed me accepting my dirt and sorrow whilst remaining itself as bright and clean as a new-born day. "Please tell me, have I harmed this place that has cherished me? I have given it nothing but the darkness of my soul."

"Nothing can defile that which is truly pure," he replied. "Darkness is but the negative of light. You know that any manifestation requires both positive and negative aspects. The outcome of this union of the land's positive and your negative is Perima reborn. You must stay here a while and consciously give some of your new light to enhance that of every flower, tree and blade of grass. The birds will sing more sweetly and the balance of Nature will be restored, for that which has been taken by you will be returned in a higher form. It is thus that evolution takes place."

❊ ❊ ❊

As I performed this act of gratitude each plant and bird seemed to grow, or at least I thought it did, and my confidence returned for I knew that I was ready for the next adventure that Life would soon make known to me.

The call came one morning as I was making my joyous obeisance to the Eastern Light.

"Come." The command came out of the sky and I felt myself being drawn towards the Sun and entering it. When consciousness returned, I found to my joy that I was taller by at least two inches.

Where was I? – and more important – where was I going? A puff of wind lifted me and gently conveyed me towards a large building of scintillating beauty, and my excitement grew as I approached a maze of corridors but I always knew the way, or rather I moved in the right direction for an unseen force was guiding me.

❊ ❊ ❊

He stood before me and I prostrated myself; indeed I had no choice, His light blinding and His Power overwhelming me.

"Arise Perima."

I looked at Him in wonder. How magnificent He was. His gentle eyes gazed on me with love; one hand was raised in benediction and the other was held towards me. I had never previously been in the immediate presence of a great Angel but I was not afraid; only filled with wonder that this experience was mine because I had earned it, for that is the only way that Man or Fairy can come face to face with a Shining One.

"You have done well."

"At the time I was conscious only of failure, for my achievements were so small that they seemed of little value when placed on the Eternal Scales of Justice."

"Success when realized through constant striving against almost impossible odds weighs more than that which is easily won through a stroke of apparent genius at a propitious time. You are to work under my guidance here to prepare you for your next task."

I stared at Him in disbelief. "I am of so little account," I eventually managed to whisper.

"Little accounts when walking hand in hand with Wisdom and Experience grow into Big Accounts." He smiled and although the surroundings were already filled with His Light, the brightness seemed to explode, reach out and find my core for a moment of ecstasy sublime, never before experienced but becoming mine many times in the future.

* * *

This was the beginning of one of the most rewarding times of my existence. The work was new to me, for at that time I was completely ignorant of the art of creating Thought Formations which was to become the main interest of my future life. Each formation is composed of a number of thoughts provided by several or many people to fulfil a particular purpose. They are woven together to make a composition of great beauty and power, which is no easy task, as thoughts have a life of their own. And, though on a single theme, may not be in harmony with one another.

To give an example, one of the projects given to the working group of which I became a member was to be used for the promotion of peace in a quarrelsome community. Of the many ideas discussed we selected "Affinity" as the nucleus and we chose "Kindness" as the first addition. All was well, in fact there proved to be a mutual attraction between the two and they blended naturally. Next a less gentle thought "Determination" was offered to the two already joined but they began to tremble and would have parted had we not given them power to keep them together. We considered many aspects of "Determination" but each, when presented, was rejected.

On separating the original two, we found that our third thought blended happily with "Affinity" but "Kindness" remained aloof. Should we give up and start again? No, the Formation needed Determination and a link must be found. We decided to relax and meditate, after which we tried "Friendship" which combined with "Kindness" but refused the other two. "Success" joined with the "Determination/Affinity" section, "Love" with "Friendship/Kindness," and "Endeavour" with the other two.

In fact we now had opposing sections instead of a single Formation. "Resolution" although repelling neither, failed to draw them together. "Good-Will" induced a slight narrowing of the intervening space and finally "Understanding" proved to be the required connection, and we witnessed a gradual closing of the gap. We held our breath as "Determination" hesitated as though it might break away; it is a somewhat wayward quality, intent on success whatever the cost; but the last thought proved the stronger and, acting as a magnet, "Understanding" firmly drew all the other thoughts together into a whole which at first gently glowed and then became a steady flame.

Every day we gathered to give the Formation power and the flame leapt with renewed life but it always diminished to a mere flicker during our absence and we knew that an essential quality was still missing. Many ideas were produced and discarded, sometimes by ourselves, at others by the Formation. Examining it from every angle we could find no obvious fault or deficiency and we began to suspect that our power was not adequate to complete the project. We discussed taking our problem to our Teacher-Lord but we knew that this would not please Him, not because we had failed but because we lacked diligence.

"That is what the Formation needs," I eventually dared to say. I was the youngest and among the least experienced in our group at the time. "No thought is missing," I continued. "It is our diligence that is lacking."

"You are right," a fellow-worker agreed. "We have an inanimate model and now our diligence must turn it into a living instrument. This is the beginning of a new phase in our work. We have been too easily satisfied when we have succeeded in persuading a few compatible ideas to join, become one and keep together, only to perform some modest function. We have become too complacent with these minor successes and I now realize that the projects we have been given have been suitable for our student status. This is our most difficult assignment, in fact it is a test to prove whether we are ready to become regular operators or to remain mere amateurs.

"We have now learned that this work requires more than suitable thoughts; we have to find within ourselves the quality that the Formation lacks and to provide it from our own being so that it will have a life of its own without frequent replenishment from us."

❧   ❧   ❧

On completion, the Thought-Formation was placed in a prominent position in the centre of the village. Although the inhabitants were unaware of its presence, it nonetheless performed its function. As is normal, there was no instantaneous change in the attitudes of the villagers towards each other but slowly they became more tolerant of one another's foibles until the time came when disagreements were no more than is commonplace in a community of varying types and age groups, and we were happy that we had been instrumental in bringing about this change which made life more pleasant for all concerned.

— PART II —
TEPI AND I

CHAPTER 8
I ENTER TEPI'S LIFE

Now that we understood that facets of our own being were a necessity for the success of our work, we felt obliged to examine ourselves minutely so that in future we would know which one of us would be most likely to produce the required attribute, thus saving time and energy.

Our leader, Eremus, was evenly balanced in all qualities but he did not have that flash of genius often required to bring a project to a successful conclusion enabling it to perform its prescribed function.

One of the group whose name was Tepi had this ability although he was, at that time, far from the calibre required for leadership, being often sullen; and yet it was this brooding tendency of his, which lifted him above us all with his talent to produce a seemingly unconnected idea, which would eventually lead to the welding of all the other thoughts in the Formation. I was drawn to him because he was unhappy, and having known the near-depths of despair myself, I understood his doubts and fears and the mental depression in which he so often found himself.

"Allow me to come with you," I said to him one day.

"I am not going anywhere," he growled.

"I know. You are already there."

He looked at me with animosity. "I do not want your interference, or your presence except when our work necessitates it."

"You seem to be under a misapprehension. I am not offering to help you; I want you to help me."

"What can an ugly creature like me have to offer a beautiful fairy like you?"

"You have genius. I only have talent and I need a spark of your flame to turn my talent into genius too."

"You are mocking me."

"No, truly, I am serious. I have extra-vision and I can see your genius which is not present in any of the others. It lies in the darkness of your mental wanderings, buried in the depth of your subconscious; and I know that if you will take me with you, no matter how appalling the conditions, together we will find it and force it into the Light in which we live and work."

"I do not understand what you are saying. My wanderings are uncontrolled. I do not want to go where I go and I refuse to take anyone, especially a female, with me."

"I am hardier than I look," I said. "For many years I have been a teacher among the most depraved of Fairy-natures. They knew nothing of Beauty. I know that somewhere in your life you have known Beauty or you could not produce the thoughts that you do for our work; indeed you would not be here at all. You are a different person when you are with the group. Why must you hide yourself away during our leisure hours?"

"I am two people. That is my curse."

"We are all two people, and it is the task of each one of us to force them to live in harmony together."

"I hate myself," he said bitterly. "How can I expect anyone to like me."

"I love you," I said gently. "I love you for what you truly are and not for the facade you present to the world." He broke down then and wept and I rejoiced for tears are the great conveyers; they can carry the darkness of the soul from the underground caverns where it dwells into the light of day to be purified and returned to its proper nature and enhance the whole.

* * *

I left him then for I was well aware that I must not urge him too far or too fast.

At our next Formation-gathering, instead of lurking on the outskirts of the group, he came and stood beside me. I smiled at him but he gave no sign of having absorbed any of our conversation. The session went well and Tepi seemed even quicker than usual with his contributions.

A short cycle of time became a longer one and still he remained silent; then one day he said: "Since we talked I have sunk even deeper into the abyss – where will it end?"

"Here and now," I said sharply. "You are deliberately wallowing in your despair and degradation. You are verging on a Death-wish and if you do not stop, you will die, for you are not sufficiently advanced to prevent your disintegration and return to involving matter."

This, I confess, was not true, for his genius was a certain anchor against any fragmentation, but it was necessary to frighten him. "Let me come with you and together we will rout the ghouls which desire to devour your soul to augment their own lives."

Almost disappearing in his terror he cried out "Do not leave me. I cannot see you any more."

"It is you who have left me. I promise I will not forsake you until we have won this battle. Come back at once."

❊ ❊ ❊

It was strange, I had never given anyone in our group a direct order before, but had politely asked them to act according to whatever I thought would be to our mutual advantage. A new decisiveness had entered me and immediately he returned to my side.

"Do not leave me," he repeated urgently.

"Literally hand in hand we will go together wherever your evil genius leads us until we have found its shining twin." I held out my hand towards him. He looked at it nervously.

"It is so white," he murmured as he touched it with a nail bitten finger.

"Hold it. It will not strike you." As he took it I kept my gaze steadily on him because I sensed he was tempted to crush my fingers until I cried out. He not only controlled his sudden sadistic desire but bending his head, he kissed them one by one. I knew then that he was mine and I prayed that I would be worthy of his trust and strong enough to lead him away from the darkness of ignorance and despair.

❊ ❊ ❊

Our journeys commenced quite soon, but first I was summoned by our Teacher-Lord.

"Are you fully aware of the dangers of this path which you have chosen, Perima?" He asked. "You have no experience of the Dark Places."

"I know, but this is a task I have to perform. Tepi is so vulnerable and he could become sufficiently incapacitated to be of no further use to the group."

"There are many capable and willing to take his place."

"They have not his genius."

"Why is his genius so important to you? Others have potential genius too."

"But his is mature. It is ripe like a fruit ready to fall from a tree, but it is almost smothered by his past and is all but extinguished. It must be saved and brought into the light or Tepi will become a useless moron."

"You could be seriously injured, and you are of greater value to the group than he is."

"I am prepared to take the risk, so strong is my conviction that the freeing of his genius is not only a necessity for him, but for the group and me personally."

"Are you not afraid?"

"In Truth I had not considered that aspect of the venture – but yes, I am."

"That is good for otherwise I would not allow you to proceed. I will be with you wherever you are, and together we will render Tepi and the group a great service."

❋ ❋ ❋

I bowed and left His Presence, but not before I had imprinted on my mind His beautiful image as He stood and blessed me, so that we should have a talisman to protect us wherever we were led, for now I knew that the project was no longer mine but that He would Master-mind its execution from beginning to end.

I called on Tepi the following day and asked him if he was ready to begin our search. He shook his head.

"I refuse to take you with me – the experiences are worse since you asked to come with me."

"I do not accept that," I said. "I think that the idea of my presence has given you a double fear. You are afraid for me as well as of the conditions themselves. You have no choice; our Teacher-Lord sent for me and he has given the project His Blessing. Come, you must allow me to enter your aura."

He removed the natural barrier which everyone possesses as a protection against infiltration by unwanted beings and I found myself surrounded by a confusion of images, some beautiful, some malign but none in its appointed place.

❋ ❋ ❋

Everyone, unless sufficiently advanced to be able to cast out undesirable thoughts, has all past experiences within his subconsciousness, but the bad should be kept in separate compartments from the good in order that they may be controlled.

"We must first restore some order to this chaos," I said. "Let us begin with a single quality – Beauty."

"That is easy," he smiled. "Beauty is present. I have but to think of you." He closed his eyes; the whirling atoms gradually settled and we found ourselves in a scene from his youth where he was filled with happiness. The environment was delightful and, like most young fairies, Tepi performed his task of giving power to the plants, enjoying himself with friends in play and expanding his knowledge with the help of kindly teachers.

"Now let us take one of your negative traits. You choose, dwell upon it and we will see where your thoughts lead us." The sunny fields and flowers vanished to be superseded by choking, Cimmerian night. The atmosphere was so thick that I could not breathe and I would have fainted had not Tepi put his arms around me. "Oh! Perima, I warned you. I did warn you."

His anguished voice and concern gave me the will to conjure up my talisman, the image of our Teacher-Lord as He blessed me. Immediately a faint beam of Light pierced the gloom to shine upon us and I was able to breathe once more, returning to normality just in time to see a great beast with slavering jaws and blazing red eyes leaping towards us.

"Stand back," I commanded. "Who are you?"

"Jealousy," it roared and the sound ricocheted around us. "Jealousy – jealousy – jealousy."

"Be silent. Normal jealousy is not a very intimidating aspect of the mind. You have an inflated opinion of your importance. Look – I will show you mine." A little creature with sad eyes lay at my feet, tethered to my ankle with a silken cord.

"A tamed jealousy" it snarled, its wart-strewn nostrils twitching in disgust. "I will devour it in a single gulp." Purposefully it paced round us preparing to attack, snapping its teeth in anticipation of so tender a meal. I drew on the ray of light surrounding us and whispering to Tepi, "Think of protective love," I guided the power-thought towards the prowling beast, which stopped in its tracks in confusion, then slunk away.

"Come back," I ordered it. "We do not want to lose you. Stay where we can see you, and behave." It lay down a short distance from us, baring its fangs intermittently and lashing its tail in frustrated rage as we poured thoughts of peace and love towards it until it fell asleep.

❖ ❖ ❖

We returned to our rooms and when I had rested and recharged my weakened power I went to see Tepi.

"I have come to thank you for saving me." He turned as white as chalk.

"Could you have died?" he asked, his lips trembling.

"No, for you would have carried me home within the safety of the ray, but I could have been incapacitated for a time. I made a grave error by making an instantaneous descent from the beauty and peace of the scene of your childhood into conditions I had not previously experienced, without making due preparation. I almost paid the penalty for my folly."

"But I did so little. I only put my arms around your shoulder."

"Dear, dear Tepi. It was not your supporting arm that saved me but your love." He closed his eyes, overcome with emotion. Then he smiled, and I continued. "You helped me Tepi; I could not have tamed that unruly brute without you."

"You made it seem so easy. I have often tried to control them by shouting and hitting them but they are stronger than me."

"Did I strike it or shout?" I asked him. "You need power, not noise or strength – and the right power. You know, do you not, that this fearsome beast is but a personified aspect of the negative side of your nature. Always use positive goodness to overcome negative failings. Each positive quality is a tiny beam from the Prime Force manifested by a Shining One. Form a link with the appropriate angel when confronting an antagonist and you will not fail."

CHAPTER 9
TEPI'S PAST AND HIS BEASTS

Whenever our Formation-work permitted, we returned to the dark recesses of Tepi's subconscious to seek out more of his beasts. Sometimes none came and when this happened we drew on the power from our Teacher-Lord both to enhance and enlarge the area of the light which we had produced when dealing with Jealousy. Eventually we were able to discern the outline of the surrounding rocks, as they oozed an evil smelling liquid, and later, passages presumably leading to other caverns which we could not see. As we worked, we could hear grunts, groans terrifying roars and howls as the beasts preyed on one another and fought for supremacy.

The increasing light seemed to frighten and yet at the same time to fascinate them and, as they became bolder and ventured nearer, we were able to shine a beam on them. We always knew, or perhaps we were told, which adverse aspect they represented; and by adding our own positive thoughts to the ray provided, we eventually obtained a degree of control over them. Intolerance succumbed to Patience, Malice to Goodwill and Selfishness to Generosity.

While we encouraged those we knew to enter the area of light, others were skulking in the surrounding gloom. One of the crevices in the rock was occupied by Avarice. We examined its home during its absence and found a heap of rubble, bones and scraps of furred flesh torn from other beasts. When it returned from its excursions, its mouth was always filled with objects to add to its hoard, and when in residence, the slightest sound or movement would elicit furious roars and spurts of flame as a warning to any with ideas of stealing its treasures.

We often heard squeaks and scuffles behind us and we would catch a glimpse of a pair of bulbous eyes peering at us from a fissure in the rocks, but our attention would cause their immediate withdrawal. I do not think that the creature had a body, for we never saw more than the terrified eyes or a bedraggled tail, which it turned towards us as it fled screaming into the darkness; for this was Fear.

We were eventually able to gather the partially tamed beasts within the circle and continued to give each the appropriate ray, until one day Tepi asked me if he could try to control them without my aid.

I was somewhat apprehensive as to whether he had the ability to protect himself, but with a word of encouragement I finally withdrew from the scene, using my extra-vision to watch from a distance. As he eyed the beasts one by one, he appeared to be somewhat nervous, until he remembered to invoke the aid of our Teacher-Lord. With his arms raised above his head in supplication, he concentrated his thoughts on bringing the power down. As soon as he removed his will from the beasts, they sprang to their feet snarling; then crouched ominously ready to attack. Tepi stood motionless, oblivious of the danger, and I was about to speed to his side when a broad shaft of light passed through him to divide so that each creature was caught in its calming ray. For a moment they were dazzled and began to slink away, but one by one they returned as though to a magnet. Tepi now looked like a beacon as the beasts circled him, snarling now at each other rather than at him. Gradually their mood changed and they began to play, cuffing each other with their great feet, as they rolled about, roaring amiably, their tongues lolling in unwonted pleasure.

❊   ❊   ❊

The light gradually faded and when Tepi returned to his sub-conscious he looked with amazement at the incredible scene before him. He began to laugh loudly and uncontrollably. Because of its novelty this sound, which the beasts had never heard before, pierced the greater noise of their game: they stopped their antics to gaze at Tepi in astonishment before they turned and fled.

"I did it. I did it!" I sensed his excitement before he actually reached me.

"Well done, but you could not have gained your victory alone."

His face became grave. "I know. He was with me."

"Indeed He was; we would not have succeeded without His power. Power has many aspects as we know, and in the final phase of the session, you involuntarily chose the right one – Laughter, so now you owe the beasts a debt for they have given you back your sense of humour. When you used to hit them and shout you failed firstly because your actions were prompted by fear, and secondly they are accustomed to tremendous clamour and much greater pain than you could possibly inflict on them. The strange sound of your helpless laughter made them afraid of you, not an ideal reaction I admit, but a promising start to a new relationship. Another time let them play for a longer period, for this too is a new experience for them; then laugh and when you have taught them to laugh with you, they will be amiable companions rather than enemies."

❊ ❊ ❊

Tepi made excellent progress and before long he was rolling about on the rocky ground, boxing and playfully snarling at his beasts. This was a great step forward but one cannot leave undesirable aspects of one's character deep in the sub-conscious, but must bring them to the surface where the logical thinking mind can analyse and eventually control them.

We decided to tame each creature separately, but first Tepi had to develop its positive characteristic in his work and life on the conscious level.

"Which shall we endeavour to tame first?" I asked him. He sighed. "I am ugly, greedy, malicious, jealous and yes – cruel, among other failings. You have met my negative traits in their brutish forms."

"Your looks accrue from your defects. When you laughed you were transformed because temporarily you realized how ludicrous your present nature is. You were really laughing at yourself, not them."

"It is both strange and frightening to see oneself dissected into a crowd of hideous beasts. 'Know thyself' our Teacher-Lord frequently tells us but as it is all but unbearable to know myself, I cannot expect the others to want to do so. They all dislike me."

"I have seen what the others only guess and I love you, but now I want to know you in your true light. I can see your potential, the light side of your darkness and one day all will see it too."

"You are just being kind. You are sorry for me."

"I am being neither kind nor sorry for you. We need you. Do not forget you are a necessity for the ultimate success of our work, for within you is the radiance which will bring to life that which is at present but an embryo."

"You love to talk in riddles."

"It is the way my mind works. Images have to be found to clothe thoughts in order to make them intelligible. We will work on your light so that eventually it will manifest as a replica in miniature of the Light of the plane where your higher self lives. Now, Tepi, which of your beasts shall we endeavour to bring obediently to heel first?"

"Jealousy."

"Of whom are you most jealous?"

"Our leader, of course. He has my rightful position."

I smiled at him. "That is true, but not yet. One day you will be leader and a worthy one. Go to Eremus and tell him of your jealousy and ambition."

"You are mad. He would dismiss me from the group." He paused. "I will go but only if you come with me to plead my cause."

"I will do as you wish this time but you must learn greater self-reliance. We will go now," I added firmly before he had time to consider the risk involved in my suggestion. Would Eremus's pride in his position overcome his better nature? Having returned to our own plane, we entered his dwelling and bowed.

"What can I do for you on this unexpected visit?" he asked.

"Tepi has something he wishes to say to you." We waited but Tepi said nothing, his eyes remaining fixed on the ground.

"What is it? Have you been doing something of which I would not approve?" Again silence. "Tepi, I have work to do, and while I am always willing to consider any suggestion or listen to difficulties being experienced by a member of the group, I have no time to waste."

"I want to be leader." Tepi blurted as though spitting out an angry wasp.

"And what are your qualifications?" Eremus asked good-humouredly.

"At present none, but I have this burning ambition which will destroy me unless you give me some hope."

"On the surface you have little to recommend you and my first reaction is to dismiss you from this interview, but I feel prompted to advise you; learn to do your work with better grace and to establish good relations with the other members of the group, for without these two essential attributes you will never be promoted let alone become a leader. And yet" – he paused – "there is something in you which, against my better judgment, keeps attracting my attention. You produce the most unlikely suggestions for linking two unwilling components together, and nine times out of ten, they succeed where more orthodox methods have failed. From where do you get your ideas, Tepi?"

"From my heart. My heart tells me the answers when all the others are using their minds."

"That is a good reply. I suggest that you give your heart to Perima and between you, you may succeed in making a leader of you yet." Tepi looked at me and then at Eremus. Was he laughing at him? I was not sure.

"The heart is the seat of the emotions," Eremus continued. "It is a symbol of love, which is the centre of your being. When you have linked its beat to the sonorous rhythm of the Universe, you will find not only yourself but the path of your destiny. Think about this truth and come and see me again."

❧ ❧ ❧

"What did he mean?" Tepi asked me when we had reached his room.

"Eremus has many good qualities and I have to confess that he has more insight than I thought."

"Why do you both talk in riddles?"

"Because that is the only way that one can speak when being inspired to give the right answer. We must work on his advice until we can both hear the music which he described."

I had myself often heard the music of the Spheres in the wind soughing in the trees, the roar of the sea, the melodious tinkle of the flower-bells and in the beating of my own heart in both joy and sorrow. "We must search for this sound" I said decisively although I was uncertain how to begin, for Tepi was far from musical. "What resonance do you find the most beguiling?"

"Yours," he replied promptly.

"I was thinking more in terms of Nature. The sea, the wind, the rain all have their song." He looked doubtful.

"When you were young, I know you were happy for I have seen you as a child. You knew Nature's melody then; how did you lose it?"

A sullen expression came over his face. "I have forgotten."

"You have erected a screen to conceal something which happened. It has formed an impenetrable barrier which not only protects you from what you wish to forget but also deprives you of access to the happy memories in your life."

He sighed. "I know that I suffered beyond my capacity to bear. Do not force me to go through the experience again. It is finished."

"That is the key which makes it possible for you to bring back this memory. It is finished yet, at the same time it has contributed to your present being and is thus part of you. Do you want access only to the beasts in the hidden depths of your sub-conscious?"

"I refuse to think of, or discuss it."

"And what about your heart? Is it to be deprived of the memory of an important part of its growth? Go now; attune yourself to its vibrancy and perhaps it will tell you what I have failed to explain."

❧ ❧ ❧

After he left me, I played my lute, hoping that the music would somehow help me to solve Tepi's problem. Sound is potent. We all have a Mantric Note, given to us at the moment we enter manifestation; in truth in the beginning it is all that we have, I had known my own for many years but I had not listened for Tepi's. Indeed I would not do so without his consent; for it is a precious possession to be shared only with chosen friends.

Several days passed and I saw Tepi only at work. He was obviously reluctant to carry out my suggestion of recalling his past, but as I had much to do I was willing to wait, knowing that Higher Forces were operating.

Eventually he sought me out. "I think I am ready now, but you must come with me."

"I will come whenever you are in the mood to set out."

"Now," he said urgently. "Let us go now."

We sat in my room facing each other. "I must enter your aura again. Have I your permission?" I asked. He nodded his head but when I tried to do so, I was unable to pierce even the outer perimeter. "Tepi, I need more than a nod, you must add will. Open the door of your mind, otherwise I cannot enter."

"I have never shared my being with anyone. I am nervous."

"I have not asked to share your being; neither of us is ready for that experience, I am but seeking to enter your subconscious mind at a different level from that to which you led me when we met the beasts, and in the brief episode before that, when you were a child. You must search for the sequence of events which led to your tragedy. When you have found it, call me and I will come."

He turned his thoughts inwards and after a short while he willed me to join him. We became part of a beautiful landscape with mountains, a lake and fields radiant with wild flowers; the breeze was gentle yet it also emanated the energising quality of snow on the distant peaks that reflected the light of a summer sun. Many Nature Spirits were giving power to the flowers as Tepi and other fairies mentally controlled their actions. After a while he withdrew his will and the little workers began to dance and gambol among the plants they had recently been tending. How changed he was, his almost permanent scowl, etched by his suffering, being replaced by an infectious grin. Later he met his friends to discuss the day's work and decide which area would receive their attention the following day.

Suddenly dark clouds began to form. I noticed that the storm-controller had an evil face which indicated that the next half-hour would test the young fairies to their capacity. At the first sign of change in the colour of the clouds all the fairies gathered together and ordered the nature Spirits to take shelter below the larger plants in order to have some protection. They themselves stood in a series of circles facing outwards with their hands raised palms upwards in the banning position as they used their tiny wills to combat the coming storm. Great drops of rain fell on them, the gale blowing the water among the flowers, which bowed their heads to the ground.

The fairies too were flattened, but each time they rose up through the deluge to join hands and re-form their circles. Beams of light pierced the storm-clouds and entered the fairy-rings, spreading to the surrounding land until a single radiant sheet reflected upwards and dispersed the clouds. Even when the main danger was past, there was much work to do and the exhausted fairies ran or flew among the plants willing them to raise their drooping heads. Unlike those on Earth, fairy flowers do not break and a little encouragement will cause them to raise their faces and rejoice in the Light that ever plays on them. This Light is dimmed only when dark forces temporarily escape from their own domain and try to wreak havoc wherever there is unity.

❀ ❀ ❀

When we had returned to my room I said "Thank you Tepi, you and your friends did well."

"That was just routine. After the event was over we realized that we had enjoyed it in spite of the drenching we received and the terror, for we had faithfully followed the storm-pattern and enabled our angel to overcome the enemy through our actions. He always impressed on us that he was unable to do this unless we assumed the correct battle-stations; the rings are not haphazard formations but are set in a specific design that causes the reflection of the Light to break the power of the storm and at the same time to disband its instigators together with their servants the black clouds."

❀ ❀ ❀

Sometimes when we were working in the circle of light preparing the conditions for another training session, Greed would shamble past us with its extendable proboscis snuffling up and down the boulders in search of spattered blood. When it succeeded it let out hysterical yelps as it tore at the surrounding rock with its granite teeth and iron claws.

When it had hacked off a blooded chunk, it would crunch and crunch and finally dispatch it, not without difficulty, into its overfed belly, which already dragged on the ground.

This meal was often regurgitated with a clatter, recrunched and swallowed; these actions being repeated several times until eventually its strange sustenance would remain in the hidden recess of its nether regions. Sometimes another beast would attempt to steal some of the vomit, but would turn tail after it had been clawed and bitten with amazing dexterity, considering the bulk of its protagonist.

Tepi and I, although revolted by these scenes, were astonished at the determination with which this enormous creature scrambled over the rocks, often crashing to the ground with angry roars as it searched for its seemingly endless meal. Its cries were piteous when its trunk-like snout detected the blood it so relished, but its cumbersome body prevented the fulfilment of its craving in spite of repeated efforts.

In the peace of our own sphere, we often discussed how we could contend with this beast's voracious appetite.

It was obviously beyond reasonable expectation that we could succeed by beaming Generosity towards it – the gap was too wide. We therefore decided to use Satisfaction in its Satiety aspect. We also realized that we must not allow Greed within the circle of light as we did the others, for it might well transfer its desire for blood-strewn rocks to the life-force within the enclosure. If it used its seemingly indefatigable hunger to satisfy this new craving, it could easily drain the entire area. Whereas we could withdraw to our own plane, it would be disastrous for the other beasts as, without the influence of the beneficial rays which we were giving them, all progress would be lost.

On our next descent into Tepi's subconscious, we directed Satisfaction/Satiety thoughts towards Greed as soon as it appeared, but no effect was achieved on that occasion, or during its following three visits. But later, after the second disgorgement had taken place, it paused, snuffled at the steaming pile it had ejected and turned away leaving it for others. We felt we had achieved a minor victory or at least won the chance of eventual success.

The beast had ignored us; in fact its mind was so occupied with filling its stomach that I do not think it was even aware of our presence. Then one day its eyes turned towards us and it waddled in our direction until it reached the barrier which we had erected to prevent it entering the circle of light. It peered at Tepi in a puzzled way then went back to its foraging, returning on several occasions and trying unsuccessfully to come closer to us. Finally with deliberation it emptied the contents of its belly with a rattling squelch as near to Tepi as the barrier allowed.

This vile hotchpotch was indescribable and the stench nauseating, for this time not only had the blooded rocks and scraps of fur and flesh been ejected but all its entrails as well, heaving and squirming as though they were alive. It proceeded to push by giving sharp jabs with its snout, until the steaming mess came through the barrier and lay writhing at Tepi's feet. He leapt back with a horrified "Ugh!"

"Tepi," I said, "The beast is presenting you with a gift."

He turned towards me; his jaw dropped at so grotesque a concept, then he covered his mouth with his hands as he rocked silently backwards and forwards in his effort to control his mirth. At last he managed to blurt out: "Perima, what can I do?" I looked at him with my eyes twinkling. "You must thank Greed and show your gratitude."

Tepi skirted his unwanted offering and walked out of the circle. The beast towered above him and for a while Tepi was uncertain how to deal with the situation. Then he stepped on to one of its great feet and pulled himself up the leg by grasping clumps of hair until he reached the matted chest which he proceeded to scratch as he repeated "Thank you, thank you my very dear Greed." The beast's jaws opened and I quickly absorbed sufficient light to direct a shot of anaesthetising power should it be required. Slowly it drew its lips back from its teeth. Greed was grinning. Then an extraordinary sound like pebbles hurtling down a mountain erupted from its throat. Greed was purring.

Tepi leapt clear as it slumped to the ground in a haze of delight and we continued to pour Satiety upon it until eventually the beast staggered to its feet and lumbered away trailing the empty sack of its belly between its legs.

✿ ✿ ✿

On the next occasion when Tepi and I went back in Time, he had left his work in the depths of the country to enter a school where he learned greater control over the nature Spirits. He had known how to direct them to the next phase of their work according to the life-pattern of a comparatively small number of field plants. Now he was taught that of cultivated flowers which are more complex in their being. Later he moved to a larger garden where he became a member of a happy family group which worked side by side under the instruction of a guardian – thus they were learning and also imparting their knowledge to the little nature Spirits under their control. He was still a member of a group but his individuality was growing and he was developing preferences among both plants and the fairies with whom he worked.

He then went to an experimental garden to which plants from a higher sphere had been transported. This was in order to test them in the less rarefied atmosphere than that to which they had been used. Their delicate bodies would absorb some of the surrounding raw material thus enabling them to exist on this lower plane. A gradual descent into ever coarsening matter was experienced until eventually the plant would be able to live on Earth. This change in conditions, though gradual, would sometimes prove beyond the capacity of the more fragile ones; the life particle would break away from the new constricting form and return to the Essence of the Species to begin another cycle of descent into matter. This was testing work but Tepi instinctively seemed to know which of the few rays he had learned to administer was the right one to stabilize a wavering plant.

His next move was to a more advanced experimental garden where lifeless plant-forms, consisting of no more than a vague outline, awaited impregnation by soul-particles. A minute fragment of life would alight on one of the misty frames and either accept or reject it. Sometimes a potential plant would be entered, only to disintegrate as the life-particle rebelled at even so slight a restriction. It would remain free until its instinct for manifestation would cause it to approach another form. There might be several unsuccessful attempts before a compatible body was found and the soul-particle "housed." This acceptance of restraint would be of a very temporary nature and soon the life-fragment would escape from its prison. However, even so brief a union served to quicken the plant-form, ensuring its survival until the inevitable return of its particle which was now incomplete in itself having left some of its essence with the plant-form during its brief visit. Inherent desire for wholeness and manifestation would force it to rejoin its body, encouraged by the fairy-attendant. Once again Tepi proved his ability by aiding life-particles to find a compatible form and when its period of temporary freedom was over, guiding it back to its chosen body.

The happiness of these gardens of new growth is wonderful to experience. The life-particles are a force from a Higher plane and plants which have been but a concept in the mind of an Angel become a reality. Tenuous matter is given a degree of stability, and is transformed into a beautiful living organism for the delight of all. At the same time, this enables the life-particle to manifest itself according to its nature for even at that stage it has a choice, though a limited one, of the colour and perfume that it will give to the world.

Chapter 10
Overcoming Cruelty

O n one of our visits when no beasts were with us and we were replenishing the power within the circle, we heard in the distance a tumultuous noise. Always there was discordant clamour, but this was beyond our previous experience. Immediately we invoked more protective power and assumed our "alert" position, which is back to back, so that we could visually cover each entrance to the cavern.

The first to dash past us was Fear, squealing hysterically as, with eyes and tail telescoped together, it fled from its pursuer. Avarice was already in its lair; its red eyes peered out for a moment but quickly vanished. Then a group of howling, whimpering, screaming creatures, some of them known to us, careered past, unseeing in their terror.

I could feel Tepi's shoulders tense against mine in trepidation. Although I knew that nothing could harm us within the circle, I could not think which of the many beasts that stalked each other, or at times belligerently paced round us, could be causing such pandemonium.

With resounding bellows something was crashing from side to side up one of the tunnels. We quickly changed our position so that we both faced whatever danger was approaching. The noise became stupefying as a monstrous brute lurched through the entrance to the cavern. Unlike any of the other beasts, except when they were foraging among the higher rocks, this one was standing upright; his legs were as thick as the trunks of small trees and were covered with coarse, black fur. Tepi and I both gasped as it turned towards us, for the face was that of a man; it was stub-horned and mainly covered with hair, but nonetheless it was human. His mean eyes glowed like small coals in the darkness and he was armed with an array of clubs and a large catapult made from the skins and bones of beasts.

It was these weapons which we had heard crashing against the walls as he made his way up the tunnel.

"Do not move," I warned Tepi.

"Is that m-m-my c-c-cruelty?" he stuttered in horror.

"No, this is no ordinary embodied trait of an individual but a personification of group-cruelty."

Cruelty proceeded to hurl rocks down every passage, each assault being followed by terrified howls and screams from the beasts which had neither the time nor dexterity to take adequate cover. Half of Avarice's tail protruded from its lair, but not for long as a blow from a club ensured its speedy withdrawal to the accompaniment of a piercing shriek.

After a while Cruelty stopped his roaring in order to listen. The silence was, if possible, more frightening than the din, because it held menace-in-waiting. Tension grew and we knew that nerves must soon crack. First a whimper came from a cleft in the rock. Cruelty thrust in a hairy fist bringing out a small rat-like creature which he held squirming and squealing for a full minute before putting it in his mouth. One crunch and it was dead – at least its body was dead. Nothing dies in the Dark Places; in time it cloaks its being in another form.

Cruelty took a club in both his hands and systematically covered every inch of rock with resounding blows until the floor was covered by small, terrified creatures which had slithered from their protective fissures. They ran or wriggled hither and thither trying to escape but they were scooped up by the handful and either eaten, trampled on, or thrown against the rocks until all perished.

He tried to reach Avarice cowering in its lair but his arm was quickly withdrawn dripping with blood after a vicious bite, followed by a shower of stones. Avarice must indeed have been desperate, to part with some of his precious hoard.

This event seemed to sober Cruelty somewhat, and with a few final kicks at the dead creatures on the ground he disappeared groaning and cursing up one of the tunnels.

* * *

We returned to my room dazed and horrified that we had been able to do nothing to prevent either Cruelty's vicious assaults or to alleviate the suffering of the beasts and smaller creatures. Oblivion soon mercifully claimed us and when we later returned to consciousness, we were filled with determination somehow to protect the beasts with which we had originally been in conflict.

"Who were they all? Where did they come from?" Tepi asked in bewilderment. "They cannot all have been mine."

"No, of course not. You would have recognised your own instantly. The cavern where we work is part of your subconscious mind but, as you know, there are many tunnels leading in and out of it. These link it to the group subconscious of those with whom you work and to other 'divisions' such as the inmates of the plane where you live, your species and, eventually, the Universe. All are interpenetrating. As a rule inmates of one cavern or division stay in their prescribed area and that of their group or family, but given certain conditions they have access to regions beyond. The denizens of the larger caverns can also enter and pass through smaller ones and vice-versa. This Cruelty must come from some large criminal group and should certainly not be entering our area, which contains misdemeanours rather than evil."

"Should we go to our Teacher-Lord and ask for His aid? This monster is obviously beyond our powers to overcome." I considered his suggestion and then replied. "It would ease our problems but He expects us always to do our utmost before asking for anything but power. What does your heart say, Tepi?"

"I must listen to it again and perhaps it will tell me."

"And I will play my lute and hope that music will reveal the answer."

We parted but I was unable to play. I was too weary for one must be fully alert to receive a message through music when it manifests without thought from the player.

Tepi and I met at work but each time we were obliged to admit failure, indeed, whenever I tried to play, my fingers refused to pluck the strings.

❖ ❖ ❖

After a week had passed Tepi came to me and said: "The beasts that we have partially tamed are to act as intermediaries. That is all I know."

"Intermediaries," I repeated. "Surely not between us and Cruelty for they would be disembodied. We must meditate on the word, or rather I will, while you attune yourself to your heart once more."

"Intermediaries?" I mused. "Between who and what? Each beast's intermediate state lies between its basic fault and its opposite quality. As their defects are different, so are they separate; therefore they prey on one another. Could the latent good within each combine and overcome Cruelty?" I picked up my lute and this time my fingers plucked the strings but only jangling discords emerged. Disappointed, I was about to call Tepi, when he entered the room.

"The beasts are to work together," he told me.

"My meditation indicated this too, but my lute gave me only harsh, jarring sounds."

"There will indeed be strife but my partially trained beasts will act as intermediaries to gain help from the untamed ones in the adjoining caverns. They must all know Cruelty and be terrified of him. If, instead of running away, they all stand their ground and eventually attack him, some bringing him down while others steal his weapons, they can overcome him."

"Must we use savagery to overcome even evil?" I asked doubtfully. "Should we not try to use the Light to attain our purpose?"

"Power will flow to and through the beasts and in its coarsened form will become the strength and strategy to overcome their enemy." I looked at Tepi and realized that he was 'away.' When he returned he answered my previous question. "Yes, that is a problem but I doubt if Light alone..."

"Tepi," I interrupted him, "you have just provided the answer, or rather your higher self did. You have been 'away'."

"Away? Yes, yes, I remember now," he said excitedly. "Ask your lute for confirmation." My fingers plucked the strings but it was not I who was playing it. First there was an uneven beat which gradually changed to a regular rhythm. My fingers became frenzied and tore at the strings to produce violent dissonance, chords be interrupted by a chromatic ascending scale played crescendo, symbolising, we hoped, victory.

As there was much planning to do we met every day to discuss the best way to talk to the half-tamed beasts. We decided that Tepi should be their Leader as they were part of his make-up, and I should act in an advisory capacity.

We built up a brighter than usual area of power and invited the beasts in as though for a normal treatment. When play-time came, Tepi stepped forward and embraced them all in turn.

"Dear beasts," he said, "the time has come for action." They grinned and began their usual antics.

"Stop" Tepi commanded. Although surprised, they obeyed, regarding him quizzically. "I want to talk to you about Cruelty." The change was dramatic. Some covered their heads with their paws; others would have fled had not the light held them; the rest stood motionless as though frozen in terror.

"Be calm. You are mine. I will not let you be vanquished by another."

Avarice removed a paw and peeped at him with one frightened eye. Jealousy came and lay at his feet seeking comfort to assuage his terror.

"We need an army," Tepi said.

"An army?" they repeated without understanding.

"An army is many. Cruelty is one. Many can overcome one, however powerful. Cruelty has no friends. You have friends and also enemies. Join with both – make friends of your enemies through this communal need and we will advise you step by step."

"Make friends with those who have preyed on us for years?" asked Malice incredulously.

"And have you not preyed on them?"

"It is a matter of survival."

"Do you think any of you will survive now Cruelty has invaded your territory? He has weapons to destroy you. We must use guile and numbers."

Their powers of understanding were not great but these clear facts they could assimilate.

"You within the circle are now living in amity" Tepi continued. "You must not at any time work alone except when approaching known friends. Lure your enemies into this cavern and enter the circle of light where we will be waiting to help you."

"They will follow and steal our light" complained Selfishness.

"The light acts as a barrier against those who have not yet received it. Light itself is inexhaustible; there will be enough for all." They looked doubtful but they agreed to talk to their friends.

* * *

After they had gone, Greed entered the cavern. We had not seen it since the presentation of its strange gift to Tepi and we were amazed at the change. Its stomach no longer dragged on the ground and its gait had become almost springy. It licked the slime off the rocks and nibbled the sparse lichen which somehow grew in the darkness.

Tepi left the circle and stroked it. "How handsome you have become." Greed grinned, its eyes rolling in pleasure. "Come with me and meet a friend." We opened up the circle to let it in for the first time. When it saw me, it dropped its front legs on the ground placing its head upon its feet, leaving its great rump erect; Greed was bowing. This sight was indeed comic but I was both touched and gratified that respect had entered its consciousness. I placed my hand on one of its legs and dribbling, it licked my fingers almost removing their surface in its pleasure.

"Greed, you are indeed redeemed," I said. "Partake sparingly of our light and you will one day become a leader."

It did not understand but a great shuddering breath of pleasure shook its frame and, with the breath, it inhaled the light. A look of wonder filled its eyes as it stood gently waving its tail. For the first time in its life it was feeling joy. Greed was happy. What a triumph for all three of us.

After a short time its legs crumpled and it slumped to the floor asleep. "Happy dreams" murmured Tepi, as he kissed the spot between its eyes; this was no haphazard action as this is the seat of enlightenment which if awakened could speed Greed's deliverance from the Dark Places.

In the days that followed we met our beasts, their friends and later their enemies, to impress on them the necessity to forget individual animosity and to combine their forces to overcome the common foe.

During this period Cruelty made several forays into the area, creating havoc and inflicting pain and body-extinction on more of the beasts and smaller creatures; this caused many waverers to join us.

❖ ❖ ❖

The time was now ripe to ask a number of those already working in the Dark Places to help us to increase the light in both volume and radiance. The beasts were now receiving training to play their specific parts in the conflict but we were well aware that fear and excitement could overcome their ability to do so. We therefore sought the aid of technicians to programme the power with the proposed action for every beast taking part in the plan. Each would have its own individual ray for its protection and to ensure that it performed its function from the moment it took up its battle position.

We of course had no idea when Cruelty would decide to invade our territory again but we had scouts on duty, covering a wide area to make certain that we had sufficient time to collect our beast-battalion together. They had been primed to be ready to flee, screaming in supposed terror as soon as the scouts warned them that Cruelty was in their vicinity; he thus would have no inkling that the situation was different from usual. They had also been forbidden to kill or mortally wound him, and this was difficult for them to accept after all the suffering and body-loss he had inflicted on many of their group. We explained that if Cruelty's form was destroyed, another would eventually take its place, and he would wreak terrible vengeance, if not on them, on the unfortunate inhabitants of another area. The fundamental intention must be that he would be tamed although this would take many years. Eventually they gave a solemn promise to abstain from doing anything that would lead to his death. In fact their individual rays would prevent any such action taking place, but it was important for their own development that they should prove willing to accept instructions.

❈ ❈ ❈

The scouts relayed to us the information that Cruelty was moving in our direction and, after a while, we heard yowls and squeals from the apparently terrified beasts as they ran up the tunnel towards us. Cruelty was charging after them bawling abuse.

On entering the cavern, he was temporarily blinded by the light. Roaring with frustration he blinked and rubbed his eyes. As vision slowly returned, instead of the fleeing whimpering creatures he expected, he saw that every tunnel was filled with defiant, snarling antagonists; the walls of the caverns were lined with them, their lips drawn back and teeth snapping as though with intent to tear him to pieces. Shouting invectives and bawling with rage, he wielded his largest club aiming at the head of his nearest contestant, which dodged the blow, backed then stood its ground. Raising the club he struck again and again but each time its ray protected his intended victim by shining in Cruelty's eyes, impairing his vision.

During these distractions, Greed crawled on his belly behind him and with one bound, seized the club which was raised above his head, wrenching it from his hands. The larger beasts then launched their attack, hurling themselves at him, battering him from the back, the front and from both sides so that he was constantly off-balance.

Smaller rat-like creatures played their part by climbing up his legs and gnawing at the thongs of his weapon-belt. As soon as Cruelty seized one, another took its place and the captured rodent, instead of being paralysed with terror bit and scratched his hand until he hurled it against the rocks but it came to no harm as it was either cushioned by its ray or by the bodies of the larger beasts.

Other rays also activated the hundreds of fleas and bugs that lived in the black fur of Cruelty's legs causing them to run through the hairs, biting and stinging the underlying flesh, so that he hopped first on one foot and then on the other bellowing like a maddened bull as he beat his legs and thighs, but the fur was too thick for his blows to affect the insects.

By this time each thong of the belt had been chewed through and the weapons carried away in triumph. No mortal wound had been administered but all were using teeth and claws to inflict gashes and lacerations from which blood, black and evil-smelling, flowed.

The final blow was delivered by Greed who, standing on its hind legs and still holding the large club firmly in its granite teeth, swung it sideways and struck Cruelty on the back of his skull.

At last Cruelty had had enough. Holding his head in his hands, he staggered down the tunnel up which he had earlier stormed with such confident belligerence, chased by a horde of nipping, clawing, yapping, trumpeting beasts which now knew the value of communal attack.

As all were both over-excited and weary, they were herded back to the cavern to be bathed in a calming blue light until sleep enfolded them. This was the last time that Cruelty ventured into our territory.

Alas, I cannot claim that thereafter there was peace among the beasts but some had proved themselves ready to receive training and power, and others, having worked together, were no longer enemies. A modest start had been made on their long journey out of the darkness of ignorance.

CHAPTER 11
THE VAIN FAIRY

The next step that I witnessed in Tepi's evolution on another journey into his past was obviously quite a long time after I had seen him in the Experimental Gardens. He had grown in both stature and maturity, and had become more fully individualized rather than being a member of a group.

He had now volunteered to tend trees which were failing to adapt themselves to adverse conditions. Normally a period of training would have been required but his unusual instinct for the needs of plants in his care earned him his desired task without this usual procedure.

I watched him as he stood in front of a young sapling. "What ails you?" he asked the attendant fairy as he patted the slender trunk. "You have moisture and light, and a continuous flow of power from your angel. What more do you need?"

There was no reply. He ran his fingers up and down the delicate bole. Then he bent to peer at a spot near its base. "What is this?" he asked. "Your form was unblemished when you entered it. What has happened?" He pressed the defect, and with a scream the young attendant fled. "That is better" said Tepi soothingly. "Make the most of your freedom and explore your surroundings while I mend your tree-form."

Casting off his own body, he entered the sapling and became it. Being more advanced than the departed nature spirit, he was able to locate a blockage caused by a marauding insect, which had entered and made its home in the trunk causing discomfort to its rightful inhabitant.

"My friend," Tepi addressed the insect, "I understand that life is hard for you. You have a delicate body, easily buffeted by wind and rain; perhaps the light is too strong for you, but you must learn to counteract these inconveniences by sheltering under larger forms, not by entering them as an unwelcome guest. As I know that you will refuse to leave of your own accord, I am about to expel you. Prepare yourself, for you will not like being forced from the refuge you regard as yours." He invoked a ray which banished the insect and soon the blemish on the trunk faded leaving only a small discoloration. Then he emitted a summoning note that recalled the legitimate occupier, who returned and settled into his rightful home with a tiny sigh of contentment.

*   *   *

When fairies are sufficiently advanced, they become "guardians" of trees or shrubs. However, some form such a deep affection for a particular species of flower that, instead of changing to those members of the Nature Kingdom whose lives often exceed that of the Human race (except when their true cycle is curtailed by Man for his own purposes) they remain with that group and care for an increasing number of members; later joining others who are experimenting to improve the species by enhancing its colour, size or perhaps longevity.

Those who become guardians often form an alliance which lasts the life-cycle of the tree, but as they grow in knowledge and stature, he or she may become interested in other work, perhaps involving Man. And so young fairies serve both the Nature Kingdom, which is their prime function, and also the Human Race.

*   *   *

The next problem that I watched Tepi solve was a dual one. A fully-grown tree had begun to wither. He examined it in some perplexity because, at this stage of its growth, its guardian should have been able to deal with the situation herself, as their alliance had been functioning satisfactorily for many years; in fact, ever since they had come to the forest.

He addressed the tree-spirit. "This is a puzzling case Gopron. You have done so well with your charge until now. The tree is beautiful and has produced many flowers but then have fallen before the fruit has properly developed. What has gone amiss?"

She pouted and said with a sigh: "I am full of woe."

"Woe is woe and duty is duty," said Tepi cheerfully "They should, however, be kept apart."

"Those who have come to advise me have already expressed in exactly the same way," she said pertly

"Have you, by chance, loved and been rejected?"

There was a slight pause before she answered. "It was not I who was spurned. I rebuffed my suitor, and now I am lonely."

"How can you be lonely in a forest?" Tepi asked incredulously.

She waved her hand scornfully at the surrounding trees. "They are aliens." He took a close look at the different varieties growing in the vicinity and he saw that the tree which had now been put in his care was the sole representative of its species.

He gave a shout of laughter. "It is you and your tree who are the aliens; and how proud you should be. You have been brought here for a purpose."

"I know my purpose. It is to supervise the growth of my tree and to aid it to come to flower and fruit. But I am bored with it all; the cycle is always the same. My suitor who fell in love with me brought a little excitement into my life but I sent him away."

"If you were compatible and he loved you, why did you spurn him?"

"He is only a shrub" she said disdainfully.

"Shrubs are shrubs and trees are trees, but there is no truth in your idea that, because your charge is taller than his, you are therefore superior to him."

"Angels are of tremendous height and they are superior."

"That is because of their purity, intelligence and power; not because their bodies inhabit a vast area of the atmosphere."

"I am superior to Mello, nevertheless," she insisted. Tepi shook a finger at her. "Even if you had been superior at the time your spurned him, you are inferior to him now because you have failed in your duty to your tree. Think about that," he said and flew away.

Tepi made enquiries as to where Mello's shrub was growing and paid him a visit. He explained to him that he had been given the task of trying to save Gopron's ailing tree, and repeated the conversation he had had with her.

"She is so beautiful," Mello sighed. "I was over-daring, I should never have approached her."

"Do not confuse foolishness with modesty," Tepi chided him gently. "Come, leave your charge and stand by me."

Mello was a good-looking fairy, and his shrub was beautiful and prolific.

"What a wealth of flowers you have helped to produce."

"They are bigger than those last year and there are more of them," he said with a proud smile, "But it worries me that we have ceased to grow in stature."

"I am not an expert on your species, but could it be that you are fully-grown?"

"No, I have seen many of our kind which are much larger."

"But what of the environment? Were the other shrubs in open country with ample space to spread? Here you must share the light with the trees, and the ground with many small flowers and mosses. Each is entitled to its rightful portion and should not take more. That is the lesson of dwelling in a forest."

Mello was now smiling with satisfaction. "You are right, my brother and sister shrubs were growing in open country, but to tell you the truth I had not thought about sharing. I took as much light, space and moisture as I could."

"Think about this idea then. Take only what you require and perhaps some more weakly plants may survive longer than they otherwise would have done, without depriving you or your shrub of your needs for growth."

❖ ❖ ❖

Tepi allowed about a week to pass before he again went to see Gopron.

"Still full of woe?" he asked cheerfully.

"I am weary," she replied languidly. "I have tried to save my few remaining fruit but they continue to fall."

"Why not pay Mello a visit? His shrub is strong and in full flower. Its invigorating scarlet colour could both cheer and strengthen you and your tree."

"I have never visited him. He has always come to me to pay his respects."

"If it were not a fact that you are the only tree of your species in the forest, and it is essential that some fruit should be saved for reproductive purposes, I would suggest to my superior that you should be allowed to die with your tree."

"Fairies don't die. I know that." she spat at him.

"You would die as a tree-guardian, although it is possible that you might be allotted a few yards of moss to care for." At last Tepi had frightened her as he had intended.

Her eyes blazed. "Moss is only fit to keep my roots cool," she screamed. Tepi, although he had heard her remark, had vanished and the air was the sole recipient of her ensuing rage.

❖ ❖ ❖

He left the two of them to ponder on his suggestions and carried on with his other work until, on about the third day, he saw Mello coming towards him. "I have been thinking that perhaps a gift of my flowers would be more acceptable than my presence. Would you take some to Gopron for me?"

"No," Tepi replied. "The idea is good, but you must present them yourself. On second thoughts, perhaps one perfect bloom would be suggestive of your feelings for her. But I warn you, she is no longer beautiful."

"How can that be?" he said in bewilderment. "She is the most exquisite fairy I have ever seen."

"Then you cannot have looked far."

"Oh! But I have, I assure you. I have met hundreds of female tree-guardians all over the forest."

"I used the wrong expression. I should have said 'deep'. You have been looking at her surface and seeing only what she desires people to see; for she is vain and spends much thought and will on her appearance."

"But many fairies do that. Are you saying that it is wrong to make an effort to manifest beauty when it gives so much pleasure to others?"

"No, no. I am a great admirer of a pretty female face but I have learned not to be fooled by it. Gopron is in great distress and her mind is on matters other than her personal appearance. Her face and form are now her natural attributes."

"Why did you not tell me before? I will go to her at once." His face fell. "But what is the use? She hates me."

"She has spurned you it is true, but that is a different matter from hatred. She has a false idea of her superiority, built up by the adulation she has received from males because of her self-manufactured glamour. The truth is that she has spent so much time on her appearance and entertaining the admirer that she considered temporarily acceptable that she has been neglecting her charge and it is failing; perhaps dying. In a forest this is normally no great tragedy, apart from the fact that a guardian may have been neglecting essential duties and would be suitably demoted. But in this case, her tree is the only one of its species, as you know."

"That was how I knew that she was not only beautiful but also worthy; otherwise she would not have been given this important mission of trust."

"That was true at the time when she was chosen. Where she was working, there were only a few young males more interested in their work than in female fairies, whereas here she has received too much attention for her own good. Never far from Beauty walks Vanity, which should always be kept in its proper place – that is two paces behind. When it is permitted to stride ahead so that the view of Duty is obscured, you will find Trouble as an unwelcome Intruder."

At first stubborn disbelief was printed on Mello's face; but as Tepi continued to talk, concern took its place. "What can we do? I will gather together every friend I have and march to the rescue."

"It is not a question of your friends marching to the rescue. Where are hers? The answer is she has none. She dislikes the female sex and one by one she has discarded all her admirers. That leaves only you."

Mello's eyes opened wide with joy, then dimmed in sorrow. "But she spurned me too. What is to be done? I am so ignorant. I can only admire her from afar, firstly for her beauty and her regal manner, but now that she has lost her looks and is in distress, I realize I truly love her."

"Love is our only hope and you alone possess it" Tepi said solemnly. "Now for some action. First we will go to your shrub and pick one perfect bloom."

Much time was taken over the choice. Tepi found many that he considered of the first quality but each time Mello shook his head. One had a tiny blemish underneath a petal, another a slightly damaged stamen and a third had a seed which he doubted contained sufficient power to grow. At last he looked up, beaming. "This is the one," he said, and Tepi could feel the glow of growth-determination emanating from it.

They set out together but as they neared Gopron's tree he held Mello back. "Look at your 'beauty' now."

"That cannot be my love," he said, and for one moment Tepi thought that Mello's devotion had been extinguished by the sight of the distraught figure, exhausted by giving power to the single fruit which still remained on the tree. Then his face lit up."Now that I am no longer her inferior, perhaps she will accept my flower." Timidly, he walked toward her and laid his offering at her feet. "I bring you the gift of the finest bloom on my shrub as a tribute to the loveliest fairy in the forest."

All anger had gone – despair now ruled. She gazed at Mello in amazement, then burst into tears. "Do not add mockery to my hour of anguish. I am finished as a Tree guardian. I am only fit to tend a few feet of moss." Tepi smiled to himself but without malice.

"To me you are always beautiful," Mello told her earnestly. "The flower is but a reflection of your true self." She picked up the bloom and as she gazed into its heart, some of its perfection was reflected on her face.

"Thank you, Mello," she said quietly. "What I have seen in the flower has given me back some faith in myself even though I am doomed. That one fruit will fall like all the others for I have failed in my duty in search of Beauty." She sighed. "Tell me, Mello, is it so wrong to seek for Beauty?"

"It cannot be. We all seek for Beauty and I have found it in you."

"Then I have not completely failed." She paused, her mental capacities returning. "I have done this service for you, so why should your flower not do the same for my tree. But how? It is so small and my tree is so large. The fruit" she cried and flew up to the branch which bore it, and gently held the flower and fruit together.

Tepi, while retaining invisibility, drew nearer to watch as the power from the strong red bloom, so filled with Mello's love, entered the weak fruit.

"Add your power, both of you," he ordered, the command coming as though from Heaven itself.

They worked as long as their strength remained and then, collapsed in each others arms, they fell asleep at the foot of the tree, which made history, for not only were both fruit and tree saved, but years later a new species came into being, a tall tree with flowers which raised their blazing, scarlet glory above all the other denizens of the forest.

CHAPTER 12
TEPI'S LAPSE

When the time came for Tepi to take on other work, he was given the choice of becoming an under-leader of a large group or a leader of a small one. He considered deeply before reaching a decision because, although success had been his in the various consignments which had been entrusted to him, he knew that he still had much to learn. Which would lead him to greater knowledge for the ultimate benefit of both the fairies and plants in his charge?

Eventually he decided to accept the greater responsibility of being leader of a smaller group, and he was allotted a lonely tract of land in the depths of the country. The task involved would be more difficult than any he had previously experienced because the field was not very fertile and it would be part of his duty to study the soil structure and the prevailing weather conditions, and also to endeavour to increase the number of species capable of growing there. During his period of research he learned how to manipulate many new forces in order to enrich the earth and to make tests with various plants, which were subjected to different powers including his own will, to help them to adapt to conditions other than those to which they were used.

Armed with this knowledge, he eventually took the place of the retiring leader and began his new duties by examining the temperaments and capabilities of his group which consisted of three males and two females. All of them had been working in the field for several years, tending the sparsely growing plants and trees with no thoughts of either expansion or change.

At first they were apathetic as they were convinced that the Lord of Nature planted seeds where they were meant to grow, and that their sole duty was to help them through their cyclic waxing and waning. Tepi told them that if they did not wish to cooperate in this project which had been entrusted to him and them, they must leave and others more open-minded and enthusiastic would be sent to take their place. Faced with an even more radical change, they all agreed to stay and the work began.

At first progress was slow because minds which have stagnated for many years require effort from both pupil and teacher to force them into allowing new ideas to enter, remain and develop, for a while the fairies' little minds were unable to expand and they rejected anything not already known. But as each concept was frequently presented, at last familiarity overcame suspicion, and it was able to find a permanent home. Very slowly progress was made, and the time came for power-sessions to commence on a patch of soil which was to become the experimental nursery-garden.

* * *

Fairies always invoke the angel of their area at least once a day. Normally this is to request a blessing for themselves and the plants with which they work. Now they were taught first to ask for enrichment for the soil, then to note the colour of the power which the angel used and finally the result – whether it quickened or slowed down the action and reaction of the earth's component parts. They were enthralled by their ability to discern the workings of the miniscule particles of life involved and eventually, under Tepi's guidance, they became competent to ask for the specific power required to make the ground suitable to receive a new species of plant and then stabilize it.

Each fairy had innumerable nature spirits in his charge, and these acted as generators for the incoming power. Others made and changed the cells in the plant to enable growth to take place. There were at first many failures, which led to disappointment and even to near-despair, and sometimes the fairies longed to return to their previous, easygoing way of life, when they had followed their simple instructions and obtained the same modest results.

At last they achieved their first success and a new flower accepted the conditions and flourished. Indeed enthusiasm nearly led to its early death as too much power was given, but Tepi managed to save it by reversing the procedure and extracting some of the surplus until the conditions once again became compatible.

During this time the temperament of the fairies was gradually changing. Instead of their having near static minds, their growing enthusiasm and modest successes added new colour to their auras, showing outwardly that mental growth was taking place.

Eventually their successes and failures became about even and they were able to make minor decisions for themselves, provided that they had first gained Tepi's approval for the main project. Their lives too were altered – instead of routine work being followed by play, dancing or riding the air currents, they would of their own free will form discussion groups to decide how the next few days' work would be allotted, and how further improvements could be achieved to save energy and eliminate failure.

As their success ratio grew, more fairies were drafted into the area and these were taught all that the original group had learned. The tract of land became a centre of activity instead of a sleepy and somewhat infertile field; and the nursery was greatly enlarged to become a show place where other fairies came for a period before taking over similar daunting conditions in other parts of the country.

❋ ❋ ❋

Tepi was now the leader of an expanding, changing group which taxed his ability to the limit. His work had always given him both joy and fulfilment; but now the strain of increasing responsibility made him doubt his competence to deal with further development, although he had known, when making his choice, that this had always been the prime factor of the project. Indeed it was this challenge which had influenced his final decision. Had he been wise, he would have taken his problems to his Superior. But he had been loth to do this as the indication would have been that he was incapable of completing the task which up to that time he had taken forward with all its problems so successfully.

Weary and no longer confident that his decisions were either wise or practical, he continued to work beyond both his physical and mental capacity, his exhaustion preventing him from realizing that, without his diligent supervision the fairies' work was also deteriorating below even reasonable efficiency.

The plans for the next stage of expansion were placed before him and, as always, he was asked for his comments. He gave them a superficial examination and decided that they must be put into immediate action or he would be considered a failure. A water network was to be added to the soil improvement programme; so he set about plotting its course throughout his domain. This kind of project had always stimulated him, and he was temporarily filled with renewed energy.

A stream ran beneath his land and the water would have to be drawn to the surface through an artificial duct.

Waterways are not dug or dredged in our realm, but made by thought and will, a meticulous plan being followed. The main canal bed was brought into being, running the length of his tract with a network of rivulets leading from it to the many plants and trees. When filled, their previous reliance on rain in this naturally somewhat dry area would be greatly diminished.

✽ ✽ ✽

At last, after many weeks of planning and mental exertion, the connecting link between the subsoil stream and the overground canal was in place. Many jewel-coloured boats ready for launching lay on the banks; in fact all was ready for the opening ceremony and water carnival.

As always a blessing for the project was invoked by the many who had gathered from miles around. Then all used their will to draw the water up the artificial duct to the surface. It arrived as a small jet, which was greeted with prolonged cheers; gradually it rose higher and divided, to become a fountain. The main stream bed began to fill, and eventually reached the rivulet channels until all were running with the sweet smelling life giving liquid.

The boats were launched to the accompaniment of singing and dancing. The fairies being land dwellers entered the water a little nervously at first; but soon, during the fun of splashing and ducking each other, they became more adventurous and dived to the bottom to examine the stones, which shone like jewels from the reflection of light through the stream above.

Gaiety and the excitement of this new experience made them careless; so none noticed the gathering of black clouds on the horizon. The ripples of laughter continued until simultaneously there was a clap of thunder and the light of sun was extinguished.

A moment of mass shock followed; then the clouds disgorged their contents like a vast cataract. Laughter changed to terrified screams as all endeavoured to flee the scene; the frail boats were smashed to pieces, the flowers and plants broken or swept away by the ruthless torrent. Fairies do not drown but many lost their bodies and reverted to small pale lights either floating precariously or battered underwater until the malice of the storm demons propelled them to the surface to be carried far away from their homes and work.

Tepi had been with his under-leaders in the largest boat, wending its tranquil way along the main stream when the storm struck. He had noticed that the horizon had become dimmed by clouds but there had been no indication that they were moving towards his land.

He later described the affair as a sudden onslaught. The clouds had not advanced in the normal way; it was as though black sheet lightening had driven them across the sky in a single flash; and simultaneously they had discharged their element in its negative destructive aspect as a deluge.

He did everything within his puny power to mitigate the inimical forces but to no avail. Though all but disintegrated he remained at the scene of devastation, which had brought ruin to his work of many years, and disembodiment and terror to all the fairies.

He worked until the last flickering light was found and he supervised transportation to centres of rest or healing according to the needs of each, and then he "died", not as humans do, but he lost his will, already weakened by overwork, and remained in a state of coma for many months.

Tepi's awakening was long drawn out. He had no desire to face the events which had led to the disaster and he continued to slip back into unconsciousness each time his eyes opened. Many methods of resuscitation were tried, rays, the vibrations of friends and the will of his Superior, aided by others of his status. Eventually they found a method to prevent him from regaining oblivion. A constant barrage of sound, beautiful, loud and containing a message of hope to offset his despair, surrounded him from sunrise to moon set. He was allowed brief periods of freedom from this music, and at first he slept, the sleep gradually becoming less heavy until eventually he began to respond rather than trying to escape from it and later he became aware not only of the notes but also the message.

* * *

After all catastrophes there follows an enquiry and when Tepi was considered strong enough, he presented himself before his Superior and Members of a Council of Justice. He readily confessed his refusal to accept his inability to carry the plan for his tract of land to its proper conclusion. He agreed that although it had been beyond his capacity, he had avoided full recognition of this fact, because he was loth to admit failure.

It was explained to him that his Superior had always known that the full project had been beyond his present powers to complete and the test had been to discover how much of the plan he could organize, and whether he had the necessary character to admit his limitations and appeal for help and advice, which would have been gladly given.

"Are you saying I was never meant to succeed?"

"We do not set impossible tasks and expect success, nor do our plans fail to come to fruition. Many expand indefinitely and each organizer must take the work as far as he is able, using all his diligence, imagination and strength. We do not know when this point will be reached, and it is the responsibility of the leader to tell us."

"You mean I was permitted to bring destruction to the plant life on my tract, and for all my fairy helpers and others to be maimed because I did not understand the terms of the assignment?"

"That is what the acceptance of responsibility entails. You failed in your responsibility, not in your work on the project, which you brought nearer to completion than we had expected."

"I shall never forgive myself. Never," said Tepi bitterly. "All that toil, all the Celestial Power used, and so much energy and will from everyone concerned in the work, wasted."

"It is not wasted." The High Justice spoke. "Your work is indelibly imprinted on the land. It is still there beneath the devastation, and in time the fragments will reform themselves into the pattern which was present before the disaster. This storm was not of our making and had you sent a precautionary invocation the moment you noticed the black clouds massed on the horizon, we could have prevented the dire results."

"What can I do to make amends?"

"Only you can find the answer. After the deluge and for much of the time before it, your conduct was exemplary. There will be no disciplinary action. I can only advise you to seek earnestly for the ability to forgive yourself, for we regard what you call your failure merely as a lapse for which no reprimand is needed. We know that those black storm clouds will obscure your many talents for some time to come. It is expedient that you find a way to disperse them as soon as possible."

✽ ✽ ✽

Tepi returned to the scene of the devastation and his tears were added to the waterlogged soil, for not a plant remained. He endeavoured to conjure up the scene as it had been, hoping that his repentance would give it renewed life, but no change took place and he left with the aftermath of the moment of destruction firmly imprinted on his mind.

CHAPTER 13
THE RECOVERY

He joined many groups as a humble labourer. No one knew who he was, so his failure remained his secret.

The years passed and gradually the tragedy reached the edge of his memory and floated away. As he lost the reason for his unhappiness, moroseness and bitterness took the place of despair. He knew that the work he was doing was far below his potential, but his will was at such a low ebb that he had no desire to take part in more important projects or to lay before his various leaders ideas of his own.

He changed his modest tasks frequently, wandering from one group to another. One day he decided to turn towards the west but somehow he found himself roaming along yet another unknown path in the opposite direction until, in the distance, he saw a town. He felt nervous for he knew that towns were not like the countryside – they gave out different vibrations and were places of enclosure rather than freedom. As he drew nearer, the vibrations mingled with his own and as panic seized him, he turned and fled. Before he fell asleep he decided to retrace his steps and take the path leading to the west as he had originally intended, but on waking a curious fascination impelled him towards the town once more.

His progress was slow because each time he felt its vibrations he experienced terror and ran in the opposite direction until the day came when they not only blended with his, but surrounded him and refused to release him. He was trapped – there was no escape. A continuous scream added to his hysteria until the truth dawned – the scream was his own. This knowledge caused it to die to a whimper, as amidst tear and sobs he at last fell asleep, cradled in the welcoming embrace of his future home.

Tepi awoke feeling strangely refreshed and timidly began to test the invisible barriers around him. He found only one direction was open to him – that which led to the town. He sat down with his back towards it, sulking in spite of the beauty of the countryside before him.

Eventually he sighed despondently and began once more to move slowly along the path. Because, during his sleep, he had blended more deeply with the town's vibrations, this time he felt no panic, and he soon arrived before two silver, jewel-embossed gates. Here he was brought to a halt having never previously encountered such a visibly solid barrier; and he had no knowledge of the usual method of gaining entry, which is to ask for permission to pass.

As he found he was unable to retrace his steps, he began to examine the gates, which he found intriguing. Here was an object constructed of metals and precious stones which he had often found in rocks. But because of the intensity of the light and the potency of the love and will of both metal workers and stone polishers, these revealed an astonishing brilliance; and he was transfixed by their beauty and no longer wished to escape, indeed he wanted to know what was behind this gleaming obstacle. He tried climbing, but after reaching a certain point, the metal and jewels became slippery and he slithered back to the ground. He began to search for a suitable tree branch to lean against the doors to aid his ascent, but there was none.

For the first time for many years, here was something he wanted to do and he began to use his long abandoned will. He willed a series of stones to leave their settings so that they protruded sufficiently to enable him to gain a foothold, and by this method, he achieved his purpose and reached the top. At first the light dazzled him and he remained seated on the gates until his eyes and the substance of his body became in tune with the new conditions. After a spell of dizziness, during which he was obliged once more to use his will in order to retain his position, he opened his eyes and the scene became clearer.

Grassland with flowers, shrubs and trees were interspersed by beautiful buildings, all glowing like pearls, with intersecting paths of all colours of the rainbow. He was enchanted, and floated down from his perch. The whole town seemed empty so he moved forward and examined some of the houses more closely. He was amazed at the energy emanating from the plants which seemed to be leaping from the ground to meet those gracefully trailing from the roofs. In fact some of the buildings were constructed solely of brightly coloured massed flowers. He wandered up and down the rainbow paths until he came upon an avenue leading to a much larger structure, that was giving out vibrations of great activity, which felt different from anything within his previous experience.

As he approached the door, it opened. He hesitated but when he heard the sound of laughter, he lost his fear and entered. To the right of a large hall was a gathering of about twenty fairies making music and dancing.

No one noticed his approach, so he stood and watched – he even smiled to himself for the first time since the disaster. Suddenly the music stopped, and with no rhythm to follow so did the dancers. The fairies looked round and one shouted, "He's here." They all ran towards him.

❊ ❊ ❊

It would be gratifying to be able to say that, as we ran to welcome and embrace him, he happily returned our love and entered our life, which was now to be his also, with joy. But he fled until he reached the gates, but this time the stones refused to obey his will; and once more he began to scream in terror at the conditions which, such a short time before, he had found so enchanting.

"Leave him," a voice commanded. So we returned to the Hall, but not to dance for we were too sad; and we wondered why such an unlikely and unwilling student had been brought among us.

The days passed but there was no sign of Tepi. He spent most of the time in hiding and only ventured into the streets when we were asleep. Eventually he once more approached the scene of our music making and dancing, and again the sequence of notes stopped in the middle of a bar.

We turned as before and there again stood Tepi, but this time we made no movement as step by step be came timidly towards us. As he approached, we slightly changed our positions, forming a half circle and leaving an escape route so he would not feel trapped. He stood looking at each of us in turn. We smiled but made no move in his direction. He sighed and turned to go. He was not wanted.

"Please stay with us," we whispered in unison. He hesitated. "I will come tomorrow – if I may," he added doubtfully.

"Yes, yes," we said gently so as not to frighten him.

❊ ❊ ❊

Day by day he came during our recreation period and gradually he learned to tolerate us. Despite our efforts to make friends, he always remained beyond our reach, alone, sad, if no longer frightened, young fairy. He began standing on the outskirts of our classroom and here he gradually came to life.

During our Thought Formation Sessions, he slowly drew nearer, watching intently as the constituent thoughts were either attracted to or repelled by each other, to blend or break away. One day, after we had failed to draw two completed sections together, in spite of trying endless ramifications, Tepi nervously made a suggestion.

"You do it," our Teacher said, smiling his encouragement. Interest overcame any remaining timidity and he walked between us and altered the position of a single thought in each section Slowly the two came together.

"Well done," our Teacher said.

"Well done," we echoed.

"You are ready to join us. I shall expect you to take your place at tomorrow's Session," our Teacher continued.

"Yes," was all Tepi replied as he left the hall; but he came the following day and took part in our work from then onward.

* * *

I pondered deeply over the revelation of Tepi's past in an endeavour to find a way to help him to face the facts and eventually forgive himself for his lapse in procedure and responsibility.

We saw each other daily during our work on the Thought Formations, but I was not yet ready to suggest a meeting to discuss his problems as I had no idea how to advise him, let alone how they could be solved.

* * *

One day when I was musing in the woods near my home, a thought came into my mind. Tepi had deliberately banished the memory of his failure for many years, but now that he was fully aware of the cause of his moroseness and despair, he should be encouraged to find the solution himself.

When he arrived at my apartment at my request, I was amazed at his sullen expression and attitude.

"You obviously despise me," he said beligerently.

"How can you make such an unjust accusation, Tepi?"

"Why have you not made the slightest move to discuss my past, which you now share?"

I sighed. "I am deeply distressed that you should harbour such a misconception. All my thoughts have been of you and your problem during the periods when we are not working. But I have to confess that I am no nearer a solution than I was before you permitted me to enter your subconscious. How could anyone despise you when you worked yourself into a state of exhaustion on your project and later lost your will in your endeavour to correct your error? Only you can find the answer. You are more mature now; whatever the negative side of suffering appears to do, the positive aspect forces evolution even against a person's will. You were led here for a purpose, but you cannot fulfil your potential doing this work on which we are all engaged, and for which you have an extraordinary aptitude, until the problem of your Self-hatred is resolved."

"At least, my dearest Perima, I have learned to love."

"The grace of love is bestowed on both giver and receiver. Together we must somehow use this love to disperse your hatred of yourself and your animosity towards most of those around you; the cure emanates from the heart as does also love, the heart being the centre of one's being."

"I am not deficient in love, Perima; I love you, you know that."

"But that love is not yet strong enough to overcome your Self-hatred. Now, let us consider carefully your past life. Success always came easily to you. You had youth, good looks, a sense of humour and well-earned praise for your work. You also possessed a natural authority over both plants and people, even before you became a leader. Let us try and find out where and how these assets became lost."

Tepi turned his memory towards his final project which had led to his downfall. "At first it was all so exciting, he said. "The fact that I had been offered this great opportunity was in itself electrifying. I was proud to have been chosen out of many applicants." Our eyes met.

"Say that again."

"I was proud to ..." I raised my hand to stop him finishing his sentence.

"Is there anything wrong in that?"

"No, Tepi. It is a natural reaction and one that I myself have felt upon occasion. It is a positive response, which spurred you on to ever greater effect and achievement. When did this positive become negative?"

"Ah!" He sighed. "Perima, beloved Perima, I believe you have helped me to find the answer. It was my pride that led to my refusal to admit even to myself, that I could not carry the whole responsibility of planning and bringing the project to a successful conclusion with only the help of my resident workers, who were willing but only moderately skilled. Why did I not ask for a trained organizer with whom I could have discussed my plans, and had more experienced workers drafted in to carry them out, instead of overtaxing my mental and physical capacities to breaking point?"

❊ ❊ ❊

A long silence followed. I analyzed its content and found it to be without bitterness. A tear fell on Tepi's cheek as he sadly shook his head.

"So simple a solution. When we found the memory, and I watched myself working – working, then creeping away to drop from exhaustion, I kept saying 'What a fool!' forgetting that it was I." He gave a rueful smile.

"You are smiling, Tepi," I said, "smiling at your own foolishness. When you can laugh at it, you will be ready to go into the darkness and find that beast of yours, Self-pride and bring it to heel – and when it is following you obediently instead of leading you into folly, we can turn our attention to your Self-hatred."

"Let us begin now," he said, rising to his feet.

"You must first learn to laugh, not only with your tamed beasts but at the absurdities and small misfortunes of everyday existence. Then you will be able to accept the adversities of life, and in striving to overcome them, you will both evolve and find fulfilment."

❊ ❊ ❊

Many moons passed, before even the first part of my surmise became fact. I sang funny songs to Tepi, and although he joined me at my request, his eyes were sad and his body drooped. We went for long walks together during which I would point out to him the amusing shapes which the cloud-people were making in the sky. We watched the antics of young fairies and animals playing games, but nothing seemed to stir the fun-spark which had all but died within him.

One day I took him to see a friend who made comic cartoons although I had little hope that they would have the desired effect on Tepi's depression; usually the theme was of the fairy who could do nothing right; disaster followed disaster, but always he survived to begin another adventure, which led to further misfortune, and once again he found himself in a hopeless situation from which he was only extricated by an unexpected trick of Nature, or the miraculous appearance of some bird or animal which carried him to safety and further trials.

After watching these moving cartoons gloomily for some time, a flicker of a smile appeared on Tepi's face, to be quickly extinguished. I laughed almost continuously and at last he joined in and we were hugging each other in mutual enjoyment.

At the end of the performance, which was of course far from the end of the fairy's predicaments, Tepi turned to me and said: "I was not as bedevilled as that chap anyway."

"Bedevilled is a good description," I said, "and you still have a little demon sitting on your shoulder. His influence is not on outside events but only on those made by yourself for your own discomfiture. Can you laugh at that?"

"Not yet, but I promise to try. Can I come here by myself to see if I can find the cartoons funny without your laughter to encourage me?"

❋ ❋ ❋

Tepi visited my friend on several occasions, and each time he laughed more. Eventually he asked him if he could borrow some copies of the more preposterous incidents in order to test himself each day. He began inviting some of his co-workers to come and see them, and immediately they too fell under the cartoonist's spell: Tepi's room became a popular centre of merriment. Together they would invent new disasters for the unfortunate fairy, which the illustrator brought to life, providing an endless supply of fun for them all.

Tepi's talent gradually became a positive skill as the months passed. During this period, he frequently asked me if he could face Self-pride, but I was not sure whether his renewed sense of humour would be obliterated by the surroundings that he would encounter in the lower depths of his subconscious, into which he would have to plunge. Eventually he overcame my remaining doubts and we set out together.

The conditions gradually worsened until we had difficulty in breathing, but we knew that our Teacher-Lord was with us; and by thinking of Him we were able to maintain the channel through which the Life Force flowed, enabling us to continue our search.

"It is hiding," Tepi gasped.

"You have driven it into the deepest recesses of your mind, for pride hates derision. We must rest awhile. I can go no further without replenishment." We relaxed side by side and drew in the blessed power which quickly built up around us.

"Call the beast forth!" We both heard the command.

"It is yours, Tepi," I said. "You call it."

"Show yourself, you vile wretch! You who have been the cause of my misery for many years!" His voice was harsh with anger. We waited but there was no movement anywhere in the vicinity.

"I know it is difficult when you are almost choking, but we agreed to laugh," I reminded him.

"How can we laugh at it when it is not here? Perhaps we should try to go deeper."

"No. This is the place and the time, I feel sure," I said although I was both puzzled and disappointed at our failure to find it. There was a sudden loud click. We both stiffened.

"What was that?" Tepi whispered as we both renewed our efforts to pierce the gloom. And then we saw it – not the terrible monster we were expecting, but a flickering cartoon depicting the unfortunate fairy of the many dilemmas, and one of his foolish companions. This time, however, the faces were Tepi's and mine. It showed our journey to our present locality as we struggled to wade through murky streams which were not there. We were felled to the ground by rocks made of air and hurtled head-over-heels down precipices which were in reality but holes in the road. We began to laugh at our absurdity and tears fell as we clasped each other in mutual enjoyment.

Suddenly my mirth froze as Tepi let out a shriek of pain and fell to the ground. From him emerged the fearful monster we were seeking – a large grey shape with gaping jaws and burning holes instead of eyes, rearing above us like some enraged, inflated cobra as it ejected streams of venom towards us. When it discovered that it could draw no nearer to us, it circled the light and began to squeeze it, so that our area of protection was gradually diminished. Tepi was still prostrated, but somehow I felt no fear, and then I began to laugh because I could see that the creature's vast body was only its imagination.

I shook Tepi and cried, "Look, quick, look! It is only a puffed up Pride!" Together we watched the bulbous form gradually shrink until all that remained was a small, writhing strip of matter.

"It is so small," Tepi giggled. "Hey, was it really you that caused me so much misery, you – you worm?" The creature hesitated; then began to wriggle away.

"Stop! Stop!" Tepi shouted as he began to follow it.

"Do not leave the light," I warned him. "It will get gradually weaker now that it no longer has you to feed on, and when we come again, it will do us no harm."

✤   ✤   ✤

Tepi's attitude towards those around him now improved. He became more companionable with his fellow workers and not only asked them to view his cartoons but accepted several invitations to join in their various leisure activities. Nevertheless I sensed that all was not well. Something was affecting his concentration, and his work was failing to maintain its usual high standard.

With me he was always loving and kind, but when I endeavoured to find out what was troubling him, he insisted that nothing was amiss. Then one day he came to see me and announced abruptly that he was leaving. For a moment I was stunned. The tide having apparently turned in his favour, he now wished to forsake the conditions which were helping him to find his true self once more. To me this made no sense.

"What has caused this radical change Tepi? You are making good progress."

"Something is happening to my inner being, causing a pain I cannot ignore," he said pressing his solar plexus as though trying to assuage it. "I must get away or it will destroy me."

"Did you escape from the pain of the beasts during your many years of wandering before you came here? You must be more explicit or I cannot help you."

"Perhaps pain is not a good way to describe it. It is more like an aching void."

"This is good news," I assured him. "Voids are meant to be filled. For years you were harbouring a disease which could have destroyed you. Now through the partial redemption of your beasts this dangerous condition has almost vanished and you are left with what you describe as a void. We must discover what is seeking to occupy this valuable space."

"Not other beasts, I hope," he said ruefully.

"Do you know who I think is knocking at your door? – the counterparts of the beasts. Every quality has an opposite: Pride – Humility, Avarice – Generosity, Greed – Self-Restraint. I think these entities wish to claim their counterparts, which although tamed, are still living in the darkness of your subconscious. Now they want us to help them to reach the light, which is their rightful home."

Tepi regarded me doubtfully. "Then, why did they leave it in the first place?"

"That is indeed a long story. Every power has a positive and a negative aspect. Before it can become a functioning whole, one aspect dwells in the light and the other in the dark. They are where they are because of their respective natures. There is a 'thread' which joins them, through which the positive supplies life, and the negative gives stability through its experience of matter. Owing to our work with the beasts they have enjoyed a glimpse of the light through the circle of power, which they have been allowed to enter for gradually longer periods. The transference of Power is not a one-way action; it flows from its angel source, its purity being polluted by matter on its journey. But during its return the contamination is cleansed and only the experience remains, giving the a transitory view of another world, towards which it is slowly being drawn to enable it to evolve."

"It sounds very complicated."

"Knowledge which has not been properly absorbed always appears to be complicated, but when it is transformed into understanding, it becomes simple because Nature itself is in reality simple."

"Perima the Wise, I accept your word while still failing to comprehend your explanation," he said as he mockingly gave me the salute normally reserved for the Presence of a Shining One. "What do we do now?"

"Another pearl of wisdom is about to fall from my lips. I have no idea."

"Perima, you have plummeted in my estimation. Your dissertation was so positive that I thought you were about to lead me and my beasts from the depths to join their glowing counterparts in a land not yet experienced by either of us."

"I wish I could, but there is one small truth which you are forgetting – the ultimate success of any project depends on the initial planning and the amount of enthusiasm and energy expended on it."

"How can you make such a ludicrous statement? If that were true, all the work I put into my scheme would have ensured its rightful conclusion."

"And so it would have done without that inflated worm you were harbouring."

Tepi looked pensive for a moment; then he grinned. "I wonder how it is getting on without me; I almost feel sorry for it."

"In spite of all the anguish it caused you?"

"Almost."

"Then you have indeed evolved through the experience." His face suddenly clouded and a scowl obliterated his previous good humour. "For myself, almost, but for the suffering and devastation affecting others – Never."

❖   ❖   ❖

We often discussed possible methods of getting into touch with the beasts' counterparts, and we tried meditating together at my home, and again in the darkness of the cave; but we had no results. We then decided to see if we could purify the bodies of the beasts through longer exposure to the light. In order to do this it was necessary to devise some scheme to keep them awake for longer periods, so we organized games which would stimulate their powers of thought to take the place of their random play. Although these were enjoyed, they provided nothing towards finding a solution to our problem.

We then divided the cave into sections, one of which was kept in darkness. Others were flooded with different coloured lights; and one of these provided a stimulating ray to encourage vigorous exercise. Another promoted peaceful relaxation and a third produced a gentle sleep during which we hoped the beasts might be raised to a slightly higher level of consciousness. They were led singly from one section to another to test their reactions, which naturally varied. Our efforts proved to be no more than an interesting experiment, which failed to give us the knowledge we required

Our next endeavour was to locate the thread which linked each to its counterpart for without it no beast could exist. This proved totally nonproductive, and after several sessions we reluctantly came to the conclusion that the lifelines were undetectable at such a deep level.

Our plan of campaign changed once more and we decided to work from my home. First we concentrated our thoughts on the beasts lying or playing in the circle of Light surrounded by darkness. We then imagined their counterparts as beautiful "beings," but were unable to produce more than a hazy image as we did not know whether they possessed any bodies or were but Intelligent Forces. We persevered for some time without any result. So we decided to turn our thoughts on the beasts once more – or rather, one beast.

We had noticed that Greed had obviously gained great pleasure when in the sector on which a yellow ray was playing, so we established a pool of this colour in my apartment. We then mentally made a facsimile of Greed's form the size of a small sheep in the centre. For many sessions it lay sprawled motionless. Then one day, I observed a slight twitch in one nostril. I looked at Tepi and, from the expression on his face, I knew that he too had seen this miniscule sign of life. Excitedly we watched for what seemed an age, but Greed remained as though dead. Through the following months the second nostril joined the first in its twitching. Then one of the iron claws was retracted into the foot and later an ear flicked. Although still unconscious its body was very gradually coming to life, until one day, a bleary eye opened and then quickly closed. Later first one eye opened;

then the other joined it to look round vaguely, but recognised neither of us. Finally both half opened together and gazed blankly into space. Suddenly they widened in seeming amazement and Greed began to grin – but not at Tepi or me; it had seen and recognised something or someone that we could not.

Naturally we were elated at this eventual success after so many failures in spite of the fact that the body was vitalised for but a few seconds. Each session began where the previous one had ended until total animation was complete on the plane where we lived. It lumbered round the room, sniffing at each object as though to learn something from it; it turned on its back and grinned, rolling its eyes in pleasure as Tepi ruffled the fur on its stomach. Its actions for some time remained typical, but its body was gradually changing from the grotesque to a more normal animal form. Its clumsy feet became paws, their iron appendages claws. A nose replaced the elongated snout, and the rough, granite teeth diminished in size and became smooth and white. All knobs and warts disappeared and its normal, slightly inane grin became a joyous smile.

Finally, intelligence entered the now kindly eyes, which gazed at us questioningly as though in expectation of some specific action which should be taking place. We would gladly have done anything to help Greed to achieve what we had been striving to bring about for many months, but we were at a loss to know what this could be.

Then one day, its eyes became focused on something in the distance; it stood motionless for a few tense seconds, then began to sway its now supple body while emitting a low and musical sound which it had never produced before. It continued to wait expectantly, and then, at some signal which we could neither see nor hear, it gracefully bounded away and disappeared.

❖ ❖ ❖

We waited in silence for some time not knowing whether he – we could no longer think of this beautiful creature as "Greed" or "it" – would return or if he was permanently reunited with his counterpart, and also whether the beast part of him we knew and had helped to tame was still in the darkness of the cave. This, at least we could ascertain and after preparing ourselves for the descent into gross matter we plunged into the depths. All was normal there. Jealousy, Avarice, Intolerance, Malice and Selfishness answered our call one by one but when we summoned Greed, the only response was a faint yellow glow which came towards us and then disappeared.

Tepi and I clung to each other in delight for having achieved the redemption of one of his beasts. We now knew that we could perform this service for the others too and at the same time clear Tepi's subconscious of these traits which were holding him back from developing his potential.

* * *

So one by one we worked on them, watching their gradual refinement on one plane until each joyfully obeyed the call to join its counterpart in a higher sphere – that is all except Self-pride, which we had not seen since it had deflated and disappeared.

During this period which covered about a year, Tepi's looks and temperament were changing. Instead of being a person of whom to be wary because of his unpredictable moods and intolerance, he became one of the most popular members of our group, always ready to laugh or to help anyone in difficulty over work or emotional problems. My love for him deepened, and as I had been able to help him, so he now spent much of his leisure time teaching me the intricate art of creating Thought-Formations, of which he seemed to have an instinctive knowledge, including how to cajole, command or gently ease a difficult thought into taking up its required position and thus enhance the whole.

* * *

One day Ereraus sent for him and this time Tepi did not ask me to accompany him, a sure sign of growing maturity and confidence.

Later, he burst into my room, his eyes shining. "He wants me to teach," he said.

I smiled. "If you have the ability to teach me, why you not be capable of teaching others?"

"But this is official. I am really excited."

"And that is what you need, for your excitement is caused not by the offered task but by the approval of your leader."

"Yes, that is true. My dearest Perima, I owe everything to you. As your encouragement has carried me through the terrible time of change, which eventually led to the taming and redemption of my beasts, so your precious gift of love has been the sole cause of my deliverance from despair."

* * *

This proved a time of happiness and progress for Tepi. I already had proof of his flair for teaching and our co-workers soon received benefit as well. We were now being given more difficult work, which stretched our powers to the limit. We also won awards when we entered competitions, a gratifying experience especially when we had sacrificed our hours for leisure in order to perfect the work in hand.

When our daily tasks were finished, our activities took on a different guise. Instead of dancing, putting on plays or indulging in sports, such as joining the water fairies in acrobatics or the cloud fairies in challenging the wind we divided into groups and raised our consciousness to a higher plane to seek new ideas and new forces to conjoin those already in the Thought-Formations we were constructing.

Strangely Tepi and I missed his beasts and we wondered whether we would ever see them again in their rarified forms, but we were too busy for this to become more than an idle conjecture.

Occasionally Tepi would disappear during our leisure periods, but I did not ask him where he had been as I knew that he would tell me when he was ready to do so. Sometimes we would spend these times together exchanging power, a very beautiful experience when love is present between two fairies.

This was no substitute for my love of Sulic, but an extension of it. A great love is expansive and can take in other loves which in no way diminish the first. I thought of Sulic often, but I could not reach him, in spite of using my extra vision when taking solitary walks, which I always hoped would lead me to him if only for a moment. But Time was not propitious.

❊ ❊ ❊

At last the day came when Tepi came to me and said "Perima, beloved, it breaks my heart but I must leave you."

I looked at him in dismay.

"But the work, Tepi. We cannot do without you now."

"I promise you I have spent hours in thought before coming to this decision. I cannot be worthy of your love until I have conquered my Self-pride. It is still with me you know. I am proud of my work with the group. My pride becomes inflated when we earn awards and acclamation and, above all, when you give me some of your precious love."

"But that is permissible pride, Tepi."

"Not to me, I must efface it utterly so that I can work without any reward, unlike a tamed beast waiting for a pat after performing a clever trick which has pleased us."

"Where are you going?"

"Back to my tract of land. Where else? I must recreate all that was there and was destroyed."

"Let me come with you."

"My dearest heart, nothing would give me greater joy than for us to perform this act of renewal together but the group truly could not do without you. I am a teacher. There are other teachers but you have an inbuilt wisdom. We all possess this too I know, but somehow yours has come to the surface in a miraculous way before its normal time in relation to your age and experience. How is it that you are so wise, Perima?"

"It is a question of adoration."

"What an extraordinary thing to say. What do you adore? – certainly not yourself."

"When I was young, my guardian taught me to love – firstly Nature – the flowers, the trees, the wind and sea, my little birds."

"And then?"

"The Angel-Lord of Wisdom."

"But many invoke Him."

"I did not say 'invoke'. I said 'love'."

"And did He answer?"

"Of course. It is a Cosmic Law that love begets love."

"And did it turn to adoration?"

"No." I said – "Adoration is reserved for The One."

"You actually reached Him?"

"That would be impossible Tepi dear, for many years to come; but my adoration reached Him."

"How do you know?"

"You have already said it: because I have wisdom beyond my years."

CHAPTER 14
THE REDEMPTION
OF TEPI'S LAND

After Tepi's departure I felt as though a part of me had been torn away. I was also worried about him because I was sure that alone he could not resuscitate the ravaged land, which had been lying fallow since the disaster. But I had my own work to do so I gave it all my energy and put into practice the new skills which Tepi had taught me. The group was going from strength to strength and projects of increasing importance were sent to us with requests for Thought-Formations to help bring them to successful conclusions.

I had heard nothing from Tepi for some time and when he came to see me he looked haggard and ill. He had spent most of this period brooding over his land and praying for inspiration to solve his seemingly insuperable problem.

"The whole area lies in the grip of a rapacious darkness," he told me despondently. "I had meant to do most of the work myself, but obviously I need help. I cannot seek the aid of those who suffered so much because of my Self-pride, and I am not sure to whom I should turn."

"Why not ask Eremus? He is your present leader and must therefore be a link in the chain of the land's rehabilitation, or you would not be here."

"Yes," he agreed. "It cannot have been pure chance that led me to you, to the Thought-Formations and our work with the bea..."

"Thought-Formations." I interrupted him. "Of course. They are the answer and it is the group who will become your helpers."

"But they no longer work with the Nature Kingdom – if indeed they ever did. They know nothing of plant compatibility with certain soils nor of the necessary powers to promote their growth."

"But Tepi, do you not realize the work will be no different from what we are already doing; except that here we are creating the thoughts that we use, whereas there it will be facts – plant – atoms already proven in matter – which will be at our disposal?"

Tepi's vibrations began shooting in all directions.

"Calm yourself, " I laughed, "or you will get nowhere, not even to Eremus."

We requested a meeting which was instantly granted, and Tepi told him about our idea.

Eremus smiled. "Your development is going according to plan," he said. "But first we must ask the rest of the group whether they are willing to work on this project. You realize, do you not, that we have been climbing the ladder of progress with our Thought-Formations. We have been competing successfully with other groups and the resultant praise and rewards are being enjoyed by all."

Tepi's face fell. "How selfish of me – I have only been thinking of myself and how to rectify my personal blunder. Why should they give up all that, for which we have been striving over a long period of time, for my benefit?"

"You are learning Tepi and I am glad to admit that Perima was right about you and I was wrong. Come, we will approach your co-workers, whom we can now call your friends, and I will address them."

As soon as the group was gathered together Eremus began: "Fellow craftsmen, I am here before you with a story which no one in the vicinity but Perima, Tepi and I know. You have watched Tepi change from a broken personality, who had been wandering in a self-made wilderness for many years, to an admired colleague, and now a respected teacher. He perpetrated a grievous error which brought disaster to both the land under his jurisdiction and the maiming of the fairies in his charge." All eyes left Eremus' face and turned towards Tepi, but he remained calm and met their gaze with dignity.

"The details are unimportant but I must impress on you the fact that it was not lack of dedication which led to his downfall. He performed his duties with both diligence and success. His error was his refusal to admit even to himself that to complete the latest part of the plan for his tract of land was beyond his ability and strength. In fact his superiors had not expected the success he had already achieved. Thus although it was partly exhaustion from overwork which led to his error of judgment, the prime cause was a flaw in his character known as Self-pride. He admits that this defect has not yet been eradicated in spite of all his efforts."

❋ ❋ ❋

Tepi turned and looked at me with pain in his eyes. I shook my head to assure him that I had not betrayed his trust.

"He realizes that the success of the group still gives him both Self-pride and pleasure when awards are won followed by congratulations and praise. It is his aim to learn to work with no desire for reward or applause, as his next priority in self-improvement. 'Splendid' I can sense your reaction. 'We hope he succeeds.' Now Tepi's land, which is on the surface destroyed, cannot be restored to its proper form by himself alone; he needs help. It will mean sacrifices for those who volunteer, but I am not going to bring pressure to bear on anyone.

"As you all know, each Thought-Formation that we make serves a special purpose. It may act as either a catalyst or as an anodyne; as an aid to bring success to a worthy cause, or perhaps to bestow peace or advantage to a deserving individual or group.

"I want each of you to put some questions to yourself. Why are you working so diligently in this your chosen vocation? Is it for the group? For the satisfaction of taking part in this creative art form? For the recipients you are trying to aid? Or for the resulting rewards of success and acclaim? Are you too suffering from Tepi's disease Self-pride? If this is so, do you like him wish to eradicate this flaw from your character? I do not want your answers now. Go away, and in the quietude of your rooms consider carefully all that I have told you. Then those of you who wish to help Tepi come to me; and we will formulate a plan."

❊ ❊ ❊

Tepi and I returned to my apartment to discuss the meeting.

"I was embarrassed," Tepi said. "I did not realize that Eremus knew about my past and now everyone else knows it too."

"In reality this is a good thing because now we will be certain who your true friends are. Knowing has not affected my love for you; in fact it has enhanced it. I see no reason why the group should turn against you. None of them is perfect."

"No, I suppose not, but somehow I feel more vulnerable now that they know. Whereas an unsuccessful student might be acceptable, a failed teacher could become a figure of fun."

"What is that?" I interrupted as we become aware of a mass movement, gradually drawing nearer. My outer door is always open, and now into the room came all our fellow workers, who crowded round expressing sympathy and offering their support. Tepi was on the verge of tears. "I doubted you," he said. "I thought you would be ashamed of me, and now I'm ashamed of myself for my mistrust."

"I thought you were supposed to be in your rooms considering the situation in order to make up your minds as to your future actions," I smiled.

"It was not necessary for us" they choroused. "Our determination to help is unanimous. Tepi has made us what we now are – the most successful group in the area. Without him we were merely a number of students learning the art of creating Thought Formations."

"Did you notice what Eremus called us, 'Fellow craftsmen'? He has never honoured us with that description before. We have always been 'Students' or 'Co-workers'" one said.

"We want to hear it all" said another. "Please tell us, so that we can share your unhappiness instead of merely giving you our sympathy and love, which is all that we can do at the moment."

✿   ✿   ✿

By this time tears were running down Tepi's cheeks and, I confess, mine too. Such a unified expression of friendship had not been expected by either of us. "What can I say? Tepi gulped. "How can I convey my heartfelt gratitude for such unqualified support?"

"Your tears, Tepi; they say it all."

"It will be no sacrifice anyway. It is a most exciting project, which will take place in new surroundings giving us greater experience."

"The conditions will certainly be new and much more primitive than those to which you are used – no individual homes or comfortable workrooms – only the naked land and the elements."

"Tepi, do not exaggerate," I laughed. "You forget we are the Thought Formation experts! We will make our own dwellings – replicas of the ones we have here."

"Of course, my emotions have overcome my powers of rational thinking," said Tepi, actually smiling at last.

"When would you like me to tell you about the disaster?"

"Now;" I said firmly. "It is always better to share a burden than having to bear it alone."

Tepi looked at me. "Well, nearly alone. Then we can go as a united band, and confront Eremus with our decision."

Tepi began his story from the time when he was making up his mind whether to accept the task of being under-leader of a large group or leader of a smaller one, through his slight initial difficulties with his helpers and his early success. When things began to go wrong for him, the situation changed.

His audience was no longer merely listening with interest to Tepi's narrative. Each one became him, suffering his doubts, his failure to supervise his workers because of his exhaustion, his errors of judgment and the horror of the final destruction when the Storm-demons swept away the result of years of labour in a seething torrent of water.

When he had finished, all were unconscious on the floor, sharing Tepi's coma prior to his appearance before the Council of Justice. For a while they remained motionless and then, one after another, they began shaking their heads and holding their breath.

"They are trying to escape from the music as I did," Tepi said. Eventually they returned to our world looking rather dazed.

"Poor Tepi."

"If only we had known, we would not have been so unfriendly."

"Had we been told, we could have helped you."

"Apart from the Council of Justice and those who suffered in the disaster, nobody knew except me," I told them. "It was all locked up in Tepi's subconscious. I think that it was only when he allowed me to enter it and together we released his past, that even Eremus knew about it."

"What happened after you came to life again?"

"I returned to my land and tried to resuscitate it by giving power firstly to the whole and finally to a single dead plant. How ridiculous I must have appeared to the mourning, presiding angel. Then I left and wandered wherever my feet led me."

Tepi then took us mentally to the divided road and on his journey along the path which led to the jewelled gates – and finally to his entry into the room where we were dancing.

"He's here," repeated the fairy who had said these words so many years ago. They all moved towards Tepi, and this time he did not run away but held out his arms in gratitude as once again they offered their sympathy and determination to help the barren land to bloom once more.

Then there was silence.

"You know" one began "I have learned a lot about my own shortcomings. I realise now, that I too suffer from Self-pride. It is largely the adulation we receive for our work that spurs me on to greater efforts."

"I think that we are all guilty in this respect in varying degrees" I said. "It is difficult not to enjoy praise."

"Jealousy, that is my main flaw," said another. "I used to ask myself continually 'What does she see in him?' I am better looking, better tempered and would do anything to please her. I am jealous of Tepi's success with Perima."

"And I. What did you see in him, Perima?"

"I saw a great soul, his genius enchained. I recognised one who will be a distinguished leader, not only of this group, but of many. One who will give his all for the redemption of the suffering, the weak and those who are lost by the wayside. One who ..."

"Oh Perima" Tepi was squirming with embarrassment. "How can you know all this? I only want to put right a terrible wrong, of which I alone was the cause, and there is nothing very noble about that."

"I am right, I know, and in the future all who are now present will agree with me. Now let us return to our self analysis; for any lesson we may learn from Tepi's past failures will add to our debt to him; and we can pay off these debts with the diligence we put into the work ahead."

"When Tepi changed in character and became our teacher, I was jealous of Perima," said one of the girls.

"I, too" the others echoed.

"I am truly flattered," Tepi smiled at them "but do not cause me to add Vanity to the rest of my defects."

"I realize that I also have a fear of failure, but I had not realized that this is an aspect Self-pride."

"And I am avaricious – I am envious when our teacher – now Tepi – praises someone else."

"Come now," I interrupted. "If we are to continue in this character analysis, we should really balance the flaws in each with the qualities possessed. I can assure you that if the latter did not greatly outnumber the former, none of us would be in this town called 'Onward' nor would we be capable of creating Thought Formations to aid those in distress."

"You are right – as usual – Perima. We were getting positively morbid in our self accusations."

The mood had now lightened and laughing I said: "Let us all arise, resolute though chastened. We will march to Eremus, confess our faults and declare our resolve to bring death to our sins and life to Tepi's land."

❊ ❊ ❊

Several weeks of planning were needed before we were able to set out for the ravaged ground. Although I had already seen it in his subconscious, the factual desolation was far greater than I remembered. A weeping angel hovered overhead and administered power – to no avail. Darkness and a sinister depression permeated the area and we knew that these must first be dispersed before we could live or begin our work there.

We tried to comfort the angel by telling him that we had come to help him resuscitate the land.

"It is accursed," he sighed despondently. "Ghouls come and gorge themselves on the devastation. You are too small and too few to affect them."

"Revered brother," I said: "Replenish your hope. We know the art of welding power and thoughts together, and we have studied the prevailing problems for many weeks. We do not come unprepared. Dry your tears," I pleaded with a smile. "There is sufficient water here already without your personal rain."

✻ ✻ ✻

At one of our many meetings we decided to invoke the Higher Angels to help us disperse the darkness through which the sun's rays could no longer reach either air or soil. We approached our Teacher-Lord and He agreed to be present during our next visit, when a down-rush of Light would permeate the area. He told us that first we must study each type of demonry present, and prepare a Thought-Formation that would contain the necessary power first to counteract and then expel every one.

Eremus suggested that Tepi and I should carry out this investigation as the others had virtually no knowledge of the forms taken by malevolent forces. Although our experience was limited to Tepi's defects rather than the embodiment of evil, we were capable of dividing them into different categories for analysis.

Each day Tepi and I returned to his land, forcing our way through the clinging darkness, under the protection of our Teacher-Lord. Everything appeared extinct; but we knew that, although the vegetation had died, the Life Force ever flows into matter, and it was from this that the ghouls were gaining their sustenance.

They were of all sizes; some as small as the ratlike creatures in Tepi's cavern, others as big as Greed. They sucked in the air with shrieks of maniacal laughter voraciously gulped the putrid water or clawed at the earth with horny nails, scooping up fistfuls of rotted garbage. They champed, grunted, slavered and belched, until they were two or three times their normal size when they flopped down in turgid pools of their own excreta and slept.

It was at this stage that Tepi and I were able to examine them. Some were offshoots of Defilement or Destruction; others of Tyranny, Pillage or Rape. We looked at each other with but a single thought – in comparison, his beasts at their worst had been pleasant companions.

On our return home we visited a Cleansing Unit where we discarded our bodies and slept, while a perfumed breeze blew through them removing not only the filth but the evil as well. We awoke refreshed and began our search for the opposite attributes to offset each embodiment of sin. When we had found what we needed, we were ready for the rest of the group to join us, and we all set to work to make the Thought-Formation which would free the land from its marauders.

❊   ❊   ❊

Our task was not easy because we now had to weld totally opposing thoughts rather than the merely incompatible ones which we used in our normal work. Tepi, as so often, found the key. We flooded all the destructive aspects with light and cast those which were contra-evil into shadow, so that the entire Thought-Formation was in various tones of grey. Eventually after frequent failure and much anxiety, it was completed to the satisfaction of our Teacher-Lord, and we began the difficult task of transporting it from the tranquil atmosphere of Onward to the very different conditions of Tepi's land.

For the duration of the journey the Formation was reduced in size, so that we could keep it within the protective light made by our bodies and power in case of attack. All went well and on our arrival, we placed it over the centre of the area; and as we moved away from it we drew the Formation after us, so that it expanded and reached its full size as it hovered steadily over the murky field.

We then stood at intervals beneath its perimeter; and by giving out power, we connected our bodies to form a large circle of light. We invoked the host of angels which was gathered overhead; they too gave power, and the Formation was flooded from above and below.

Silently we watched the effect; the particles of darkness gradually disintegrated leaving the ghouls exposed in their various hideous forms. Tepi and I were inured to them, but the rest of the group let out shrill cries of horror as the ghouls rushed towards us in their endeavour to escape from the Light.

"Be still." We all heard His Voice and were calmed, for He had already promised us total protection.

When only few paces lay between us and the ghouls, it was as though a solid wall stood in their way. They turned and stampeded back to the centre, snapping, snarling and clawing each other.

Some flapped bat-like wings to flounder upwards a yard or two, but the Thought-Formation drove them back. There was no choice; they had to go down, but the earth refused them with constant eruptions, which hurled them into the air again; back and forth, back and forth they rushed as in some macabre contest with no one the winner. Rage and terror produced a cacophonous roar as scaly, slimy, bloodstained bodies hurtled past us.

As the Formation slowly descended, hysteria became rife.

Beneath the incessant onslaught of running, burrowing, clawing feet, the land in the centre collapsed and from the crater leapt Fire. Light had appalled them but Fire they knew. Like a rampant rabble gone mad, they charged towards it and all were engulfed in the avid abyss. But still the flames leapt and spread; they vaporized the stinking water that was churning and bubbling like some sinister brew in a witch's cauldron, and consumed the excrement that defiled the ground, leaving it naked and cleansed. We watched the Formation's journey downwards until it rested on the steaming, shrivelled earth as a permanent barrier against further invasion from the dwellers in the Deep.

*　*　*

For a while, we stood dazed looking at each other. Although the Light had protected us, we were blackened by evil and scorched by flames. Gradually we relaxed. Silence crept over us all like a beautiful dream as each was wrapped in the ray of an angel and transported home to rest.

It took us several days to recover from our ordeal, for we were not only exhausted but our mental faculties had been severely battered by the deafening clamour and fear.

When we regained our equilibrium, we gathered together and exchanged details of our reactions to all that had happened. Some had eased their tension by concentrating on the Thought-Formation, while others had accepted the horror as an experience to increase their knowledge of a world outside their normal lives. All felt gratified that we had managed to bring to a successful conclusion the first phase of the plan to return the land to its proper state.

Tepi asked for permission to view the result of our combined efforts alone; this pleased me greatly for it showed that he had acquired more selfconficence than he had previously possessed. When he returned, he invited us to a meeting at which he began to thank us.

"No, No, Tepi, we do not want thanks. We are working only for the land," we insisted.

"But what about me? I have all this gratitude inside me. I cannot keep it. Please, please accept at least some of it." This was an aspect that we had not considered, and it was quite a problem. One should feel gratitude for a service rendered or one is at fault; but if the intended recipient is unwilling to accept the proffered thanks, what is the answer?

There was silence for a while and then I said "We were but instruments. One does not thank one's mind for providing thoughts, or the matter which will be moulded by those thoughts according to our will. Without the Power flowing through our Formation, it would still be hovering ineffectively over the ghouls. Tepi's thanks, and ours too, can only be offered to the Angelic Forces to whom we owe our success. Let us go and perform a ritual at the location where victory was granted us."

On arrival we again formed a circle round the perimeter of the now purified field. We raised our arms towards the sky and with thoughts of love we asked the angels to accept our gratitude for our safekeeping and success, and we requested that our heartfelt thanks should be proffered to the Shining Ones who had provided the Higher Power. A rush of Light enveloped us, and we felt a wonderful sense of dedication – an urge to give selflessly of our strength, knowledge, and experience to our task.

A form slowly descended and stood in our midst. It was the weeping angel, his smile now as bright as his renewed Light. He began to move within the circle and then he said: "It is good to feel the earth once more. I was wrong when I told you that you were too small and too few to affect the ghouls. With my brothers and sisters I have endeavoured to oust them with our power and love for many years. We realize that this was not enough, for we lack the knowledge and experience which you have put to such good use. But we have learned much. Our lives were all joy but now that we have suffered, our joy is much greater, and for this gift we thank you."

We bowed in loving respect and, as the angel withdrew, the light faded. We then broke the circle and gathered closer together to discuss future plans.

Eremus arrived unexpectedly among us. "Already you have understood the problem of Self-pride and are endeavouring to eradicate it. Well done. And now to work."

�֍ �֍ �֍

It was difficult to realize that the stretch of barren earth could contain the un-manifest form of every flower, tree and shrub of the garden that had been. Tepi alone was the interpretor for he was the only one of us who had given his thoughts, love and energy to it. He was part of it and his memory would restore it; but first he must brood over every inch of the land and make a thought-form of each plant that had grown there.

It was decided that he should go into retreat and, without disturbance, regain an image of the whole. He would then make a thought-formation and later we would join him and construct a full scale model on the actual site. This would of course be an inanimate version of the garden and each flower and tree form would then have to be ensouled. We asked Eremus if, during this period of Tepi's musing we could gain some experience of this work. We could not become proficient in the time involved, but at least we would be better equipped to follow his instructions and be of some assistance to him.

He spent each day recalling where every plant had grown, and where each streamlet of the watercourse had flowed. He confessed to me that he sometimes wept when he thought of the backward sweep to near chaos that the land had suffered in place of the steady progress towards perfection that had been planned.

"Stop, Tepi," I said sternly, although I felt like weeping too. "You cannot alter the past but you can influence the future. We will make that land and all the region round it into a miniature paradise, containing both animals and birds, as well as new and exotic plants."

"I have only recently learned to share your love of these creations of a more advanced nature than the plants, whose beauty has always tugged at my heart. I had no room for anything else, not even my fellow fairies. I had not realized this defect until this moment." He paused. "I wonder why there was no equivalent beast within me."

"Because it was not a defect. At that time the Plant Kingdom was your life. You had not the capacity for anything else. The situation has now changed; first you let me into your subconscious and more recently, the rest of the group. You are expanding, Tepi."

"I hope I do not explode," he said with a grin. I put my arms round him. "My dear love, you have gained the ability to laugh at yourself and that is the most effective weapon to use against Self-hatred."

❊ ❊ ❊

As had been planned, we left Tepi and set out for the Experimental Garden how to help ensoul plants. We were of course more advanced than Tepi had been when he had done this work by using his natural instincts, because we were able to call upon our more highly developed will and selection ability. We found the operation both interesting and rewarding, as we were not only adding to our knowledge, but were ensouling plants for their future benefit as well.

We then made our way to Tepi's land to construct our homes for our future work there. With thought we each made an exact replica of the dwelling that we occupied at Onward, and also our communal recreation rooms. All were at last ready, but Tepi had not completed his part of the plan; so we asked Eremus if we could begin to work out designs for the area outside the original garden, where new exotic plants would grow. We explained to him that we wished to make this special contribution as a gesture of thanks to Tepi for all he had done for us.

The Council of Justice was approached and gave not only its permission but also its blessing for the project, so we set to work making many thought-formations, all of which included birds, butterflies and colourful insects. Of course these were not necessary for pollination as on Earth because we use other systems for plant propogation, but they are loved for their beauty and often graceful movement. We also planned a heavily wooded area where small animals would scuttle happily among the moss and wild flowers, or leap about among the branches of the trees.

Tepi burst into one of our sessions gleefully. "It is finished. Every single plant is now recorded and the watercourse plotted. Here is the plan," he said as he placed the completed model before us.

We were filled with joy. It was truly a beautiful garden with each section fulfilling a purpose, which Tepi explained to us in great detail.

When we had finished, we told him that we too had something to show him, and we assembled our thought-formations round his model. Ours had not individually portrayed plants or trees, for we needed experts to complete our plan but it gave a reasonably accurate idea of what the final result would be.

Tepi was ecstatic. "Truly a miniature paradise," he said "And how right you were Perima about the animals and insects. They will enhance the whole in a beneficial as well as an artistic way because they will add unrestricted movement, and this will encourage growth in the plants."

* * *

Many months passed before completion was attained, during which time we worked day after day until we dropped from exhaustion. But at each dawn when the Sun's incandescent orb rose above the horizon, we were all present to offer our salutations and gratitude for His power and light.

The garden had not only reached the stage of its original beauty before the disaster, but with our added contribution it bloomed as never before. Everything was now ready for the Opening Ceremony.

Tepi asked me whether those who had suffered with him should be invited to participate in the celebrations, or whether it would be cruel to conjure up a memory which hopefully, would now be almost forgotten.

I had in fact been thinking of this problem for some time. "I think that they should come if they wish, for any memory which they may still retain will be one of horror and fear. If we can show them the land as it is now in all its beauty, the new vision should completely obliterate their past image, and be a comfort to them."

"How can I find them?"

"The Council of Justice will surely know where each one lives and, when the information reaches us, we will go to the Dissemination Centre and request them to convey our love to all, together with our hope that they will join us at the Ceremony of Blessing." The required data was supplied and to our great joy, the Council requested that they themselves should also be present.

Tepi and I went to the Centre and asked to see the Chief Organiser.

"My name is Tepi" he began.

"I have been expecting you. The Council of Justice has already sent us particulars of the Ceremony and we are now preparing the invitations in readiness for their dispatch to all who were involved in the ... er the ... er ... the ..."

"Disaster," said Tepi firmly.

"We had, of course, heard of the wonderful gardens you have been creating, and it had been our intention to interview you, but we were forbidden to do so. It is only now, after we have heard the whole story, that we understand it is not just a place of great beauty which you have made, but a rebirth, through penitence, suffering and years of striving against adversity. I would like to ask your permission to make public the history of the garden past and present, and your association with it."

Tepi visibly drooped. "How can you ask me to go through the whole terrible experience yet again? The loyalty of my friends and the reality of this new garden alone have helped to balance the wasted years of wandering as a nonentity when I refused to remember the event."

"Tepi, I truly understand your misgivings," the Chief Organiser said kindly, "but the story could be a wonderful inspiration to others who have failed. We all fail at some time in our lives, and this could uplift many who are, even now, in the depths of despair, as you yourself have been."

Tepi was silent for some time; then he said: "I will agree on one condition and that is that all those who suffered with me should also give their consent. Mine was not the only life that may have been ruined."

"I accept your proviso and shall await your advice with patience and hope. Before you go, you may like to know that the invitations to the Ceremony of Blessing are to be sent out in the name of the Council of Justice."

Tepi and I were speechless. What an honour for us all.

✤   ✤   ✤

As the day approached, we became increasingly excited. A Ceremony is always a great event for us of the Fairy World and on this occasion, the intended presence of the Council of Justice ensured its success.

Crowds began to gather, and all Tepi's previous co-helpers told him that, strangely, their experiences had somehow enhanced their lives. Great kindness had been shown to them in the Homes of Rest to which they were sent and new and interesting work had been found for all. This news was a valuable contribution towards the elimination of Tepi's guilt, and as the time for the reopening ceremony approached, he was shining with happiness.

The Members of the Council of Justice were in the position of honour close to the fountain which was to provide the water for the main canal, and everyone present was in his designated place. This time there were no omissions. We all held our arms up to the scintillating sky, and asked for protection from evil and a blessing for the Miniature Paradise, which had now become its official name. Immediately the firmament flashed with light as angels gathered above and around us.

A single note – the mantric note of the garden – rang out from an instrument made specially for the occasion, and this was acknowledged by an answering note from the garden itself. Simultaneously power poured downwards and a great jet of water rose from the ground, to divide and fall like a multitude of flowing, translucent rainbows. The canal filled, and the water gurgled and chuckled its way through all the gullies that we had made. The boats were launched by a happy, excited crowd; Tepi was in the leading craft with all of us who had contributed to this, the culminating event. We completed the route and halted in front of the Council of Justice.

"Come, join us," the Chief Justice called to Tepi, who smiled rather nervously at us as he obeyed the summons. He was escorted to the rostrum and the Chief Justice began to speak. "Fellow Associates, friends, craft workers and all lovers of beauty, welcome. This is a momentous occasion which everyone present will never forget. I think you all know that Tepi had the misfortune to make an error of judgment many years ago, and this beautiful garden was lost in a storm of evil intent. But now, through his own endeavour and that of his friends and the presiding angels, all has not only been restored but enhanced a hundredfold. Tepi, stand before me." He held his left arm above his head and a flash of light came out of the sky and descended on Tepi, completely enfolding him so we could no longer see him. As the ray gradually withdrew, we saw that he had grown at least six inches, an instantaneous honour to prove and display his worth, for height in our evolution is of great importance. "I now name you 'Farrilim,' a title which I know you will bear with distinction." Tepi bowed low and turned a beaming face towards us. I do not use the word 'beaming' idly, for he was filled with light, a light that was part of him and was only now revealed.

Everyone leapt with excitement and filled the air with their cheers. Colours flashed, music played and breezes drifted or bustled through the trees and flowers. The garden was open for all to enjoy, and each gave power to the plants until the area glittered with effulgence and movement.

Tepi was a hero, and we, his friends, rejoiced with him. He had been invited to become head supervisor, and those who had been with him before the tragedy were eager to join him. They too had grown in enthusiasm and ability during the intervening years, and felt an urgent need to work in the garden, as all had experienced guilt because of their inefficiency and failure to give Tepi the support he had needed.

What a wonderful, rewarding day it had been, not only for us but for the many who, through the years, would visit the garden and learn its history.

❉   ❉   ❉

The time had now come for Tepi to seek out his Self-pride and to transmute it in readiness for its union with its counterpart.

We had visited the scene of its disappearance several times but had seen no sign of it. Again the cave was empty and I suggested to Tepi that he should make a thorough search. As this was unsuccessful, we decided to stand in the circle of light, while Tepi called it. "Self-pride, come to me. You have nothing to fear; indeed we are here to help you." After a short pause, we observed the small flattish strip of matter crawl from a crevice in one of the rocks, slither stealthily towards us, and collapse. Tepi picked it up and carried it within the circle where we made a thought-form so that we could reproduce it accurately when we arrived back in my rooms. The little eyes and nose were running, and it was so weak after its journey of only a few feet that it could scarcely move. We decreased the volume of light to a mere glow and left what remained of Tepi's defect for several days.

We then carried out the procedure which we had used for the other beasts but this time the result was somewhat different. The flattened strip of matter became tubular in shape and we realized it was turning into a caterpillar; this gradually transformed itself into a beautiful butterfly, which fluttered round my room for nearly a week. Then one day, on my return, I found that it had flown away to integrate with its counterpart, thus enabling it to evolve according to Natural Law.

CHAPTER 15
ON THE HATREDS' TRAIL

Tepi's combined work in the Miniature Paradise and at Onward had been carried out successfully for six months, when he visited me in order to discuss his greatest problem – Self-hatred.

"I have seen no sign of it since the Blessing of the Garden," I said.

"I can truthfully say that I no longer hate myself. My suffering has reaped a rich harvest. All who were participants in the disaster have regained their happiness; the garden is more beautiful now than before the storm, and I have once more been established as a worthy leader."

"Do you think it could possibly have been an illusion? It is strange that it was not with your other beasts. Perhaps it was, in reality, no more than bitterness."

"No, it was definitely real. It had me in its clutches it dominated me totally. It was a tyrant."

"Do you really believe that? If you are right, the problem is even greater than we thought. Tyrants live with others of their kind. Do you realize, it is no longer a case of gaining freedom from your Self-hatred; we now have the added task of segregating it from its equally ruthless brothers?"

"I am filled with fear," Tepi confessed.

"And I, with terror." We clung to each other in our mutual dread of the hazardous prospect ahead. I had not previously been confronted by terror, but I knew what was before us – a descent into matter more Stygian, more dense than we had ever experienced.

"We must approach our Teacher-Lord, " I said decisively. "It would be sheer recklessness to face a group of Hatreds with our power alone. We need advice and training as well."

We bowed low before Him and, as always, I was awed by His beauty and height. He welcomed us and drew us both within His Aura. "My beloved victor-saviours" he greeted us "You are small in stature but great in spirit. You are wise to seek My counsel for you need my help. Hatred and Cruelty are two of the most venomous opponents of Order, equalled only by Lust-for-power. You have already had contact with Cruelty but it was outside its own territory and thus vulnerable to our concerted attack. This Hatred is in fact, not one of your defects, Tepi; you unknowingly became its vassal because you had mentally sunk to the depths, and had not the power or knowledge to ward off your invisible assailant. It is a member of a group, as indeed was Cruelty, its brothers in iniquity will not lose a part of themselves without a bitter struggle. They practice self-mutilation, and perpetrate unspeakable horrors on each other in their endeavour to assuage their own Self-hatred."

"My Lord, have I your permission to speak?" I asked.

"I am always willing to hear you, Perima, whether you make a request or an observation."

"I know that we will perform any act which is necessary to extricate this particular Hatred from its group, but you have said that this is not one of Tepi's failings, as were the beasts. We had no responsibility for Cruelty, a similar group member. Why is this case different?"

Our Teacher-Lord turned to Tepi. "You tell her, Farrilim."

"Because I owe it a debt."

I looked at him in astonishment. "It ruined your life for years and you say you are indebted to it?"

"The torment I suffered caused me to wander in a futile endeavour to escape from it. Eventually my seemingly endless journey led me to you Perima, and through you I learned to love. Is that love not worthy of repayment, no matter what the cost?"

Tears came into my eyes as I put my arms around him. "Our mutual love will more than compensate us for whatever horrors we experience."

We stood hand in hand as our Teacher-Lord continued.

"I have already formulated a plan, and this time you will need more than My Power and Guidance; a Presence is necessary – the Presence of a Man."

"A Man?" We both gasped simultaneously. Neither of us had considered this possibility. We knew, of course, that the Human Evolution runs parallel with, and is complementary to ours. We had examined thought-formations and thus knew what some of them looked like, but we had never made direct contact with one. The prospect intrigued and excited us.

"As you know, Man's vibrations differ from ours and allow him to enter and work in much denser matter than we can. I know of one who will help you. He lives in the deepest sector of Gehenna, giving his life to those who dwell there. He is a combination of compassion, courage and strength; with these attributes and My Light he will be able to force his way through conditions which would be impenetrable to you. Together you will find and enter the region where the Hatreds live."

Again terror assailed me.

"Do not fear, little one. Your training and ability to obey orders from a distance will enable you and Tepi to carry out the plan which will release him from the possibility of future attacks, and fulfil his obligation to this personified evil. The brute-fiends which will confront you will be stunned your beauty Perima and will loathe you for it; but Vigilance, Light and Man-power will bring you victory; I promise."

✽ ✽ ✽

On returning to my home, Tepi and I could think and talk of nothing else but the man that we were going to meet. What would he be like? Courage and strength obviously indicated someone tall and of athletic build: a warrior in armour perhaps. Compassion; he would have a kind face with a noble expression. What a wonderful person he must be. And to work with a member of the Human race would undoubtedly be the most exciting experience of our lives.

Our Teacher-Lord eventually sent for us, and we entered His reception-area filled with both curiosity and expectation. Standing beside Him was a slim man of small stature; his feet were bare and he was clad in a plain home-spun garment with a thin rope tied round his hips. But what a face. His eyes revealed his experience of suffering, but when he smiled, he lit up and his aura covered several feet around him. His light was different from ours. Fairy power scintillates; his was steady and bright.

"This is Augustine of whom I spoke on your previous visit," our Teacher-Lord said, as He led the man towards us. We bowed deeply before him, then we gazed at him in fascination, touched with amazement that so frail a figure could possibly be strong. He held out his arms towards us and we both reached up and took one of his proffered hands in ours.

"It is difficult to believe that such small people can have achieved so much through dedication, determination and the power of will. You can teach me a great deal," he said.

We had rarely met such humility before, but the size of his aura established the fact that we were in the presence of a great soul. We waited breathlessly for his first instruction which would set our training in motion.

"Let us enjoy ourselves," he said, his eyes twinkling. "We will go for a walk and you can show me some of the treasures of your beautiful land."

We took him first to see the Miniature Paradise where he frequently bent down to whisper words of encouragement to the younger plants. He gave praise to those which were doing well and he soon demonstrated to us that his knowledge of herbs and their healing powers was very extensive.

We travelled for miles over the countryside; we soared over mountains, dived into streams or sat contentedly in meadows, surrounded by flowers. He noticed tiny insects struggling to carry pieces of foliage from here to there, and sometimes back again. Our butterflies with their jewel-like wings entranced him, and little animals and birds gathered round us chattering to him in their different ways.

It was obvious that he loved them all and understood what they were telling him.

"I think I miss the animals almost more than anything else, where I live," he said a little sadly.

"There are beasts there, are there not?" I asked.

"Oh! yes, and I love them too. But I am starved of most beauty; that is my most baneful loss."

"Are there any compensations for your great sacrifice?" Tepi enquired.

"Yes indeed, when I can give the 'lost ones' a glimmer of hope and watch them lose their fear of me."

"Fear of you?" we asked in amazement.

"You see, I cannot dim my aura enough, and they are afraid of light. But I lie down and keep very still, sometimes for days on end, and curiosity eventually over-rides their fear. They creep nearer to see if I am dead, perhaps hoping that I am," he chuckled. "Then they shake me to make sure and once they have touched me a little of my aura stays with them."

"How long does it take to rescue someone?" Tepi asked.

"It depends on the level at which I am working. It may be a year, sometimes but a few weeks."

"How can you live so long in the Darkness? We can manage to stay for only an hour or two."

"I leave for a few days of replenishment when my inner light begins to fail. But after a short while, I feel compelled to return. I am so fortunate to be able to leave at will unlike those I strive to save. The pleasure we have enjoyed today will compensate me for many weeks in the Dark."

Our hearts were touched by his simplicity, as they would be on many future occasions.

"When do we begin our training?" Tepi asked.

"I will speak to your Teacher-Lord, and together we will form a plan, for He knows your capacity for endurance better than I. We will commence as soon as possible, I promise you."

"What should we call you? What is your title?" I asked him.

He smiled. "I do not think we shall need titles where we are going. Call me Augustine."

* * *

Tepi and I waited impatiently for nearly a week, and then our Teacher-Lord summoned us and told us that our training would begin the following day. He suggested that we should take Augustine to the Cavern of the Beasts and spend the day there without the circle of light. He assured us that we would be quite safe, as his personal power would be ample protection against any minor evil that might endeavour to harm us.

When Augustine met us at Onward, we asked him if he would consent to meet Eremus and our co-workers who had helped us to make the Miniature Paradise. "I am more than willing; in fact it was my intention to request not only that a meeting should take place, but that a committee should be formed, because your leader and friends are an important part of the Plan." We greeted this information with enthusiasm because it meant that we would continue to work as a group.

They were already gathered together because Tepi and I had been certain that so kindly a man would not refuse our modest request; modest from his point of view, but it is always an important event for a fairy to meet a man for the first time.

We entered the recreation-room and all rose to their feet and performed the obeisance reserved for a Shining One, although Augustine was not a member of our Evolution.

"You honour me too much," he said. "Please accept my heart-felt thanks for making me so welcome. Your Thought-Formations will be a valuable contribution to the success of the Plan, and they will save us a good deal of preliminary work. It is often necessary for me to use my will for many hours to enable me to penetrate a rock-face, or ford a raging river. But you of the Fairy Evolution are the wielders of Will-Power. You are also trained to weld thoughts together and, in combination, they are far stronger than each individual one. Perima, Tepi and I will take up temporary residence in the Cavern of the Beasts. We will be there with the direct protective Light of your Teacher-Lord, and we will rely on you to supply the power necessary to sustain us when we plunge into the spheres where Darkness is not only present, but also rules.

"Your annihilation of the ghouls, when purifying the land which is now the Miniature Paradise will have been a valuable experience. I understand that you have not been to the Dark Places even for short periods. Tepi and Perima did not give you a detailed account of their conflict with the Beasts as they feared that the conditions they suffered, even second hand, might contaminate your innocent vision which provides an essential attribute for the Thought-Formations you create.

"But Time is not static. All must march forward with it. Your Teacher-Lord has agreed to allow me to take you mentally into a World of which you know almost nothing. Innocence is an attribute of the Angels; they can only gain experience through reflection, unless their own territory is violated. You will remember how the one you named the Weeping Angel and his brothers thanked you for your help, because their own suffering during the invasion, followed by their active participation in the routing of the ghouls, had enabled them to acquire a greater joy than they had previously known.

"But first I must request and also gain your permission to help you to lose your innocence and gain wisdom and fulfilment through experience. You will not at any time be with us, but even from a distance, the stench and the evil will reach you. It will not surround you as it will us. Your experience will be but a pale shadow of the reality. You must grasp this fact and hold it firmly through every eventuality, to enable you to remain steadfast, whatever may follow. I cannot say that you will not be afraid, because the reflection will appear to be real. I can sense no weaklings among you. But you must think about all I have said and any who wish to withdraw from this project are not only permitted to do so with no loss of dignity, but must do so for the safety of Perima and Tepi whom you love so well."

"Gracious and noble Sir," Eremus said. "We are a group welded together by years of love and service. Our minds are so in tune that if even one leaves, there would be an unbridgable gap." His eyes scanned all those present. "There is fear but no wavering in their determination to do your bidding in order to separate this terrible Hatred from its brethren and free Tepi from its domination."

All eyes continued to gaze at Augustine with wrapt attention. None looked down or even blinked.

"A full-scale model of the Cavern of the Beasts has been constructed outside the entrance-gates of Onward. I want you to spend an hour or two each day exploring not only the main cave itself, but every passage leading in or out of it, so that you become familiar with each rock and the position of the fissures or any structure which could either hide or produce a hazard.

"Together we will practise, Tepi, Perima and I in reality, you in reflection, blasting our way through boulders and other obstructions. We will then stage mock attacks from beasts, demons and ghouls. None of these will be real, but merely forms moved by automation. All your future work on this project will take place in this model. Its contour will frequently change to become a facsimile of the terrain through which our underground journey passes on our way to the realm of the Hatreds.

"After we have reached a certain point, and we do not know where this will be, Perima, Tepi and I will be in constant danger and a warning from you could save us from mutilation or unconsciousness. Artificial darkness will be introduced and gradually intensified so that the conditions will at all times be similar to ours. You must learn to combat this black menace which will encircle you so that you cannot see one another, with the Light of your Teacher-Lord. This Light will be conveyed by you to us; in fact you will be power-transmitters for the whole operation at whatever level we are working."

His voice ceased and silence followed; it was not a negative pause but one filled with many emotions; elation at being chosen to take part in the project; apprehension concerning their ability to perform whatever would be required of them; fear that they would lack the necessary courage; but above all there was the will to prevail, whatever hazards had to be faced, for how could they fail with our Teacher-Lord and Augustine leading us.

Eremus asked when they could explore the model of the cavern.

"Now, if you wish. I will take you to it, and later Perima, Tepi and I will go to the real cave, and you can watch us as projected images."

❊ ❊ ❊

We left Onward through the great jewelled gates, and at first we could see only the usual scene. Then Augustine showed us an opening in a rock through which we passed to find a tunnel leading downward. We made our way along it until we reached a large space, an exact replica of the Cavern of the Beasts. We showed our friends every passage, the hole where Avarice had kept his hoard, the area where we had placed our circle of Light, and the shaft up which Cruelty had stormed and down which he had been driven in defeat.

"We will leave you now and go to the real cave." Augustine said. He turned to Tepi and asked him how we usually made the journey. He told him that we always started from my home, and it was agreed that Tepi and I should go first and that Augustine would follow us.

We were soon all within the circle of light. "I think you know that you must learn to dispense with this power as an ever present protection, to prepare you for conditions in which it will not be possible to establish a stable light. We will have to rely on individual rays administered for our particular need at any given time."

"We know that your aura will be enough to guide and protect us," we assured him.

"It will be adequate here. But remember, we shall be entering territory which is new, not only to you, but to me also. Mental alertness will be essential. You must understand that whatever ray is sent to us must have a prepared focussing point for its particular quality provided by our thoughts. If it is not there, the ray cannot manifest."

"This will be very different from what we have been used to," I said. "We have always been given the ray that we need in answer to our plea for help, or even when an unexpected event occurs."

"As we work together you will acquire the ability to follow my thoughts, and eventually yours and mine will be as one. We will practise with mock attacks coming from unexpected sources, and you will learn to react automatically. You will bring into being a new set of faculties of which you have previously been unaware."

"This sounds exciting" Tepi said.

"And essential for both our mutual and self-preservation. You can rely on me to supply the primary reaction to danger, which you must detect, translate, and take immediate steps to eradicate, because I shall be preoccupied with the hazards surrounding us. There will be many of them, and I may be unable to send you a conscious warning."

"We are gratified to have your confidence in our ability to do what is vital for our safety," I said.

"I am not relying solely on the reports given to me by your Teacher-Lord," he said. Then he turned to me. "You are not the only one present who has extra-vision, Perima." I then set mine in motion and ascertained that this was not a gentle rebuke, but a little joke.

* * *

Our training and that of the rest of the group continued for many months, until we had exploited to the full everything that could be learned from simulated Reality. We achieved a degree of at-one-ness with Augustine which he was satisfied would be adequate for the next phase of the Plan, which included learning how to penetrate ultra-solid matter. We practised concentrating on prepared masses which were impervious to normal will-power alone. We learned to use rays that pierced, pulverized, melted or caused explosions until at each level, we became masters of the matter around us.

Deeper and deeper we forged our way – the air becoming as thick and foul as stagnant water. We learned to breathe by drawing from it the pure inner aspect which is present in any element, however polluted.

It was an exhausting experience, but we also enjoyed periods of relaxation when we returned to planes to which I had previously been transported only in meditation. These spells of replenishment were like beautiful dreams in which we knew rapture and the satisfaction of attainment, although at the time we had in fact achieved very little. Our determination was intensified, and trust and love grew steadily between us. In the Dark Places we were three people working in absolute accord. In this higher sphere of consciousness our thoughts, actions, and intentions were identical; we were perfectly blended; we were one.

These Utopian interludes soon came to an end, having achieved their main objective – the one-ness which was essential for our survival and eventual success.

❊ ❊ ❊

At this stage, we still did not know where the Hatreds lived; and our search now began from the Cavern of the Beasts.

Tepi was the generator of the seeker-ray that was being used and there was little that we could do to help him. I could get nothing but a downward reaction, we decided to make a tunnel. No tools or mechanical contraptions were used – only rays and concentration. Before beginning, we moved away from the Cavern, because it could be dangerous to make a real opening leading downward which could also be as an entrance by undesirable denizens of the nether regions and thus cause harm to the beasts in the vicinity.

We travelled for many days down subterranean passages and along sluggish near empty river beds. Alternatively we were hurled on our journey by raging torrents until eventually we reached open country once more; a vast tract of wilderness where nothing grew and no beasts roamed; the sole evidence of life being rock and fire.

This was the terrain we were seeking, so we lay down to rest close to Augustine and the protection of his light. How comforting it was. How safe we felt. We dreamed of clear, sparkling waterfalls and lush grass and the memory of these sleep-images were to sustain us for many weeks.

❈ ❈ ❈

We awoke to reality and set in motion our inner-breathing technique as the air was stifling outside Augustine's aura. We scanned our surroundings and chose a site from which to start the hazardous enterprise to which we were pledged.

We used a boring ray, which thrummed its way downward, scattering the resistant earth in all directions, until we reached impenetrable rock. We then sent splitting rays which probed and revealed any weak point or points. One penetrated deeper than the others, so we returned to the borer again. We made slow but steady progress following both rays through each aperture produced, pausing only to replenish ourselves with power beamed towards us by the group, before continuing the work.

Eventually we heard a clattering, crashing roar and we knew that the rubble displaced by the rays was falling into a large crater. The beginning of our search was ended.

After we had rested, Tepi again used his Seeker-ray in a further endeavour to find his Hatred's direction. This time he felt a pain below his solar plexus when he was facing north. We marked the direction on the rock face and went gratefully to sleep and our dreams.

❈ ❈ ❈

Our journey continued. Sometimes we travelled up steep and stony paths, at others downward, and Tepi's pain became increasingly severe as we drew nearer to our goal. The conditions steadily worsened and we were forced to take longer and more frequent periods of rest.

At last we knew we were nearing our goal. We could hear nerve-shattering screams, rattling groans, pitiful shrieks and whining, pleading cries in the distance.

To my horror Tepi joined in this barbarous chorus, Augustine endeavoured to soothe him but he bared his teeth and screeched "I hate you, you vile, sanctimonious soul-saver. I hate ... hate ... hate you."

Augustine took him in his arms and cradled him like a child. "Well done, Tepi beloved. You have achieved what we could not. You have found your Hatred, but you must not give it dominion over you again. You know that it cannot seize control. It can only possess it as a gift from you."

Tepi was sobbing in great, choking gulps. "Augustine, what has happened to me? How could I revile you when, apart from Perima, I love you more than anyone I know."

"And that is what will save us. Love. Alas, one cannot conquer Hatreds with Love at this level, because they are surrounded by their own kind and are generating their malevolence in a free-moving, magnetic circuit. Even though we are but three to their many, our love is both indivisible and indestructable. It is our strength and with this strength we will prevail."

We made direct contact with our Teacher-Lord asking that a large volume of power should be generated through the group, in order to build a barricade around us; this could be taken forward with us when making surveys of the conditions in which the Hatreds lived. It was essential to know whether they were incarcerated in an enclosed area, or were free to wander in the vicinity at will. We felt rather than saw the light, and its presence both comforted and reassured us.

❋ ❋ ❋

Our progress was slow because we knew that the area ahead might be filled with embodiments akin to the Hatreds' in nature.

Our fears seemed to be justified when red eyes peered at us from all directions. We were not attacked, but we were followed by snorts and snuffles wherever we went. We wondered whether they were made by sentries, who would warn the Hatreds of our approach, or were members of a separate group. We sent out a testing ray, which caught several of them in its beam. There was no reaction, which proved that they were not evil, but merely denizens of the Dark in their normal evolutionary sphere.

Augustine told us to stay where we were while he endeavoured to gain their confidence in the hope that they could be used to aid us, should the necessity arise.

He moved towards them and began to intone wordlessly in a low, soothing voice. The red eyes blinked and heads were cocked first on one side and then on the other. The creatures could obviously hear and liked what they heard.

Slowly, they crept forward on their bellies until they reached Augustine's feet. He bent down and fondled those nearest him. "Welcome, little brothers," he said gently as he held his hands over them with the love-ray beaming from his fingers. They rolled on their backs in a similar manner to Tepi's beasts when we played with them. Augustine called to us and we joined him and rumpled their fur and tickled their ears. They wriggled and yelped with pleasure and we began to laugh. They shot to their feet in instant alarm and assumed defensive positions with their heads down, teeth bared and back legs bent, ready to spring.

"Now, now, little brothers, we mean you no harm. Relax. Soon you will learn to laugh with us." Augustine's voice assumed a crooning tone. "Now sleep. Carry our laughter into your dreams, and it will lead you to a higher plane." Lids drooped and red eyes were eclipsed as the creatures collapsed on the ground, unconscious.

Day by day, we directed rays towards them and introduced them to the beneficial vibrations of our laughter. Like Tepi's beasts they began to play with each other as well as us, while emitting strange sounds, which were certainly not belligerent.

We decided to set up our headquarters with them, and during this time we taught the creatures to enjoy themselves, and Augustine left us for short periods while he explored the terrain ahead. He found it to be a vacuum as far as living things were concerned. This was good news indicating that it was probably a prohibited area, inaccessible to the Hatreds as well as to any other forms of life which dwelt beyond it.

❊ ❊ ❊

We became accustomed to living in the darkness, which was complete apart from the faint glow of our restricted auras and the redness of the creatures' eyes which were now objects of comfort rather than fear.

Soon we were allowed to accompany Augustine in his efforts to find a weakness in a seemingly endless circular wall of rock and fire which formed a barrier between us and those we wished to observe.

"We must look for sentries," Augustine said. "Their presence will indicate a position which cannot otherwise be protected. There must also be an entrance, for the Hatreds need newcomers for their maintenance: fresh blood is essential to them."

A terrible uproar followed his words. It came from far away on the other side of the fortified enclosure.

"This could be a new intake," he said. "Let us be guided by it." Our progress was slow owing to the density of the atmosphere and the sulphurous fumes arising from the fires, and the daunting shrieks and cries died down in the distance when we were still a long way off.

We returned to our headquarters to rest, and then set out once more; we circled the entire wall, but found neither sentries nor an entrance. By this time Augustine had come to the conclusion that our normal sight was inadequate and that we should use our extra-vision in an endeavour to find the hidden entrance, which must be in existence though invisible to us.

Tepi accompanied me, and our progress was a little faster than before because we had become more used to the new system of breathing and were able to extract the essence from the atmosphere without being affected by the fumes from the fires. But any real speed was impeded by the necessity to will our protective power-barrier to move with us, and to keep it replenished by signalling to our group at Onward.

Tepi skirted the wall itself with his seeker ray, while I moved at a distance using my extra-vision. We found several deep crevices, but none was sufficiently large for use as an entrance. I floated above the fires to see if access could be obtained beyond them, but their smoke formed an additional barrier and I could see virtually nothing.

After the time allotted to us by Augustine had lapsed, we returned to our headquarters disappointed by our lack of success. But we were comforted by the welcome given to us by the creatures. Augustine arrived shortly afterwards and he too was obliged to admit failure.

We continued our search until eventually we met on the far side, having circled the entire wall between us. Augustine too had examined the area above the fires, and apart from the smoke, he did not think that the Hatreds' body-density would allow them to travel above ground-level. It was then decided that we must return to our digging operations.

❈ ❈ ❈

So once again, we asked for the probing , splitting and explosive rays and set to work. But first we used our extra-vision to see if we could locate an existing underground tunnel. Again we separated, and after a while we received a call from Augustine to join him. He told us that he had located at least one, and he thought that there could be a network which would make our task much easier.

We employed the same techniques which we had used on our journey, and when we heard the clatter of debris falling into space, we slithered down with the rest of the rubble and found ourselves, as expected, in a tunnel.

Augustine suggested that we should stay and replenish our inner-forces while he endeavoured to find out where the passage led. But we asked if we might accompany him, as we did not yet know what dangers to expect. So the three of us moved silently and wearily forward, until we came to a cavern, which appeared to have been uninhabited for a long time.

Augustine decided that we must rest before continuing our exploration, so we sat together, grateful for the peace and comfort of his aura. When we had recovered sufficiently, we began to examine the surrounding walls, and we found several passages leading out of the cave. There was no sign of life anywhere apart from the groans of the rocks, suffering from their ultra-solidity, which restricted the intake of sufficient power for their needs.

*   *   *

We had searched five of the tunnels and were proceeding along the sixth, when we saw a flicker of fire coming through a crevice.

"There must be an aperture with moving air; otherwise there would be no flame," said Augustine. Somehow the glimmer of light cheered us and, for a while, we watched it in silence, hoping that it would disclose something.

"Little fire," intoned Augustine, "reveal your secret to us. Whence art thou? Whither goest thou?" The flickering faltered and then was extinguished, enabling us to peer up the cleft to see a light from an obviously large conflagration. "Honoured Great Fire" Augustine called out, "pray send an emissary to lead us to you."

We waited tensely for a sign that our plea had been heard and we were rewarded. What had appeared to be a solid rock facing us became transparent and we could see a brilliant, flashing Light.

"Enter."

We walked through the transformed boulder, not without fear as far as Tepi and I were concerned. Perhaps it was a cunning trap and we would be scorched or burned.

"All is well, little ones. The Elements do not deceive if they are addressed with respect."

We advanced until we stood before a vast sheet of fire, which covered half of a large cavern. To Tepi's and my amazement we found that it was not hot. Augustine bowed and we followed his example. Two arms of flame shot out and surrounded us and then withdrew.

"We thank you for permitting us to enter your Princedom, and also for your courteous welcome." Neither Tepi nor I had received any instruction on Fire-lore, so we read Augustine's mind in order to follow the conversation.

"You are indeed welcome, Wise-Man. My name is Ra-onus. My Princedom has been invaded by evil ones; I withdrew to this cavern because they continually robbed me of my resources when I was resting. They forge tools from the ore in the rock, and with these they mutilate one another; they also use my fire-children to inflict terrible burns."

"We grieve deeply with you for being a virtual prisoner in your own domain, but pray tell us where the Hatreds live."

"Ah! so that is what these half-human devils are. I guard the entrance between us myself. They are unable to overcome me here, because they cannot surround me."

"We wish to observe them, for we are here to rescue one of their members and, hopefully, to destroy the others, or at least invalidate them."

"How many of you are there, to perform this awe-inspiring task?"

Augustine smiled. "At this level we are only three, but we have instant access to many Forces from the higher Planes. "

The Fire-Lord lost some of his brightness from shock. "But there are hundreds, maybe thousands of them," he said. "How can so few overcome so many?"

"By whatever strategy is required – perhaps with guile. We are image-makers and can make ourselves look like a small army."

"Tell me, what role I can play, Wise-Man."

"You can help to activate our images if you are willing."

"I will do everything in my power to help you overcome these fiends and, at the same time, you will be aiding me to regain my Princedom."

"That will be an additional reason for us to strive for victory. Will you now permit us to pass through you so that we can examine the Hatreds' territory and study their activities."

"Certainly," Ra-onus replied, "and I will provide sanctuary for you any time you need it. The devil-men burn when I touch them with intent."

"Come," Augustine said to us, and Tepi and I followed him, this time without fear. We walked for about half a minute accompanied by the Fire's friendly roar, masking the demonic clamour, which battered us as soon as we reached his boundary.

⟅ CHAPTER 16 ⟆
THE HATRED'S DOMAIN

The brightness of the Fire's light at first prevented us from observing the scene which we had taken so long, and driven so hard to reach. And we were obliged to leave the safety he provided and stand as though blind, until our eyes and breathing became used to the darkness and the pitch-thick air.

Without the Fire's protective roar surrounding us the sounds which assaulted us made those emitted by the ghouls seem like music in comparison, and our minds became temporarily nullified by the pandemonium.

When we had gathered ourselves together once more, we slowly opened our eyes. Tepi and I quickly closed them again and we were forced to use our willpower to prevent ourselves from turning and running back to the Fire.

The ground as far as we could see was littered with torn-off, hacked-off, gnawed-off limbs. Decapitated heads lay shrieking or groaning, and vomiting blood. Bodiless legs fled from weapon-wielding pursuers to stumble into fires, which crackled and belched smoke every few yards. White hot irons were drawn from the flames to brand exhausted bodies that could no longer move. Pointed flints were hammered through stomachs driving the entrails before them. These were pounced on, torn apart and greedily gobbled as they writhed on the ground, as though aware of the gruesome fate about to befall them. There was a constant movement of lusting pursuers shouting obscenities, and demented pursued shrieking vainly for mercy as they fled through the fires.

At first we stood, petrified with horror, watching the general scene without being aware of individuals. When we recovered slightly from our near torpor, having invoked the aid of our Teacher-Lord, we saw that most of their heads were animal and their bodies human, but some were entirely animal. All were repulsive. Some were like pre-historic reptiles; others like crocodiles and rhinos with crowns of horns which were used to gouge out their victims' eyes. Still others were similar to giant stag beetles, shrews and bats. Many were creatures we had never seen before and all bred terror and disgust in both of us. Their bodies were caricatures of the male human form; some being as gnarled and knotted as old tree trunks. The head scales of others spread, like a terrible disease, over the rest of their skin. All were scarred and bleeding. Gaping wounds, spurting streams of near-black blood, were sucked by gruesome apertures – I cannot call them mouths – until the victim's body was drained. There were some which were blind, their eyes gaping holes, or lids sealed together with congealed blood. These used their snouts, which swivelled ceaselessly to sniff out their prey; but how they could single out a specific victim from the stupifying stink of pus and excreta which flowed, dropped, or spurted from every orifice, I shall never know.

❈ ❈ ❈

Augustine signalled to us to retire and we re-entered the flames. This time we stood for a while in the centre of the Fire while he performed an act of purification, so that, when we emerged on his far side, the stench and ordure had disappeared.

We stood looking at each other in silence. Then I burst into tears. "You were so calm" I said to Augustine. "I am deeply ashamed of my disgust and terror. I found myself hating them. You must despise me."

Tepi put his arms around me. "You are a female; it is a natural reaction for you. But I am a male, I should be strong and able to protect you, but I was frightened too."

"My beloved ones, I would be dismayed had you not been afraid," said Augustine gently.

"On Earth, it is the animals' fear of predators that often saves them from instant death. It is the young and inexperienced that are the most vulnerable because they know not fear. I may appear to be calm because my mind is vigilant and my danger instinct active for our safety; I have no time to be afraid."

"I watched you briefly and you did not hate them," I sobbed.

"That is due to my knowledge that they are but thought-creation made by my fellow men. They are not of themselves evil. They are like puppets at first, manipulated by their human inventors and later motivated by their Group Mind."

"Do men really behave like these Hatreds?" Tepi asked.

"Not many act thus physically, but mentally, yes quite a number do. A Hatred performs the actions that its creator's mind imagines. When many of them are gathered together, as they are here, a Group Mind forms and takes charge, influencing its members to obey its will. The one here is both powerful and evil. It is our real enemy. Come now. Dry your tears Perima and cast aside your disappointment in yourself for I am proud of you. The fact that you stood your ground and observed the horrific scene is a great credit to you. Many would have fled into the Fire's protection." He embraced us both fondly, then said: "Come, we have work to do."

❖ ❖ ❖

After discussing the alternatives, we decided to make bodies for ourselves similar to those of the Hatreds, so that we could go among them without detection.

"What about your aura Augustine?" I asked him, "Tepi's and mine can be hidden but not yours."

His eyes twinkled. "I shall be the biggest Hatred they have ever seen – and the fiercest."

"But you could never be fierce," Tepi said.

"My inherent ferocity is buried in the Vaults of Time, but I can produce the outer signs of savagery and venom. I shall fool them, I promise you." He turned to me and asked "What animal body is your choice Perima?"

"I shall be an outsize vampire bat; I can at least escape from those that cannot fly," I answered, trying to smile.

"A very good idea, and from above you can also pounce. We shall be obliged to perform many actions alien to our natures if we are to trick them into believing that we are one of them. What about you Tepi?"

"I rather like the idea of gnashing my teeth; a crocodile is my choice." He grinned.

We set to work making thought forms of the frames of our chosen animals, consolidating them with atoms from the surrounding atmosphere and leaving a space in the centre for our own bodies. I made my bat with a wingspan of about three feet. The eyes changed colour and swivelled in all directions, partly to enable me to see what was taking place behind me and also, hopefully, to frighten any minor Hatred with belligerent intent. The mouth gaped to show teeth as sharp as cactus spines, and behind them were secreted sacs containing a supply of blood.

Tepi provided his crocodile with a variety of sounds: it rattled when it moved and it grunted, bellowed and made sucking or disgorging noises at will. He gave it sharp retractable claws for use as potent weapons and it could thrash its tail sideways or flip it over its back and bring it down again in a stunning blow.

When they were completed to our satisfaction, we turned to Augustine and asked him what form he had chosen.

"I must think of something that will really frighten them." He paused, then he triumphantly announced "I shall remain a man."

"But they will attack you as soon as they see you," we objected. "They will know that you are not a member of the Hatred Clan."

"I think that it may be necessary for me to remain behind the Fire until the final phases of the battle. Before it begins, I shall be in constant communication with those at Onward and also with you two through thought transference. My mind will work more efficiently if I am not encumbered during this period with a body I am not used to. When I finally appear I shall carry weapons for my protection which the Hatreds have never seen before: an innocent-looking staff will spray fire; stunning rays will pass through my fingers; my arms will elongate and my hands clutch them round the throat or seize them as they are about to destroy members of our forces."

"But what if they attack you as a pack?"

"They are not a pack; that is their weakness. They are divided by their virulent hatred for each other. Have you witnessed one attempting to help another in distress? I promise you, they will only fight to protect themselves."

"Will you be just a large and ugly version of yourself?" Tepi asked.

"No, my normal appearance would not be sufficiently impressive to fill them with fear, even if it was many times enlarged; and I may need to scare them in order to attract their attention away from one of you, perhaps when you, Tepi, are involved in the removal of your Hatred to safety. It is absolutely essential that you should find it before the battle begins, even if you are unable to complete the rescue."

"You are assuming that I shall know which one it is. How shall I recognise it among so many when I have no idea what it looks like?"

"In the same way that you knew your defects among the beasts."

※　※　※

Augustine stood for a while in deep thought and then a giant figure appeared before us.

Fire hissed in apprehension while Tepi and I stood petrified for a moment before we realized that it was only an image. The body and legs appeared to be made of granite. The arms of twisted metal clanked as Augustine manipulated them in our direction and seized first Tepi in one fist, and me in the other. Sitting on the side of the great hands, we examined the face of this gruesome figure.

The head was that of a hideous man with small, squinting eyes and a bulbous nose like a gnarled turnip. The mouth was hanging open in a permanent leer exposing fangs as black as ebony which manifested menace in the light of the Fire.

Although we knew that our disguises were for a serious purpose we all burst out laughing, including the Fire who expressed his mirth through a series of small explosions.

"This is what we need when the time comes" said Augustine as he placed us once more on the ground. "Excluding mine, the bodies we use will be recognisable to them, but the sound of laughter will be a new experience. This element of surprise could be to our advantage, perhaps by giving us time to put into action our next strategy. We shall, of course need much more laughter than we and the creatures combined can provide. Some must be supplied by the group so that, at our signal, wave after wave of joyous sound will envelop the remaining Hatreds and, we hope, cause a change in their dispositions or failing that annihilate them."

❖ ❖ ❖

Tepi and I set to work to help Augustine build his ogre. When it was complete it proved to be very cumbersome and we wondered how he would manage to manipulate its massive limbs.

"I intend it to be impregnable rather than athletic," he said. "Come, let us enter our new bodies and learn to operate them so that they perform any action we may require of them."

❖ ❖ ❖

Our next task was to construct the individual units for our army. There was such diversity in the Hatreds' forms and so many of them that we had no great difficulty in making images that would rouse no suspicions during the short period when they might be visible before going into action.

When we had fashioned enough of them for our initial purpose we contacted Eremus and the group. We asked them to animate the units and also learn how to move them in any required direction, because at all future times they would be manipulated by remote control from Onward, leaving Tepi and me free to play our parts as leaders and strategists.

In order to obtain experience of battle conditions, we coloured some of our images white to represent our forces and others red, which they would operate as the enemy. Ra-onus watched the proceedings with increasing interest and asked when he could take part.

"We shall need your help when we have learned more about Hatred behaviour," Augustine replied. "We do not know what the Rulers among them will do when they are attacked, nor the degree of authority they wield over whom. There is always a fluctuating ascendency-descendency pattern in gangs such as this one, when rank is not gained through merit but by strength and brutality. Incoming members, although strong, are less experienced than those already in possession of an area and at first they are always ruthlessly subjected to the prevailing system. Eventually some will acquire sufficient cunning to raise their status by overcoming those weaker than themselves. Having gained vigour by sucking blood and vitality from their victims, they begin to challenge, through savage attacks, the less powerful of the lordlings; later, a few will become Tyrants until eventually they too are overcome. At the moment, you can create what will be an element of surprise for them. The Hatreds are obliged to handle your stolen flames with care lest they get burned. If you will activate our images to enable them to eject fire in all directions, this will be a new experience for our adversaries and many will be destroyed before they learn to take cover behind rocks. Once they adopt this evasive procedure, they will doubtless counter attack by hurling boulders at our units and crushing them. We must, therefore, have plenty of reinforcements hidden in the cave to replace them."

The Fire crackled with excitement. "When may I begin?"

"Now! We will stage a mock battle with the group at Onward manipulating the 'red' units, and you can operate the 'white' using your new spray-fire technique. We can then ascertain what defences our co-workers will bring into action when taken by surprise."

We did not warn them of our new weapon, but merely asked them to operate the red automata. As soon as the Fire had completed his preparations, we sent a signal to Eremus and the 'reds' began to attack. As soon as they came into range the 'whites' opened fire. The 'reds' dropped in their tracks and for several minutes, confusion reigned. Then it was the Fire's turn to be taken by surprise because the remaining 'reds' retaliated by shooting great jets of water on the 'whites' and the spray fire was quickly extinguished.

"Invalid," Augustine signalled to Onward. "There is no water here".

"We will try again," Eremus replied. "Give us time to formulate a new stratagem."

✳   ✳   ✳

We quickly replaced both the drenched 'white' and the burnt-out 'red' units with others from our reserves, and comforted Ra-onus who was very dejected because he had been vanquished so soon. Augustine explained to him that his defeat was unfeasible because the element of water was present nowhere in the Hatreds' domain.

Once more the 'reds' began to attack and the 'whites' used the scatter fire again, but this time the enemy failed to ignite as planned.

"Invalid," Augustine called once again. "You are using a higher aspect of fire to protect your fighters than that available here. But we can use it to protect our own automata. Please set to work and fire proof each one as it is made."

* * *

For days the cavern became a miniature battle ground, each side intent on out-manoeuvering the other. Sometimes Eremus and the group proved themselves more inventive, at others we gained mastery over them; and all the time we were learning to adapt ourselves to confinement in our respective forms and to use them to the best advantage.

We returned to our original headquarters in order to capture the laughter of the creatures for future release at the appropriate time. And what a welcome we received. They leapt high in the air screaming shrilly as they turned somersaults and performed the strangest capers to show their delight at our return.

We gathered them in our arms and petted them until each had received its share of love. Then we played our usual games, running, jumping and tumbling with them. As we laughed, so did they, and we imprinted our impressions of happiness on the sensitized matter which was already prepared. A much greater sound would be needed to pierce the clamour of battle, and other reproductions would be made using the laughter of the group. All of these would need live vibrations to activate them, and for this purpose we chose six of the most intelligent among the creatures and took them back with us to the Fire's Cavern.

We had to keep them in the dark for several days after our return because their eyes could not stand the light. We put them in a deep hollow over which we placed a screen. At first the darkness was total in order to simulate the conditions in which they normally lived; we then allowed a few chinks of light to infiltrate and finally we made an opening through which the Fire could be seen. We hoped to persuade them to pass through this gap into the cavern, but for some time they remained cowering in the darkest corner. So we called and whistled to them until at last a little nose appeared, then two. Four red eyes followed and then two whole bodies, but as the full glare shone directly on them they quickly disappeared. It was finally Ra-onus himself who solved the problem. He sent little darting flames into the hollow; they undulated towards the cowering occupants like dancing caterpillars, then turned away to form glowing patterns on the ground. The creatures were fascinated by these new playthings and soon they were leaping on them and poking them with their little muzzles. These were followed by shining balls, which were soon chased and patted all round their home. The Fire gradually withdrew them from the hollow and the creatures followed, squealing with excitement.

Day by day they gambolled closer to the main fire mass until they were chasing their toys in and out of the flames. Ra-onus was most inventive in devising new games to amuse them and they were able to spend longer periods in his care. After a while we noticed that their eyes were no longer red but a brilliant blue, bringing a touch of Heaven to our infernal home.

❉ ❉ ❉

During this period Augustine was primarily occupied with distance consultation with our Teacher-Lord concerning the Higher Forces and which aspect of each should be used in the coming battle. Those from above a certain level would be unable to manifest at the depth where they would have to function, and those too low in vibration could be invalidated by the enemy. It was, therefore, the Fire who acted as our guardian when we were away from the cavern: little fingers of flame followed us wherever we went, ready to signal to Augustine should any danger befall us.

We naturally did not wish to exhibit any unusual accomplishments; so Tepi lumbered along slowly as though on a foraging expedition, shoving his snout into any mess which might be considered edible. In spite of my wings being empowered by members of the group, I found that I was unable to raise myself more than a few feet from the ground, owing to the inhibiting leaden texture of the atmosphere. But by clinging to the surrounding rock face I was able to climb in all directions as I sought for crevices in which to hide not only the creatures when the time came, but the matter on which their laughter had been imprinted. This restriction was probably fortunate, because I soon discovered that none of the Hatreds could fly; had I succeeded in doing so, I would doubtless have drawn unwelcome attention to myself. I kept as far away as possible from my fellow bats as I did not know whether they had a method of communication which would be unintelligible to me.

Both of us displayed a variety of bloody scars to demonstrate that we were among the attacked and not ourselves belligerent; but when any Hatred came too close to us, I swivelled my multi-coloured eyes and emitted high-pitched, warning squeals while Tepi bared and snapped his teeth while thrashing his tail from side to side. If the Hatred was still undeterred, we signalled to the Group to send a special ray which would either stun or temporarily blind a would-be assailant; when he recovered we were no longer in sight and no memory was retained of the incident.

Tepi always carried Seeker rays with him, now reduced to two red beams shining through his crocodile eyes, but he had no success in locating his Hatred among the many who surrounded us.

During these sorties, although we failed in this our main purpose, we were learning a great deal about the Hatreds in general. The largest and most repulsive among them were the leaders – Tyrants who ruled by their superior strength and barbarity. Each cavern was the domain of a separate Tyrant who held sway over all the inhabitants. Frequent fights took place between them when one tried to infiltrate another's territory with the object of gaining greater power and a larger number of vassals under his control. Power and lust were the dual motivating forces in this Tartarean abyss where hope had never been. Each had his personal sycophants who tended to his needs – finding prey for his lechery and seemingly unassuageable hunger. They held down the victims for his sadistic practices and wrenched or hacked off limbs from underlings, sometimes holding them in one of the fires before presentation and at others, delivering them still raw and dripping blood. Although servants to the Tyrants, these were Hatred Chiefs, subordinate only to their direct despotic Ruler. They had absolute authority over all the other Hatreds, who were slaves; they acted as overseers to those who mined the rocks to extract the ore which others forged into primitive tools and weapons in the flames stolen from the Fire.

The miners had a degree of dominion over the serfs who, bent double from overloading, carried the ore from the sunken shafts to the surface; and the blacksmiths had subordinates, who lay on their bellies all day perpetually blowing the reluctant flames into activity. Even more menial in rank were the food-providers who acted as butchers, dismembering the Hatreds who were too weak to work and were useless for anything but to provide fodder for all. So there was a constant frenzied movement of the slaughterers chasing their victims as they endeavoured, by crawling away with any remaining strength, to escape from the descending axe or plunging knife.

More wretched still was the fate of those kept for sadistic purposes; every orifice was subjected to prodding tools, fingers, horns or sexual organs, flesh being split, eyes gouged, limbs broken until bodies as such were unrecognisable, and were dragged away to we knew not where.

Those with animal forms were obviously regarded as the lowest form of life. They were allowed to feed when all the others were replete, and then only on the pallid remnants of what had once been breathing flesh and blood. Fortunately for them, animal meat did not appeal to the Hatreds in general being too tough in texture and rank in flavour in comparison to the more tender flesh of their own kind. But that did not prevent the animals from being subjected to all forms of sadistic brutality, and they themselves attacked and devoured each other.

* * *

Our search for Tepi's Hatred took us through many caverns until eventually we entered a new sector, which was piled high with mutilated bodies; all were white, sucked dry and flacid like empty sacks. Yet some of them still showed faint signs of life as a limb twitched or a feeble movement of the chest showed that a minute quantity of the choking air was being inhaled. This was the vault of the dying victims of sadism.

I was floundering over Tepi as he lumbered round the cave examining the bodies and pushing some aside in his search for his Hatred, when from my slightly higher viewpoint my eye fell on one that bore no wounds, almost hidden in a far corner. I was on my way to make a closer examination when one of the Tyrants entered the cavern and in passing kicked two of the scavenging animals; they immediately turned and attacked one another and several of the others joined in. I flopped down on Tepi's snout and said

"I have something to tell you. Let us go."

I pretended to dig my teeth into one of his nostrils and he let out an awesome roar. He continued to bellow and toss his head as we made our way back to the Fire in an apparently vain endeavour to remove his tormenter. About half way through the final cave I left him with blood streaming from my mouth and clung to the rock to make sure that we had not attracted undue attention. Such situations occurred so frequently that none of the Hatreds had even paused to see what was causing the commotion, irrespective of whether they were forging some new murderous weapon, chasing an underling with a burning torch, or clawing at a neighbour's limbs to make a meal.

I signalled to Tepi that all was well and separately we slipped into and through the Fire. When we had removed our Hatred bodies, he asked me what I wanted to tell him.

"I saw one among the bloodless ones that bore no wounds."

"Ah!" said Augustine.

"What do you mean by 'Ah'?" queried Tepi.

"You tell him, Perima."

"I think it was either dead or dying."

"Well, they all were, were they not?"

"My attention was definitely drawn towards this one. Do you remember telling me that you had no self hatred left – in other words it no longer exists."

He looked at me for a moment in bewilderment, then his face became drawn and white.

"All this time I've been looking for a savage and loathsome brute and now I have found it, it is just a corpse."

"Not quite; it must have been alive and mobile when it was admitted," said Augustine.

"It was doubtless debilitated and because its hatred was disintegrating, it had no bond with either its surroundings or the inhabitants. Somehow it must have managed to hide and gradually became weaker; when it was eventually found by a body disposer, it was thrown away with the ravaged ones. Hatreds are only interested in the quick that have life and blood flowing through their veins."

"Are you telling me that our suffering on the journey and our deprivations since we have been here, together with the time and energy expended on the planning of my Hatred's rescue have been wasted? That all the work of forming the images and the power poured into them to make them mobile, not only by us but by the group, have been for nothing? Do you mean that we are too late and that the debt I owe to my Hatred can never be paid?"

"Calm yourself Tepi beloved. Firstly that which started as a single objective, a rescue operation, has become something far more complex, the obliteration of a vast horde of personified evil, man made, dangerous and with the ability to seize, ravage and hold a large area intended for the evolution of the element of Fire. Secondly, I fully understand your distress, but I do not think that your Hatred is dead. You were receiving reactions to your Seeker ray throughout the journey. There are so many cross vibrations here; this coupled with its extreme weakness would account for the lack of response to the ray since our arrival. You must go at once and give it some power so that its deterioration will cease."

We set out immediately, and when we had attended to the Hatred's needs, we examined it more closely. Its human body was covered with matted hair but it looked less un-healthy than most of the others, possibly because it had not been mutilated. Its face was that of a gorilla, its eyes glassy and sightless but it did not possess the evil expression of the other Hatreds we had seen.

We were afraid that the bodies would periodically be either burned on the fires or disposed of in some other way, so we hid it under a heap of other Hatreds that were still breathing. In fact we need not have worried for we found that no-one took any notice of them once they were dumped in the Vault of the Dying; and the corpses gradually disintegrated until nothing remained but hair and bones.

❖ ❖ ❖

After our fourth visit, I asked Tepi if he had noticed any change in his Hatred's face. "I nearly asked you the same question," he replied. "The gorilla look is not as pronounced as it was; the features appear to be flattening out, and its eyes seem less dazed." He turned to Augustine who was standing near us.

"What does this mean?"

"It means that its redemption is beginning, even here."

"Can we bring it to this cave now?"

"Alas no. It would not survive passing through the Fire. It needs more power and time."

❖ ❖ ❖

We continued to move among the Hatreds in order to find out if there was a pattern in their habits and movements, which might be of use to us when planning battle strategy. But they seemed to live by their appetites and whims alone and apart from the workers their actions appeared to be unpremeditated; a sudden pounce here, a buffet there, a kick, a punch for no apparent reason filled their days with the brutal activity they craved.

We dared not stay in any of the caverns long in case it was noticed that we were always together. I began to have a strong feeling that it would be safer for us both if I were able to fly and could watch the activities taking place over a wider area.

With Augustine's approval I started to practice in our cavern behind the Fire where the air was not as viscous as elsewhere. Each day I made progress, lifting myself further from the ground, my wings becoming more obedient to my will. Higher and higher I flew until I made the surprising discovery that I was no longer confined by rocks: in other words the compartments were not true caverns for they had no roofs. All above was Stygian darkness apart from the glow from the fires far below. I was able to land on the top of all the granite walls and watch what was taking place beneath me. This was a definite asset and I pondered how we could turn this new situation to our advantage.

"Bats!" I let out a wild, exultant scream as I rose in the air and flew back to our cave. So great was my excitement that I clasped Augustine between my wings and squealed in his ear. He smiled as he extricated himself from my clinging embrace.

"I do not understand bat language," he said. I stepped out of my body, still breathless with excitement. "None of the divisions are true caverns," I told him. "They have no roofs and are open to the sky. The atmosphere became less dense the higher I flew, and I was able to see, though dimly, over the whole area. By landing on the top of the rocks I had a good view of what was taking place immediately below me. And then a thought came to me."

"And what was that?"

"We can make a regiment of bats, that can swoop on the forces below."

"An excellent idea. We will set to work immediately to make the images and inform the group that they must now think in terms of a second division that flies. They will have to take into consideration the changes in the density of the matter through which the bats will be required to dive. They must also be automated to attack only bodies of flesh and not our own thought units."

"This will cause problems for them," said Tepi."And problems are there to be solved, especially when our necessity is so great. I have every confidence that they will succeed. I only hope that there will be sufficient time for a solution to be found."

"Do you think the battle is imminent?" I asked.

"Frankly, I do not know. Something might happen at any time to make a clash unavoidable. Our greatest need at the moment is to discover when a new intake of Hatreds is expected so that we can find out where the entrance to the Domain lies. We can then marshall our own forces nearby so that they are ready to join the next batch of replacements and pass through the entrance with them. Your ability to fly over the whole precinct now, should make this task easier."

✳ ✳ ✳

Our image making for our ground forces continued and to these a host of bat forms was added.

During this time we were also training the creatures to stay in crevices until we called them. This was achieved by placing several automata on the ground below them; if any of them left its niche, it was gently nipped and chased back again.

A regular time was set aside for play because this was a much needed recreation for us as well as for them. We taught them to laugh when one of us called out "Games Time;" they were quick to learn that we would not romp with them until they produced this sound, which we needed to set off that supplied by our friends already imprinted on sensitized matter. After this initial exercise we played our own games of chasing and being chased. They rolled on the ground and galloped their paws at us accompanied by high pitched cries from them and hilarious laughter from Tepi and me in which Augustine would often take part. We enjoyed the fun as much as the creatures, and for these short periods we became as carefree as children again.

I regularly overshadowed Tepi when he went to give power to his Hatred and escorted him back to our cavern when his expeditions were completed.

One day I was flying high over the area when I noticed a large group striding purposefully in our direction. I glided down until I was near enough to see that they were very large, ill shapen and ultra hideous – obviously Tyrants. I wondered where they were going; perhaps a meeting was to take place to invent new forms of torture to inflict on their victims; or maybe they were about to evolve some diabolical plan to subjugate other Tyrants who were flouting their authority or plotting to overthrow them.

I followed them as they passed through several caverns and finally reached one which I knew was adjacent to an outside wall, where they abruptly settled themselves on the ground. There was no communication between them but they appeared to be in a state of expectation. I landed on a rock above them and waited too.

A shout rang out from a sentry and the Tyrants lumbered to their feet. Some of the accompanying Hatred Chiefs moved in the direction of one of the many large boulders leaning against the rock face and began to push and heave with their shoulders until it started to move to one side. Then followed the disclosure for which we had waited so long. The boulder had been hiding the entrance to the Hatreds' domain and I realized that I was about to witness a new intake of replacements. I glided over the outside wall and landed on a rock. The darkness was total and I was obliged to use my extra vision before I could discern a group gradually drawing nearer. They were quarrelling among themselves, kicking and punching one another as they trudged along. By this time the boulder had been removed sufficiently to reveal a faint glow from the fires within.

"Ere tis. Us'll show 'em 'oo's 'oo. Us'll bash 'em. Charge," their leader shouted and they swaggered through the entrance, waving their clubs and shouting obscene oaths.

The Tyrants had grouped themselves round the cavern walls and thus were invisible to the newcomers. As soon as they were all inside several of the Hatred chiefs barred the entrance while others heaved the boulder back into place. The waiting Tyrants hurled themselves out of the darkness in a concerted attack. Although taken by surprise, the newcomers defended themselves savagely by wielding their clubs and flinging rocks at their assailants, but they were confronted by better weapons, including flaming torches, hatchets and knives, as well as superior knowledge and numbers.

Those that were the first to succumb were either dragged or flung outside the conflict area, while the strongest and fittest continued fighting the Tyrants and their lackeys. When the newcomers were finally defeated, the victors did not fall on them and gulp the blood which was streaming from their wounds, as I expected; lechery and sadism had first to be gratified. Sickened, I covered my eyes as tears flowed down my cheeks. How could such monsters ever be redeemed? I blotted out my vision, but lustful grunts and growls accompanied by shrieks of pain invaded me, and the stench of their orgiastic antics assaulted my being. My will ceased to function and I was unable to escape from the repulsive scene.

※　※　※

At last a silence of satiation fell, and I forced my wings to bear me away from the glutted, entangled bodies. Still weeping I sank down at Augustine's feet. He extricated me from my bat body and held me in his arms as I described the depravities I had sensed taking place around me. "I feel not only degraded but in despair," I sobbed. "We have set ourselves an impossible task."

"My poor little one," he said, passing his hands gently through my sadly tarnished aura, "You have witnessed so many horrors for one so sensitive, but you will bear them for the sake of the few that we shall save, including the one which is still a part of our beloved Tepi. Everyone will be given a chance. Remember Fire purifies. All the corpses will be burned. Not only will their material manifestations be destroyed but their hatred as well. Fire is the all-consuming element. Earth absorbs, Water conveys, Air dissipates but Fire assimilates, transforms and returns the indestructible essence of all Life back to its source."

I slept in Augustine's arms and awoke with my memory of the recent past dimmed and my despair gone.

✳ ✳ ✳

A few days later, when I was keeping watch over Tepi from the top of a rock, my concentration was diminished by a commotion coming from the adjacent cavern. I rose in the air and glided in the direction from which the noise was coming. A group of Hatreds was making its way in Tepi's direction, waving clubs and hurling abuse at anyone unfortunate enough to be within reach.

Tepi looked as though he was foraging and he was well equipped with self defence mechanisms should he be noticed. I was, therefore, not unduly worried as an animal scavenging among the corpses was no unusual sight. As they drew level with him, I received a warning signal and continued to hover overhead. The Hatreds all strutted past without giving Tepi so much as a glance and I was about to return to my perch on the rock, when the last one in the group suddenly turned, swung his club above his head and brought it down with a sickening thud on the back of Tepi's crocodile skull. Even then I was only slightly concerned because the blow had struck only his outside covering, and he was safe within.

However, the ear-splitting crack had excited the Hatred and with a belligerent shout he began to raise his club once more. In the same instant I realized that Tepi was taking no evasive action and that the impact of the blow must have stunned him. I sent a lightening call for help to the group, folded my wings and plummetted downwards to land on the attacking Hatred and clamp my vampire teeth into the back of his neck. Great yowls of pain and rage filled the air as he tried to beat me off with his club. But I brought my wings into action, lashing them against his face, temporarily blinding him. The other Hatreds stood like stolid blocks of stone as they watched and I suspect, enjoyed witnessing the distress of a fellow member of their clan.

During this time the group had succeeded in reviving Tepi. I had been anxiously watching his inert form through my wing flaps and to my astonishment, instead of creeping away, he suddenly seized his tail in his jaws and began to rotate like a wheel, covering the ground at tremendous speed and scattering the Hatreds in all directions.

The Chief let out a frenzied bellow. "There's summat odd goin' on. Bats don' fly. Crocs don' roll. Them two don' jus' stink, them thinks. We'll clobber 'em arter we's fed. You an' you." He seized two of the nearest serfs by the scruff of their necks and lifted them to the level of his glowering bull's head. "Chuck all o' us outer 'ere, an' watch th'ins an' th'outs so them don't whip orf. Truss up that crazy bat." He hurled the two trembling Hatreds off to the ground and they all lumbered off to their fodder of blood and guts.

One of them dragged himself to his feet and began to stagger in my direction so I quickly removed my teeth from Tepi's assailant, who hobbled after the others screeching in pain. I tried to fly but I was too close to the rock face and as I clambered upwards, the serf seized the end of one of my wings. By twisting my body and bending my head downwards I managed to sink my teeth into his hand. He released me with a yell and I was able to clamber safely to the top of the wall without being hit by the club which he repeatedly threw at me until I was screened by the blackness overhead. Their attention was then directed towards the other occupants of the cavern, who were quickly dispersed by the club and a whip, and the two took up their positions as guards in front of the exits.

Tepi sent me a signal as he waddled towards one of them and I clawed my way along the rock face so that I was poised immediately above the other. Both the sentries were watching him intently as I flashed a message to the Group requesting stunning rays. Tepi set his in action when he was still at a distance from his target, but it was as effective as mine, and both the guards slumped simultaneously to the ground.

"Tepi, we haven't a moment to lose now that they realize we are not normal animals. We must rescue your Hatred now," I said. We went to the Vault of the Dying and Tepi set to work immediately to push the almost lifeless bodies away, so that his Hatred was fully exposed. I endeavoured to heave it on to his back with my head and wings, and succeeded in getting its top half into position. But when I tried to raise its legs, it slid off the other side. "I need my arms," I told him, "I must leave my body for awhile."

"No, no", he said decisively. "The pressure of the atmosphere here may crush you. I would rather leave my Hatred."

"Never," I said. "Our whole life for months has been planned for this moment. We have toiled through many dangers to reach this ghastly place; we have suffered near-lethal shocks to vision and senses; we have used both the mental and physical energy of our friends and the priceless gift of the power of Life which has sustained us through all our afflictions. To give up now is unthinkable." I rubbed my hideous snout against his. "I too owe your Hatred a debt, not only for leading you to me but also for bringing Augustine into our lives."

I stood free and as I concentrated on our Teacher-Lord, I felt the great surge of protective and energising power which already surrounded me but which had failed to pierce the coarse matter of my bat body. I bent down and as easily as lifting a small sheaf of corn, I raised the unconscious Hatred and placed it on Tepi's neck. Once more as the bat, I covered the body with my wings and with my teeth fastened just above Tepi's eye, we started on our journey back to the Fire. Once we had left the empty cavern with the two unconscious guards, Tepi began to bellow and roar to demonstrate the suffering caused by his fictitious wound which was leaving a trail of blood behind us but his performance only gained a few casual glances.

As we reached the Fire, he divided, leaving a path through which we took our precious burden to safety. One might imagine that a sense of triumph would have been ours at this moment; but we were too weary to feel any emotion because although we had rescued Tepi's Hatred from its kindred, we still had a battle to win.

Augustine was waiting for us somewhat anxiously although he had kept us under constant surveyance with his extra vision from the time we had left him. He had sensed danger from the Hatred which had knocked Tepi unconscious and had sent me a warning, and he had also dimmed eyes, which were noting something unusual on the homeward journey.

He gathered us in his arms after we had discarded our animal bodies and praised us for carrying out our plan successfully. We now had time to examine the Hatred as it lay in the comforting warmth of the Fire, and we saw that it was no longer white but tinged with the shades of living flesh. We also observed with slight discomfiture that where its face should have been was only a blank.

Tepi and I exchanged nervous glances. We had seen many faces without bodies but never a living body without a face. What did it mean?

"It is good," Augustine reassured us. "It has lost the evil hatred that was the nucleus of its being. It is now a no-thing. When the battle is over, we will watch it gradually becoming a some-body and our task will be complete."

❃ ❃ ❃

After we had rested for a while, we awoke refreshed, and Tepi turned to me with a grin. "What did the Hatred Chief mean when he said 'Them two don' just stink them thinks!' I call that very insulting!"

"We were wrong when we came to the conclusion that the all-pervading stench would prevent any of the Hatreds from noticing that you smell different from them," said Augustine. "We must ask the group to manufacture some extremely offensive odours with which we will impregnate our automata. I will send a signal to them immediately. We must also make a new body for Tepi now that the crocodile is a known enemy."

"What about me?" I asked.

"Your bat body suits you well," he said his eyes twinkling. "One bat looks much like another and it gives you the mobility and vision without which we cannot work. Be careful to keep out of the Hatreds' reach and sights until you are actually taking part in the battle."

CHAPTER 17
THE BATTLE

We now began to place our forces in position ready for the next intake, which would herald the beginning of the conflict. The images had been motivated to follow us, so we asked Ra-onus to reopen the surface of the rock through which we had originally passed, to enable us to lead them into the outer darkness and round the ramparts to the entrance of the Hatreds' Domain. We checked that all the mechanisms reacted to the willpower with which the group controlled them, so that they strutted, loped, crawled or hobbled along, to the accompaniment of the appropriate grunts, growls, bellows and howls.

We had already found a suitable cavern and other smaller cavities near the opening, and into these we led our automata. We also placed Tepi's new body in a separate aperture so that he could disguise himself quickly. No longer a lumbering crocodile, he would lead the attack in an upright position with his Hatred's original gorilla face.

My army of bats was removed by remote control from Onward, up the walls behind the Fire's cavern, to positions that overlooked the rest of the territory. We then put the creatures in their crevices high above the reach of the Hatreds; they had been trained to stay there for gradually longer periods each day to accustom them to the noise and incessant movement below.

Eventually every unit of our forces was at its appointed post, ready for the arrival of the next batch of replacements. I regularly flew high above the area on the look out for sentries, who would doubtless be waiting to convey to the Tyrants the news that their prey was approaching. I also made sorties over the surrounding territory in the hope of locating the newcomers at a distance; this would allow more time to give our forces a final inspection and take up our own battle positions.

I was fortunate to find a large group straggling over a wide area when still a long way from the Hatreds' Domain. Its members appeared to be both exhausted and dispirited, unlike the braggarts of the previous intake; they were making very slow progress in spite of being thrashed forward by their jailer's whips. As I flew back to the Fire's cavern, a faint hope crossed my mind that perhaps some of these captives could be saved. I quickly relayed to Augustine and Tepi my impression that these new replacements were loathe to continue their journey, and it was agreed that Tepi should endeavour to protect them from the waiting Tyrants instead of allowing them to be destroyed, which had been our original intention.

We proceeded to recheck the creatures in their crevices and our reinforcements still in the cavern; we also tuned the communication system between us and our Teacher-Lord to its most sensitive level.

Augustine entered his ogre form which contained apparatus enabling him to view the battle wherever it was taking place. According to the plan, Tepi and I would gradually drive the enemy towards Augustine in the area in front of the Fire, by which time it was hoped that many of the Hatreds would have been destroyed or maimed either by our forces or their own.

After I had inspected all my bats once more I flew towards the main access, over which sentries had been posted. As I approached, they let out a ferocious howl of excitement and the Tyrants who, with their chief, were now gathered together, rose to their feet and as before, took up positions round the dark walls of the cavern so they would be unseen by the replacements coming through the entrance.

I swooped over the outside wall, passing over Tepi who was on watch in his gorilla-faced body, awaiting the time for his forces to join the intake and enter with them. As the boulder slowly moved away, the newcomers came to a halt; some, overcome by fear, tried to flee but whips cracked, lashing them onward to their doom.

Suddenly to my amazement all the jailers dropped to the ground, felled by stunning rays; the possibility of rescuing some of the reluctant prisoners had obviously led to a radical change of plan. Tepi led his forces out of the cave and said to the cowering prisoners: "Fear not. A battle is about to take place. Hide until I return. But first use their whips to fetter your jailers" but there was no time to ascertain if they did so.

Thus, instead of a bedraggled, cringing group passing through the entrance as helpless prey for the persecution and lusts of the Tyrants, Tepi and his automata walked, waddled, slouched and jumped into the cavern. The Tyrants were totally unaware that anything was amiss, as with tumultous roars and obscene shouts, they rushed at their intended victims to be met not with the expected ineffective defensive measures, but by a sustained assault from weapons belching smoke and flames. Although taken by surprise, blinded by smoke and choking with fumes, the Tyrants fought back savagely, wielding clubs to bash and knives to slash all within reach. Many of Tepi's units were felled to the ground but others from outside quickly replaced them.

The Tyrants were gradually forced to retreat and join the Hatreds in the next cavern. They seized flaming brands and hurled them at our forces, but as they were already proofed against this element, they failed to ignite and continued to attack.

Some of the Hatreds then took cover from our firepower behind boulders and indiscriminately hurled large chunks of rock, incapacitating their own combatants as well as ours. Others endeavoured to escape by climbing the walls, but the Tyrants dragged them down and flung them back into the fray. Some of these aimed malicious kicks at their masters when their backs were turned in retaliation for past atrocities inflicted on them. Serfs and animals were no longer subservient; the accumulated venom caused by years of oppression exploded in acts of vicious revenge.

Howls, bellows and screeches rent the air, already surfeited with deafening sound. Hearing the uproar, Hatreds rushed from other caverns to join the battle, cracking whips, brandishing axes and waving clubs like gale-struck windmills. Contenders on both sides fell in their hundreds as the fighting spread; it was no longer a contest between Good and Evil – Evil had turned against itself in a desperate battle for survival. The clamour and perpetual motion excited the fires, which crackled and spluttered, their flames leaping upwards as they consumed the bodies which were flung in their midst.

The battle zone resembled a seething volcano, erupting malignity. Those without weapons seized blood-soaked corpses from beneath their feet and wielded them as truncheons. Decapitated heads were used as weapons to shatter other skulls. Feet wedged down gullets caused gurgling death from choking. Arms hacked from trunks rose from the ground of their own volition, to clutch their assailants' necks in a strangler's grip. Gouged and heaving intestines evolved a life of their own, as they writhed and hissed like nests of rattlesnakes; they uncoiled themselves to become whips that flailed, or wound round necks and chests ...tightening ... squeezing, until breath faded to a choking whisper, a gasp, then nought.

Life persisted in dismembered bodies that continued to fight, the Group Mind using the communal venom to vitalize the fallen, even when dead. Malevolence multiplied and bred new forms which zipped and zoomed like demented wasps, stinging whatever they touched.

The Tyrants were triumphant wherever they fought, but their numbers were few and their strength was flagging. The plan to drive our foe towards Ra-onus was slowly being achieved.

I made frequent flights above the combat area and found that not many capable of continuing the struggle remained in the caverns close to the entrance; and the sight of my swooping black form with its swivelling eyes and buffeting wings soon drove these few in the required direction. I judged that our forces in the central sector required some action from my bats as they were gradually being overcome. I signalled to Eremus, and immediately an ear-splitting, high-pitched screaming fractured the air and pierced even the incessant din of the clashing weapons and raucous shouts below. The Hatreds paused in their death-dealing pursuits to gaze in the direction of this unusual sound coming from what they had always known as black, untenanted space.

I led my bats in a vertical dive; they swooped – dozens of snapping, clawing horrors – sinking their teeth in the nearest flesh. The Hatreds were not only torn asunder but were thrown into utter confusion by this attack from above, but they continued to wield their axes and clubs, hurling their assailants through the air or flinging them to the ground. When I at last withdrew my forces, pandemonium reigned.

❊   ❊   ❊

I returned to my point of vantage on top of the wall and watched the ensuing carnage take place. Then, having signalled the group to activate my reinforcements, I continued my reconnaissance flight. Tepi was in complete charge of events in his area; hastening to aid any of his fighters in trouble, directing fire at the Tyrants – although they seemed impervious to its heat, ducking away from any assault and contacting the group concerning the number of new automata needed. He seemed to be leading a charmed life – as indeed he was.

The main cavern was my next objective and there I found that Augustine's fire and ray power had obliterated most of the original inhabitants; but others were continually driven towards him. His ogre form towered above the fighting Hatreds; his metal arms were often extended, not to seize and destroy the combatants but to divide the weak from the strong. He lifted the weak and placed them in crevices in the rocks, safe from their torturers forever, leaving the strong to slaughter each other.

The battle had raged virtually non-stop for days, our foes sustained by the hatred generated by the Group Mind; its ferocity seemed to grow rather than diminish because it was now manifesting through less forms in a smaller area, giving each combatant an added fury.

Few of the Tyrants had been destroyed in spite of being constantly attacked with dexterity and will as well as rays and fire. Wherever my bats swooped, chaos followed. Ground fighting temporarily ceased while the Hatreds attempted to beat them off. Many fled before their onslaught, and always they were driven nearer the Fire.

Strangely, my senses were not affected: I felt neither excitement nor pity. I did not even utilize my power of reasoning to wonder why I felt no compassion for these man-made monsters, which were destroying each other to our advantage. It was as though I had lost my power of volition and was merely programmed, as were my bats, to perform certain acts like a machine. But I never lost the certainty that our Teacher-Lord was protecting me and, however many of my units were battered by clubs or hit by missiles, I was invulnerable, and for this reason my squealing became a paeon of praise.

The main fighting was now taking place in the cavern next to Augustine; and as the Tyrants and the remnants of their personal retainers were all together, they were successfully destroying the other Hatreds who were still on their feet. Tepi was holding his forces on the far side of the entrance and my bats were activated ready for the final attack, which we hoped would drive the Tyrants towards the Fire.

We plummetted downwards, once more drawing the attention of the enemy towards us, as Tepi's troops charged through the gap to attack them at ground level. After a savage and bloody assault from our combined forces, the Tyrants' appetite for the carnage ceased and they retreated, still bellowing with fury, through the final entrance there to come face to face with the Ogre.

For a moment they stood in astonishment before the huge, hideous figure towering above them.

"Charge!" roared the Tyrant Chief as he hurled himself at Augustine. But the image was not made of flesh and blood and the granite and metal withstood the attack, the Tyrant's body rebounding several feet before falling to the ground. None of the others had followed him; Augustine was right: the Hatreds were not a pack: they fought and would die as they had lived, for themselves alone. He heaved himself to his feet and retreated to the entrance, not in defeat but to belabour his retainers into action. Reluctantly they moved forward until the Ogre was surrounded.

During this time Ra-onus had been crackling and exploding in the background, red flames shooting out to engulf any Hatred who was foolish enough to come within reach. He now clarified himself and I could see Augustine standing safely in the centre of his light. The Tyrants surged forward and began to dismantle the Ogre, their energy restored. They now had new weapons with which to fight and this they proceeded to do with mounting rage.

Augustine moved slowly forward. "Stop!" he commanded but his voice was unheard through the tumult of combat. Our final reinforcements poured through the Fire to augment our diminished units on the ground while my bats still swooped and screeched overhead. The fallen formed a groaning, bloody carpet over which the contestants floundered and fell.

"Games Time!" Augustine's voice rang out clearly. The shock of the unknown voice bewildered the Hatreds, causing a pause in the fighting long enough for the creatures in their crannies to begin to laugh. This set off the mechanism of the imprinted matter which we had placed in many of the clefts in the rocks and peal after peal of joy rang through the cavern causing a cessation of activities and panic as well. Brutal blood lust was replaced by fear; the Hatreds ran first one way and then another, covering their ears with their hands as they tried to escape from the unknown sound. But always the laughter followed them. Screams of pain replaced their usual howls of abuse as they rolled on the ground. Clutching their heads and bellies they leapt in the air and hurled themselves against rocks in a hopeless endeavour to rid themselves of their ghastly affliction.

One by one they dropped down dead – killed by laughter, the song of joy they had never known. But still the Tyrants and their attendants remained, impervious to fire, blows and now, the death-dealing laughter. They appeared to be indestructible, protected as they were by the diabolical power of their Group Mind. "Come Tepi. Come Perima!" Augustine called. We entered the Fire and shed our Hatred bodies, to stand together in full view of the remnants of our enemy.

The jaw of the Tyrant Chief dropped when he saw us, not in awe but to thunder out a soul-rending roar. His particular venom was aimed at me and I remembered the words of our Teacher-Lord "They will be stunned by your beauty and will loathe you for it!"

All the Tyrants gathered round, not to give their Chief support, but to glower at me with abhorrence. As they drew nearer, Ra-onus hissed to keep them at bay. Something compelled me to step slowly forward. I knew that they craved me and their desire could destroy them.

Augustine called urgently "Stop, Perima!" but I continued to move towards them until only a thin sheet of flame divided us. The Chief's arm shot out to seize me; the Fire exploded forward, and the Tyrant's arm was no longer there. He sprang back with an agonised shriek, clutching the hole where his limb had been. But his bestial eyes still leered at me as saliva streamed from his champing jaws; his great phallic-horn was erect, ready to plunge, gouge or destroy. Edging towards me, some of the Tyrants pawed the ground, while others clenched and unclenched their blooded hands in time with their pelvic thrusts of infernal lust. Their brute voices were silent; their bull bellows, wolf snarls, and hog snorts became like the baying of hounds, mad for the kill. I again moved forward, this time out of the Fire's protection. Yes, I was afraid but I also knew that I could come to no harm because I was still surrounded by Light.

"Get 'er!" the Tyrant Chief bawled.

They all leapt towards me, and the Fire leapt at them. A communal shriek ushered their end. Nothing remained but a sickening stench which was quickly consumed by the flames. Augustine and Tepi moved swiftly towards me and held me in their arms.

"I had to do it," I said.

"I know," replied Augustine. "Although we were unaware that it was part of the plan, Tepi and I were immobilized; our feet rooted to the ground. Those that are left owe you much."

I caressed Ra-onus and he sighed with contentment.

"Thank you dear lord for saving me."

"The four of us are now one. I could do nothing else," he said, as he stroked me with little tendrils of pink flame which curled about my face and arms.

*   *   *

It was as though a great weight had been lifted from us, and for the first time for many days we laughed with joy – the joy of achievement; that for which we had struggled against so many odds for so long had now been accomplished. Ra-onus too joined in with great splutters of mirth. Augustine gave a shrill whistle and the creatures jumped down from their crannies and still laughing, ran into the Fire. We played with them for a while and then returned to our task.

"Come forward any of you who are not maimed," Augustine ordered. A few rose from the ground; others who had been hiding came out of the shadows, and those which Augustine as the Ogre had thrust into cavities in the rocks now scrambled down and stood before us in a frightened group.

"Be not afraid," he said. "This has been a battle between Good and Evil. You have proved by your existence now, that you have sufficient potential worth for Good to recognise His own. Go to the Vault of the Dying and bring back with you any of the 'white ones' who still breathe." They limped and shuffled away to return later carrying the near-corpses with them and stood just inside the entrance.

"Bring them here," Augustine said. They hastily dropped their burdens and cowered close to the walls. "There is nothing to fear," he assured them once more. "See your living clansman here, and these little creatures playing around us. "Five of the group crept slowly forward on their hands and knees. They dragged two of the bodies with them to the edge of the Fire, but would go no further. So the three of us, with the Fire's ever vigalent eye guarding us, left his protection, lifted one of the bodies and carried it into the flames.

The watching Hatreds whimpered, some holding their hands before their eyes, peering through their fingers. We gently laid the 'white one' down, and the creatures scampered over him, firstly to sniff and then to lick him. A sound ensued – like a great agonised sob. One by one they came forward, bearing the remaining bodies and walked with them into the fire. They looked at each other in disbelief; "Over?" one asked tremulously.

"You go and search the rest of the Domain for any who are wounded or have fled the battle and are now in hiding. Call loudly, search diligently; we do not wish to lose even one that has suffered and can be saved. "They left the cavern obediently.

"Augustine," Tepi said doubtfully. "There may be some who fled, not because they had lost their hatred and no longer wished to fight, but because they realized that the battle was going against them. They are cunning and may have planned to become Tyrants after we have gone, and all the misery will start up once more."

Augustine smiled at him. "You forget the final tests."

"But they could lie to us, pretending that they are anxious to help bring the new life into being, when in reality they are already plotting their own future as despots."

"The tests will not be by interrogation. Neither Laughter nor Fire can be deceived."

Tepi grinned. "Of course; we have two infallible arbiters. All are assured of impeccable justice."

"While we are waiting, I will request the group to stop the laughter; otherwise some of the Hatreds may refuse to enter the cavern to enable judgment to be passed on them," Augustine said.

Silence fell; the first silence we had experienced since we had set foot on the Domain many months before. There was no hammering on anvils, no curses, no shrieks of loathing, lust or pain. Even Ra-onus was quiet. While we waited, we gave power to the 'white ones' who, even in the short space of time they had been lying in the Fire's light, showed signs of slightly less laboured breathing. Then we relaxed and enjoyed a much needed period of calm in the unaccustomed stillness.

The Hatreds whom we had sent out returned in ones and twos, accompanied by others. Some were wounded and were being carried; all were in distress and terrified. But there were three which we mentally divided from the rest; they still maintained the arrogant walk of Hatred Chiefs, but were most ingratiating, standing with downcast eyes, and bowing low before us.

"Welcome to the Cavern of Justice," Augustine addressed them. "There are neither judges nor jailers here. You are witnesses who will not be required to give evidence except by your natural reactions to two tests which will be applied. All of you are present here because you have escaped annihilation by the forces of either Good or Evil. You have thus proved yourselves to be suitable candidates for the new life which will be offered to you. You will remain here under the rule of the original, rightful overlord – Ra-onus; you will work in the mines and as blacksmiths as respected citizens. Your skills at present are crude and used solely for the purpose of destruction. You will learn to demolish only in order to rebuild. The ore which you mine will be fashioned to make articles both pleasing and practical; those not needed for your own use will be transported for the benefit and enjoyment of other communities.

"You will never be ill-treated, but you can expect mild chastisement from your ruler for any attempt to usurp his authority, for sloth and for all forms of cruelty perpetrated on others. Disagreements and minor misdemeanours will be accepted as differences in temperament and as reasonable expressions of inadequacy or self dissatisfaction.

"You will all start as equals but those showing aptitude and enthusiasm for their tasks, the ability to co-operate with others and later to form friendships, and provide assistance for those less able than themselves, will eventually achieve higher rank and the advantages that go with it.

"I will allow you a short time to absorb my description of the new conditions which will prevail in this Realm of Amity, and then the first test will be applied. Those who have already passed both of them can come and stand closer to the Fire."

They separated themselves from the others, this time without obvious fear. Augustine continued: "For your first act of non-hatred I suggest that you discuss what I have said, with those nearest to you."

They looked warily at one another. A few exchanged a remark or two but most remained in stunned silence. We watched the three suspects moving among the erstwhile slaves, ostensibly speaking to them, but all the time they were making their way to the back of the cavern.

"Games Time!" Augustine called as he left the Fire followed by the creatures, who immediately began their chattering laughter; this activated the imprints in the rocks and the joyous sound rang out again. A wailing and whimpering began as the vibrations reached the Hatreds; some clutched their ears or stomachs rolling about in agony. A strange look spread over the faces of those who had survived the original test and were now standing near us; their nostrils twitched and their mouths stretched to display blackened and bloody teeth. This new reaction, we realized, was the travesty of a smile; there were even a few extraordinary gurgles emerging from some of their throats. Could this possibly be laughter?

The creatures running about at first caused fear, but none dared raise a hand against them. I watched the suspects who had disappeared behind separate boulders with my extra vision. One seized dirt from the ground and stuffed it into his ears in order to deaden his hearing; the second tunnelled his way under a mound of corpses, while the third bashed his head against a rock, presumably as a counter distraction. When the sound was switched off, we viewed the scene. The ones that had rolled about in obvious pain now lay on the ground exhausted, but they had not died. There was enough will for the new life to temper the lethal effects of the laughter.

The suspects again became visible.

"You have all passed this initial test, proving that you have the rudiments of good will, enabling you to escape the eventual doom of all Hatreds. When you have recovered, the second test will begin."

In ones and twos they sat on the ground or rose shakily to their feet, fearful of what was to befall them next. Ra-onus ceased flickering and became a still, white light.

"Look into the Fire," Augustine directed them. "You will see the bodies of many 'white ones'; they are those among you who have suffered such terrible affliction that their will to live has been all but extinguished. I now ask those who have already passed both tests, thus proving their desire and ability to take part in the new life, to enter the Fire and stand in full view of you all as proof that their inherent worth is greater than their former sins." He paused. "You will be invited to follow them. I guarantee safety to all those who cross the threshold with the intention of working within the group for the good of the whole, with the expectation of rewards when merited. I do not know what is in your minds, but the Fire; Ra-onus who is your rightful ruler, has the instinctual aptitude of discerning whether you are truly desirous of a drastic change in your life pattern; and he has the right to accept or refuse your admittance to his Realm. "Come!" he addressed one of those who had previously passed through the portals of flame, "You lead."

This time they all moved forward with little signs of fear, and went and stood in the centre of the Light.

"The rest of you stand one behind the other in a line," Augustine continued to those scattered over the rest of the cavern. They obeyed, but were obviously filled with terror as to what was about to take place.

"We'll all o' us burn," one wailed.

"You passed the previous test, which has killed many. You are now being offered the chance to accept the rule of a just and kindly overlord instead of suffering, as you have in the past, the brutal whims of those who have now paid the penalty for their crimes. Look at your erstwhile fellow Hatreds who now stand in the Fire – whole. If you examine them closely, you will see that already some of their wounds have been healed."

"Com' over 'ere wiv us," one of the ex-Hatreds encouraged them.

One stepped forward nervously and held out a finger which he slowly moved towards and into the Fire. His hand followed it into the flames, then a foot and finally his whole body. He hugged himself and let out a whoop – a sound we had never heard any of them utter before.

"It don' burn. It feel good," he called to the others, and one by one they followed his example of testing the Fire's effect on a small part of their body before joining him. All were inside except the three suspects.

"Us be Chiefs. T'aint on ter tell us wot ter do afore them clods of serfs," one said.

"Your days of giving orders are over," Augustine informed them. "You are humble vassals of your rightful overlord, Ra-onus; until you have proved your worth through ability, not force."

"Us don' take no orders from yous."

"Nor t'e Fire."

"We goin' to make a noo life som odder place." They had forgotten the obsequious role they had been playing and their voices had risen in frustration and rage.

"No," Augustine said. "There is only one new life for the survivors of this Reign of Evil. You have lived and ruled by force and cruelty. I now give you one further choice – whether to live under the new conditions – or die."

They looked at one another and all muttered "Us'll live."

"That is good. Now, to perform your first act of obedience: enter the Fire."

As one, they turned and began stumbling towards the exit as fast as the dead bodies would allow. But Ra-onus with split-second timing reached it first and blocked their way with a sheet of flame. The Hatreds were unable to check their headlong flight and three plumes of black smoke spiralled up the walls; and three small mounds of ash formed on the ground – the sole evidence they had ever been.

A hoarse shout rose from all the ex-Hatreds; then they went down on their knees before us, their hands clasped in gratitude for their deliverance from the monsters who had caused them so much suffering and fear. We moved among them, patting their ugly heads and stroking their blood-stained bodies as gestures of goodwill and encouragement.

"Your days of being Hatreds are over," Augustine told them. "You are now inhabitants of the Realm of Fire. You will be known as New Lifers while you serve your apprenticeship. When you have proved yourselves to the satisfaction of your ruler, you will be entitled to a new name which is amity. If you later fail to live up to its meaning, you will be banished.

"You have been introduced to laughter, the expression of joy, which you will one day know; also to justice and hope, neither of which you have experienced before. With these three blessings and with the guidance and protection of Ra-onus you have the chance of becoming new beings. Go now to the cavern behind us and rest for you must be weary."

As they crawled and hobbled away, Augustine turned to our faithful guardian. "Beloved friend," he said, "this Realm is now yours once more.

Let us go together and reclaim it."

We moved slowly forward to the stench and sizzling sound of burning flesh as he consumed the mangled bodies. Tongues of fire licked up the walls, cleansing each crevice of the clinging corruption which defiled every corner of the Hatreds' Domain. Not the smallest crack was left unpurged.

As we finally drew near the exit, and the last corpse went up in flames, a macabre, dark mass, gyrating like a whirlwind, leapt into the blackness overhead. Ra-onus roared in pursuit. A gargantuan explosion rent the air. The instigator and generator of all the horror, hatred and carnage, dissolved into a cloud of stinking debris which slowly drifted downwards, into the heart of the flames.

The Group Mind was dead.

∽ CHAPTER 18 ∽
THE ANHUMANS

I stood gazing at the falling flakes as they wafted like black snow around us. This was the grand finale, the goal for which we had striven and given of ourselves to the last particle of energy and will. And now we were free.

This sense of liberation was the most rewarding experience f I had ever known. I felt like a goddess who, out of chaos, has produced a bright, new star. I began to leave my body; up, up I soared towards the Sun-behind-the-sun.

"Our task is not yet finished." Augustine's voice reached me from far away and ended my flight. He held me close. "The time for ecstasy is not yet, beloved. It will come. We still have work to do. We must release those who sought refuge outside before the conflict began, and ascertain their attitude of mind so that we may plan their future. Come Tepi. Don your battle garb so that they will recognise you when you return to their cave as promised."

Once more, disguised as his gorilla-headed Hatred, he stepped through the exit. We followed him into the outer darkness, and the surroundings became illumined by Augustine's aura and the light of the Fire. Tepi walked to the mouth of the cave where the Hatreds' prisoners lay hidden and called out: "The battle is over. Come and present yourselves to those who have fought and won."

The group that staggered or crawled into view was not what we had expected. Instead of gross, deformed bodies with hideous faces projecting either ferocity or guile, they all had heads of gentle herbivores – kangaroos, antelopes, asses and sheep. Although they were dirty and in rags, they were fully clothed; and were obviously exhausted, bewildered and afraid. Leading them was a stag, who came towards us with arms outstretched; and as he entered Augustine's aura, his antlered head vanished and we saw that he was a young man of great beauty.

"Greetings master," he said, bowing to Augustine. "My name is Nicholas. I am a Teacher-guide and I joined this group of Anhumans to teach them how to help themselves. We are tillers of the soil, growing our own food and spinning yarn for our clothes. We have no weapons; indeed none live near us who would do us harm. We are people of peace." He paused and his lips trembled at the memory. "One day monsters with Whips came to our settlement; they herded us together and drove us here for what purpose I do not know. Good sir, my people have eaten nothing since we left home. May I beg some food for them?"

Augustine embraced him and smiling, said: "I shall have to be chef. My battle comrades are fairies and do not eat."

The young man looked at me in amazement. "Did this gentle beauty truly take part in the conflict?"

"She fought valiently as a vampire bat. Alas, one cannot overcome Hatreds at these Cimmerian depths with love – only with stratagem and will. All our opponents are dead, except for some of those who were their slaves; their suffering fanned the potential spark which lies within all that exists, and saved them from extinction.

"Now I must set to work and feed your hungry companions. As no plants grow here, the meal must be conjured from my mind. Tell me: do they like cooked food? As you can see, we have a fire with us: a large and friendly fire, who will be more than willing to help."

"Yes, we eat both cooked and raw food. I too need solid sustenance at this low level of existence. May I also partake of your magic meal?"

As we watched Augustine concentrate, a large iron cooking-pot, which was held off the ground by chains fastened to struts, came into view before us. He turned to Ra-onus: "May we borrow some of your valued heat?"

Immediately flames darted forward and settled themselves beneath the cauldron, shooting up the sides until a delicious aroma of herbs, vegetables and grain pervaded the air. This soon reached the nostrils of the Anhumans, who crept slowly towards us, licking their lips in anticipation of their much-needed meal.

Before each of them a pottery bowl appeared; these gradually filled and the soup in the cauldron receded. This quickly regained its original level and replenished the bowls as soon as they emptied. Most of them had three helpings, some of them four, but at last all were replete and they came and bowed before us, murmuring; "Thanks, thanks, blessed saviours," as they caressed our hands and feet with their tongues.

We stroked their heads and ears as we gazed into their gentle, grateful eyes. Some of them were weeping in relief at their deliverance, and I laid my face against their cheeks and my tears mingled with theirs. They curled up on the ground and were soon sleeping peacefully while their leader related his story.

"I was sent to this group seven years ago when they were still living like animals, travelling for miles over infertile country to find sufficient food for their needs. They were docile and kind to each other and mentally fit to live like primitive men. I came to them as a stag so as not to disrupt their view of life too much. I arrived bearing seeds, plants and simple tools, and I led them to a region which had been chosen as suitable for the next phase in their evolution. It was pastureland; and had I not learned their language and restrained them, they would have eaten the grass and moved on as they had always done.

"I explained to them that the time had come for them to use their hands. They looked first at them and then at me without comprehension because they already used them for scratching and caressing one another, for plucking berries from trees when they were available and cracking nuts between stones.

"I then took a spade and turned over some turf. They watched in amazement. I planted a little tree in the hole I had made, and told them that in time it would bear fruit. They twitched their ears and exchanged glances because they knew that fruit grew on trees which they had not planted.

"I then drew a small plough across part of a field and demonstrated how we would grow grain for them to eat, because it was more suited to their human bodies than grass. I also gave them some of the seeds to taste, and they enjoyed the new texture and flavour. These became part of their regular meals to prevent them from cropping the grass before it was long enough to cut and make hay for bedding.

"As they had always followed the sun in their travels and their bodies had a thin coating of fur, they had no need of clothes. But the site of our new Homestead was subject to the seasons, and at times they required covering for warmth. At first garments were provided, but then we grew flax and reeds, which they plaited into material and later they learned to spin. They also cut their fur and wove it in with the grasses to give them extra warmth. When they had worn clothes for about four years, their fur moulted naturally and they grew human hair on parts of their bodies.

"We slowly became self sufficient; we worked all day, ate well and ran and jumped for joy at our happy, simple lives. I had decided to shed my antlers gradually and revert to my man's head, when disaster struck.

"We were used to the storms which sometimes battered our fields; these had been sent as a challenge to test the Anhuman's ability to deal with the problems relating to crops grown for their needs. But this storm was different; black clouds gathered but there was no rain. They hovered for days, descending slowly until we felt stifled by the compressed air. This was no seasonal dimming of light. Menace loured above and around us.

"I mentally sent an urgent request for help to my Leader, but the clouds increased in density and for weeks we lived in total darkness. Although we were afraid, we continued working by the light of torches. If we had not made this effort, most of my companions would have died from despair.

"Then one day – or was it night? – we heard a noise. I knew that it was shouting but the Anhumans who had never heard the sound before became petrified with fear. They cowered close together, their heads covered by their arms while I stood and faced the danger whatever it might be; I did not have long to wait.

"Fifteen loathsome creatures, armed with whips, came pelting out of the darkness: they roared foul oaths at us such as I had not heard for years, and which my charges could not understand apart from their evil intent. They were flogged to their feet, herded together and driven weeping and stumbling blindly through the satanic gloom. Some fell and would gladly have died, they told me later, but they were thrashed onwards by the lacerating thongs with only brief periods of rest after they had fallen to the ground and were unable to move in spite of the pain of the whips and the onslaught of blasphemy. You know the rest, master. You have saved us from I know not what dire fate."

"It is preferable that you do not know," Augustine said. "Truth is sometimes better when she is not unveiled."

Nicholas looked at us in near despair: "What is to become of us? Our home is a dark nightmare to which we can never return."

Augustine looked at Tepi, who rose to his feet and put a hand gently on the young man's knee. "I too had a land that was invaded, but now it is rightly called the Miniature Paradise. It was desecrated by ghouls; but, with the help of the presiding angels and our friends, it has now been redeemed. Do not be despondent: we will help you."

At last Nicholas smiled, although, his eyes were filled with tears. "You have given me hope, which was all but extinct. When may we talk?"

"I am eager to start now."

"A moment please," said Augustine, amused by their youthful enthusiasm.

"First, tell me Nicholas, where are your jailers?"

He looked uncomfortable. "Master, I regret – no, I do not regret – they are all dead." He sighed: "I instructed some of my Anhumans to use their whips to tie them up, as Tepi had instructed us. They obeyed me but the thongs were tight – including those round the jailers' necks." He smiled ruefully. "They do what I tell them; I should have been more specific or supervised them myself; but I was occupied shepherding the rest of the group into the cave, soothing their fears and tending their wounds to the best of my ability without equipment or water. Those who were not badly injured then joined me in a rite of thanksgiving for our rescue, and in prayers that victory would be bestowed on our liberators in the coming battle."

"There were but three of us – your new friend Tepi, Perima, myself and, of course, the Fire."

Nicholas looked bewildered. "But Tepi had many followers, who entered the cavern with him; I saw them."

"They were automata, manipulated from afar by our superiors and co-workers in the project of the rehabilitation of the Miniature Paradise, about which Tepi has told you."

"I am truly amazed," he said. "I know about Humanity and Anhumans, but magic lies beyond my ken."

"Magic is but knowledge of the Natural Forces, which are ever ready to come to the aid of those who know how to invoke them."

"May I be instructed in this lore for the good of my dependants?"

"We will teach you all you need to know to enable you to repel invaders and keep them at bay; and also how to resuscitate your stricken land so that your people can live in peace and evolve into Human beings."

We heard little snorts, grunts and whinnies, quite different from the travesty of animal voices to which we had been subjected for so long. Heads were scratched and limbs stretched as the sleepers twitched their ears and blew through their nostrils. But when they became conscious and opened their eyes, fear returned as their alien surroundings were revealed; and they felt the unfamiliar hardness of the barren rocks on which they lay. We went among them and stroked their furry heads, and gently held our fingers, from which healing rays were beaming, over their scars; and gradually their anxiety was allayed.

Large troughs, filled with water by Augustine's thoughts, appeared so that they could first drink and then wash themselves. We asked Nicholas if they would be content to stay alone for a while so that he could accompany us and see for himself the aftermath of the battle and the cleansing of the precinct. He called to two of his under leaders and gave them instructions; then he eagerly followed us into the Fire's Realm.

The air smelt fresh; there was no stench of burning flesh or excrement, and no visible remains of the explosive demise of the Group Mind. We walked through soft ash until we reached the main cave, which was now permeated with the friendly warmth of the Fire, who had preceded us. Nicholas hesitated on the threshold of flame.

Tepi and I each took one of his hands in ours. "Come," we encouraged him, and trustingly he walked forward between us.

"Do not hold your breath," I smiled up at him, "'Ra-onus is our ally. Although he has swallowed a thousand corpses, he smells sweet." He began to inhale normally, then more deeply and a look of wonder entered his eyes.

"What power!" he said in amazement and awe. "I know that fire keeps us warm in winter, cooks our food and bestows contentment when we sit around the dancing flames, but I have never experienced this..." he paused.

"The Essence," I prompted him.

"Welcome to my Realm." The Fire's voice echoed round the cavern. It sounded different from that with which he had always addressed us; it still bore the kindly inflection of a loving friend, but now its sonority conveyed majesty.

This Nicholas recognised, and wishing to perform the correct obeisance to convey his respect, he turned first one way and then another as he sought the source of the sound. A merry laugh rang out – no longer expressed through small explosions but by an all-pervading fanfare of joy.

"You are within me. I surround you; and now that you inhale me with every breath, I am within you too. We are friends."

Nicholas, still uncertain of the direction from which the Fire's voice was coming, held out his arms in an all-embracing gesture. Then he bowed deeply. "I am both honoured and blessed," he said. "I hope that one day I shall be worthy of your precious gift — en-light-enment."

❊ ❊ ❊

We returned to the Anhumans outside and found them either sitting in small groups talking as they groomed one another, or playing a game, throwing and catching a large, smooth stone that they had found. They came towards us eagerly, asking when they could go home. Nicholas looked at Augustine for instructions.

"We still have work to do here," he said. "And as we do not know the way to your settlement, we must ask you to remain with us until we have finished." They shook their heads and shuffled their feet in dismay. "On second thoughts, perhaps you could leave one or more of your good people to act as our guides; that is if they remember the route which you took? Your journey was long and filled with suffering. Perhaps none of you noted the direction in which you travelled."

"The Anhumans have retained many of their animal instincts; I myself will need them to lead me home. I will leave a small group with you, and if you will conjure up some food for us to take with us, I am sure that we can forage sufficient plant life from the wayside to keep us alive when we are nearer home. Not all the surrounding land was ravaged; I could feel grass beneath my feet for part of the way."

"Do you fully realize that it will take months to dispel the dark menace and the intruders who always gather in such conditions; and it will take even longer to make the earth bloom once more? Would it not be better to settle, at least temporarily, outside the perimeter of the infiltration of evil?"

Nicholas looked crestfallen. "All our implements and dwellings are there. Surely these solid assets will not have been destroyed?"

"They will be contaminated, and will cause disease, or at least depression, to those who go near them. I think it would be better if you stay here until our mission is finished and we can travel together."

"My people are used to work; it is their life. I thank you most sincerely for your suggestion, but there is nothing for them to do here with no soil or light." He smiled at them affectionately. "They may get up to mischief if they are not employed. I must beg your permission to leave."

"Then I suggest that Tepi goes with you." Augustine turned towards him. "How do you feel about this proposal?"

His face lit up; then he looked uncertainly at me. I smiled and nodded to him with apparent approval although it was as though an arrow had pierced my heart. I felt myself starting to disintegrate from shock; then I gathered myself together under Augustine's tender gaze. I had always known that this moment would come when our allotted tasks would divide us. I also knew that our parting was essential; although we loved one another, I also loved and belonged to Sulic. We two had sprung from a single Spark, and according to Cosmic Law, we will one day become one again.

Tepi's excited voice infiltrated my suppressed despair as he answered Augustine. "If you do not need me here, this opportunity to work with

Nicholas will be another challenge, which I gladly accept." He flashed one of his endearing, impish grins. "I think that I can trust you and Perima to bring our project to a successful conclusion." Then he added: "I can also be of help, making food by thought. I watched carefully when you were cooking the stews, and although I may prove to be an inferior chef in comparison to you, I am sure I can provide meals that they can eat."

"Then the matter is settled. Nicholas, when your charges are sufficiently rested and their wounds healed, you can begin preparing for the journey."

❊ ❊ ❊

During this brief period, Tepi practised preparing food under Augustine's supervision; and with his experience of, and ability in the making of thought formations, few problems occurred. Once, through lack of concentration, he allowed a concoction to bubble over the top of the cauldron; and another time, the liquid boiled away while he was talking to Nicholas, resulting in burnt food and pot. But both errors were quickly rectified; by lowering the flames in the first case, and by obliterating both container and stew in the second, and replacing them almost immediately.

We stood in two groups facing one another: Tepi, Nicholas and the Anhumans on one side; and Augustine, Ra-onus, myself and our future guides – a horse and two females with the heads of a camel and a zebra – on the other. We had already said our farewells and I had promised Tepi to take good care of his ex-Hatred until the time came when we would be together again.

As they began to move away, Tepi came slowly towards me with the look of a lost child in his eyes. He took me in his arms and we clung together as though we would never become two again.

"It has to be," we murmured simultaneously. "It is our destiny." We gazed at one another in both tenderness and pain; then with an effort of will we both managed to conjure a fleeting smile. With a final exchange of power our bodies parted, and my beloved Tepi set out on his journey to what was to become his life for many years.

CHAPTER 19
THE AFTERMATH OF BATTLE

Augustine thought it advisable to leave our guides outside the precinct of what had so recently been the Hatreds' Domain while we carried on with our work. They had already joined their friends in a meal before they had set out on their journey, and now we talked to them while waiting for them to settle down quietly. When we saw their eyes beginning to droop, we gave them rays that would put them into a deep sleep, in which they would remain until it was time for them to lead us to their companions.

As we entered the Fire's Realm we found that although the natural darkness was still dense, it was now relieved by many small flares, all of which were popping merrily. They appeared to be paying each other visits, as little streaks danced from one blazelet to the next. Flames whirled upwards from crevices in the rocks, creating light, colour and a sound like whispers of laughter.

My leaden heart was lifted as we walked in wonder; not only were our eyes and ears enchanted by the flickering beacons as they strained upwards towards their source, but our own thoughts too rose Heavenwards. We stood for a while in silent wonder in which the fires joined us, ceasing their cheerful crackling for a while as an act of gratitude for their release from bondage and reunion with their beloved lord.

As we moved towards the cavern from which we had witnessed the climax of the battle and the death of the Tyrants, the news of our approach was relayed by spurts of flame, which flashed from one fire to another until Ra-onus surged forward to meet us. He returned our bows gravely.

"Welcome to my Realm as it was and as it will be for many thousands of years. You came here as weary travellers with a mission, and you found a lonely, dispirited ruler, wrongfully deprived of his Princedom. You gave me the will to fight and the means to achieve its liberation. How can I thank you?"

"We owe you gratitude as well," Augustine replied. "You have been a loving friend and protector throughout our ordeal. You provided the only light capable of piercing the darkness because, apart from that of our auras, we had none that could manifest visibly and give us comfort. We are proud to have such a staunch and able ally."

We turned our attention to the sleeping new-lifers and awoke them with rays, allowing them a short period in which to gain full consciousness. Snorting and snarling, they tossed their ungainly bodies from side to side as they thrashed their arms about in imaginary combat. But when they finally opened their bleary eyes, although they peered at their neighbours with distrust, not one attempted to molest his fellows.

Augustine and I stood in the centre of the cavern. Curious eyes were fixed upon us; then all who were physically able to do so heaved themselves to their feet and bowed.

"There is much work to do, but not all of you are yet strong enough to perform the necessary tasks," Augustine told them. "You need nourishment and rest. You have been used to sustaining yourselves with the flesh of others; this is now forbidden. Food is already on its way but it will need preparing. It is known as grain. It grows in the light and contains the goodness of that light. There will be a continuous supply of this nutritious fare as long as you live in your present conditions, but in the new life that which you receive will not be free. We will give in exchange for mining ore from the mine and other products of your labour. You will learn to make pots in which your meals will be cooked, and the instruments which are needed to prepare the ground in which the grain is grown. Until the food arrives you must rest and enter the Fire for specific periods, partly to gain sustenance from his light, but also to receive healing for your wounds. You know the element only as something which relieves the darkness of some of its terrors, as heat with which you temper weapons and as a giver of burns. Your Fire lord has many attributes and you must learn to use them for good, not evil." The first lesson was over and as the sleep rays were applied, heads began to nod and the sound of snoring filled the air.

"Where is the grain coming from?" I asked.

"From the nearest point where it can be grown. It began its journey before the battle commenced."

"But how did you know when it would be needed?"

"My 'Augustine' personality is only part of my whole Being, who knows much more than I. I commune with my Higher Self and that which is required appears at the appropriate time. Have no fear that our new workforce will starve."

"Why cannot you give them thought-food as you did the Anhumans?"

"Because they do not know what grain is. I could conjure up a roasted human leg for them and they would eat it, but that would hardly fit in with the plan for their rehabilitation," he smiled. "When the grain arrives, they must find or fashion flat stones between which it can be ground. I have asked that two should be transported with the other necessities, and these will serve as a pattern; but more will be needed."

"Does not cooking require water?"

"Liquid, not necessarily water," he replied. I remained puzzled.

"Urine is quite suitable for making bread which will constitute their main diet until they have earned more appetising fare."

"Do humans use urine for this purpose?"

"Not unless they are obliged to do so, because it is considered to be a waste product of the body, and only desperate circumstances would normally cause them to utilize it; but it has been done where no water is available. I am sure that the ex-Hatreds will not be squeamish over its employment."

❊ ❊ ❊

Augustine and I were only too happy to enjoy the luxury of a respite from continuous exertion. We relaxed in the Fire's light and gave power to both the Anhumans and the new-lifers. Gradually the latter's wounds were healed and during their frequent periods of applied sleep, dreams of their future work were placed in their subconscious to filter into their waking thoughts. My sadness at Tepi's departure began to abate as Ra-onus and I listened to Augustine as he interpreted for the benefit of both of us some of the mysteries of the Ancient Wisdom. The creatures too played their part with their frequent demands for attention, and their comic antics roused my laughter; a healing balm in itself.

We now had time to turn our attention to Tepi's Hatred, who was still unconscious, as were the 'white ones'. They were all permanently resting in the Fire's light and progress was being made. Their bodies were now the normal colour of flesh which never sees the light of day – a dull grey with darker blotches – and their breathing was regular and deep. They began to emit animal grunts and groans and to make twitching movements with their noses and ears. We were confident that they would awaken from their death-like coma within days, and we asked for volunteers to spend periods with them to watch for increasing signs of life. Their presence would also ensure that some of their own kind would be within sight when the 'white ones' regained consciousness.

I spent a good deal of time with Tepi's Hatred while Augustine was teaching new skills to the miners and blacksmiths; and as I combed the matted hair on his head and chest with my fingers, I wondered what form his face would take; I also noted that his body seemed to be shrinking. The first change that took place was hair starting to sprout on his chin, and thick eyebrows appeared above the blank eye-space. Then features began to form: large pointed ears, a bulbous nose and small eyes which remained firmly closed. At first I thought that this was the head of an old and ugly man, but then I realized it was a gnome. I do not know why, but this discovery gave me pleasure: that Tepi's ex-Hatred was to follow the line of the Fairy evolution and not the Human race.

Augustine was watching over my patient as keenly as I, and we rejoiced together over his progress until it became almost stationary, as though the experience of inhabiting a changing form had taken all his growing strength. At last one of the attendant new-lifers called me from the far side of the Fire.

"On' o' d'em's not 'arf gruntin'," he told me as he pointed in the direction of Tepi's gnome. We bent over the writhing figure. One eye opened, but it registered nothing as it swivelled from side to side; then it closed and its owner returned to oblivion.

"This is very good," I said. "You can help to awaken him by stroking his head and moving his limbs. Speak to him: tell him that the Tyrants and Hatred Chiefs are dead, and talk to him of your work and of us, your friends, who are here to help you."

At the final words, his mouth opened in a genuine grin. He nervously put out a knotted hand and touched me with the tip of one of his fingers.

"You's luvverly pal to all o' us. I do all o' wot yous sez, alwez."

I stroked the back of his hand and said: "We will be good friends as long as you need us. Even after we have left you, we will come back and visit you, and you will show us what you have been making during our absence."

He began stamping his feet on the ground; then he turned round clumsily three times as he executed a lumbering jig. He was dancing! I had inspired a new talent.

❀ ❀ ❀

One day when we were playing with the creatures, Ra-onus said: "Augustine, I am overjoyed with the present condition of my Realm. My happiness almost overwhelms me when I visit my fire children and they surge towards me in love. I am also eager to help with the rehabilitation of those forms of life which issued from evil on the involutionary path and are now at the Nadir before entering the evolutionary cycle. I will watch them diligently, giving them praise when it is due, and chastening them when it is necessary to remind them of their past pain, in order to keep them on their way to the stars. But...," he paused.

"What troubles you dear friend?" Augustine asked him.

"I cannot imagine my life without these little creatures; they brought laughter with them and I shall need them to cheer me when you have gone."

"Dear Ra-onus; they could not return to the circumstances in which their own kind normally dwell, now that they have lived in your radiance. They are part of you. They are yours."

He beamed with pleasure, covering the floor with shafts of light, on which the creatures pounced and slid.

"Perhaps you would be agreeable gradually to adopt the rest of the colony. They would settle quickly now that other members of their breed are already here. This would enhance their evolution and provide playmates for the new-lifers as well. But first we must be sure that there are no reversions to previous habits."

"My ever-watchful eye will protect my little friends wherever they may be; and my fire children are in every cavern and they too will act as their guardians."

❊ ❊ ❊

We posted a sentry on the ramparts to watch and listen for the approaching supply train, while we continued to attend to the wounds and welfare of the new-lifers. During sleep they were drained of any remaining hatred, and they gradually became obedient through respect and gratitude, not fear.

Augustine proved himself to be a man of many talents; and he began to teach them not only how to chisel bowls from the rocks but to temper metal and make chains and ornaments for their personal use. These were burnished until they shone in the firelight, providing both pleasure to the wearers and a sense of achievement to the makers. At first there were mild quarrels over who should possess the more successful pieces; so Augustine settled the matter by confiscating them and explaining that they were needed as part payment for the supplies which were on their way. They were then allowed to keep only minor trinkets of a set pattern for themselves, and eventually each was the proud possessor of a single chain from which hung a plain iron disc; and from then on there were no more arguments.

As they now had no material food, it was necessary for them to rest a good deal, so that the light essence from the Fire could do its work of purification and sustenance.

CHAPTER 20
THE HUMANANS

At last we heard the awaited shout from the sentry as he came panting into our presence, having run all the way to tell us the good news. "Oi 'erd creakin' an' rumblin' loike yous said," he announced triumphantly.

All the caverns were astir with the news, and we gathered followers from each as we made our way to the exit. We did not have to wait long before the first ox-drawn cart arrived, to be followed by eleven more.

The new-lifers watched in wonder as two great flat grinding stones were unloaded by people who, like themselves, had men's bodies and animals' heads; but there the resemblance ended. These were magnificent specimens, who radiated health and good humour; the muscles in their legs and arms rippled as they strode about or lifted enormous loads with ease and enjoyment. They were Humanans, a breed which our survivors would one day become.

They laughed and sang as they worked and gave their gaping audience playful punches in the ribs to demonstrate their friendship. At first we wondered whether belligerence would return and our workers react with vicious kicks or blows, but they just stood and shook their heads in amazed admiration. "Com' on; give us an 'and," one of the Humanans called out cheerfully; and several of them ambled forward and began to hoist the heavy sacks on to the backs of their fellows, who staggered with them towards the caverns. But they soon tired and were obliged to rest; and others willingly took their place while they sat gazing at the action going on around them with as much interest as if they were watching an exciting play.

During this time Augustine was discussing future barter with their governor, who told us that he had made the journey with members of his community in response to an urgent appeal from Higher Realms.

"We are somewhat isolated in our underground world," he continued, "but at present my Humanans prefer to live in a close-knit group in semi-darkness. We have many contacts though, including those with Anhumans, who grow our food and who, of course, live in the light. I think my

Humanans will one day become shopkeepers because bartering goods is their main interest and pleasure. We have a large warehouse which contains merchandise of every description, and I am in constant communication with the Higher Realms, where messages of the goods available, and also those needed, are documented and passed on to the nearest depot. It is in this way that I heard of you and your exploits with the Hatreds and Tyrant Chiefs. Those that have survived seem amiable enough."

"They are already half tamed by suffering, and I am most anxious for them to have suitable associates who will claim their interest and widen their horizons."

Augustine asked him if a regular exchange of wares could take place, and their governor gladly agreed, especially when he was shown the metal jewellery.

"These will please my workers; they have no other source of personal decorations; the females particularly will enjoy wearing them." He then told us that another wagon train was on its way and others would follow. Stageposts would be set up so that in future, the travellers would have a little more comfort than on this, their first journey.

"I have another request," Augustine said. "Can you help us to find replacements for Perima and myself? Our destiny lies elsewhere, but these people have become so much part of our lives that we cannot leave them until they are more settled and have others who are competent to teach them how to improve their modest skills. Fire is the prevailing element here, and Fire is their overlord. It will be necessary for at least one of those who come to be an Initiate, so that full communication can take place."

"I will tune in to the Higher Realms on this matter and as soon as I have a satisfactory answer, I will send word with the next wagon train."

"We are both expert in the art-science of long-distance thought transference." Augustine's eyes twinkled. "I think it would be quicker if we used this method of communication."

The governor laughed. "How foolish of me; I am unused to the company of those with minds capable of piercing the confines of the Underworld. It will be a pleasure to do so with you."

❊   ❊   ❊

At last the unloading was complete, and the Humanans unpacked large, rush hampers containing loaves of bread, honey and raw root vegetables, which they spread on the ground and invited the new-lifers to share. They thrust their noses into everything available, and followed their hosts' example by dipping chunks of bread into the bowls of honey. Great smiles spread over their faces as it ran from their jaws on to their hairy chests, to be licked up again with relish; then they crunched up the vegetables with obvious enjoyment.

Augustine and I exchanged glances of relief. Their purification had already begun and their bodies were now sufficiently cleansed to accept the fruits of the earth. Their days as cannibals were over. When their meal was finished, chests were thumped and great gusts of digestive gas rose through their gullets and shattered the surrounding air.

The Humanans began to load the mined ore, which had already been stacked outside the cavern together with the other goods for barter. The workers who had fashioned the bowls out of rock and the pots from iron then presented their wares to their new friends, who tested their strength and admired the workmanship which, although crude, was sound.

Then came those who had made the pendants, some of which bore simple patterns cut in the metal. These were greeted with enthusiastic acclaim, and made the occasion a memorable one for those who had made them; for the first time in their existence they were receiving praise for their work, apart from that given to them by us, who were their friends.

"Wen you's commin' agin?" they asked.

"Wen you's ate all de food. So keep guzzlin' an' us'll be back fer mor' o' dem jools." They roared with boisterous laughter and the new-lifers tried to emulate them but the sound that emerged from their throats was more like retching than an expression of pleasure; however it was a genuine attempt to demonstrate amity – their prime goal.

✳ ✳ ✳

One of the wagons, laden with rough-hewn planks of wood, was left behind for our general use and also to serve as a model from which to make others. All the new-lifers wanted to take the place of the oxen between the shafts or alternately to push the cart from behind. We therefore drew up a rota so that each had a turn. They required strict supervision over this new occupation because their renewed strength after their regular meals of bread, coupled with unbridled enthusiasm, caused many a near accident; the cart's own velocity on sloping ground ran away with them on several occasions, and almost crashed into the rocks.

However they soon realized that it was one of their most precious possessions, saving hours of arduous labour, and it became an indispensable aid to their work rather than a large and amusing toy.

Their rehabilitation through work and recreational activities went smoothly until the next wagon train arrived. Augustine received the news of its approach from the governor and excitement ran high. We all went to meet it when it was still some distance away, and escorted it back to the cavern with cheers and much back-slapping good humour. A carpenter was among those who accompanied the Humanans so that our workers could learn how to make a second wagon.

Large vats of honey augmented the grain supply, much to the joy of our friends, who had continually extolled the virtues of this new food as they smacked their lips at the memory of its sweetness.

The visit with its attendant feast of good things to eat, accompanied by many jokes, passed all too quickly, but this time they had the stimulus of learning a new skill from the carpenter. They were clumsy with the tools that he had brought with him, but made up for their inefficiency with willingness and interest. Augustine and I were filled with wonder that latent talents should have blossomed so quickly, once the shackles of hatred, suffering and fear had been removed.

❊   ❊   ❊

Some of the 'white-ones' were now twitching, sighing and showing other signs of approaching consciousness; but closest of all to obtaining a new life was Tepi's gnome. I visited him several times a day to hold his nobbly hands and stroke his hair and beard. He occasionally opened his eyes but they were sightless, and they soon closed and stertorous snores rent the little brown aura which was forming round him.

Augustine came to add his power to mine, and at last the awaited event took place. The gnome opened both eyes and focussed them first on Augustine and then on me. A little glint of life appeared. Was it fear? No, it was a twinkle. I clapped my hands with joy and the vibration seemed to reach him because he shook his head from side to side. We waited breathlessly, but his small store of strength faded and he returned to his dreaming with a smile on his lips.

Progress was made each day and soon he was standing shakily on his bandy legs, then taking a few wobbly steps before collapsing with exhaustion.

"We must ascertain his name," Augustine said decisively. "If we repeat it over him, the moment of birth-stabilization will come sooner."

Above the planet of Earth, a name is not bestowed by parents on an unwitting child. Each individual has its nominal identity built into his or her being at the moment of becoming. As he evolves and has existence on more than one plane, he has several names, that in current use being the one that is compatible with the vibration of the dimension in which he is functioning.

Augustine and I stood, one on each side of the recumbent gnome. We emitted a small vibration to quicken his almost non-existent life impulse, but for several days we received no reaction, and then I felt a minute sensation of something extraneous. I cloaked my excitement as I kept murmuring: "Who are you? Tell me; what is your name?" After quite a long period of concentration I received my reward. The sound was weak, but decisive – the single word: "Koog."

"His name is Koog," I whispered to Augustine.

"Welcome Koog," he said.

"Welcome Koog," I echoed breathlessly.

"The Past is dead. The Present is born," Augustine intoned on a single note. "You Koog have within you the latent qualities of him who saved you. You will serve Tepi faithfully to atone for the unlawful infiltration of his aura and the resulting disorder you caused him." He bent down and touched the gnome's brow. "I bless you in love." He looked towards me.

"I give you my love, as I have bestowed it on him you will serve," I said.

Koog opened his eyes and gave his first conscious smile. I could not fail to notice the resemblance to Tepi's own impish grin. He held out his arms towards us just like a child. Augustine fondled his head as I gathered this ugly potential bundle of mischief into my arms and kissed him.

❊ ❊ ❊

"Tell me," I said to Augustine, "why did you intone your utterance and blessing, instead of chanting them?"

"While you were listening for his name, I was searching for his mantric note. The sound which I produced was as near to the original as I could make it. At the moment his own sound is harsh, but it will mellow in time until it eventually becomes as pure as that which I heard and endeavoured to emulate."

The arrival of the little gnome enhanced the enjoyment of all in the Fire's Realm. He was so droll and caused much laughter as he tottered about, continually falling but always picking himself up with an infectious grin. We never had the usual problem of having to watch over a young one in case it does itself injury, because there were always volunteers ready to look after him and the little fires would hiss and withdraw if he went too close to them.

The creatures also became willing playmates to all once they had been accepted as part of the daily routine. At first they had been regarded with aversion – similar to that felt for the animal Hatreds, who invariably bit and received kicks and punches in return. When the creatures put their little paws on the legs of erstwhile serfs and scrabbled to gain their attention, they were at first surprised; but after they had held out tentative fingers, which were invariably licked to the accompaniment of wildly wagging tails, they first stroked them and then picked them up in their arms and carried them as they had frequently seen Augustine and me doing. Eventually the creatures joined in all their activities and became welcome members of their clan.

The wounded and the 'white ones' still lying in a state of coma also received attention. A number of their kindred often wandered among them when Augustine and I were giving them power. They would prod them in a jocular way and say: "Com' on; 's time ter get up an' do som' work; then us'll lie down an' get more sleep." They would then prize their lids open and examine the white eyeballs, the irises still being invisible.

"'E ain't got no eyes," they would say to us. Each time we explained that the seeing part of the eye was hidden behind the top lid, but they did not believe us until eventually one of them looked straight at his investigator. All of those gathered round him were amazed. "'E's got eyes arter all."

They then enthusiastically increased their aid by moving the limbs of the one regaining consciousness, and I became certain that the receiver of so much attention struggled back to life only in order to get some rest.

❅ ❅ ❅

"Them's comin'. Oi 'ears de creakin' o' wheels." The sentry came careering among us, eyes blazing with excitement. Pandemonium followed. Some of the workers dropped their tools and rushed to the exit while others paused to bellow the good news to the miners underground. The scene was similar to a flight from a building after someone has shouted: "Fire. Fire." They hurtled through the caverns, gathering momentum as others joined them. Many stumbled and fell panting to the ground, as their gross bodies failed to answer the will of each to be among the first to welcome their friends, who brought good things to eat and implements to ease their labours.

But the apparent chaos was very different from that which followed the death-dealing swoops and screams of my bats. There was no panic; only an excessive eagerness to reduce the period of time between receiving the information and experiencing the pleasure that awaited them. They ran in the direction of the sound, which was gradually coming nearer, and some of them mounted the oxen while others seized the shafts and pulled or pushed the carts from the rear, shouting:

"Com' on! Faster!," as the animals began to stumble at the unusual speed being forced on them.

They were all laughing and out of breath when they arrived at the entrance to the Fire's Realm, to be greeted with cheers by those who had fallen and been unable to catch up with their more agile comrades. Their enjoyment was obvious; and again my thoughts reached back into the past and I was amazed that this jostling, good-tempered crowd could be the surly, maltreated slaves who, when the opportunity had arisen, had swiftly become savage fighters, sweating hatred from every pore.

❈ ❈ ❈

This time our people were in better condition after their meals of bread and honey, and they were able to make a larger contribution to the work of unloading the supplies than they had before. Root vegetables had been brought to add variety to their staple diet and sweet cakes with dried fruit were included in the meal which the Humanans shared with them.

After stomachs had been filled to saturation point, loading of the barter goods began. When the ore, iron pots and various implements had been produced and lifted on to the wagons, the Humanans said: "Com' on. Were yous 'idin dem jools?"

"Ar luvvies is pest'rin we ter get som' more."

"Dere warn't 'nuf fer all o' dem."

The trinket-makers grinned. "P'raps us is goin' ter keep 'em fer arsel's dis time."

They then proceeded to jump on one another in a boisterous game. Heads were buffeted, and chests and bellies pummelled. A great deal of noise was generated but humour remained high. As swiftly as it had started, the unarmed combat ended and they all sat or lay, panting, on the ground.

"Us fixes oo' 'as 'em wid straws."

I repeated this strange observation to myself and I am sure that my face must have mirrored a similar lack of comprehension as those of our charges.

Augustine was endeavouring to conceal a smile. "There were not enough trinkets to go round; so they decided who should have them by drawing lots with straws."

The Humanans were trying to mime the proceedings, but to no avail. So one of them made his way over to an ox and picked up some of the straw that it was placidly munching, and took it back to the jabbering, gesticulating group. He offered it to one of the new-lifers, who took a single stalk and raised it to his mouth in order to eat it, but the Humanans expressed their disapproval by relapsing into their animal neighs, grunts, growls and whoofs. One of them seized his other hand and told him to put the straw on his up-turned palm. All his companions also took one and proceeded to gaze at it fixedly as though it were an object of great rarity and beauty.

One of the Humanans came striding towards us purposefully.

"De man alwez sez 'long' or 'short'," he said to Augustine.

"Ah! Your governor decides which straws will be the winners."

"No 'un kno's; on'y de man." Obviously 'de man' was a title of greater importance to them than 'governor'.

"I will be happy to help you in this matter." Augustine stood for a while, holding his chin in his hand, as though deep in thought. Then he began pacing up and down as if unable to come to a decision in this important matter.

"The long ones," he eventually decreed.

The Humanans returned to the waiting group and gave Augustine's decision.

"We's won," shouted about a third of the contestants while the others proceeded to eat their straws.

"No; t'aint done yet. De man mus' say 'bent' or 'straight."

Augustine closed his eyes, and then raised them upwards as though he was invoking the Angel of the Harvest herself. Judgment seemed to weigh even more heavily upon him this time, and the new-lifers appeared to be holding their breath in anticipation.

"Straight," Augustine said in his most authoritative voice. This time, eight of them were decreed the winners.

"Wot's us goin' ter git?" they asked eagerly.

The Humanans guffawed and slapped their thighs in amusement.

"You's arn't goin' ter git nothin'. Us was on'y showin' yous 'ow us doos it. You's larnt somp'thin' tho', 'asn't yous?"

It was there and then decided that all future disagreements would be settled by the 'straw draws,' so great was the enthusiasm over this novel way of satisfying all concerned in an argument that I fear Augustine would have had little time left for teaching or carrying out his many tasks. He complied with their requests several times and then he reminded them that Ra-onus was their rightful lord and it was he who should really determine the winners. This task was happily accepted by their amiable ruler and so, in his own Realm, Fire took over the decision making in the straw draws instead of Man.

The 'jool' makers then fetched their wares. There was a marked improvement in their workmanship and little pieces of shiny metal had been cut and polished, under Augustine's instruction, so that they looked like semi-precious stones. These were greeted by many an "Ooh" and "Ah", interspersed with "Whoosh" which we presumed also signified approval.

What a happy day it had been for all and perhaps especially for us because we now had proof that the rehabilitation of the ex-Hatreds was progressing according to plan.

❖ ❖ ❖

The carpenter was proving himself to be a patient and able teacher. A second cart was now in use, and a third about halfway to completion. He was also teaching those who wished to learn, how to make simple furniture, such as tables, shelves and stools. Each new article created great interest and many of his pupils began to develop a modest degree of skill. Some, under Augustine's tuition, were proving to be competent bakers; others applied their growing energy to grinding grain between the two flat stones which had come on the first wagons train, or chiselling facsimiles from the rocks.

The comic jig performed by my admirer inspired me to teach singing, dancing and simple gymnastics. This final sport encouraged some of the new-lifers to construct, with the carpenter's help, a crude apparatus to enable them to climb the rock face. None of them had previously reached the top, and although there was only empty darkness when they had hoisted their panting bodies over the final overhang, they were far from disappointed because their pleasure in achievement for its own sake was growing every day.

The carpenter knew how to wrestle and although he was much smaller and of lesser strength than most of his pupils, he made up for these deficiencies in agility and technique.

We made forays into the surrounding terrain to look for small stones, which, when fashioned and polished, were set in the metal jewellery. These expeditions proved to be a popular diversion for those who took part, particularly when we loaded the carts with hampers of food and they enjoyed the equivalent of a picnic.

The perpetual darkness was far from ideal for an alfresco meal; but the flaming torches and the new-lifers' attempts at singing provided a festive scene, and my bruised musicality was assuaged by their obvious pleasure.

*   *   *

Augustine and I continued our work with them and there were few moments when we were not either teaching, supervising their recreation, or answering questions from groups or individuals, except when they were asleep.

Those that had been known as the 'white ones' had all become conscious. When they had regained some of their strength, we endeavoured to persuade them to join one of the work groups. But all they wanted to do was to sleep or alternatively, to gaze blankly into space. These unfortunate half-men-half-beasts had never known peace of any kind; this they now enjoyed as they relaxed in the Fire's light, and they wanted nothing else.

After Augustine and I had applied stimulating rays over a period without success, we decided to ask some of the workers to help us to rouse their comrades from their comatose condition. They set to with a will. If verbal encouragement failed, they seized their protesting kin and either carried or dragged them by their feet into the caverns and, holding their eyes open when necessary, they showed them the various activities taking place.

At first the sound of laughter and the scampering creatures frightened them. But when they discovered that the strange noise was not a prelude to an attack, and the creatures licked rather than bit them, they gradually lost their fears and joined in the pursuits of their companions, who were delighted to become teachers as well as craftsmen. This success was due far more to the determination of the new-lifers than to our more gentle persuasion; and for some time Augustine and I remained as aliens to them and were treated with distrust until they eventually realized that we wished them no harm and we became accepted as a part of their everyday lives.

Augustine contacted the Humanans' governor at regular intervals to tell him of the expanding mental capacity of our work force so that the equipment necessary to extend their activities could be carried on the next wagon train.

During one of these telepathic sessions the governor relayed the information for which we had been waiting. Three replacements had been found; a welder of ornamental metalwork, a woodworker and a woman who would attend to the new-lifers' general welfare and recreational activities.

Augustine and I embraced one another: our part of the scheme, on which we had worked so long, was at last coming to its close. And yet we were sad; because at this period, when what had been an intractable nightmare had become a project which held promise of enduring success, we would be leaving to resume our own lives once more.

We gathered our charges together and broke the news of our impending departure to them. They all wept, wailed, moaned and beat their chests in anguish. We had frequently told them of the necessity of returning to our other work, but they had merely shaken their heads and twitched their ears in disbelief; and we realized that they were unable to assimilate anything that did not refer to the current day's work or play.

Tears seeped from my eyes at their uncontrolled expressions of dismay; and Augustine spoke calming words to them as he gave them tranquillizing rays – but to no avail.

Ra-onus then showed his growing understanding of their natures. He exploded into a display of fire dynamics. Forked lightning streaked overhead to strike the rock face, and rebound to form intricate patterns which twinkled and twirled among them. Fireballs shot skywards, to burst like shouts of laughter and descend: in cascades of coloured sparks. These settled on their bodies and tickled them until they collapsed into helpless gurgles, their distress, at least temporarily, erased.

The Fire now accepted more responsibility in the lives of his vassals. Having discovered that he could divert their attention with his display, he devised other ways of interesting and amusing them. His fire-children joined them as gyrating wisps of flame whenever they expressed their exuberance in an impromptu dance, and they crackled as Ra-onus roared, to augment our musical sessions.

He now led the way on expeditions deep into the surrounding terrain. These would have been ill-advised without his presence because darkness in the lower depths is not merely absence of light – a negative condition. It is peopled with hidden dangers; fiends lurk round every corner ready to pounce, not only to frighten but to maim. A sudden start of fear could send a victim hurtling down an abyss; a fall might lead to an attack by many of the demonic forms which prowl the infernal regions. None of them can endure white light, and the Fire lord's presence guaranteed the safety of his more adventurous subjects, who were eager to expand both their knowledge and territory.

He also taught them how to keep the caverns free from contamination. They made hundreds of torches, which they held against the walls. At a command from each, flames leapt to the top of the rock face, ensuring that no intruder obtained more than a temporary foothold. In the day of the Hatreds the Domain was filled with internal corruption and had been so well guarded that no intruder could force an entrance. But now the situation had changed, and infiltrators were destroyed by fire before any seeds of evil could be planted and multiply in the countless cracks and crevices in the rocks.

The new-lifers not only approached Ra-onus with their straw draws; other problems which had previously been brought to Augustine and me for advice were now referred to him. We had always insisted on his mental presence on these occasions, and now he took over these duties, we were released for other tasks.

Koog was making some progress. Most of these primitive members of the Fairy evolution manifest little consciousness until they work with the earth and live in the proximity of trees, the roots of which they often tend. His movements were very clumsy but he did not fall so often. Gnomes are usually very inquisitive and Koog was no exception; he was frequently prevented from receiving more than minor burns, only by the hasty retreat of the little fires every time he attempted to put a hand or foot in their flames. He played happily with the creatures, tumbling and turning somersaults; but his attempts to emulate their acrobatic leaps always ended in failure, with Koog sprawled forlornly on the ground.

CHAPTER 21
OUR REPLACEMENTS

When we heard the sentry's call, it was far from triumphant. He ambled disconsolately across the cavern and stood before us instead of shouting from a distance. "Dem's commin'," was all he said, his ears drooping. When we walked through the caves, we found that all their inhabitants had dropped their tools and stopped work; they stood and stared at us but made no attempt to follow us to the exit.

"Your behaviour is unworthy of you," Augustine said sternly. "What will your new teachers think when none of you are there to bid them welcome? This is against all the rules of hospitality among evolving people. They know that Perima and I have been with you for weeks, and they will be shocked at your lack of progress. Perhaps they may even regret answering the call to help you. Do you really wish to be left alone here with no hope of learning further skills and with no contact with your new Humanan friends except on a strictly business basis when you exchange your wares for essential supplies? There will be no feasting together; no jokes, games or fun. The Humanans will not understand when they are obliged to enter the caverns to seek you out and find you standing with scowling faces when they expect embraces and cries of greeting. I am deeply disappointed in you."

Augustine beckoned to me and we both turned to go back the way we had come.

Cries of protest clattered about us: "Grrrr. Haugh. Re-te-te-te. Woomph."

"No, no, no. Us be sad," one blurted out.

"Perima and I are sad too; but we are not lost to you. We will return, and I know that you will amaze us – as you do each day – with the progress made during our absence. I have explained to you and you have understood the principle of reciprocal exchange, when each gives according to his ability. Although the offerings may not be equal in excellence, they are in worth if each has done his best. You have gained much from our presence here, I know; and our rewards have been great; but the greatest gift that you can grant us now is to dry your tears and meet your friends and teachers with dance and song, portraying the spirit of welcome."

An uneasy silence charged with emotion followed, and was eventually broken by sniffles and sighs. A quavering voice started a song I had taught them; then others took part as they stamped and gyrated towards us.

Augustine and I walked slowly through them and they followed, the sound of song and dance increasing as their fellows joined them. By the time we reached the exit, the first of the wagons was coming into view, and we fanned out forming an arc large enough to contain the entire supply train when it stopped.

All were now filled with excitement as they recognised their friends and surged towards them. Augustine and I waited until the three teachers had climbed down from one of the carts, before walking forward to greet them.

The two young men had pleasant, intelligent faces, and the woman possessed a sublime beauty. She ran towards us with her hair flying like a golden banner behind her; and she curtsied to Augustine before presenting her companions to us. The three men were immediately surrounded by new-lifers, who propelled them towards the caverns to escort them round the Fire's Realm.

The woman stood and gazed at me as though I were an apparition from another world – as, in fact, I suppose I was.

"When I was told your story, I could not believe that a female fairy could possibly have taken a leading part in a ferocious battle, and gained victory over the forces of evil with but two fellow combatants, and little else but will and courage. And now that we have met and I witness your ethereal beauty, gentleness and dignity, I am even more incredulous.

"The fairies that I know and love are those that tend my flowers and the great trees under which I sit and meditate when my day's work is done. I thought that Nature's growth was the sole task of your evolution. Can you truly have fought as a hideous vampire bat, witnessed scenes of bloody carnage, and emerge unscathed?"

"I am touched and flattered by your unstinting praise," I said. "Your description is partly true; but we had many unseen helpers, who from afar manipulated the automata which followed us into battle and overpowered our foes. We also used rays which destroyed the Hatreds, and we were at all times surrounded by protective forces. Others later healed us and readjusted lingering mental disorders caused by performing acts which were foreign to our nature. And of course we had the Fire-lord with us; we could not have won without him."

"Oh, how I wish you were not leaving; I am sure we would be friends."

"We are already friends," I said, "and I am certain that we shall remain so. It is so apt that you bring with you such exquisite beauty. Your future pupils need it, and I know that the affection which so miraculously came to life in such ugly frames, was nurtured and bestowed on me, will now be transferred to you. Come with me, and meet some of them."

"May I greet them in my own way?" she asked me. I inclined my head in agreement, and she drew from her belt a small pipe, which she raised to her lips, and from it enticed sounds of sheer enchantment. I was beguiled into instant joy, and also amazement that such sweet tones could manifest in the cloying darkness which engulfed us.

Those within range of the music, turned as though hypnotised, and began to dance towards us. Higher and higher rose the notes until they hovered over our heads as twinkling, coloured lights. They uttered their "Oohs" and "Aahs" of approval as they pointed at the phenomena. The lights began to move, diving and climbing as they wheeled over and under each other in a frolicsome caper. The watchers raised their hands and tried to catch the magic spheres but, like flies, they always escaped. As swiftly as it began, the melody ceased on a high-flung note, which shot upwards and vanished in the endless night.

After much bowing, grinning and clapping, our audience dispersed to seek other excitements, and the piper and I were alone,

"You are the Fire Initiate," I said.

"Indeed, yes; my name is Ra-eena. To me fire is power, light, passion and adventure. It enables me to leap into the Unknown in my search for Wisdom. When I was told the conditions in which I would be working, I knew that there was a purpose for me here apart from helping the Hatreds. I pondered on the reasons for the urge I had to answer this call and suddenly the answer came; through my music and dancing notes, I would take a glimpse of the higher spheres to these people, and in the depths where they live the mystery of the Essence of Fire would be revealed."

"I have touched their hearts," I said, "but you will unveil their souls. Come with me now, Ra-eena, and I will present you to the Lord of the Realm."

❊ ❊ ❊

We walked through the empty caverns. "This is magical," she cried as she gazed at the countless beacons, flashing and flaring up the walls. She caressed the little fires that streaked towards her, climbing her body to form a dazzling halo round her head.

"I only know fire in the light," she said. "But in the endless night it will divulge hidden wonders, I know."

We reached the Fire's Cavern; and I could sense that he longed to expand towards us, but he restrained himself. This was an official occasion: the meeting and blending of an Initiate with her chosen Element, in the Ceremony of Immersion.

I stood in silence and watched Ra-eena as she gravely arrayed herself in a robe of flame. She remained for a while with her eyes closed, and when she eventually moved, it was not of her own volition; she was gently propelled towards her ritual union.

As she entered the Fire, he quivered, and gossamer-fine filaments spiralled upwards to form a vaulted path for her to tread. Her advance was slow and dream-like; as though each step fulfilled a yearning. And as she reached his core, Ra-onus exploded into a white, blinding blaze as though the sun had turned inside out and disclosed its innermost being.

I stood in awe – a welcome witness of the mystic union of positive and negative forces: of a male Essence of Fire and a female member of the Human race.

The white light wavered; then died to the whispering sound of an ecstatic sigh; and Ra-eena became visible once more as she lay asleep in a pink haze of love.

The ritual was over: the marriage had begun, and I knew that this woman had the power and resolve to continue successfully the work which Augustine, Tepi and I had started.

* * *

I returned to the milling crowd outside. The unloading was still in progress and jokes flew backwards and forwards; not only between the Humanans. The new-lifers were beginning to learn the pleasure of making droll comments of their own. I joined Augustine, who was deep in conversation with the two teachers.

"Stephen and Raoul have come well equipped both mentally and physically," he told me. "They have had experience working in similar conditions to those that we have here; and they have brought with them implements which will enable their pupils to make many new objects for their own comfort and for barter.

"Stephen is also a physical training instructor and I have no doubt that he will help them to change the unwieldy hulks in which they at present live, into strong, flexible bodies like the Humanans'."

Raoul turned to me and said, "You need harbour no doubts that we have the ability and desire to help these people. You have already changed their lives from complete subjection under despotic rule to that of benign obedience through trust and affection. Now that we have met a number of them, we are confident that we can guide at least some to the stage where they will work with only minor supervision. They can then be given a degree of liberty; and once they have learned to protect themselves from the demonic dangers which lurk on every route, they can travel and meet others of a slightly higher grade of intelligence, and absorb new ideas and eventually think for themselves."

We led them through the caverns and showed them their modest quarters in the cave behind the Fire, where all our planning and training for the battle had taken place. We saw that Ra-eena was now stirring and we watched her as she rose to her feet and made her obeisance to Ra-onus before leaving his presence with little curls of flame enveloping her feet and head.

"A truly amazing experience," she murmured softly, "and one which will reveal more during meditation. Ra-onus has been vanquished: a condition I have never met in other rituals. I told Perima that fire, to me, was power, light, passion and adventure, but this lord has revealed not only despair but tenderness, patience, and most surprising of all – love. I did not know that the Elements included love among their attributes."

"No entity can give what it does not possess," said Augustine. "Each Element has the characteristics of its state of being. Fire is the outward manifestation of solar power; it stimulates mental activity; it is the courage of those who march against aggressors to defend principles, people or land. It destroys temporal forms and transmutes the energy thus released into a dynamic force.

"We restored to Ra-onus his will to fight for his rightful position as prince of the Realm. He learned the joy of healing when we gave the wounded 'white ones' into his care. We introduced him to laughter, and above all, we gave him love for his friendship, for his protection and unfailing support both before and throughout the battle; and for the comfort and safety he provided when we slept within him.

"Other Fire lords are his superiors in strength and status, but Ra-onus has qualities which they do not. And these, Ra-eena, you discovered when you became him."

"I have not previously worked with a Fire lord," said Raoul. "I only know the physical power of the element, which I use in my work of metal casting."

"Would it be possible for us to be accepted as pupils, with the ultimate aim of becoming Initiates?" asked Stephen.

We heard a sound which I had never heard Ra-onus emit before – almost like the purr of a giant cat.

"What does that mean?" they asked in unison.

"He accepts you willingly," Augustine told them. "But I must warn you that long hours of study will be required of you: and also soul searching. The mysteries that you seek are dangerous and are only revealed to those who prove themselves worthy. You have both spent many years helping others, and I think you come within this category. You are fortunate to have with you one already experienced in Fire lore and you must discuss this matter seriously with Ra-eena before you make a final decision. The knowledge that is granted is a sacred trust and must be used only with sagacity in the service of the Element and not for personal gain. Nevertheless it will aid you in your work and eventually, it can give you the power to raise you from whatever depths your destiny leads you, to the source of Fire itself, the Sun-behind-the-sun."

"We thank you, Master," said Stephen. "I confess I did not know of the inner implications of my request. I watched Ra-eena on our journey here. In spite of the presence of our husky Humanans, who are well used to keeping demons at bay, many women would have quailed as we passed through hostile territory. But I sensed within her a hidden fire, which made her glow with confidence when danger threatened; and her good-humoured kindness whenever such minor misfortunates as a grazed knee or a small wound needed her attention, endeared her to everyone."

"Ra-eena never goes unnoticed, wherever she appears," Raoul said. "We naturally had many meetings with experts to discuss curriculums which would suit the temperament and lack of skill of the new-lifers, and always she stood out like a goddess among lesser beings." He smiled at her and then continued. "For some time I have felt that my work among the needy, although both useful and fulfilling, was not enough. I made enquiries at several Schools of Occultism and Mysticism, but I did nothing about enrolling. And now I understand my apparent laxity; it is here in the depths that was once a Hell, and not in a Hall of Advanced Studies that I shall learn what I need."

❖ ❖ ❖

After enjoying the usual meal with their Humanan friends, the new-lifers bade them and the carpenter farewell. The latter was the recipient of a jocular display of goodwill, including mock wrestling tactics and hearty thumps on the back, to demonstrate their gratitude for his help.

One of the wagons was left behind for our use on the journey to the Anhumans' Homestead; and during the interim period the oxen received a great deal of attention. Straw draws were held to decide who would have the pleasure of looking after them, and their coats were daily groomed and horns and hoofs polished until they shone.

Throughout the days that followed, Augustine helped Raoul and Stephen to set up their apparatus. A demonstration took place and all were astonished at the decorative objects that could be made by experts in beaten metals and carved woods.

Ra-eena spent much of her time among Raoul's and Stephen's pupils, encouraging and consoling those who were clumsy and praising others whose finished products showed that care, if not skill, had been employed in their making. During their periods of recreation, she played her little pipe and set many feet stamping and hands clapping. She also showed them the two other instruments that she had brought with her: a lyre, and one that I had never seen before. It had only three strings, which emitted cheerful sounds when a silver bow was drawn across them.

As I passed or paused among them, eyes became misted and tears fell as they gently stroked me with their gnarled hands. I patted them in return and spoke soothingly to hide the heaviness of my heart. My sorrow was not for them but for myself, because I knew that their present teachers were more expert than Augustine or I in the skills which would eventually lead them to the achievement of self-expression and to Manhood.

＊ ＊ ＊

Raoul accompanied me when I returned to our original headquarters in order to collect more of the creatures to augment the group which had been so successfully transferred to the Fire's Realm. We took two of these to give confidence to the ones which we would take back with us.

As we drew close to their home, I left Raoul holding the two little animals in his arms while I walked forward. As soon as I called them, they rushed towards me with excited squeals of welcome; they leapt and gambolled about me with their paws scrabbling the air in joy. I knelt down and picked up as many of them as I could hold in my arms, while the others climbed over me, licking my face and hands. After they had calmed down a little, I called to Raoul to join me, and he too received a great welcome. But when he placed the two creatures that he was carrying on the ground, the others took one look at them, froze, and fled in terror into the darkness.

"Have they forgotten their brother and sister?"

"As you can see, they remember me; they would be most unlikely to forget members of their own race so soon. I am frankly puzzled."

The two creatures were quite undismayed being scorned by their relatives. They gazed up at us, wagging their tails and talking to us in their own prattling language.

"I know what is frightening the others," I said. "It is their blue eyes. They changed from red to blue after they absorbed the Fire's light. They are now aliens to their own kind."

I placed my hands over their eyes and willed a faint film to form over them; this was sufficient to mask the colour, but left them with enough sight to leap and scamper without colliding with anything. I held them in my arms and called the others, who responded to the familiar sound and moved slowly towards me. But they were far from confident, as they peered and sniffed around for hidden foes. I gently threw the two I was holding towards them, and this time the familiar smell reached them before their reflex action to danger came into play. They began to romp together and to emit excited "eek-eek" sounds to express joy at their re-union.

We had taken a box, which Stephen had made, and in it we put the two creatures that we had brought with us and six of the remaining group. We did not choose these for their individual intelligence as we had on the previous occasion, because this time the transfer was purely for their own good, and eventually all of them would be collected and become members of the Fire's colony.

❊ ❊ ❊

We explained our departure plans to Koog, but his only response was to turn a somersault and peer at us roguishly with his head upside down between his legs.

Augustine and I took him with us when we awakened the sleeping Anhumans. As I watched them play with him, I knew that they would compensate him for the loss of his other new friends. The little gnome watched with interest as we helped them to exercise their muscles, which had become weak during their long sleep; and he insisted on pummelling their backs and legs, much to their amusement. When we told them that we would soon be beginning our journey to their Homestead, they showed their teeth in delighted grins. Then they rose to their feet and cocked their heads on one side and twitched their ears as they listened for something which we could not hear. There was only one track with high rocks on either side, which led up to and away from the Fire's Realm; so their senses must have been tuned in to the far distance.

"Us knows the way," Horse-head told us with confidence, and the others nodded in agreement.

Augustine cooked them a final meal while they played with Koog, and when they were replete, he advised them to relax, as we would be leaving in a few hours. We spent most of the time that was left before our departure with Ra-onus. He was still in a state of bliss after his union with Ra-eena, and retained his amazement that this unexpected joy had been granted to him.

"You have both shared my form and our minds have intermingled," he said. "We have also given and received love, and for these blessings I shall always be grateful. But Ra-eena is a suprema. I have no thoughts to describe my feelings for her."

"Your experience with Ra-eena was quite different from the frequent occasions when Perima and I blended with you. It is true that I am a Fire Initiate and Perima a beautiful member of the opposite sex, but Ra-eena possesses both these constituents, which are essential for a true union."

"Now that she, Raoul and Stephen are here to help you, our departure deprives you of nothing except our physical presence. Our mutual respect and affection grows and will never wane. You have acquired a companion with whom to explore the unknown reaches of love and wisdom. Your two new disciples are eager to learn Fire lore from you and they will teach their own skills to your subjects. The new-lifers and the creatures will be constant reminders of the testing time we spent together. An unbreakable link has been forged between us; this will be strengthened every time we see a fire or you meet a Human being or a Fairy."

"It is strange that I can now rejoice at the loss and despoilment of my Realm; when bereft of power I was unable to fulfil my function and became a feckless fire-body. I shall never forget the time when, steeped in despondency, I heard your voice, Augustine. You greeted me with respect and politely requested an audience. Was it a trick? I decided not. Brute strength and not chicanery was the Hatreds' wont. But I was not without fear, I confess. Had I misjudged your intentions, my body as well as my Realm would have been invaded, with what dire results I dare not think. When I uncovered my secret entrance and I beheld a Wise man and two fairies, I knew that my Lord, the Sun-behind-the-sun, had knowledge of my straits and had sent you to succour me.

"I have also learned a lesson," he continued. "Never despair. I was close to it many times during my solitary incarceration, and it touches me again as I lament your impending departure. But now I know I am not merely one fire among countless others, but a fire that possesses the mind of Man. As each Human being is born with the attributes of all the four Elements, sadly I have nothing to give you in return."

"You have given us love, and no being can bestow a richer gift on another."

"There is a paradox to this blessing," Ra-onus mused. "The more of it one gives, the more one has."

"It is a circle," said Augustine, "And a circle is eternal; and therein lies its infinite grace."

I stroked the Fire's quivering flames as he enfolded me in his radiance and love. Augustine blessed him with the sacred sign of his Element and we slowly withdrew, leaving within his consciousness many plans for the future. Some of these he could not at that time understand, but we knew that meditation and determination would eventually quicken them, and ideas would become reality.

We then took our leave of Ra-eena, Raoul and Stephen, who insisted on remaining in their quarters while we bade the new-lifers a fond farewell. In the short time that we had known them and watched them at work, we had become increasingly certain that all three of them had the temperament, desire and ability to take their pupils into the next phase of evolution, and that they would learn from Ra-onus many truths that were at present veiled.

We clasped one another affectionately and I began to look forward to our next reunion.

❈ ❈ ❈

When the hour of our departure drew near, Augustine gathered everyone together outside the caverns. It was no longer the dark, forbidding territory of the past, because Ra-onus had spread his fire children outside his Realm as well as within, and beacons blazed out of crevices from the ground to the topmost rock.

"Dear Friends, " Augustine said, "this is an occasion tinged with sadness because we are all parting from those we love. Perima and I have both experienced this sorrow before, but for you it is a new emotion. You will therefore doubtless be surprised when I tell you that I rejoice for you, because this emotion has been awakened by affection. Before we came to this Realm, you knew only fear, hatred and suffering. Now you have assets which you do not wish to lose: among them – us. You value our friendship and I assure you that it will remain yours as long as you need it. It is only our physical presence of which you are being divested. We will return I promise you.

"Our sojourn with you began with a quest – the rescue of one of your clan; this we planned to achieve by stealth. As we travelled towards you, we were unaware of the existence of your vanquished ruler, who was powerless to regain his Realm; or of the magnitude of the battle we would be forced to fight.

"I need not describe the horrors, because you shared them; but out of this abyss of corruption, torture and anguish came not only the rescue of Tepi's Hatred – now the gnome, Koog – but the liberation of each one of you that is now present. And this occurred because you held within you a spark of True Life, which proved to be indestructible despite your cruel suffering and despair.

"You are important people. You saved yourselves. We could not have performed this service for you however much we had desired to do so, had you not guarded that precious fragment of Life with such tenacity.

"Tears are the expression of many emotions – of happiness as well as gloom. Therefore shed them. but let them mainly be tokens of joy for your release from bondage and fear; pride in your just and kindly ruler; pleasure in the friendships you have formed with each other; and also for the presence of Ra-eena, Stephen and Raoul, the teachers who have left their groups of artists and seekers to help you to enhance your skills and to achieve the physical strength and muscular flexibility of Humanans.

"Spare some of your tears for us, that they may wash away our own as we remember with gratitude the miraculous change you have brought about in yourselves. From being detested members of the Hatred Clan, feared by all who live in these regions, you are now people worthy of welcome wherever you go, not only for the skills which you have acquired and make manifest in your wares, but for yourselves. This success is the result of our combined labours; so we leave you now with our heartfelt thanks for enabling us to complete our part in this project, which could well have proved beyond our powers."

❊ ❊ ❊

We were surrounded by the sound of ill-concealed sniffs and sobs as we passed through the crowd, and eager hands stretched out to give us a final caress. Augustine was deeply moved although he remained outwardly calm; but despite my efforts, tears coursed down my cheeks.

The oxen had already been harnessed, and the Anhumans and Koog were waiting for us in the wagon. We joined them, and then turned to wave our final farewell to those whom we had fought and later come to love.

From the back of the crowd the trilling notes of Ra-eena's pipe rang out and, at the same time, thousands of multi coloured lights burst from the Fire. The oxen strained at their traces and as we began to move, the final scene for ever etched on our memory was of our clapping, stamping, singing friends, who, despite their distress, were determined to cheer us on our way.

CHAPTER 22
THE ANHUMANS' HOMESTEAD

A s we knew that our journey was to be a long one, we administered sleep-producing rays to Koog, so that he would be neither bored nor frightened.

When we reached the end of the gulley, which led from the Fire's Realm, we came upon a wide, open space of dark, potentially dangerous terrain. The Anhumans jumped from the wagon and set out in different directions, raising their heads to sniff the air and frequently sneezing as they inhaled the fetid, sticky substance to which they were not used.

"Tis what me thought. T'e way is to t'e right," Horse-head informed us. They set the oxen's course in the desired direction and then joined us in the wagon. We talked to them and told them as much as they could understand about our work; and they revealed to us their apprehension about their return to their home, which held such frightening memories.

"Can you not think of the many happy years you spent there rather than of the weeks of terror?" Augustine suggested.

"'Tis all t'e black. Us can no t'ink what light look like no more," said Zebra-head sadly.

"I think I can help you," I said. "But go now; walk with the oxen for a while; they will enjoy your company."

Augustine joined me in providing thoughts of waving fields of corn, through which whispering zephyrs blew; trees laden with brightly coloured fruit; and chortling brooks, which rippled through lush grassland as the sun shone from above on Annumans at work.

I wove them all into a thought formation, which we placed against the inside, protective covering of the wagon. There was of course no real light, such as they craved. It was a semblance, but perhaps it would quicken their memory and enable them to capture thoughts of what had been, and what would be in the future.

We called to them and as they drew the flaps aside, all three of them gasped.

"T'e sun," Camel-head sighed.

"Corn," grinned Zebra-head.

"Apples. Can us have som te eat?" asked Horse-head eagerly.

"Alas, no," I said. "It is all an illusion."

"I will make you apples that you can eat," said Augustine; "but first I must concentrate. There is colour to be considered, texture and, above all, taste. I have not eaten material food for a long time; so I may make mistakes. Cooked food is easier to conjure up, because I can rely on the memory of familiar smells. But I will do my best."

A lengthy discussion followed: on colour – should the apples be green, red or variegated? Would the Anhumans like the texture to be crunchy or soft? Did they prefer a sweet flavour; sweet with a sharp tang, or sour? Augustine applied his thoughts to their final decisions, which had been worked out among themselves. If there was any difference of opinion, two to one carried the vote.

"You are learning about majority rule, too," Augustine said with a smile. "Perhaps Nicholas will not approve."

"Nicklus like what us like," said Camel-head. "He alius ask us what us want; but us say, 'you say,' an' he shake his head." They all laughed happily at their communal harmony.

❊ ❊ ❊

There is little of interest to relate about our journey. It was ebony gloom all the way; but we were not attacked by the demons prowling round us because we were surrounded by the protective light wielded by our Teacher-Lord and our friends at Onward, which was now able to manifest as a transparent glow.

The infallible instinct of our guides led us along stony paths which sometimes had an abyss on either side; across sluggish, oily rivers in which sinister, horned fish floundered and died; and across fields over which dark grey vegetation nervously crept, until at last we saw, in the distance, a haven of light produced by hundreds of wavering beacons. Another phase of our journey in the Underworld was coming to its close.

The Anhumans leapt from the wagon and ran, snorting and neighing joyfully, towards their friends, while Augustine and I followed at the more sedate pace of our plodding oxen. Those at the Homestead had heard the sound of our creaking wheels, and Tepi raced to meet us, passing the panting guides as they careered in the opposite direction.

We clasped and clung to one another as we gazed into each other's tear-filled eyes. Our love flowed, enveloped and held us in a rapturous embrace within a rose-hued haze, which even the darkness could not hide. Augustine watched our reunion and shared our joy; then he gathered Tepi in his arms and held him tenderly.

For a while we stood silently looking at other. The three of us were one again.

❖ ❖ ❖

Tepi was the first to regain his personality. "Quick, show me my Hatred. Is he handsome?" he asked with his eyes twinkling.

"That is for you to judge," I replied, and Augustine opened the flap at the back of the wagon to reveal Koog sprawled on the ground. His eyes fluttered as he began to regain consciousness and Tepi stared at him in amazement. Whatever he had expected, it certainly had not been a gnome. He began to laugh and Koog, roused by this sound, which he had so often heard since his rebirth, blinked, wrinkled his bulbous nose and scratched his beard. He turned his squinting eyes in Tepi's direction and frowned uncertainly. Then he rose to his feet and tottered up to him to take a closer look. He obviously liked what he saw because he began to chuckle and held out his arms towards him. Tepi picked him up and hugged him. "What is his name?" he asked me.

"Koog."

"Well Koog," he said, "as we shall be together for many years, it is important that we should be friends. I will therefore give you some power to seal our relationship of big and little brother."

As the green ray of the Fairy Evolution flowed, Koog clung more closely to Tepi and began to stroke him, an act I had never seen him perform before. Soon he was asleep and Tepi gently put him in the back of the wagon and the three of us walked beside the oxen as we completed our journey.

Nicholas and his charges were waiting to greet us, standing in front of some rough shacks, which were now their homes. One of these had been set aside for our use, and Augustine and I rested while the Anhumans unharnessed the oxen and unloaded the wood and tools that we had brought with us. After a brief sleep we all gathered between the huts, and Nicholas and Tepi took it in turns to tell us how they had fared since their arrival.

❖ ❖ ❖

They had made no attempt to cross the perimeter of the land, mainly because it was occupied by a horde of obstreperous demons, who were determined to keep its rightful owners at bay; and also because they feared becoming contaminated, or even incapacitated, by the highly active malignity which radiated from them. However they had placed pillars of fire in a circle round the intruders to imprison them, and prevent them from attacking, while they were working or sleeping. They had watched them trying to extinguish the flames by beating them with iron bars and throwing earth and their ordure at them, but they were composed of no ordinary fire. They had been gifts from Ra-onus and possessed intelligence. When the demons came too close, the red-hot pillars roared forward and chased them away.

Tepi had taught Nicholas the Banishing Ritual, with the correct actions and accompanying chants; and together they had trained the Anhumans to produce various sounds from their animal throats. Some of them had shown an aptitude for producing high notes, others low; so they had been divided into different sections as in a choir. All agreed that the results had not proved as tuneful as they could have wished; but they had made a start in learning what would be required of them later.

Tepi, with Nicholas' aid, had endeavoured to contact the angels, but they had failed to reach them because they could not produce enough power to pierce the darkness.

"Now that we are together again, I am sure that our Teacher-Lord will find a way," I said. "With our friends at Onward forcing their power downwards, while we send our thoughts and will upwards, eventually they must meet. We succeeded when we were in the Hatreds' Domain where the matter was much denser than here."

Augustine turned to Nicholas. "Are your people able yet to visualize the sun, moon, fields of waving corn and the fruit-bearing trees?"

"Alas no; their memory is only of the horror of their capture by the Hatreds and their journey to the Fire's Realm and back."

"Us can do it," said Horse-head proudly.

"Com wid we," said Camel-head.

"Us shows yous de sun" added Zebra-head.

The three of them ran towards the wagon, drew aside the flaps, and pointed inside. The others looked at each other in bewilderment at their friends' strange behaviour because nothing was visible except benches, the floor, the protective covering, and Koog.

"Watch us," commanded Horse-head as they directed power from their bodies towards the now faded thought formations I had constructed for them.

A glimmer of light appeared, followed by images of plants, trees and the sun: and finally the facsimile of the Anhumans working in a field of corn came into view.

"'Them's we," they shouted; lips were drawn back and teeth displayed in delighted grins. They jostled each other to obtain a closer look and Horse-, Zebra- and Camel-head were almost crushed by boisterous hugs.

When they had calmed down, Augustine said: "Come now; we have work to do. This semblance of light that we have shown you, is but a reminder of what was and what will be again. But only after much physical and mental endeavour will the reality be able to manifest. The fact that your three friends – our guides on our journey here – have learned to recreate these representations in such a short time, has led me to believe that we can quicken the process of returning the land to its original state much sooner than I had dared to hope.

"First, Tepi, Perima and I will make thought formations similar to the ones which you have just seen, but on a much larger scale. We will place them in the vicinity of the huts so that there will be a little light, apart from the fire beacons; and the reproductions of the flowers and fields will cheer us while we work. But, as you have witnessed, the images fade. To keep them visible, you must give them power."

"Pow-er?"

"What is dat?"

"Where do's us find dis?"

"You tell them," Augustine said to our guides, who repeated what he had told them during our journey.

"Pow-er is life. If yous got life, yous got pow-er. If yous uses it, dis keeps your body strong. But if yous don' use it, it sleep. Yous mus' wake 'un."

Immediately their companions began to beat their chests and slap their neighbours' backs as they made loud encouraging noises. We managed to mask our smiles, but our guides guffawed in derision.

"Yous am simple," they said. "Pow-er aren't woke up like yous doin', wid thumps and hubbubs. You must shush."

Eyes widened in wonder, but silence reigned. Horse-head tapped his brow: "Yous mus t'ink. T'ink ob a star. It arn't still. It twinks. Take de star and put it in yous 'tomach."

All eyes were now on their instructors: such a novel idea obviously appealed to them. After a while some looked down.

"Don' see no star," one said.

"Yous don' sees it, yous feels. Twink, Twink. Wait for it."

Time passed. The Anhumans were frowning with the effort of such unusual concentration; then one or two of them began to grin; others swayed their hips or made little leaps in the air. "Me's got 'un."

"Aren't got nuthin," the others wailed.

"You are doing well," Augustine encouraged them. "It took me longer to make a star twink inside me than it did our guides; and now some of you are succeeding too. Gather together in small groups and practise. The stars will come, I promise you."

                                    ❄ ❄ ❄

They took their new task seriously and often when they passed us, instead of waggling their ears and smiling at us, they appeared to be unaware of our presence. As they strode about their business with downcast eyes, they would rub their stomachs, murmuring: "Com-mon. Twink fer me."

Eventually when about a quarter of them had achieved their goal, a group arrived outside our door. None greeted us; lips trembled, ears drooped disconsolately and I detected a tear or two trickling down some of their cheeks.

"Us no goods," one of them declared.

"Now, what has happened to distress you so much?" Augustine asked them.

"Odders got twinkums. Us no got twinkums. Us jus' big know-nothin' boobies."

"Come now, dear friends; we cannot all lay claim to similar degrees of talents. Now you," he turned to one who had the head of a cart horse and fetlock hairs still growing round his ankles, "you possess magnificent strength. You can carry three times as much wood as any of your friends. You,'" he pointed to another with the head of a gnu, "your speed and leaping power saves much time when you go on scouting expeditions. And you," he addressed another with the head of an ibex, "your sure-footedness when climbing the rocks to seek out the position of the demons is invaluable. Each of you has a talent not necessarily shared to the same degree by others.

"If time were not an important factor, you would all eventually find your stars, but as we must free your land as soon as possible, we will take a short cut. Perima, Tepi and I will make a thought form of a star for each one of you and we will place it on the outside of your stomachs. You can then look down and see it at any time. But you must bring it to life by your thoughts. Imagine it shining like the stars in heaven. Your friends will help you, and in time it will twinkle like those which are already inside some of their bodies."

"Wen us got 'un, wot do's us do wid dem?"

"That is a secret to be revealed when you are ready. All knowledge begins as a secret; it is unveiled only when the seeker for truth has worked hard and earned his prize."

✳ ✳ ✳

We spent a good deal of time endeavouring to make a link with our Teacher-lord and our friends at Onward, but we had little success. We needed those twinkums.

At last a sufficient number found their stars through their own endeavour, and the others proudly displayed the thought forms we had made for them.

We had already chosen a tract of land, farther away from the Homestead than the huts, so that we could practise the Banishing Ritual without the demons gaining knowledge of our activities. Round it we placed many beacons, and we took our places between them.

"Now all must concentrate and will their stars to grow," Augustine told them. "Instead of being either inside or outside your stomachs, they must become so large that they surround you." They grunted and groaned, and contorted their bodies as they panted and gasped for breath, as though they were giving birth – as indeed they were. After many weeks we had what we needed – a circle of large stars, which shone brightly between the beacons.

At our next session, Augustine instructed them: "Think high. Send your thoughts soaring above the black menace of the clouds. Think higher than you have ever thought before. Think of a star so enormous that if it descended amongst us, it would overlap the land on which we stand and us as well. Tell me when you have a clear vision of this Super-Twinkum."

After much groaning and stamping of feet, they began to whinny, baa and moo. Others called out: "Got 'un."

"Now let your stars address their mother. Call 'Mother-star' and at the same time, will a beam of light to leave your stars and travel to Her. Eventually she will answer you."

They intoned "Mudderstar, Mudderstar," first softly and reverently, but gradually increasing in volume to a roar in their desperation as no answering ray pierced the darkness. But their efforts caused tiny wisps of light to emerge from their own stars, although these faded before they had reached no more than an arm's length.

* * *

Day by day we practised until at last a few beams of light, so pale and weak that they were scarcely discernible, pierced the brooding clouds in about a dozen places. A great cheer rang out; this added to the power of the beams until the rays conjoined with ours, and we could see that the light was travelling in both directions, from our stars to Motherstar and back again. Active circuits had been formed.

We then worked until a good contact was gained and also maintained with our friends at Onward; and at last the feeble currents which we had achieved widened until they became one; and a bright, steady light shone over the whole circle.

We were now able to call the Motherstar and the group at will. This success hastened the return of joy to the Anhumans, who showed their delight by running, leaping and patting the glowing stars of their friends as well as their own.

"Us got no corn ter grow; so us grows Twinkums," they kept repeating with satisfied snorts of laughter.

* * *

Then it arrived – the Day.

We awakened our fellow ritualists, impressing on them the necessity for absolute silence, so that the demons would have no warning to enable them to conjure evil from the clouds above or from the sub-earth beneath their feet. We lit the brands from the beacons surrounding the huts, and diminished the resulting light by willpower, until only intermittent sparks remained, these being masked by our hands.

As we scattered and moved stealthily across the sterile fields towards the pillars of fire, we could hear yowls, trumpetings, honks and yelps – the invaders were awake and active. Silently we took up our well-rehearsed positions between the beacons, with Augustine, Nicholas, Tepi and me quartering the circumference.

We removed our hands, which were screening the sparks, and flames leapt from the torches as we began to move, waving them in front of our faces. The sparks flew and settled on the demons nearest to us, but although they were startled, they showed no signs of fear as snapping and snarling they hurled themselves at the dimly-seen figures behind the zig-zagging brands; but the flames kept them at bay.

Our advance continued and they began to retreat, gibbering as they attacked us with their horns and hooves; some turned round and ejected jets of stinking, excoriating fluid towards us. This caused some of the Anhumans to vomit; they broke ranks, but not for long; their whole future was at stake.

When the circle became sufficiently reduced for our purpose, with the demons herded close together, we stopped. Augustine opened the Banishing Ritual by intoning a single note accompanied by the appropriate actions. I have never learned how a man, small of stature and slight in build, could produce such a deep resonant sound: it must have issued from the pit of bygone time.

The Anhuman next to him reproduced the gesture and raised his voice a tone, to be followed by his neighbour doing likewise. This formula was repeated round the half circle until it reached me. As a member of the Fairy Evolution and the element of Air, I can produce much higher sounds than the Human Race. Through the second arc of the circle the notes were stepped down the scale until they reached Augustine again. Then the wave began its upward surge once more, the volume increasing as each cycle became complete.

The vibrations of the first circuit struck the demons; they held their hands over their ears and howled, moaned and screamed. During the second cycle many hurtled through the air, crashing against each other before falling to the ground in a writhing mass of tangled limbs and fury. Others endeavoured to burrow their way to freedom until their claws fell out, and black blood gushed in glutinous streams.

While the third round was in progress, the power of the Ritual took its toll and the invaders became deranged. They rolled on the ground, tearing each other with fangs, horns and talons. They spewed great spurts of bloody pus and ejected clouds of viscous vapour with the stench of depravity and decay. All began to gasp and choke; and the surface of the land became a heaving conglomeration of contorting, fermenting evil.

Above the sonorous rhythm of the intonation and the pandemonium made by the demons, we heard in the distance a booming rumble, which gradually drew nearer. The Anhumans standing between Augustine and

Nicholas drew aside; and through the gap stormed Ra-onus with the roar of an erupting volcano, his flames rearing like wild stallions into the sky.

We withdrew to the perimeter of the land and watched him sweeping in ever-widening circles from the centre to the circumference marked by the beacons, until we felt his heat on our faces. As his flames flickered and died, and the smoke lost its density, we could see that the land, although seared, was cleansed and freed from all dross except for a large mound of heaving, wailing ash in the centre.

He enveloped us all in a soft, warm light as a wind whipped round the rocks; and all that remained of the demons was sucked into a whirling spiral, like a swarm of moaning locusts, which forced its way through the black cumulus overhead.

The wind became a gale; the Anhumans groaned in apprehension until the clouds began to fragment; rain beat down and a torrent of water carried the scorched topsoil away. The lashing wind sank to a whisper and as we watched the erstwhile clouds disintegrate, we could see through a golden mist the Sun and Motherstar side by side.

We raised our arms towards them in heart-felt gratitude, and our fellow ritualists dropped on their knees and kissed and licked the earth; they scooped it up in handfuls and rubbed it over their faces and limbs.

* * *

Augustine, Tepi, Nicholas and I softly chanted the names of the angels. Two points of light appeared in the distance; these became beams, down which glided the presiding deities. The Anhumans ceased their earth-adoring and gazed in wonder at the tall, beautiful beings, garlanded with exotic flowers, their multicoloured robes and hair floating behind them. As they touched the ground and stood towering above us, the earth, so long silenced by corruptions and gloom, began its eternal song once more.

The Anhumans bowed low before them, weeping tears of joy as the Shining Ones beamed their light on each of them in turn. They gently tried to touch their robes, but angelic atoms vibrate at a greater speed than those of humans or their younger brethren, and their hands passed through them. But when they looked at their hands in surprise, they saw that they sparkled; they laughed at this unforeseen wonder and stroked themselves and one another until all glittered with ethereal light.

Tepi, Nicholas and I joined Augustine as he welcomed the angels, whose radiance grew as they rejoiced at their return, but diminished with grief when they gazed on their pillaged land.

The Shining Ones express themselves through thought waves, and Augustine translated their address.

They spoke in unison: "We have shared with you many years of fruitful happiness although you were unaware of our presence. We experienced your fear and suffering when we were all driven away by the descent of the Darkness and the infiltration of Evil. But now that we are reunited, we will work together to restore the land and cause it to bloom as never before. You will not always see us because we live and work on a higher plane, but from time to time we will invoke the power that enables us to manifest here, and we will all rejoice over a new sowing or a bounteous harvest."

They floated over to Nicholas and placed their hands on his head in blessing; then they swept round in a glowing circle, which slowly ascended and disappeared from view.

❊ ❊ ❊

A long silence followed as we pondered on the miracle of the swift dispersal of the clouds following the cleansing and deliverance of the land, and our vision of the angels.

Nicholas' eyes were shining in wonder. "My heart bursts with joy for us all. I thought it would take months of arduous labour before we could see and touch the good brown earth again."

"And so did I," said Augustine. We have received an unexpected gift from the Lords of Nature; this was made possible by the determination and dedication of you all to achieve our purpose against almost impossible odds."

"I have never seen an angel before," Nicholas said pensively. He seemed to have entered a half-dream state, overcome by their beauty, kindness and power. "I did not consider myself worthy."

"But they obviously thought otherwise," said Augustine, "and they will manifest again as promised at the first sowing and the harvest; and Tepi will help you to prepare for their coming."

I felt my whole being contract as though an iron fist had clutched my heart and the life force had ceased to flow. Although my inner self knew that he would not, my persona persisted in hoping that Tepi would return to the Miniature Paradise and work there for a while.

Augustine walked towards me and gently tilted my face, compelling me to look at him. "Both your higher and your lower selves are right. Tepi has earned his reward of rest and replenishment in your Fairy World, as indeed have you and I. The atoms of Dis must be ousted from our material forms and the horror and anguish from our minds, in preparation for our future tasks. But Tepi will later return here to help Nicholas and the Anhumans – and indeed, Koog. That is your wish, is it not, Tepi?"

He came and took me in his arms. "Your destiny and mine have blended for a while but now our paths lie in different directions. I know they will blend again, but next time your Sulic will transform our love duet into a trio."

"You are right, I know. When I am with you, my memory of Sulic fades, although I love him with all my being. Down the ages, we have been together many times but since our previous form-life, my path has led me to both happiness and sorrow, while Sulic's has been one of fun and laughter. After our last brief meeting, he chose to leave his life of pleasure in order to experience suffering. This began for both of us at the moment of separation; but mine has been assuaged by our love for each other. I do not know where Sulic's path has led him, but he needs comforting and only I can give him solace."

This in-built knowledge now rationally expressed, calmed me; we embraced tenderly, but as friends rather than lovers. A maturer, deeper devotion would be ours later.

❦ CHAPTER 23 ❧
OUR RETURN TO ONWARD

Our return to Onward proved to be one of the happiest periods of my life. We had successfully completed a difficult mission; we had received a rapturous welcome from our companions in the struggle against the forces of evil, and now we were to enjoy a period of relaxation and reward.

Tepi and I wandered hand in hand over rolling landscapes canopied with flowers, their stems entwined in love. We found exotic blooms hiding themselves in mountain clefts, their beauty reserved for us alone. We performed aerobatics with the birds; ran races on the backs of fleet-footed cheetahs; and dived into moon-flecked lakes to savour the magic of their liquiform world as we joined the fish in their endless dance.

On our arrival, the colours of our auras had been darkened and blurred, their texture coarsened and their edges frayed. But as they absorbed the sweet-scented air, their defilement gradually dissolved and they shone once more like jewel-bedecked rainbows against leaden skies.

Augustine remained with us, and when he was not conferring with the Shining Ones, we introduced him to trees that walked, flowers which fell from the sky to form and reform intricate patterns for our delight, and fields of corn that grew as tall as pines, so great was their desire to reach the sun.

When we were summoned by our Teacher-Lord, we made our obeisance and received His blessing. A beam of light shone from His brow and pierced us between the eyes. I lost myself and became Him. I was no longer Perima, but a Presence presiding over a vast tract of land, peopled by many races. When my attention encompassed a group, I knew the thoughts of every member. I studied their work patterns over many years as well as their present desires and ambitions. And from these I deduced the likelihood of future success or failure. If one was ambitious beyond his current powers, I transmitted a thought of a wiser plan but left him the freedom to accept or reject it.

I received forces direct from their Source – pure and undefiled by matter; and these were processed by my mind and will for use on the lower planes. A galaxy of angels gathered around me, eager to obey my commands. A thought flash sent them streaming Earthwards. One succoured a dying woman and led her through the misty twilight of death; others soothed the guardian of a tree, its body felled to the ground: years of growth destroyed in minutes for the benefit of Man. One tended an ailing child and others sped to temper rampageous winds in a storm.

It became dark. Roars and screams assaulted my entire being. I became aware of a bloody battle that raged below me, and I watched Perima as a bat, Tepi as a gorilla, and Augustine calmly standing by Ra-onus, beaming light wherever it was needed. I directed power to each, and then I joined a conclave of angels who gazed in sorrow on the tragic scene of Man's cruelty and greed on the Planet of Earth.

I too became sad at the Human Error, but then I rejoiced as a radiance revealed small groups of people who tended the poor, the sick, and those who had not yet reached a stage in their evolution when they could contend with the problems of their lives alone.

Between these glittered tiny, luminous specks, as though a giant sower had scattered millions of glow-worms over the land. These were men and women who, through many incarnations, had developed their inner light and reached the understanding that the Planet of Earth is a testing ground where disappointments and tribulations teach patience, perseverance and self-control. When their problems are overcome, a sense of achievement, followed by calm content are ample rewards for their striving. Most of these people were considered of little account by their richer, more powerful brethren, but in reality, they were superior to those who held them in mild contempt.

✻ ✻ ✻

We had many discussions with Augustine and our Teacher-Lord, and sometimes we were given glimpses of our future lives. Tepi would spend many years with the Anhumans, teaching them to develop their faculties of Will – the power of the Fairy Evolution. Their Homestead, having been dragged by demons to Cimmerian depths and restored to the Angels through Fire and Sound, would become a famous Centre of Progress where people at different stages of evolution would gather and learn from one another.

Those with special skills developed from their animal instincts, would teach them to those more intellectually advanced than themselves. Then their pupils would become their teachers by helping to develop their minds.

Eventually they would become Human beings and Nicholas, after a span on the Astral Plane, would return to Earth as a community leader. Koog would remain with Tepi until he reached the Elfin grade, when he would join a group which tended woodland life.

Having reached the required stage in spiritual growth through compassion and understanding of a race more primitive than his own, Tepi would leave the Homestead and become a teacher to members of his own Evolution. In the distant future he would follow the path of a seeker and revealer of the Mysteries of the Universe.

As my story unfolds, that which was then my future will gradually be disclosed. All futures are roads which lead us, and when we are young we have only one, but as we mature, two or three paths may confront us and we choose which one to follow.

❆   ❆   ❆

During the remaining weeks when the three of us were together, we explored each other's minds. I had already entered Tepi's when he had taken me back in time in order to find the incident which had caused him to lose his memory; and also more recently, on the occasions when we three had blended during our training for the battle in the Hatreds' Domain. But now that our love for one another had grown, all was freely revealed and we learned not only about the other two, but also about ourselves.

From Augustine, Tepi and I gained further knowledge of the thought processes of Man when encased in a solid body. And through us he learned the freedom of forms and minds which know the lesser restriction of more ethereal particles than his own.

We frequently exchanged power: this was always for a purpose, because it must never be wasted. Used correctly, it proliferates and releases other forces for the project in hand, which at that time was to gain a clearer understanding of our destiny,

We also blended in love. I cannot describe what happened when Augustine and Tepi were one, because they are both males; and as a female I would find it difficult if not impossible to translate their experience. Tepi always emerged from these blendings in a semi trance-like state, which remained for several hours. And then all he could say was: "The Power, oh the blessed Power! I knew everything. I was everything. There was nothing I could not achieve!"

When Tepi and I were united, our love flowed around us and from one to the other. We knew the ecstasy experienced when two opposites mingle and produce a third existence, which manifests the characteristics of both its creators. I now understood Tepi's male attributes: his love of power and achievement, and his fervent desire to bring order to chaos. Streams of ideas for the betterment of Man, Fairy and all other forms of life as well flowed endlessly without purpose until they formed a circle. They now had containment, and within this protective barrier they sped. The ideas met, conjoined or rejected each other; those that blended rushed on to form other combinations and gain experience on their seemingly endless journey until the ideas became facts, his male power now tamed by my female gift of stability.

After many unions and countless discussions, we realized that we had proved a fundamental Truth: Power needs Matter in order to manifest.

When Augustine joined us, he, through meditation and his incarnations on Earth, contributed far more knowledge of the Evolutionary Path than we could. How can I describe this microcosmic trinity? The free-flowing power became a controlled force: passion and tenderness were one: the desire to receive became an obsession to give. All grew within us, expanding outwards until, in our yearning for realisation, like an exploding star we burst. We lost our capacity to think, either as individuals, or as a Triune being, as we entered and became the Great Unknown.

❈ ❈ ❈

The joyous days flew by and as the hour of our parting drew near, Tepi and I spent all our time in each other's company and being. We became, aware that this well mitred link would not weaken, even when we lived on different planes and did not meet for many years.

Our farewells when they took place, though tearful, were tempered by the knowledge that, sometime in the future, we would be together again although, as Tepi had foreseen, as a trio not a duet.

Augustine remained with me at Onward acting as my tutor, and he led me along many paths of knowledge until it was time for us too to part.

Lost in a sea of memories, my immediate future unknown, I returned to work with my friends in their construction of Thoughts Formations. But I found that their activities seemed to me like a game when one fits small coloured fragments together to form a picture, rather than being an absorbing task, welding essential constituents into a whole which, when completed, would be used to benefit others.

The work was the same; it was I who had changed. I wondered whether my discontent was caused by some aspect of the Hatreds' venture which I had failed to rationalize or eradicate from my mind.

CHAPTER 24
THE NEXT STAGE
IN MY DEVELOPMENT

I awaited a summons from my Teacher-Lord. When it came, I stood before Him uncertain of my present ability to perform, even adequately, any task which he might allot me.

"Precious Pearl," He said gently, and I bowed low twice in acknowledgment of this unusual form of address. "You have reached a stage in your life when you are to make the decision in regard to its next phase. Up to the present each project has been given to you as a form of education; but now, your close alliance with a human being, and one as advanced as Augustine, has given you the stability of mind to enable you to decide which path to follow next."

"You have three choices: Firstly, you can go to a Temple of Wisdom and continue your studies of Augustine's teachings. Secondly, you can join your life with Sulic's once more. He is living on a plane close to Earth, receiving its contaminating radiations as he works with beings who have completed their span on the planet, but have failed to carry out their appointed tasks. He is submerged in an atmosphere of depression and despair. To you, who have been surrounded by hatred, fear and physical suffering for many months, the conditions would be easy to combat. But Sulic, the lover of jokes and laughter, finds the constant abasement of spirit difficult to overcome. I must therefore warn you that, although your presence, for which he yearns, would doubtless alleviate his dejection, it would also cause him to relinquish the struggle and immerse himself in your love. Finally, you can enter into retreat in order to learn about yourself, not through your reactions to other people and events, but by seeking and finding the Silence, and, paradoxically, eventually to hear within it the rhythmic beat of the Cosmic Heart."

To make a choice is always a responsibility. Here were three paths stretching out before me, with no indication as to which would lead me in the right direction. I longed to be with Sulic to help him through his experience of anti-joy, but to mitigate this discipline could well retard his progress for many years.

Augustine's teaching had enabled me to solve many mysteries through meditation on symbols – external forms with secret meanings, released through concentration. How would I fare when I endeavored to not lose myself in order to enter a higher state of being, but rather to relinquish my "I" entirely and become the Impartial Truth?

He smiled at me confidently. "You have decided, have you not?"

"In reality, there is no choice."

"I said 'You must choose' and you have done so. When I say 'You' I am not referring to you, Perima, but to your Higher Self, whom you have reached occasionally during meditation. She has the knowledge and experience of all your past form-lives and she knows the path which you should tread. But you have the right to defy her decision."

I sighed. "I yearn to be with Sulic, but not if my presence will hinder his evolution. I would very much like to stay with Augustine, but this chance has not been offered to me. I love him. I feel safe with him even when danger is on the prowl. But I know that I must accept your last proposal: I will go into retreat."

"Come with me then, and we will begin the next stage of your development now."

"You are to be my Mentor?" I asked in amazement. I had imagined being incarcerated in a mountain cave, far from other entities; but I was to remain and learn from Him, whom I revered and loved more than any member of my Evolution.

Again, he smiled; and when a Great One smiles, it is not just a movement of the lips and a light in the eye, but an expansion of the aura, which surrounds and enters the recipient. Always He reveals a blinding beauty; He is of tremendous stature on formal occasions. But if it is His will, He is only a little taller than I am when we are alone together. His eyes are authoritative, humourous or kind. His radiance is many-hued and His form changes with every thought.

He turned, and, as in a dream, I followed Him, unable to believe that I was to live in His Presence for the next part of my life. We walked through His Palace, a gleaming structure of light, its rooms denoted only by rows of graceful pillars, up which climbing plants wound themselves in perpetual motion of ecstatic growth. There was no roof or ceiling – only sun, moon or starlit skies according to the need or desire of those who raised their eyes to confer with nature.

We passed through many compartments, each having a special purpose.

One bestowed peace, another stimulation. A third brought symmetry to confused thought patterns. And in a fourth, the gently stirring breeze changed from a whisper to a sudden gust of inspiration. These, and many more He explained to me, and I wondered how I could ever shed my Perima-self among such opposite and diverse surroundings. Indeed, would I wish to do so?

He turned towards me. "I am here when you need me; a thought will bring Me to your side. These rooms are for your use alone."

My eyes widened. "But do I need so much space? I am not very big; I might get lost."

"That is why you are here: To lose yourself. But to be lost is not the same as being confused. It is to enable you to discard what you consider to be your attributes: Your form, your aspirations and all the exterior trappings which you regard as Perima. These are not real; they are safety-valves with which you reassure yourself."

"What will I become? How will those I love, or indeed anyone, recognise me?"

"You will not lose your Divine Spark or your prime atoms. At present you need your components as many need a home; but your desire for them will diminish until eventually in the distant future you will reach the stage when they are superfluous. Then and then only will you be free to manifest your Real Self."

* * *

He left me in my palace-within-a-Palace and I wondered with increasing amazement at the riches bestowed on me. All the materials were of ethereal silks with the texture and scent of flowers. The wall space was composed of opaque coloured light, and I knew that their many hues with their minutely graded tones would condition my mind for whatever was to come. There were stairways which both ascended and descended from the compartments. Those going upwards wound their way above the pillars, seemingly to the stars above. Others formed steep flights downwards in apparently endless spirals.

There were reclining areas which looked like the still waters of a lake. "Would I sink if I lay on one?" I idly thought. "If so, where would I go?" I experienced a moment of fear when I recalled falling down pits on the way to the Hatreds' Domain, and I realized that the memories which I thought I had erased were not dead but could return and reclaim me if my vigilance weakened. I composed myself and deliberately lay on the soft, cool surface. I did not sink, but floated as though on perfumed air, and in a moment I was asleep.

I had of course spent periods of rest and meditation over many years and the only time that loneliness had besieged me was when I had lived and worked in the Wilderness. Now, my solitude was pure joy.

My surroundings produced an infinite variety of conditions, all of which I was eager to try. After so much tumult in the Underworld, I decided to seek a balance for this surfeit through peace. The room of my choice was in many shades of blue. I wore a soft azure robe and placed forget-me-nots in my hair. I lay down, closed my eyes and breathed deeply and evenly, concentrating on the idea of equilibrium. As on previous occasions, I attained a feeling of perfect tranquility; but this was not what I sought. My need was not merely for a state devoid of sensation or thought, but for Peace Absolute. My perseverance led me close to this abstraction, but on each occasion, I fell asleep and lost the becoming and the Being.

During my recreation hours, I studied Augustine's teachings or walked in my private gardens where each bloom was perfect and every tree appeared to be watching me and following my progress with interest. The grass on which I strolled or lay emitted tiny, soothing sounds, helping me to live in peace while striving to reach its heart.

I decided to call my Teacher-Lord only if I failed to make adequate progress, and then, only after I had discovered the reason for my lack of success, and endeavored to rectify it in my way of life. All thoughts of the Hatreds had now been destroyed, not merely relegated to the appropriate area in my subconscious. And close up, it was as though they had never been, unless I deliberately resuscitated their ghosts for a purpose.

I recalled my present life span backwards, in order to discover whether any of my experiences had left aspects which had remained untamed like Tepi's beasts. But I found nothing to cause me undue concern. I had fallen below my own and other people's standards on many occasions, but failure has its purpose and from it I had learned patience, humility and perseverance. At the same time, my will had been strengthened to enable me to solve a similar problem when it raised its mocking head again.

Yet I knew that my present being contained a serious flaw and I was also certain that it was associated with Sulic. Somehow, I had failed him, and I decided to delve deeply into all my Form-lives and find the answer. I returned to our last, short time together, when I was a student teacher, and I pondered on the reason why Sulic had remembered me instantly, while I had been ignorant of our love until he reminded me. My subconscious had built for itself a protective barrier. Sulic had not revealed all, and now I must root out my failure and rectify my offence.

We were old, our auras tinged with the colours of the soil, denoting that we were humble peasants. But through this outer, somber casing, our love shone with a steady glow, and I knew that this particular lifespan did not hold the key to my problem. Many memories returned. I let them flash and fade in quick succession, until a sequence of events came to a sudden halt, and I found myself face to face with a dragon. Shock propelled me from my semitrance with a scream. I covered my eyes with shaking hands, but the symbol remained. What dire sin had I committed to be thus branded with the dreaded stigma of the dragon?

I could not think constructively. No one is perfect and I was fully aware of my faults, but this accusing image proclaimed more than an ordinary misdemeanor. I did not call Him. He came and stood beside me as I lay face downwards with my head buried in my arms.

"Stand up," He said. I rose to my feet and bowed. "Forgive me, blessed Lord, I failed to detect Your Presence."

"I do not mean stand up physically. Stand and face this error in your past, as you frequently confronted the iniquities of the World when you fought the Hatreds in their fury."

"You do not condemn me then?"

"Neither condemn nor chastise. Like everyone else, you stumbled on the slippery path which leads to salvation. Your sin was to harm another grievously, without remorse. You were not even aware of the wound which you inflicted, a wound that could not heal during that lifespan because you frequently reopened it."

"What did I do?"

"That is for you to discover." He was gone and I was left to retrace my steps into the nightmare of my transgression.

I tried every compartment in turn, hoping for inspiration or guidance that would lead me to my dragon in order to appease her. I considered asking for permission to visit Sulic so that he could take me back in time. But I knew that this was not the way. I must find the truth for myself.

❊ ❊ ❊

I was seated in the centre of an empty room, trying to free myself from shame to allow me to think more clearly, when I saw a tiny aperture in one of the walls. It was no more than a chink, and was too small for me to enter. I stood looking at it for some time. Then I dissolved my body and wafted through it.

It was cold. I began to shiver. I shook until my thoughts were whirling together like fallen leaves in a gust of wind. I was blown in a thousand pieces along a passage, coming to a halt in total darkness. Having gathered myself together, I found that I was no longer afraid. It was as though a new set of atoms now formed my body. My mind knew the purpose of my presence here, but that was all.

I felt myself propelled slowly forward towards a crowd of people in the distance. My heart leapt with excitement. I ran towards them and joined in a wild, bacchanalian dance. Drums beat, pipes wailed, cymbals clashed. Consumed by lust, I flung myself eagerly into the fray, clutching and being clutched, entered by and entering others with total abandon and ferocious zest.

I heard a voice in the distance. "My love, where are you?"

My hair was clutched in the blood-stained hands of a hideous brute with festering sores. As he dragged me closer to Sulic, I shouted: "Go away and let me alone, you fool." He clawed my breasts as I shrieked and writhed in orgasmic glee; and as the debauch became more frenzied, my lechery increased. I was violently possessed by numerous partners and transferred to many more, and gripped by a bestial joy in my willing surrender and total rejection of restraint and love.

Sulic braved the black rite and bore my shattered body home. For many weeks I lay in a coma, through which he nursed me with tender care. When consciousness eventually returned, I awoke to his gentle smile, his white teeth gleaming in his shiny, black face; but there was sadness in his eyes.

"I warned you," he said quietly as he stroked my hands.

"I had to know. I enjoyed it," I replied defiantly.

"You were overcome by the forces of Darkness – not by pleasure. You were too sure of your power to resist. I have watched you after your sessions with the so-called Master and your fellow initiates. You were as a stranger, intoxicated by the beat of the drums, the stamping feet, the nauseating stench of animals' entrails, and by repeated demands to sacrifice self to appease the gods. You only laughed when I begged you to stop. Your willfulness has led to your downfall."

"It is all part of experience," I said lightly. "You are too prudish; it would do you good to stumble sometimes."

"We have performed all these antics in our past lives. I no longer need them. Why do you?"

"I have a dragon within me, and when it licks me, I have to respond."

"We both slayed our dragons during our previous span on the lower astral plane. Have you forgotten?"

"I kept the tongue as a memento," I said, pursing my lips and wrinkling my nose coquettishly.

"Are you sorry?"

"Let us say it was a final fling. Now take me in your arms and love me."

Regaining part of my consciousness, I realized that when Sulic had said "Are you sorry?", he was not referring to my behavior; he was asking me if I regretted causing him pain. In my youthful waywardness I cared nothing for the suffering I was inflicting on him when I, whom he loved and knew so well, changed beyond recognition and willingly returned to the bottomless Pit of Degradation and wallowed in its filth.

I wept.

Our reconciliation was but a prelude to my further debasement. Sulic implored me to leave the cult and return to our normal, loving way of life, but the dragon's tongue never failed to seduce me, and I continued to take part in the black art rites.

Sulic always hovered in the background until exhaustion claimed me; then he would sadly carry me home. My craving was stronger than his love: I never tired of the corruption, and my lust remained unsated. But as the years passed by, my body lost its agility, my limbs stiffened and my beauty died. I was banned from the orgies by a younger Master, but I watched the action from outside the circle, brooding on the past and mourning my youth.

Old age finally claimed me and I sat all day outside our hut, impotent but still dreaming. On the completion of my form life, I was withdrawn to a lower plane to toil among withered trees and the grey, straggling weeds that I now resembled. Under my care, the plants eventually began to bloom – and so did I. Gradually I was rehabilitated, and I was sent to join a group that was tending flowering shrubs in a garden.

I retained no memory of my depravity, or of Sulic and his loving care. When we met again during successive form lives, we were strangers as far as I was concerned, and he never told me about my lapse, only that he loved me.

✳ ✳ ✳

I was distraught. I wandered from room to room in a daze of misery and shame, not knowing where to look or how to find a way to expiate my sin.

Ought I to ask for permission to visit Sulic, throw myself at his feet and tell him of my bitter remorse? Should I insist on staying with him in order to serve him as well as those with whom he lived and worked? But in my heart, I knew that he would refuse this act of contrition, which he would consider demeaning, because he not only loved but also revered me. Although he must have known full-well my many acts of debasement, when I had grovelled shamelessly before lust, he frequently called me his goddess during our various form lives. How could I ever repay him for his selfless devotion?

Before seeing him again, I must find and slay my dragon; she was a part of me, and it was essential that I destroy her. Then, and then only could I face Sulic, tell him I was free and beg his forgiveness.

Or should I appeal to my Teacher-Lord for advice? I was not by nature a slayer of beasts, even one of my own contriving. Was it possible that, as the black art had overcome me then, my dragon could do so even now? I decided that this was highly improbable, having witnessed the Hatreds performing many forms of sexual depravity, which had always filled me with disgust. The act of blending and exchanging power had replaced all grosser forms of coupling many life spans ago, and I was confident that I could face my dragon with the knowledge that never again could she tempt me.

How and where could I find her? It would clearly be unwise to seek her whereabouts through meditation, because this might alert her to my intention to confront and, I hope, vanquish her. This was a problem that I must take to my Teacher-Lord. No sooner had I made the decision than He was beside me.

"You are wise, Perima. You would not have defeated the Hatreds without My aid, and you will not overcome your dragon without me now. Never underestimate the forces of evil, and you will not succumb to their wiles again."

"Where is she?"

"She is within you."

I shuddered.

"You have an underworld, as has the Universe. She dwells in a subterranean cave, but she is no more dangerous than the Hatreds or Tepi's beasts. You overcame them did you not?"

"With laughter?" I asked doubtfully.

"Exactly! Laughter is the most effective weapon you can use against vice because love is beyond its experience and ability comprehend."

"I do not feel like laughing," I said, as tears ran down my cheeks.

"This is understandable. But turn your thoughts back into the past. How did you eventually make Tepi laugh?"

The memory caused my lips to twitch in a miniature smile. "By watching the cartoons of the fairy who continually found himself in ridiculous situations."

"That is true. The cartoons were right for Tepi, but I shall take you to My personal playground."

I shook my head. "Nothing will make me laugh again – ever."

"Calm yourself, Perima. Since the event of her birth, your dragon has been exactly where she is now – hidden in the depths of your subconscious. During this time, you have enjoyed much happiness.. The knowledge of her presence will not stop the spring of your laughter from bubbling into your life for long. We will give it some encouragement. Come with me."

We floated side by side above a wide sandy shore and drifted downwards to land at the water's edge, where a small boat was anchored. We stepped on board and no sooner had we settled ourselves on the cushioned seats, than we were away, skimming the surface at tremendous speed. The waves became choppy, and the boat bucked and reared like a young work horse put out to grass.

We soared through the air in a climbing spiral, somersaulting wildly before twisting downwards in a breath-stopping dive, which eased only seconds before reaching the water. The wind chuckled in my ears and the spray teased our bodies as we rode the waves at a more leisurely pace.

My Teacher-Lord began to laugh – emitting from his being, not his lips alone, a sequence of joyful, staccato notes, which caressed both sea and breeze. Excited by the speed of our aerial jaunt and relieved at our safe return, I joined him, my voice soaring up and down the scale in heartfelt thanksgiving.

The boat came to rest at the shore's edge and we looked at each other, still smiling. "It was not so difficult, was it?"

"It was wonderful. How can I thank you for returning this precious gift that I thought was lost forever?"

"Together we will laugh each day, and together we will rout your dragon."

❊ ❊ ❊

He kept His promise, and every morning He took me to a new location. Mountains provided shining glissades, down which we gently slid, or alternatively sped like shooting stars. Winding paths rose and fell, turned sharp corners, or propelled us into the sky, presenting us with vistas of snow-clad, sun-blessed peaks below.

We sometimes travelled by water, at others by air. We flew over landscapes of such wondrous beauty that my breath caught in my throat. The flowers and trees, their form expressed through light alone, reached up and touched us with tingling fingers of power, as we floated slowly above them.

Finally, we entered a rocket of fire. Crackling with laughter, it streaked skywards, leaving my mind at the starting point. When body and consciousness met once more, we were hurtling past planets and stars as though they were milestones. We dived and rolled, the flaming slipstream creating circles and loops, through which we later sped. Intricate new patterns, which burst like melodious thunderclaps into whirling eddies of colour and sound, formed and reformed in endless succession.

The speed at which we travelled and the unpredictable whims of our blazing transport released my tensions and filled me with joy. The veering winds blew away the last of my doubts and fears, and provided fresh atoms, on which to impress new exciting ideas. I lost my guilt and found my inner self once more.

"Blessed Lord," I said as we landed, "we are like children. I did not know that Shining Ones enjoyed such simple recreations."

"You are learning other truths than those expounded in mystic teachings," he explained, his eyes twinkling. "The more complex the work, the less sophisticated are the pleasures that we need, to maintain our equilibrium. And what could be more effective than delights provided by the elements? I have enjoyed our journeys as much as you; but now we must turn our minds to more serious matters."

He led me to a compartment that I had not previously entered, and showed me a flight of stairs which seemed to descend into black obscurity. "Your dragon is there," he said.

"Do I go down step by step until I find her?"

"Quests are not usually as straightforward as that," he replied. "There will be hazards to overcome. Dragons are rarely solitary beasts: they gather around them elementals, nefarious creatures, and others of their own kind, the powers of which must first be negated. This time you will not have Augustine and Tepi with you to give you tangible and visible support. But I will be here, watching over you, and my power will reach you wherever you may be. You will not, in reality, be alone."

CHAPTER 25

THE DRAGON TAMER

He left me and I sat on the top step as I probed with my mind the depths into which the stairway led, hoping to gain an intuitive idea of the conditions I was about to encounter. On previous perilous occasions, Augustine's consciousness followed me whether my bat form was flying, climbing the rock face, or crawling on the ground. How would I know when some hidden danger might pounce from the air behind me, or leap from under my feet, now that he would not be there to warn me?

I gathered my courage together and began to wend my way slowly downwards. Only the first twelve steps were made of gold; the second dozen were of iron, and the rest of crumbling stone. I waved my arms in front of my face, then all around me, but they touched nothing. The stairway seemed to meander through space. I sensed a deep, murky pit, down which I could hear small rocks falling. Beyond this, my mind could not reach.

With my next movement, I brought my will into play, to ensure that I should float rather than fall the rest of the way. My caution proved superfluous because the air was so thick that, after the first two yards, I was obliged to thrust my body downwards until I landed on the edge of a turgid pool, which gurgled and coughed, as it spewed up countless, lugubrious toads, which crouched at my feet and eyed me with venom.

Staring back at them I said softly, "Little brothers, I mean you no harm. Pray move aside that my journey to the dragon's abode may continue." Their eyes grew gradually larger until they burst, spraying an evil-smelling, sticky liquid in my direction. I willed a protective shield around me, and no harm was done.

"If you do not make way, I must force you to do so." They remained stationary, their eyes gradually returning to their normal form, then expanding for a further attack. I held my hands towards them with light beaming from every finger until they disappeared to join their companions in the heaving depths of the pool. So great was their number that I was able to walk over their bodies to reach the other side, where the waterlogged ground was covered with fetid, fomenting slime. I frequently stumbled, but each time a force helped me to regain my balance and trudge on.

I groped my way through an area filled with crawling snakes, which wound themselves round me and impeded my progress. But apart from these inoffensive, stalling tactics, they displayed no evil intent. Then dozens of bats swooped down and flapped their wings about my head. These were creatures I knew from the past; and I could understand the meaning of some of their squeals. I decided to recreate and enter my old bat form and join them. I rose from the ground and clung to the rock face, touching them whenever possible so that my thought body would absorb their smell and vibrations. At some given signal they all began to fly in the same direction with me in their midst. I hoped they would lead me to the beast I was seeking.

A female dragon lay on the floor of a cavern, lashing her tail, her eyes blazing in anger. I wondered what my companions had done to warrant her disapproval. Deep, rumbling sounds arose like giant belches from the depths of her belly, but I could not decipher their meaning.

"We f-found her. We l-l-l-ost her" one replied nervously.

The dragon threw up her head erupting a resounding "Aaahh!" A cross between a thunderclap and a banshee's wail rent the air. Her tail thrashed from side to side, fire streamed from her nostrils, and the bats near her were crushed or burned.

I carefully edged my way to the back of the quivering group and found a crevice, in which I hid while I waited for the dragon to fall asleep with her retainers on guard around her. I then flew several sorties round the cave and made a mental note of crannies in which to crawl, should she realize that I was not what I appeared to be, but rather her lost antagonist.

❊ ❊ ❊

When she awoke, one blood-red eye swiveled in all directions, checking the position of every bat, in case it was not at its proper post. Fortunately, she appeared to be unable to count, and ignored me as I clung to the rock-face behind her.

She proceeded to perform her morning routine. She reared up clumsily on her hind legs and took two or three attempts to reach full stretch, when her head almost touched the roof. Spurts of fire were then ejected with great force; these ricocheted and singed several of the unfortunate bats, which were not sufficiently alert to move out of range. She then sank to the ground in an ungainly heap, waving her tail as though beating time to some inaudible music. After a while, she straightened and began to groom herself, sticking her long, hooked claws down her ears, up her nose and finally poking them between her jaws and picking each tooth with precision. It seemed to me that there was a distinct streak of vanity in this dragon, because, when her toilet was complete, the bats were required to gather round and, I presumed, admire the results of her labors.

A stroll along various passages was her next occupation, or maybe it was a tour of inspection. She ambled along at a leisurely pace, yawning occasionally as though she was short of sleep, or perhaps suffering from boredom.

Somehow, I could not take this dragon seriously. Of what had I been so afraid? She was but the hideous personification of my lust, which was no longer active. My real sin was to cause suffering to one who loved me. Could this beast have a much more sinister twin, dwelling in the bowels of Dragonia?

I decided that this travesty of the monster that I was seeking must be changed, not slain. Laughter can not only kill; it can also amuse. Perhaps this dragon needed to learn how to laugh, as had Tepi's beasts.

I flew across the cavern, landed on her back and gently dug my teeth into the top of her horny head in order to attract her attention. She snapped her jaws together in a rather desultory manner – more as a protest against a slight discomfort than in anger. I clambered down her snout and proceeded to blow up her nose. This was obviously a new experience, and she sucked in a tremendous gulp of air and sneezed: "A-choo - A-choo - A-a-a-choooo" in a rising crescendo. The sound reverberated through the cavern, up the connecting passages, bounced off the walls and returned, until the whole area was filled with a seemingly endless succession of explosive sounds.

I had fortunately foreseen the likelihood of some such reaction, though I had not anticipated its magnitude, and I had backed well out of range. The bats had fled at the first "A-choo" and were all safely hidden. By the time the attack had ceased, the dragon was lying exhausted on her side. I crawled up close to her and tickled her by running my snout up and down and along her exposed belly. She squirmed and rolled, presenting first one side and then the other for attention. Gurgles gushed from her grinning jaws; she was enjoying herself.

Day after day I tended her, adding new agreeable touches for her pleasure. The soles of her feet proved susceptible to my attentions, as did the tip of her tail, and she enjoyed having her head fanned by my wings. Needless to state, I became her favorite retainer, and she would gaze at me with her bulging eyes. Could it have been with affection?

Obviously, I could not stay forever, amusing an amiable dragon. So, I devised a plan that would allow me to leave, but at the same time ensure that she was kept reasonably happy and therefore good tempered. I began to listen carefully to the sounds that the bats made, because, although their basic language was intelligible to me, to "speak" it was still beyond me. I did my best to copy their squeals and then watched for their reactions, if any. Eventually, they correctly followed my calls to swoop, climb or cling. At last, I learned the sound which meant "Follow me," but I was still not sure whether this could also be translated, "Do what I do."

I decided to put my surmise to the test. Gazing intently at a large male as we clung side by side to the rock face, I directed my newly-discovered squeak towards him before flying down and landing close to the dragon's jaws. The big bat followed and crouched down near me. I blew a sharp breath at him, then repeated my action very gently in the dragon's direction, in order not to disturb her. My companion seemed nervous, but he soon responded to my insistent squawks and blew, with me, up the dragon's nose. Our combined efforts elicited the hoped for sneeze, but this time it was one that any self-respecting dragon could enjoy, rather than be brought to a state of prostration, as before.

From then on, the big bat became the main sneeze-producer, while I remained by his side, encouraging him with old and newly-learned calls. The sessions proved to be of benefit to all, because the violent expulsion of breath gradually took the place of the fire-spurting; and fewer bats became either incapacitated or extinct.

I gradually initiated the big male into the art of dragon-entertaining, and when he became proficient, I trained several others, so that the great beast could sneeze and roll on her back, waving her feet in the air and exposing her belly to be tickled, all day long if she so wished.

I left, feeling that I had performed a worthwhile task in turning a bored and spiteful dragon into a contented and benign bat-mistress.

✷ ✷ ✷

I made my way back to my apartment for replenishment and a much-needed rest before setting out once more to seek my real dragon.

My Teacher-Lord was waiting for me at the top of the stairway and welcomed me home. Then he said, "The first part of your quest has now been completed. The second will commence after a period of preparation.

No effete embodiment of surfeited lust will await you next time, but a cunning and vicious antagonist, a successful attack from whom could prove lethal."

I could feel myself shrink with dismay. "You are weary, Precious Pearl, more from the oppressive atmosphere than from the difficulties that you successfully overcame. Rest now." He bent down, and because I was now of diminutive size, he picked me up in one hand and tenderly placed me on a miniature bank of flowers. After gratefully inhaling the exquisite perfume, I fell asleep.

He was still standing beside me when I awoke, and he began to describe the conditions and some of the hazards which might be encountered. "I will be with you throughout your venture, but I cannot tell you how to overcome the various problems which will confront you, because they are yours. Only a correct reaction from you can solve each one as it presents itself, and at the same time give you the experience that you need to deal successfully with those that follow."

"You said that my dragon might make a lethal attack. Could she annihilate me?"

"I used this particular term to impress upon you the very grave injury that she could inflict on you. But you are stronger than she is in will, valor, determination and the desire to overcome. She has venom, physical strength and demonic power. All these negative characteristics you met and mastered in your battle with the Hatreds. But then you were supported by the actual presence of Augustine and Tepi. Now, apart from my ever-watchful eye, you will be alone."

"You are telling me, are you not, that my participation in that conflict was not solely an errand of mercy to rescue Tepi's hatred and rid him of the trauma of past errors, but was also to train me for my own future search for redemption."

"That is true," he sighed. "If only everyone understood the value of what are considered unpleasant experiences, their suffering would be less and they would acquire the necessary knowledge to solve their future problems."

❉ ❉ ❉

During the following weeks my Teacher-Lord again escorted me round the different compartments, and taught me how to draw on the particular power of each. He also led me into pressurized darkness to acclimatize my body to a condition of constant restriction once more. He arranged mock dangers to quicken my reactions. Winged reptiles swooped from above and endeavored to bear me away in their horny talons. I was gripped from behind in the deadly embrace of a writhing python, and screaming creatures with flailing arms reared up from the ground and dragged me to the threshold of a gaping pit. But always I remembered the appropriate power in time. Talons were relaxed before I left the floor, the python was paralyzed and the creatures sent hurtling headlong into the depths of their counterfeit cavity. I became more mentally alert and acquired powers of greater potency and diversity, with which to protect myself. But above all, I developed more confidence than I had ever known before.

CHAPTER 26
DRAGONIA

The day came when I once more stood at the top of the stairway, and with his final blessing, I descended step by step until it came to an end, and I was faced with the black hole – the vertical passage that would eventually lead me to Dragonia.

Linking my mind with that of my Teacher-Lord, I leapt into the centre and again began to force my way through the resistant gloom, past the pool of venomous toads, and through a substance like stinging oil, until I was forcibly ejected and landed on my knees on an unyielding surface, where I remained, bruised and shaken, for several minutes.

When I finally looked about me, a forbidding sight met my eyes. Dark, brooding rocks, heaved out of the dying soil countless eons ago, were scattered over a barren land. Not a single plant struggled for life, no hardy insect scuttled, no snake slithered across the dusty ground, as far as my vision reached. The only movement came from the fires, which blazed everywhere. In the Hatreds' domain, the fires had consumed matter frequently fed to them by stokers. But here they gushed from the rocks, leapt from the ground, or flashed above my head in lurid streaks with tongues of flame, which dived and licked my body.

"Fire is not malign," I reminded myself. "Ra-onus was basically kind and protective; his death-dealing powers were used only against the forces of evil. I am not evil, except for this sin from my past, and I need the destructive aspect of fire. My dragon must burn out my canker before I destroy her."

The air was heavy with smoke and smuts, which settled on my body and face including my eyes, obstructing my vision. I therefore decided to travel through the fire, because my assertion that the flames would not harm me had conferred on me a partial unity with the element, even in this, its negative, aspect.

Instead of connecting tunnels of rock, as there had been in the Hatreds' domain, here there were paths of fire that streaked and crackled in all directions. I stood before the entrance to each in turn, listening, testing and tuning myself to detect the slightest response to the vibrations I was emitting.

Four of them neither caused me harm nor gave me encouragement. But the fifth roared forward in its efforts to burn me. While not succeeding in its purpose, the heat drove me back to the bottom of the black hole, where I sat, considering how to neutralize the fire's hostile intent.

Returning mentally to my miniature palace, I lay on a pool of cool, calm water. When its soothing properties had taken their full effect, I began to move slowly forward, wrapped in a protective liquid capsule. I approached the corridor of fire, and its guardian withdrew, hissing in hatred. As I was passing the entrance, flames surrounded and tried to engulf me; but they failed to pierce my cocoon of water, an element beyond their experience.

My safety cylinder bore me through and then away from the blazing tunnel. When it released me, I found myself in another cavern, dark and menacing, with the usual echoing sounds of groans, screams and roars. For several minutes I remained motionless but fully alert, as I stood in the now decapsulated water and drew down power from my Teacher-Lord. However, no owners of the voices revealed themselves and no hidden menace attacked me.

This cavern too had many exits, each one needing testing for its reaction as had those of the fire tunnels. It was as though an invisible barrier blocked the first. Another not only refused to admit me, but blew me half way across the enclosure. A third remained passive, but the fourth sucked me in like an angry whirlpool, spun me round at increasing speed, and discharged me like a missile to land on the edge of yet another seemingly endless stretch of rocky ground.

❊ ❊ ❊

It took me several minutes to re-assemble not only my body atoms, but also those of my mind, which were scattered over a wide area. But as nothing can fragment one's inner core, which acts as a magnet for its constituent parts, I soon became a functional unit once more.

After a rest I began to move, uncertain of what I was seeking. Indeed, there seemed to be nothing to find in this vast area of forgotten and abandoned matter. In the distance was a rocky promontory, which drew me towards it. Upon arrival I found a large opening. Was this the entrance to my dragon's lair?

My Teacher-Lord would certainly know what lay hidden inside this gaping hole, and ensure the right reaction.

A cold, yet searing wind sprang up as though to deter me from venturing further. I therefore turned and searched for a hollow in which to hide, and eventually found a deep depression with a short passage leading to a small cell. As there was no sign of a recent inhabitant, I crawled inside and was soon asleep.

When I awoke, a voice greeted me, "Be still. Await the dragon's exit from his lair." At first, I was aware only of the howling wind, but after a while I heard the sound of heavy footsteps as though a giant was slowly approaching. I made my way along the passage and peered through the exit to see a huge horned head only a few feet from my face. My first instinct was to scream, but a sharp command, "Silence", froze the sound in my throat. I held my breath in terror and amazement that so large a creature could be part of me. He was obviously unaware of my presence and continued on his way, crawling over my refuge and blocking my vision for what seemed like hours, as the whole length of his body lumbered over it.

At last, the total darkness gave way to the normal gloom of the Underworld. I endeavored to make up my mind what to do next. Plainly, this vast adversary could not be overcome by my puny strength, even when augmented by that of my Teacher-Lord, restricted as the flow of his force would be, by the resistant matter surrounding me. But the fairy power will was still within me, as was the latent laughter which my Teacher-Lord and I had spent so many weeks developing.

❄ ❄ ❄

Eventually I found sufficient courage to leave my burrow, though the sight which met my eyes as I peered over the rim of the hollow nearly sent me fleeing back to my cell. Dragons of all shapes and sizes, from lizards to great, unwieldy creatures twenty feet long, were emerging from a cavern in a seemingly endless procession. This was indeed Dragonia, and the giant was its king. A sigh of relief escaped me: The owner of the enormous head was not my dragon. My terror had numbed my senses: my dragon was, of course, female.

But how was I to find her among so many? "So many," I repeated. Numbers meant safety as I had learned when living with the Hatreds, and later, the bats. I would become a dragon. I continued to watch the procession as it trudged along behind its king. Each member was different, not only in size and build, but also in colour; all those of the spectrum were represented, but in their darkest aspects. Some had sharp talons, while the extremities of others were similar to the hands and feet of anthropoid apes. There were those equipped with webbed wings. All had tails, the length of which varied, presumably, according to their age. Many of them had horns or ridges of spines down their necks and backs.

Eventually they disappeared from view. During their absence, I began to plan the body that I would create for myself with the help of my Teacher-Lord. Bellowing sounds in the distance, accompanied by jets of fire, which crisscrossed the darkness in blood-red streaks, frequently disturbed my concentration, until the tramp of hundreds of feet gradually drawing nearer, told me that the dragons were on their way home. This time the king took a different route and I was not almost smothered by his horny flesh or sickened by his stench. After they had all passed through the entrance to the cavern, I was able to start on the construction of my new form. Not wishing to draw unwelcome attention to myself by inadvertently portraying a dragon of rank, I made the frame about five feet long, including the tail. The colour was mottled, one blending into another in case a particular hue denoted a clan, recognizable by its members. My feet were clawed, my body scaly, and I built an apparatus through which I could breathe and belch forth fire at will.

A small ray of light enveloped my creation, informing me that my reproduction satisfied my Teacher-Lord.

Having entered my dragon body, I peered over the top of my refuge once more, and crawled a short distance, emitting small spurts of fire to test the efficiency of my breathing-machine, before returning to my hiding place to watch the entrance to the cavern. Eventually three very small dragons emerged and scuttled out of view before I had time to take any action. A group of about twenty soon followed, travelling in my direction. When they had all passed, I followed, keeping a short distance behind them, gradually drawing closer and eventually mingling with the stragglers, who failed to notice that an intruder had joined them.

I listened carefully to any sounds that they made, hoping that they would become intelligible to me, as had those of the bats. My only reward was a series of snorts, grunts and the noise of exuding stomach gases. I contributed a few of my own, followed by modest puffs of smoke and flames. All passed unnoticed. To those surrounding me at least, I was a dragon.

After wandering somewhat aimlessly across the desolate terrain, we turned and made our way back home again. The excursion appeared to have been without purpose and I presumed that the unwieldy creatures were merely exercising.

Turning a corner round a large rock formation, we met six other dragons, which obviously belonged to a rival clan. A skirmish took place: Tails thrashed, jaws locked in savage clinches, bodies reared to their full height, crashing down on friends and foes alike. Several of my small companions crawled away and I gratefully followed them. Obviously, the young did not take part in hostile encounters.

The enemy was soon put to flight minus some scales, teeth and claws, but none was fatally injured. I rejoined the victors and we plodded back to their cavern, where I left them.

* * *

Day by day, I followed the same routine, joining groups of various sizes, and I remained undetected. Their lives appeared to consist of long treks across their barren land, without obvious intent, though, at times they stalked prey, which they killed and devoured. But although the dragons were cannibals, they did not eat members of their own clan.

The smaller ones often played together. Jaws clicked in make-believe bites, and claws sometimes caused minor damage. But apart from burns produced by fiery breath from over-excitement, their behavior was similar to that of other young creatures.

Communication appeared to take place mainly through actions: A nudge from the snout, a lash from the tail, or a show of teeth, denoted displeasure. Sharp clicking or grinding of jaws expressed anger. Rolling eyes might indicate a desire for courtship, or could mean an attack was imminent. They certainly had changes of mood but what caused them, I never discovered.

When everything possible had been learned from these daily excursions, which were identical apart from the direction taken, I knew that the time had come to gather my courage together and follow them through the entrance of the cavern, into the heart of Dragonia.

* * *

I'm not sure what I expected, but the scene that met my eyes sickened me. Hundreds of dragons, of all shapes and sizes, were crawling over each other in a heaving, snarling, groaning mass. Those with wings periodically raised themselves laboriously a foot or two before falling with a squelch and a thud on the backs of those below. They bit, kicked, tore, or thrashed each other with their tails. They wound their python-like bodies between and around one another in crushing, strangling coils. Eyes bulged and fell from their sockets, to be swiftly grabbed and consumed and breath came to a choking halt. They wallowed in excrement, made meals of their neighbors, and, to my astonishment, some even slept. These were obviously the lowest form of life, clanless, homeless – the scum of Dragonia.

The group with which I had entered this hell-hole lumbered on, using the struggling, panting mass of filth-smeared bodies as a road, until we reached a less congested area, whence we continued through several other vast caverns until we eventually entered the one which housed the king himself.

He was stretched out on the ground, the tremendous length of his body curved to assume the shape of the surrounding wall. His protruding eyes gleamed with malice and abhorrence for all his subjects. As there was no prospect of becoming a favorite sycophant here, I kept well in the background, from where I watched the procedure carefully. Several of the group were ordered to approach; they moved slowly forward and grovelled before their master. One failed, through no fault of her own, to get her head flat on the ground because of an undulation on the surface; nonetheless she was dealt a brutal blow, which sent her sprawling several yards.

"Have you found her?" I shook with sudden fear; their language of grunts and grinding of teeth was still meaningless to me, but the question was plain. My Teacher-Lord was interpreting and transmitting the king's thought. They knew of my presence in the area. Their long, plodding walks had not been aimless rambles. Each was a hunt for me.

Orders unintelligible to me were then given and I waited in trepidation until the group began to move out of the king's presence and along a corridor to a different exit. Outside, they divided and shambled off in various directions, presumably to family or community lairs. I crawled away to my refuge.

"Fear not. The plan is unfolding." I received the message from my Teacher-Lord thankfully and was comforted.

Day after day I joined different droves of dragons and took part in the search for myself, but I was no nearer to finding my own. I dared not emit seeker rays as Tepi had done when trying to locate his Hatred, for fear that one of my companions might detect the emanations, which could expose me as a dragon with unusual habits. I could only absorb the vibrations of those nearest to me, in the hope of detecting some form of kinship.

❈　❈　❈

On one of our forays I felt a sudden constriction in my throat as we passed one of the many cavities in the rock-face. I paused and opened out my sensitivity, and became suffused all over my body with an uncontrollable quickening of the flesh from snout to the tip of my tail. I began to gasp as memories of the orgies seized me, and only thoughts of Sulic's love prevented me from groveling before the nearest male.

As it was customary for single members to leave a group for short periods of rest or grooming sessions, I quickly detached myself from my fellows and crawled closer to the rock face, feeling both shaken and ashamed. I succeeded in neutralizing the passions of the past by concentrating on Sulic and our mutual age-long love. I had been so certain that my lechery was dead but encasing myself in a dragon-body had palpably vitalized it again.

I crawled through the aperture to be literally bowled over by the same obsessive craving, but this time it came from without and not within. This was clearly a site for licentious practices. A score of dragons cavorted and flung themselves at, or twined themselves round one, two or three others in an endless sequence of lewd exposure and penetration. Their contortions were extraordinary and their length and comparative mobility gave them far greater scope for diversity than the thick-set Hatreds. Their stench, which was indescribable, remained with me for hours. They were much too absorbed in their lustful activities to even notice me, and I slunk away and buried myself in my burrow.

Although nauseated and depressed, I became increasingly certain that this was the place near which I would find my dragon. I ceased joining the passing herds and spent my time gathering power, or apparently sleeping at the foot of the rock face, close to the scene of carnal activities.

After several days during which many groups passed by, a single dragon came crawling towards me. She was nearly ten feet long and moved with an unusual swaying action rather than by undulating her body up and down. Her eyes were bright yellow and flashed avidly from side to side as though searching for prey. Both nostrils and lids were rimmed with scarlet and I watched her tongue ceaselessly flicking in and out.

I tingled all over. Recognition was instant and mutual. We eyed each other warily for several seconds after which she discharged a burst of fire, followed by a piercing howl. Dragons emerged from the nearby caves and positioned themselves in a semi-circle round us, snorting and spurting flames. Fear momentarily seized me. But this was the moment for which I had waited and trained for many months. I stepped out of my scaly body and stood on its head. Extraordinary noises emerged from the watchers; they had never seen a fairy before and were filled with apprehension. Some turned and fled, but most of them stood their ground, glaring at me with their bulbous eyes.

My opponent paced backwards and forwards like a caged animal and I was grateful for the sheltering rocks behind me. My eyes followed her every movement, and I kept her at bay with my will, as she bellowed and spattered sparks towards me with every step. Holding my arms in front of me, I directed the streams of power that passed through my fingers towards the arc of dragons around us. The light was white, a phenomenon with which they were unfamiliar, and they retreated, groaning in anguish.

Moving with surprising speed, my bestial counterpart attacked first from one side and then the other, but being more agile than she was, no matter which way she swung her body, I was able to escape. I knew that her present purpose was to tire me and that she was holding the full blast of her fire power for the death blow.

Each time she tried a new tactic, the watchers honked their approval, then moaned when it failed. They made no attempt to join the affray. Surprisingly, there was a code of honor even among these primitive creatures; a contest between two was a duel, and remained so until victory was finally won.

My dragon suddenly wound herself into a tight coil and unleashed the whole length of her body towards me, with the claws of her front feet poised in readiness to rip me to pieces. At the last moment before she struck, I moved swiftly to one side and she crashed her head against the rocks. But dragon heads, with scales like armour plating, are granite hard and only minor damage was done.

She whipped round thrashing her tail in my direction. This time, instead of taking evasive action, I leapt on her back, clinging to her body with my will alone, as she charged among the watchers and scattered them in all directions. She then tried to dash me against a boulder, but I jumped safely to the ground and it was she who was injured. The unyielding surface, combined with her speed, removed a shower of scales from her side, leaving a bloody wound. While she paused to lick it, I stood motionless before her, my aura illuminating the dragon's head, clearly visible between my hips. I could feel it throb in fearful anticipation of imminent destruction.

A blinding burst of flame entered me. The pain was at the same time, violent and ecstatic. Both sensations slowly diminished, to be superseded by incredible joy. I flung my arms above my head towards the realms of light far away from Dragonia, and from my innermost being there surged a wondrous trill of laughter. It pealed out like a carillon of bells: Wave followed wave as though it would never cease. Indeed, my sole desire was that this rapturous sound would continue to flow forever.

I returned to myself with a piercing scream that was not of my creation. Still in a daze, I looked around me: The watchers had all disappeared, apart from the ends of their tails, which were squirming away in the distance.

Before me, sprawled on the ground, was my dragon – lifeless. At my feet, severed and disgorged during her death throes, lay her tongue. I stood for a while, gazing at this gory symbol, for which I had travelled far, faced unknown dangers and suffered remorse, fear, horror and disgust. No sensation of triumph followed, only an intense relief that this gruesome symbol of a past misdeed was now nothing more to me than a dead dragon's tongue. But one task still remained – to present it to Sulic and beg his forgiveness.

I had won, but I was exhausted. I picked up my trophy and moved wearily in the direction of the wind tunnels, hoping to find one willing to bear me homewards without undue violence. After testing several, I was accepted and even aided by a brisk breeze, which omitted the fierce rotary action experienced on my way to Dragonia.

Again, I encased myself in the water capsule and was transported along one of the fire paths, before dragging myself up the steps on my hands and knees, into the loving embrace of my Teacher-Lord. What bliss to be safe within His aura once more, free from the negative aspects of the elements and creatures of the underworld.

"Have I your permission to visit Sulic?" I asked after a while.

"For a brief period, yes. The gift of the dragon's tongue will finally erase the wound which you inflicted so long ago. After you have rested and replenished your power, you may join him."

❋ ❋ ❋

I fashioned a casket in which to convey the grisly object. It was made of silver and embossed with jewels. In our world, precious stones are bestowed as a reward and visible proof for work successfully completed, or for character flaws overcome. Sulic had earned several semi-precious stones, and I asked permission to add some of my pearls.

"As you two are, in reality, one, that which is yours is also Sulic's. Use your pearls by all means; they will bring joy to his heart."

When finished, the casket was beautiful. The silver was engraved with flowers, butterflies, mystic signs and runes. I lined it with white satin to denote my purification.

My Teacher-Lord then showed me an image of Sulic in a twilight world with some of the sad and frightened people with whom he worked. He laughed on several occasions and the faces of his companions lit up briefly in response. It was gratifying to watch the heartening effects of laughter, having recently witnessed its powers of destruction.

As he moved away from his charges, I followed him at a distance, until he arrived at his modest home, a little hut made of twisted branches, that stood alone on a treeless tract of land. A few climbing plants bloomed round the entrance although there was so little light. I placed the box on the ground and called his name.

He turned, and a radiance lit his whole being as he raced towards me and took me in his arms.

"My love, my lovely love," he kept repeating.

After some of our composure had returned, he asked me how long I could stay. I shook my head sadly; "the visit was granted as a special reward…"

"Reward?" he asked, grinning. "What iniquity have you perpetrated to acquire such a penance?"

"I have brought you a gift," I said as I picked up the box and laid it on the top of a small mound of earth.

"Oh Perima, it is beautiful," he said. "The pearls glow like your eyes."

"Open it." He lifted the lid and drew back in horror.

"Ugh! What is it, Perima, what is it?" He was shaking all over.

"It is my dragon's tongue," I said, and I knelt at his feet. "She is dead. I am purified and am now worthy to beg your forgiveness for the suffering I caused you in the distant past."

He lifted me and held me gently in his arms. "My dearest love, I forgave you long ago. At the time the wound was deep; but since then, our happiness has more than atoned for my original anguish."

"But there is still a scar, even though you are unaware of its presence. My expiation will be incomplete until I know that it has gone."

"How can I convince you that that it no longer exists?"

He thought for a moment. "For you, the dragon's tongue is an emblem of your sin and my sorrow. If we burn it, the last semblance of both should be removed."

We gathered some sticks of sweet-scented wood from the branches that formed his home, and I lit them with fire from my fingertips. When they were burning steadily, Sulic picked up the tongue, and with a final grimace, threw it into the heart of the flames. A spiral of foul smelling smoke curled slowly upwards for a few feet, then losing its momentum, it drifted earthwards. All that remained of my temptress was a blackened patch of soil and a blood-stain on the satin that lined the silver casket. A beam of light pierced the gloom, and when it withdrew, the ground was an overall brown, and the satin unsullied white. My dragon's effacement was complete.

CHAPTER 27

RECOMPENSE

O ur brief reunion was over and sadness overshadowed us as we took leave of one another. Yet, I had peace of mind that the invisible flaw dividing us had now been removed.

I returned to my miniature palace, wondering where my destiny lay. During my rehabilitation, my faculty to enjoy myself had returned, and the training for my venture had been a stimulating time. I loved my Teacher-Lord as no other being. He was my mentor, the savior of my lost integrity and my beloved friend.

After I had rested, he summoned me to his presence. He was sitting in a large hall filled with power, light and love, surrounded by angels and other members of my evolution. By his side stood Augustine. I longed to run towards him, but this was an official occasion, so I remained standing outside the jeweled portals, waiting for permission to advance.

My Teacher-Lord bade me enter, and I moved forward and made my obeisance.

"Welcome home, precious Pearl," he said. "Although every living being on the path of evolution has dragons to slay, when this task has been accomplished, it is always a time for rejoicing. You have successfully redressed a transgression of your past, and by your determination and valor overcome many foes and dangers on the way. There is now one dragon less in the Underworld to plague not only you, her creator, but others who through errors of judgment have become victims of the tempters of the deep. Their insidious power comes not only through their physical presence; their invitations to lust also manifest through the furtive lick of the tongue, that woos the weak into habits which become obsessions. Your dragon is dead, her tongue burned. You are now free from the lure of the Underworld – the desires of the lower body. From this day forward, you will tread the upward path, although this too has dark valleys to be crossed."

"At present you will remain here." He smiled. "That is, if this is your desire as well as mine." My whole being uplifted in a surge of joy. What a wonderful reward for fulfilling a task that was the result of my own folly.

He continued: "The time will come when you will experience life on the planet of Earth. But as you have worked in the infernal regions, Earth's conditions will be comparatively easy for you to bear. But now your reward is to live for a while in this higher level of consciousness. You will learn some of the mysteries of life and know the joy of living in a body of light, enabling you to gain experience beyond your hopes and dreams. Augustine too has earned a period of tranquility after the rigors of his labors in the Hatreds' domain, when you returned the realm to Ra-onus, its rightful lord, and saved and trained the suffering slaves. He will accompany you on your journeys into territories that are familiar to him but unknown to you."

Augustine stepped forward, his aura growing at every step. As he clasped me in his arms, I realized that his robe was no longer made of rough, home-spun cloth, but of rich, soft satin. I clung to him for a moment of true happiness, and when I stood back and looked at him again, I saw him for the first time in his true form. He had grown in stature and his beloved face, which always mirrored wisdom and compassion, was now also beautiful.

I gazed at him in wonder. "Why have I never seen you like this before?"

"Because I was wearing my work-a-day form. It was more suited to those whom I serve and seek to save. A body of light invariably fills them with fear, so I must wear a cloak of shadows to conceal it."

"Go together," said my Teacher-Lord, "and I will join you later." We bowed and left his presence.

"First, I would like to see the place from which you set out on your lone quests, and to which you safely returned," Augustine said.

I held his hand as I conducted him from room to room, demonstrating to him the powers of each and describing how they came to my aid whenever I invoked them. "And now I will lead you to the flight of steps that links the Underworld to this, my present home." I opened the door and stood silent and amazed. It was no longer there. In its place was a scintillating, golden stairway that rose gracefully upwards as far as my vision reached. The words of my Teacher-Lord were now made manifest. My journeys into the infernal regions were indeed over. Even when living my allotted lifespan on Earth, I would still be treading the celestial to the stars.

Augustine smiled. "For you it is finished."

"But what about you?"

"You are a Fairy and I am a Man. I have chosen the path I wish to tread. I have no desire to stay for long periods on the planes of light when there is so much suffering on those below. To help souls to release themselves from the shackles of their errors is its own reward. And when they bestow on me their precious gift of gratitude, I have an undeniable urge to find others who also need my aid."

"Why have I been released from this obligation?"

"It is not an obligation. The universe contains millions of paths, each being there for people to tread at certain stages of their evolution. In reality we all accept our way of life before each incarnation for a man, or form life for a fairy. Many stray from it to satisfy their personal cravings or ambitions, but those who do often find that the alternative road, which appeared so enticing, is in reality strewn with nettles and thorns. The resulting stings and pricks teach them to be wiser next time."

"But you cannot enjoy hearing the cries of anguish and pain."

"I do not like them, but my sorrow alone would not cause them to cease. I am often able, sometimes after long periods of time, to change their screams to laughter. And what greater reward could there be?"

"You make me feel guilty that I have not your strength of character and resolve."

"You have other work to do and you have the will and ability to bring to a successful conclusion whatever task you undertake. You have suffered grievous guilt over a past demeanor. Do not let it continue to spoil your present or your future. Think of it as being banished to the bottom of the flight of steps which now no longer exists, and it will quickly fade into oblivion. Do not waste precious energy on negative thoughts or on ancient flaws in your character which have been rectified."

✻ ✻ ✻

From that moment, my life changed. I was reborn. Although I had been unaware of it, my dragon's head had been hidden in my subconscious for years, haunting me. Now, I was free to lead the life for which I now knew I was destined – that of dedication to mankind, rather than to the plant kingdom or my own people.

Before I began my work with Augustine, we spent many hours in and around my miniature palace, talking. He explained that he did not wish me to be at his side in the Underworld, but to influence through thought formations the minds of those whom he was trying to save.

"We will return to Onward and form a group from among those with whom you previously worked. All must have a profound desire to serve the suffering people on the planet of Earth, and also those who lie in limbo."

"I can understand the reason for their failure, even though it may not be the same as mine," I said. "One is possessed by a madness which cannot be controlled."

"Sadly, the main cure for each is a surfeit, or alternatively such a degree of suffering caused by their addiction, that eventually they agree to be helped. Once death has claimed a soul and he is freed from the confinement of a physical body, he is automatically drawn to a plane of existence that is compatible with his present state of consciousness. If he has lived a reasonably ordered life and has dealt with problems adequately, he will at first find himself in similar conditions to those that he has left Earth, always being given the chance to change his work and environment if he so wishes. But those who have not only failed to maintain the progress, however modest, made during their previous incarnation, but have willfully ruined their bodies and minds by succumbing to their obsessive desires, thus inflicting suffering on other people, will join a group having the same kind of problems. But always within the vicinity, sometimes at first invisible to them, are helpers ready to comfort and eventually guide them back to the place on the evolutionary path which they occupied before the temptations of matter proved beyond their ability to resist.

"To our sorrow, many reject us. They are still firmly in the grip of their particular mania, and will remain so until their misery and disgust becomes too much to bear. Then, and then only will they listen to our advice and eventually allow us to lead them out of the darkness of despair."

"I realize why they so often refuse you," I said. "Did not I myself spurn the pleas, not of strangers, but of a loved one? Reason flees before lust's insistent demands."

"You will be able to explain to your friends at Onward the temptations of matter on inexperienced minds, and how they overpower the true spiritual nature within us all. Many incarnations are needed to bring into equilibrium this pair of opposites, which stand on either side of the evolutionary path."

"Do you never despair?" I asked him. "However many you save, countless others fail each minute of every day. Your task is endless."

"And so is Life. I regard my work as an opportunity to offer a new beginning to those in dire need. Those who have fallen by the wayside often rise to greater heights after rehabilitation, than those who, having completed a lifespan on Earth, show little change to that attained during the previous one.

"Sometimes apparent disasters provide the experience that people need to jolt them out of complacency. War can do this on a much larger scale. Fear and bereavement draw even incompatible people together; they cling and bring comfort to one another in shared misery, exhibiting qualities of kindness and courage previously buried beneath less likeable traits. Not that I recommend war as an ideal method to quicken the divine spark within. It is man-made, caused by the greed and lust for power of the few, leading to the suffering of the many. But spare some pity for the few; their eventual retribution will be far greater than the mental and physical wounds inflicted on the unwilling participants in these gigantic games of destruction.

"There is only one true conflict – that between good and evil. When that has been won, a sovereign age will come into being, when each man's higher self will rule his lower self. Then, all will be at peace with themselves, with nature, with one another – and eventually they will become one with God."

❖ ❖ ❖

In preparation for our future work together, Augustine and I spent many happy and fruitful hours in each other's company while we visited some of the regions into which the planes are divided. They are not separate because they interpenetrate one another, but the tasks of those who live there are different from those of either fairy or man. Because their rate of vibration also varies, one must hold the key of knowledge for each region in order to visit it.

We entered the land of music, where the flowers, trees, animals and breeze sang joyfully all day, each note blending with nature's eternal song. We met the angels who inspire musicians whether they practice this art as conductors, composers or players, or those who strive to bring harmony to the lower planes through the glorious sounds they emit, not through throats or instruments, but from the innermost core their being.

In the colour sector, we first basked in a cool, blue light to calm ourselves, relax and dream of World peace and love.

We dived into a lake of sparkling scarlet. Waves of energy conveyed us at tremendous speed to a far distant shore, where we ran together along saffron sands, as though time had mislaid us and we must race the wind to find it again. We arrayed ourselves in fairy green and followed well-guarded forest trails that led to the inner secrets of nature and the mysteries of creation.

The far reaches of the gardens of perfume intoxicated us as we danced from one flower mass to another. The savor of spices sharpened our minds, the powerful scent of the trees inspired us to perform fantastic feats of valor. We inhaled the refreshing aroma of rivers and the swiftly-changing fragrance emitted by the notes of a song. We sampled them all and many more on our endless search for the ultimate essence that will gently waft us through the stately portals of the realms of light, into the boundless beyond.

The element of air revealed countless currents, vibrations and sound waves that had travelled through it for millions of years. The excitement and speed was intense. Thoughts and ideals sent us soaring skyward. Memories transferred us from present to past history down through the ages flashed by like lightning streaks, but in that brief moment its complexities were absorbed and understood.

We observed future creations, as ideas in their early stages gradually become more tangible as they descend into matter, until they finally reach the Earth plane hundreds of years in the future, their birth there being greeted with fanfares of triumph from above, and by honors bestowed on their human "inventors" below.

The realms of mind dissolved their boundaries to allow us to enter. Here form was lost and understanding prevailed. We shed our light bodies joyfully and became at one with dancing sunbeams, swiftly travelling clouds and vast tracts land covered by nature's bounty, all in their ethereal state.

We communed with those who lived there, not in thoughts as with those who dwell on the astral and etheric planes, but in ideas wherein plans were conveyed in all their intricacies in a trice. All shared the minds of the others, yet maintained their own identity. This was true group unity, wherein desires and intentions are identical. Each member was like a beam of light joined to a central sun. The idealists' utopia is indeed a truth, but not alas, on the lower planes. I know, because I have been there as a reward for work faithfully performed, but I cannot describe it in detail now because I am residing in my etheric form, which gives me access to but a small section of my consciousness. The nearest expression that comes to my mind is bliss – that rapturous sense of nearness to the One that we seek to serve and will one day become.

Sometimes we wandered with no prearranged plan, allowing one of the nearby beams of light to select us rather than choosing one ourselves. On entry, we became it, partaking of its quality whether it was courage, determination, compassion or adoration.

Courage enabled us to leap fearlessly into the Unknown. Determination led us ever onwards, although we knew not what we sought. We followed trails leading us for miles through forests, over mountains, across swift-flowing rivers and seemingly endless plains. None went anywhere, but we never flagged, or gave up the certainty that we were being led for a specific reason. Even when we returned to my compartments having achieved nothing tangible, we were sure that, in reality, our journey had a purpose and had taken place according to a plan.

Compassion stirred our hearts to give comfort, strength and love to those in need, until, drained of our natural resources, we floated without will or desire until our power was replenished by my Teacher-Lord.

Adoration is the form of love reserved for the Highest. In its exercise, one enhances and releases the best in oneself, and offers it in all humility to the One, or the aspect of the One that is being invoked, either as an act of worship or as a preliminary to a request for aid to ensure the success of a service one is about to perform.

These rays and many others which we entered and became, augmented our own power and our understanding of their use for our future work. One such beam that immersed us was radiating so fast that minutes passed before our own vibrations began to function at a similar speed, enabling us to sense our surroundings once more.

This time, a building confronted us. It was composed of multi-coloured, scintillating air, its columns intertwined as they quivered upwards to indicate the way that we should follow. This eventually led us to a crossroads with four alternate routes, each with a glittering star at the end.

The first one that we tried was moving so swiftly, that we lost consciousness and found ourselves back where we had started. The second road was so relaxing that we fell through it and were obliged to use our will to change direction and soar back to the crossroads, and decide along which of the remaining two we should endeavor to make our way.

The one we chose carried us steadily towards the star at its end, the light becoming brighter as we progressed, until sight, will and senses were numbed. We were puppets, unable to function or comprehend anything but the resplendence of the force which was drawing us like a magnet towards it. When it released us, we floated slowly back to contemplate the final path.

"What does it all mean, Augustine?" I asked in bewilderment.

"The meaning is that which we find in each."

"I already know that speed conveys, that relaxation is a state wherein intuition can function and that light is revelation, but so far nothing has been revealed."

"We still have one more path. The first three were to prepare us for the fourth."

We entered the last road and immediately my mind cleared. Doubts regarding intellectual meanings disappeared and I stood quietly, waiting in anticipation for what was to follow.

We began to travel at tremendous speed, yet we were relaxed and completely calm. Light surrounded and entered us and I was no longer Perima, but another being. I had dignity, authority, wisdom and understanding. I was the world and its firmament: Eternal time, infinite peace, celestial power, divine love, life – death. My mind exploded. Consciousness fled until, upon opening my eyes, I found myself at home gazing at the bottom step of the golden stairway.

I was Perima once more. Augustine was Augustine, and there, standing before us, was my Teacher-Lord himself, his mind his own once more. But the part he had allowed us to share would remain with us, I knew, forever.

CHAPTER 28
OUR RETURN TO THE FIRE'S REALM AND THE HOMESTEAD

A ugustine and I paid regular visits to the Fire's Realm. At first the darkness of the surrounding terrain remained complete, but the time came when we noticed beams peeping through the overall gloom as though the sun was striving to bring a new dawn to the inhabitants below.

Our beloved Ra-onus always embraced us with tongues of fire, accompanied by gusts of joyous laughter, as he raced his faithful creatures to be the first to greet us. Their chorus of squeals, their wagging tails and acrobatic antics performed for our delight, never failed to touch our hearts.

Then it was the turn of the new-lifers, who had gathered expectantly outside the entrance to the realm. Flames leapt from the ground and rocks, turning the darkness into a riot of sparks, rockets and whirling wheels of fire. They crowded round us, clapping, chanting and dancing; those nearest to us reached out to touch us, and those too far away, kept calling our names.

When the excitement had somewhat abated, they took us on a tour of inspection in order to show us their handiwork, which improved from visit to visit. They learned to make not only decorative furniture out of wood and metal, but to weave wall and floor decorations for their living quarters. They showed us small pipes which they used to communicate with one another from a distance, when they explored the surrounding countryside, and on which they played simple tunes with Ra-eena, to which their companions danced and sang.

The gifts that we brought them added spice to an already exciting occasion. There were bales of cloth which the females who eventually joined the community made into unbecoming, baggy garments and a leather-like material out of which the males cut leggings and belts. We also gave them pieces of pottery for them to copy and the clay from which to fashion them. But their greatest appreciation was reserved for the many brightly-coloured pebbles that we presented to each of them; indeed they valued these far more than the semi-precious stones which they hacked out of the local rocks and incorporated in the 'jools' beloved by the Humanans, and indeed, themselves.

Hard work and Stephen's physical training sessions had gradually reduced their ungainly bulk; their muscles became supple rather than gnarled and they moved less clumsily. As time passed, we also noticed that their muzzles were becoming shorter, their ears reduced in size and less hair grew on their bodies. Their expressions became more gentle in repose and their eyes gleamed with interest when a new proposition was put before them. But excitement of any kind caused them to revert to snorts, grunts and other animal sounds.

They were still cave-dwellers from choice but the atmosphere of the realm gradually changed. The walls of rock, instead of rearing ominously into the sightless, ebony sky, towered majestically over their inhabitants like faithful guardians. The erstwhile reluctant fires, which had cast sinister shadows across the groaning ground, now leapt joyfully whenever the new-lifers whispered words of encouragement when they needed extra heat to temper their metals, instead of hurling abuse and jabbing them with iron bars.

* * *

When we were alone, Augustine and I sometimes returned in time to our sorry sojourn there before the battle, to the ever-present dangers and the Hatreds' brutality to one another. But the ex-serfs never mentioned their previous suffering and we knew that this part of their existence had been obliterated from their memory by the comparatively good times they now enjoyed.

Raoul and Stephen remained with them for many years as teachers and friends. During this time they both made good progress in fire lore under Ra-onus' tuition; but eventually they were replaced by others to allow them to further their own esoteric and practical training on a higher plane.

I have always had a special affinity for Ra-eena and our reunions have brought joy to us both, right up to the present day. She has worked with the fire's subjects through all their phases and body changes. Their intelligence is now that of children of about eight years of age, but their manual dexterity has improved beyond recognition. In their own world, they are renowned for their expertise in handling wood and metals, and their jewelry is no longer fashioned from crude ores, but from silver, gold and precious stones. Some of them even do their own designing.

Today they no longer live in darkness but on the lower-astral plane. They built their own dwellings many years ago, using wood that now bears a profusion of leaves and flowers. The fires, apart from those used in their homes and for work, have gone to be replaced by the gentle heat of the sun, without whose presence they existed for so many years. A large number have come and gone, but the original group have remained as firm and now, loving friends. Children have been born and have reached maturity; and with them still are some of the creatures, and their descendants. No home is complete without one or more of these charming little animals, which are also evolving within the limits of their group consciousness.

The Fire's realm is still a training ground for half-animal, half-human beings, to whom helpers such as Raoul and Stephen give many years of willing service.

✤ ✤ ✤

Ra-eena's life is now tri-form. She still spends much of her time with the former new-lifers, now known as nahums. They have taught her their skills as jewelry-makers; and she not only teaches them music in a more advanced form than before, but has introduced those interested to the craft of making the instruments on which they play. She also aids Ra-onus with those who are learning to lead an orderly existence under his guidance, their love for one another being an undying flame which sustains them both in their lives of continuous service.

All who spend a great deal of time in the lower zones must return to the higher spheres because without light their power fades and must be replenished. During these periods Ra-eena plays music with people who possess a similar talent to her own; and she also teaches those of her companions who wish to learn the inner mysteries of the element of fire.

✤ ✤ ✤

My visits to Tepi and the Anhumans were always days of sheer delight. To witness the seeds which I had been instrumental in planting produce a bounteous harvest, was both heartening and gratifying.

Over the years, they have grown steadily in intelligence and thus in the ability to express themselves; and their homestead became more fertile than ever before. They continued to produce their own food, but they also cultivated a variety of flowers, shrubs, trees and waterfalls in a garden designed by Tepi, using the miniature Paradise as his model. There were also rich pasture-lands and woodlands in which wild-life abounded. Many of the animals were so tame that they accompanied the Anhumans to work, some helping them to move heavy loads and draw their ploughs without being in any way forced to do so.

Nicholas managed his growing population with efficiency and understanding. Many came to the homestead from near and far to learn both horticultural and agricultural skills. Most of the original group remained, but some left the area to form the nuclei of other communities, and transformed their land from barren wilderness to productive beauty.

At first Koog had failed to recognise me but we soon became friends again, and whenever we met, he performed his gnomic acrobatics, which always made me laugh.

Tepi was filled with happiness because he truly loved his work and his charges. The Anhumans' heads changed less than those of the new-lifers because they had always been beautiful and able to express their charm and goodness through their gentle expressions and normal behaviour. Their bodies became like those of well-trained athletes and their mental capacity was similar to that of intelligent country-dwellers who have received no formal education.

My relationship with Tepi had changed at the moment of our previous parting from possessive love to one of great tenderness. On my first visit, I related to him the story of my past misdemeanours, and my hazardous journey to Dragonia.

He regarded me seriously throughout my discourse, his eyes never leaving my face; and as my tale unfolded, I began to wonder whether my fall from grace might dim his love for me.

When I had finished, I awaited his reaction with some apprehension, but he took me in his arms with understanding and pride; and then, with a twinkle in his eye, he said: "What a relief. You are not perfect, after all."

CHAPTER 29
MY FUTURE REVEALED

My Teacher-Lord sent word to Onward that he wished to see me. With joy in my heart I entered His Presence and he immediately drew me into His aura. Bliss enveloped me until He released me; and then He said: "A time of change is approaching, Precious Pearl. This includes good news for you and possibly that which you may consider bad. But, as you know, you have reached a stage in your Evolution when you are permitted to reject this plan if you wish. But the two parts go together. You cannot accept one and refuse the other."

"Tell me about this two-fold programme that I may give it due consideration."

"You are to go to the planet of Earth." As always, when a shock is administered, I contracted; my form diminished in size; my mind froze. Then from the far distance I heard "Sulic will go with you." Immediately my heart warmed; my body returned to its normal size, and I inhaled deeply in relief.

"Our reunion transforms our journey to Earth into good news too," I said. "When do we go and where?"

"To China. Although you know little of the geography of the planet, since childhood you have absorbed the good manners, respect for those more advanced than yourself and many other praise-worthy attributes of the oft-times incarnated Oriental.

"Your home will be with a scholar and his family; his garden is beautiful and his house spacious and richly-furnished. Scrolls of great value both materially and aesthetically adorn the walls, and prayer is part of their everyday lives."

"None of this sounds like a penance to me," I said, my eyes shining with excitement.

"There is much poverty as well as great wealth in the country, as indeed there is all over the planet. Warring factions march against each other; land is seized and prisoners are taken for forced labour; ignorance and misery are rife. But you will be living in a beautiful town, and for many years you will know peace and contentment. But first Sulic will leave the Dark Places where he has lived and worked well over a long period, and you will remain together at Onward while you prepare yourself for this new adventure."

"Am I permitted to break the news to him myself?"

"Certainly, but do so gently. We do not want our Sulic to disintegrate with joy."

I smiled. "I promise to be careful. I do not wish to transport my beloved to China in a thousand pieces at the bottom of an urn."

He lifted me so that I was on a level with his face and he gently pressed his lips on my brow. "Never forget that I am with you always, Precious Pearl. "

❖ ❖ ❖

I created an image of Sulic's modest home with my mind's eye, and immediately found myself standing outside the entrance. The climbing plants that I had seen struggling outside the cabin on my first visit, were now rampant, thrusting through the windows and trailing down the inside walls until his little dwelling was no longer a wooden hut but a bower of flowers.

As I did not wish to disturb his work, I sat quietly dreaming of our future together until I could feel his vibration gradually drawing nearer. I rose to my feet and stood in the doorway so that he would become aware of my presence as he approached. As soon as he saw me, he ran towards me: "Perima, my love; why did you not let me know that you were coming so that I could tell the flowers to brighten their colours and enhance their perfume in order to welcome you?"

"They are already blooming to their utmost capacity under your encouragement and love. We do not want to overstimulate their enthusiasm for life so that they fade from exhaustion."

"If they did so, they would be re-born as soon as you crossed the threshold. Your presence transforms my modest home into a palace."

Our auras blended in love and each was lost in the other for a precious lapse of time. When we parted, we stood and gazed at one another. "How can I ever let you go again?" he said wistfully.

"You do not have to."

"You know that I will never allow you to come and live in this scowling gloom. For a long time you endured the most squalid aspects of degradation in the Hatreds' domain when your light was all but smothered by evil and unfettered despair of those you sought to save. You now perform your work of service to those in dire need from a distance, and are able to enjoy the companionship of those who have also earned the right to live on a higher plane with its comforts, radiance and beauty."

I took both his hands in mine. "Would you be happy with me anywhere?"

"In Heaven or Hell, in the depths of the ocean, or on top of an erupting volcano."

"How about Earth?" I asked him.

"Are you serious?"

"Never more so."

"For me it would be wonderful. The sun shines there; flowers bloom, birds fly and animals play. At least I think they do," he said with a grin. "But what about you, my love? I shall be going into the light of day; but for you, although it will not be the darkness of the damned as in the Hatreds' domain, the radiance of the sun will be dim, the colours pale, the sounds will be strident and the wind feel cold in comparison to conditions at Onward."

"To be together will compensate me for any environmental deprivations we may encounter and our love will carry us through any trials that present themselves. It is not weak like an ailing plant. It is a sturdy tree that will blossom as never before." He held me in his arms and we danced round and round his hut until we fell, laughing, to the ground. When we had regained our breath, he asked: "How, when, where?"

"You will join me at Onward for a while so that the grime and sadness of this place becomes but a memory. When I am working, you can relax or wander round the countryside and enjoy the light and the freedom. Then together, we will visit the house where we are to live."

"But where is it?"

"China."

Sulic shook his head. "I do not know why I asked, because I have no idea where China or any of the other divisions of the planet are situated. What does it matter where we go as long as we are together?" He stroked my cheeks gently. "During my years here, working with these needy people, I have become more worthy of you. I have lost my frivolous outlook on life, but I have managed to retain my laughter."

"Is not this dual power of laughter strange, Sulic? You have used it to cheer, and I, to kill. But then, everything has its positive and negative state. From now on, we will use its joyful aspect only."

"Now that is a promise I can make and know I can keep. When can I leave?"

"As soon as your replacement arrives. You will need several days together so that he or she can meet your 'lost ones' and learn from you how to make flowers grow in this barren land."

* * *

Such wonderful days followed, because: Sulic was with me to share my joy in the land surrounding Onward, where nature bestowed her bounty in unending profusion. Always there were discoveries to be made – sometimes one as simple as a hitherto unknown flower, hidden under fallen leaves, bespattered with dew; at others, a visit with my Teacher-Lord to a higher sphere revealed to us a new aspect of nature's law, or provided an experience solely for our pleasure. We grew as we learned, and our increasing knowledge led to a greater understanding of one another in our present forms.

And then my crown of happiness gained a priceless jewel. Sulic and I were wandering one day in the Miniature Paradise; I looked ahead and at the end of a long green sward, banked with flowers, stood Tepi. I ran towards him and embraced him fondly, scarcely able to believe that we were together again.

Sulic and he appraised one another from a distance until I observed a flash of pink light, which streaked simultaneously from one towards the other and met in the middle. They both raced forward and hugged one another, laughing and shouting with joy and excitement. What a rapturous moment this was for me, indeed for all of us, that my love of many form-lives and my dearest companion of more recent times had now met and loved each other. Tepi had been right; our duet was now a trio.

CHAPTER 30
THE TRIO

We were together for many months. Onward had, of course, been Tepi's home as well as mine, and sometimes when I was working with Augustine and the group, he and Sulic would explore not only the land around it, but the mind of Onward itself with all its riches. Sulic blossomed under Tepi's guidance and Tepi rejoiced in Sulic's unfailing sense of fun.

Both of them became valued members of the community, joining in many of its activities, and Tepi again became involved in the making of thought-formations. His pastoral life had not dimmed his intuitive brilliance and his work with the Anhumans with their inherent innocence and charm, eagerness to learn and desire to please, had enhanced his sensitivity. Several members of the Onward group asked if they could return with him to the homestead for a period, in order to teach them to make simple thought-formations to help them with their work. This offer was gladly accepted and arrangements made for them to accompany Tepi when the time of his departure arrived.

When our many tasks and communal recreations permitted, we spent much of our time blending together; sometimes in order to find ideas for the formations, at others for love. At first my love for both Tepi and Sulic bound them together, but soon they were able to merge without my presence, and during these times they revealed much of their individual natures to one another. Eventually our union was complete and we became another being, androgynous in nature, two thirds male and one third female. In this form I became much stronger than normal, more adventurous, eager to seek, no matter that I knew not what I sought.

In this triune existence, we thought as one, and later when we became our individual selves once more, and related our reactions to our joint experiences, they were identical. Each was the "I" of this being, unaware of the presence of the other two.

✻ ✻ ✻

One day when I was viewing a network of energy-patterns, which were combining with or repelling one another in complex variations, I was seized with the desire to grow. I felt myself expand from two feet to fifty in a few seconds.

Looking down on this inwardly seething mass of undifferentiated matter, I proceeded to use my will to divide and enclose it in outlines. On my right a skeletal range of mountains stood majestically in space. Land with faintly-etched grass and flowers sloped down to a river, within which hung fish in suspended animation. From its far bank, a field of corn, straight and inert, stretched to a distant wood where animals, butterflies and birds posed on ground and branches as though still-born. High above, were curvaceous clouds, presiding over the expectant scene like sentinels awaiting orders.

"Colour," I called, and immediately flashing lights from all directions endeavoured to merge with the partially-formed matter, to be either quickly absorbed or rebuffed according to their congruity. Those accepted spread over the enclosed area, and others that were repulsed, tried another form until all had found a home, some as streaks and patches only after another colour had already found favour. The mountains were basically red, the corn purple and the water golden yellow; grass and trees were many shades of blue, mottled with all the other colours to become flowers, fruit, animals or birds; and the clouds shed a pink fluorescent light against the limpid, green sky surrounding them.

The scene that I had fashioned delighted me and anticipation grew as I gave my next command: "Move."

All the parts of my creation changed places; the earth became the sky – and their adornments annexed each other's function. Flowers gathered together and swept through the air in closely-packed masses, while the clouds crouched on the ground like large, pink birds, sitting on nests. Trees became streams, flowing upwards, and the river erupted in volcanic splendour. The mountains changed into waterfalls, down which birds skidded in joyful games. Animals and fish flew, and miniature stars fell like rain. "Wonderful, wonderful," I cried, clapping my hands in approval, but I was not yet satisfied.

"Music," I sang on a long, deep note, and instantly the air vibrated with sound. The fluidity of their rushing form tempered the normal "boom" of the mountain peaks into a rippling murmur. Breezes whipped into action, whistled through the swaying corn and whirled the trees into a tinkling spray. The flowers floating across the sky no longer emitted their tiny, single notes but sang together as a massed choir. All the sounds, whether muffled or augmented by their change of texture or site, miraculously blended in a pastoral song.

"Perfume," I willed. This time the air was not permeated as usual with individual scents such as the sweet fragrance of exotic blooms, the tantalizing zest of oriental spices, the sharp tang of citrus fruits and the soothing or stimulating aroma of herbs – they were blended together in an all-pervading perfume, which penetrated and vitalized not only my tract of land but my whole being. As I inhaled deeply, a feeling of triumph possessed me while I gazed with justifiable pride on the beauty of the rural scene l had created.

I felt like a young god: the demands of my will, governed by Nature's laws, had all been obeyed. But this was not the main cause of my elation. The changes l had effected on undifferentiated matter had released a spate of energy to be used for whatever purpose I willed. I continued to inhale deeply until the inevitable occurred. The form of the triune being split and became Tepi, Sulic and Perima once more – but the energy remained.

"What will happen to my land?" asked Sulic.

"Our land," corrected Tepi with a grin.

"Without our will to sustain and control it, it will return to its original whirling activity," I said.

"But is not that a retrograde step?" The query came from Sulic again.

"It may appear to be, but in reality the patterns have been subjected to a series of conditions: they have known the solidity of earth, the liquidity of water and the diffused state of air. No experience is ever wasted; the memory is ineradicable and has become part of each of them."

"We must not waste one iota of this precious energy that has been generated," said Tepi with enthusiasm. "Back to the thought-formations. Perhaps we will achieve something spectacular."

"Or something that is really needed," I said.

When we had been working with Augustine and required thoughts to help those in need, they were made jointly by the group. But the time would come when we were no longer with them and would be obliged to rely on ourselves to provide the ideas to combat the problems of those we were trying to help. We therefore decided to appeal to our Teacher-Lord for advice.

He at once granted our request by leading us to what might be described as a thought-bank, where specially prepared concepts on any given subject were stored in different sections. Each had a key thought which must be used before the required compartment could be contacted, in order to prevent the uninitiated from using the contents for undesirable purposes. Each was a miniature world consisting of a single theme, and when we entered one in order to experience its potency, we were immediately affected by its power.

For example, if we wished to control an unruly group of people, we would normally contact the appropriate reserve mentally from a distance, having provided the key thought; but now we were actually surrounded by thousands of ideas, all either suggesting, admonishing or demanding calm, peace, tranquility or reason. As none of us was in a state of excitement or revolt, we quickly became stupefied by inertia; we sank to the ground and would have fallen asleep had not our Teacher-Lord been with us to apply the antidote.

We next entered the section containing varying degrees of caution, which could be used to curb a desire to perform a foolhardy act. Once again, as we were not contemplating behaving in a reckless manner, we were smitten with uncontrollable dread. We shook with alarm as we turned first one way and then another, looking for hidden dangers. We even distrusted each other, fearing a sudden blow or some unspecified act of aggression.

We also encountered a miscellany of thoughts which were an antidote to despair. Tremendous energy filled us so that we could not sit still. Our minds buzzed with ideas, which our bodies tried to put into action. We began to build a house; we ran barefoot over stony ground; streams of emotion caused us to talk non-stop about – in our case, simulated woes until our minds were vacuums, ready to receive thoughts of hope, goodwill and love.

❧ ❧ ❧

After many further experiences, we began to practise what we had learned on mock cases because we not only needed to know which storehouse to open with its special key, but also which of its multitude of thoughts were the most appropriate for a particular situation; and we also needed to gauge how many should be administered in order to ensure that we did not affect the problem to such an extent that another would arise in its stead.

Series of events were enacted before us by life-like figures, to which we could send thoughts at any appropriate time, in order to try to influence the outcome if we sensed that an undesirable result was likely to follow an action or intention of one of the participants.

It is not however possible, nor indeed desirable, for us in real life or simulated enactments to try to change the course of events if a person is determined to carry out an act, however foolish or hurtful to himself or another person. Certain experiences are necessary for each individual in order that they may learn particular lessons, however unpleasant they may appear to be at the time.

In one of these mock cases there was a woman who was prostrated by grief after the death of her husband. We immediately sent thoughts to calm and comfort her, and later we encouraged her to clean her house and attend to her usual tasks. She broke down and wept many times, but each night she went to bed exhausted and usually was able to sleep with the help of our thought-rays.

A friend visited her and suggested that she might receive comfort from a small group of widows and widowers who met twice a week to talk to one another. She agreed to join them and she found that sharing her sorrow and the consoling words that she received, as well as the new friendships formed, assuaged her grief to a certain extent.

The situation appeared to us to be reaching the point when her diminishing despair would enable her to receive some happy thoughts and constructive ideas for her future life.

A man now appeared on the scene for the first time. He was good-looking, kind and anxious to help. He and his wife periodically invited members of the group back to their home in order to wean them from an atmosphere impregnated with sorrow and the constant repetition of stories of personal grief.

This we felt could be the turning point for our patient, who should by now be ready for the company of this happy couple, who were pleased to have her to their house and, hopefully, would interest her in the outside world once more. We therefore decided to allow the actions of these three people to develop without intervention.

They found that they had much in common, and visits to theatres and drives into the surrounding countryside followed. The woman still wept but she was usually able to reserve her tears for when she returned home.

On the anniversary of her husband's birthday she felt depressed and telephoned her new friends to know if she could spend the evening with them. The wife said that of course she could come but that she herself was going out; but her husband, she knew, would be more than willing to keep her company.

As he opened the door, she burst into tears; he drew her into the house and placed an arm around her shoulder to comfort her. She clung to him as the tears rolled uncontrollably down her cheeks. He held her and gently kissed the top of her head. Raising her face to his, she began to kiss him on his cheeks and eyes and finally on the lips, which led to a passionate response.

By this time we realized that we were faced with an unexpected situation. We began sending thoughts of caution and control in many forms, but we were too late. The gentle hold of the comforter had become the fierce clutch of the sexually-roused male.

The woman now went to the house less often than before, and when she did so, the wife noticed that her eyes followed her husband round the room whenever he moved. It was not surprising; he had great charm and many women were attracted to him and cast suggestive glances at him on social occasions. They often laughed together over his conquests.

The woman and the husband met and had lunch together several time a week and eventually he went back with her to her house. They were in love. The secret liaison continued for several months and then they decided that they must either part or live together.

"I can't face life without you now," the woman said. "Your wife is tougher than I am. She will become adjusted."

"Adjusted? After twenty years together and bringing up two children?"

"You will see. She has more outside interests than I. I need you. I really do."

"And she does not?"

"No, no. I don't mean that. But her need is a habit; mine is an overpowering necessity. I have a great capacity for loving and being loved."

Endless discussions followed; although he had not meant to fall in love, the woman had become an obsession. Love is unscrupulous when it has a chance to unfold, and becomes the master rather than a valued friend.

When they eventually confessed their relationship, the wife looked as though she had been turned to stone, and she left the room in silence.

"There! I told you she was tough. Not even a word of protest or anger."

"She is not as tough as you think. 'Courageous' or 'stoic' would be more appropriate words to use."

The husband went to live in the woman's house and gradually he came to terms with his rejection of the wife, whom he had loved for years, for a woman who needed him and excited him sexually.

The bad news came after two months. His wife had been knocked down by a car and killed.

"It was murder," the man said bitterly as he sat dazed with shock and grief.

"Oh, don't be silly, darling. It wasn't the driver's fault. Two witnesses said that she stepped off the pavement right in front of the car."

He looked at her with momentary hatred. "We murdered her and we will have to live with our guilt until the day we die."

* * *

"M'm. It's amazing that such a disaster should stem from a kiss, between a woman mourning her dead husband and a kind man trying to help her," mused Tepi.

"The fact that they were humans and not fairies makes the result predictable rather than surprising. With them, a kiss by no means always remains just a kiss; it sometimes has repercussions," I replied. "Now let us reverse the enactment to the moment when the woman was standing outside the house."

The man opened the door; the woman burst into tears. He drew her inside and placed an arm about her shoulder. She clung to him and then raised her head.

"Stop," I called out excitedly. "I should have been more vigilant." Sulic switched off the apparatus and he and Tepi looked at me blankly. "I should have recognised it immediately. Look at the way she is gazing at him; her eyes are not expressing either sorrow or gratitude – but desire. It is the lick of the dragon's tongue and the man accepted it."

We again contacted the compartment of caution, and as the enactment re-commenced, we set free a stream of "Beware. Beware. Beware." To us, it sounded like the howling of wolves; surely the man would hear it. He returned her gaze and recognised the signal she was sending him; he had received it many times before from other women. Her head slowly sank on his chest, and he let her weep for a while. Then he held her at arm's length and smiled at her.

"What you need, my dear, is a good stiff brandy. Dry your eyes while I get it for you."

The point of potential danger had passed. It is true that for one brief moment she had held a vision of happiness with this man, but she now realized that it was a dream without substance. She sipped her drink and they talked together of her future. He suggested that she might take a course and become a nurse, or a doctor's receptionist. She said she would rather like to take up voluntary work at a hospital.

"I'll really think about it," she promised, "and thank you for your patience and kindness." Their relationship was back to where it had been before the moment of crisis, and the friendship between the three of them continued.

❉ ❉ ❉

One of the advantages of being a fairy rather than a member of the human race when he is living on Earth, is that we need not decide where we are going before we set out on a journey. We can relax, banish all thoughts from our minds and await events.

On one such occasion, we became very hot, and when we opened our eyes, we found ourselves in the centre of a desert.

Not a palm tree was in sight; no cacti nor scrub of any description broke the monotony of the vast stretch of sand; except, surprisingly, a boat. Tepi and Sulic whooped with delight as they raced towards it, scrambled up its side and began to climb the rigging.

I wondered what a watercraft could be doing in this wasteland of heat and sand, and how it had come to be there – but not for long. The surface of the desert began to undulate; waves formed and broke at my feet, covering them with a fine grain-like spray. The sails flapped lazily in a whiff of breeze which wafted gently from behind me; they slowly filled and the boat began to move.

"Come on, Perima; stop dreaming," urged Sulic.

"This is the beginning of a new adventure," shouted Tepi.

I willed myself in their direction, and sat between them as we discussed the possible object of our journey across this sea of sand, and what we might find on arrival. All our ideas were wrong.

We saw a light in the distance which took us a long time to reach because the boat was in no hurry; and despite Tepi and Sulic slapping its sides to encourage it to increase its speed, our pace remained leisurely.

We continued to dawdle until a crunching sound beneath us told us we had beached. The shore was covered, not with sand or pebbles, but with fine particles of fiery-red coral. After testing it with our bare feet and finding it soft and resilient, we scrambled up a slope; and on reaching the top, we saw the source of the light – a domed palace, also made of coral, but this time it was a soft glowing pink.

Vociferous music burst through the entrance and assaulted our ears. Had a revelry been staged for our pleasure? We were all in one highest of spirits and eager to take part in whatever awaited us.

A stream of strange creatures erupted from the porticoed balcony and down the steps to the beach; they were like hard-shelled caterpillars, but instead of moving by undulation they rolled or somersaulted towards us, making cheerful, clicking sounds. They surged past us, then turned and charged the back of our legs. Their message was clear: we were to go to the palace.

Guided by our strange escorts, we passed through the columned entrance into a large, empty hall with an exit at the far end, through which blasted the sounds we had heard from the beach. We hurried towards it and entered the room beyond, where we saw a large orchestra of musical instruments, which were all playing without visible aid. Bows flew backwards and forwards across the strings of violins and cellos; those of harps and lutes vibrated wildly without the touch of plucking fingers. Trumpets blared, their tappets leaping up and down at amazing speed; horns tooted and cornets shrilled. Each ejected piercing notes, which ignored the tempo and tune of the others. Rat-Ta-Ta-Ta; drums joined the discordant sound, their sticks tirelessly whacking up and down as though to prove perpetual motion. Cymbals clashed and the deep-throated roar of a titanic organ split the air, hit the walls and ricochetted round the room.

This must be ultimate sound, we thought – but we were wrong.

A gargantuan crash shook the palace; we turned and darted back to the entrance to discover the cause of the clamour.

A tornado was whisking the beach into conical whirls that whipped round and through each other like dueling snakes, striking, scattering, retreating, then rallying in a raging battle between Air and Earth.

Excitement seized us as we joined in the conflict. Thunder crashed, grumbled and growled, rumbled and roared. The livid sky plunged downwards and scooped up the coral. Forked lightning smote the beach, rebounded and pierced the racing storm clouds overhead. Their instant response was a deluge of fine-grained sand like stinging insects, which spun into the desert-sea, now bubbling and gurgling like the grisly contents of an ogre's cess-pit.

Very gradually, the action slowed and the sounds abated; the wind's voice became a murmur; the black menace of the clouds writhed away to be replaced by fluffy white wisps which drifted dreamily across the sky. The coralloid whirls sank back to the beach and the sand-sea returned once more to its idle calm.

We all took a deep breath.

"That was sensational," said Tepi, his eyes shining with excitement. "I feel full of elemental power."

"I tried to out-roar the thunder," laughed Sulic.

"And I rode the lightning like a fiery, white steed," I added ecstatically. We turned around to assess any damage done to the palace, but there was none. The floor of the portico looked newly-swept; everything was in its place. It was then that we realized that only our minds had entered the storm. We had not in fact left the terrace. Not a grain of sand had touched us. Not a hair of my head was ruffled.

"What a strange experience," said Tepi.

"I wonder why it happened," mused Sulic.

"Come."

We looked in every direction but could see no-one.

"Come inside. Welcome to my home." We re-entered the palace, and at the far end of the hall we saw a figure seated on a throne. As we drew nearer, we could see that he was old and frail, his hands like birds' claws, his feet buried in sand. His foam-white hair hung in tangled strands about his wrinkled face; but his eyes were gleaming brightly and he still retained his dignity and regal mien.

We bowed and waited for him to speak again.

"As you can see, I am a great age," he sighed. "My sea of sand has now reached a stage of almost permanent calm; its movements are gentle and rare – in fact it scarcely stirs at all." His trembling lips cracked in an almost impish smile.

"But I, its ruler, still enjoy a storm. It brings back to me the old tempestuous days when I was young and strong, always on the move, bellowing my defiance to gods and devils alike. But all that is over now – my will has gone. Nonetheless I must sometimes prove that my power is intact, even though it sleeps in the depths of my being. I cannot activate it alone, and so my musicians come to my aid. Normally they play sweet, harmonious airs, which they consider congruous to my advanced, years. But, in truth, they are apt to send me to sleep, rather than bring contentment to my old and weary soul.

"I become bored when peace perpetually surrounds me. A storm stirs my memory even if it fails to revive my languid will." He smiled ruefully.

"Please tell us why we are here," I said. "Perhaps we can perform a service for you."

"You are here because you have enquiring minds. My sea of sand reaches out, sometimes I think into infinity. Many years ago, at my instigation, boats were placed at regular intervals for any curious wayfarer that passed by. Many came, but none had boarded one for years except you. You see, my magnetic power has all but left me; but you are both adventurous and sensitive, and so you felt the lure of the boat in its seemingly unorthodox location, even though you were unaware of its hidden, magic mobility. It is good to have young minds about me to stimulate my withered senses. Come nearer to me. You are right. I have a special favour to ask of you before your own world claims you."

We stood before the throne and we realized that his feet were not in fact buried in sand, but were part of it. He gazed at us in silence as though to recapture something that he had lost. He shook his head sadly and continued.

"When you leave my kingdom, I ask that each of you carry with you a handful of sand. It still has life flowing through it; you will feel it tingle against your palms. Keep it with you in your homes and test it daily. When it fails to respond to your touch, you will know my life is over. Please perform a ritual for me and intone a prayer for the dead."

"But sire, you will not – indeed you cannot – die. You will but leave your present form and become a higher being," I said.

His eyes lit up. "Thank you – oh, thank you for reminding me. I had forgotten this wondrous truth." And as we slithered to the ground; on the throne a youth of resplendent beauty sat, vibrating with energy and radiating power.

He held out his arms towards us. "May my grateful blessings go with you, my very dear friends," he said. "This essential and fundamental truth had forsaken me, and until you returned it to me, I was unable to vacate my aged shell. One day, we will meet again; but now I must leave you to begin my new life, which has awaited me for many years."

The throne was empty and below it was nothing but a small mound of sand.

❊ ❊ ❊

Sulic, Tepi and I remained together for many months – working, blending, learning, seeking adventures and enjoying each other's company. Although we knew that our tri-union was of a temporary nature, when Tepi's summons to return to his work with Nicholas and the Anhumans came, we all felt stunned. At one blow our threesome was split; Sulic and I still had each other, but for a long time we felt incomplete. However, as the weeks went by we realized that, after such devotion, although our bodies were parted, nothing could sever our minds; in fact distance caused our love to grow, rather than fade.

— PART III —
SULIC AND I

CHAPTER 31
THE GREAT ADVENTURE

Our remaining sorrow was eventually assuaged by a visit to the Chinese scholar's house, in which we were to live for many years, and at once we found that we could blend with its aura. The owner was a professor at a university, teaching painting and writing. Many of the scrolls displayed on the walls were his own work; and we were fascinated by the exquisite calligraphy, its many shapes conveying to us far more than the mere meaning of the words.

His students were always welcomed graciously, not only by him but also by his wife, when they sought advice about their work or personal problems, The family consisted of three bright-eyed boys and two little girls, who looked like exquisite smiling dolls. They were always polite to their parents, but were full of fun, and they loved playing jokes on one another. Sulic and I fell in love with all of them and rejoiced that we were to live in such a beautiful home with its erudite master and gentle mistress.

For some months our work at Onward continued, and at the same time we studied the history of what was to be our new country; and through many and varied life-like three-dimensional representations we learned about the human race in general.

The district in which the scholar and his family lived was situated on a hill with a wonderful view of a harbour. Neither Sulic nor I had lived by the sea in our present form-lives, and on our visits to the house we gazed in fascination at the constant movement of ships; sometimes our eyes would follow a particular vessel from the moment it shed the mists on the horizon until its safe arrival in port.

On later visits we made our way down to watch the boats being loaded and unloaded at close quarters. To get there, we passed through very different areas to that of the heights; here hundreds of poor and hungry people lived in overcrowded squalor, just as my Teacher-Lord had warned me.

Both Sulic and I had experienced living in the clinging misery of the Underworld, but here there was not the feeling of abject despair, nor the perpetual darkness. Jokes were exchanged by the loaders; women cooked food for their families; children played together; and the constant movement of large numbers of people at close quarters generated Life.

In our Realm also there are varying gradations of existence but they usually evolve on different planes. The inhabitants of each are there because of their state of consciousness, and not because of any impermeable division of class or intellectual ability. And always there are 'servers,' ready to go to the aid of those in distress.

We decided to visit other fairies who lived in the houses on the hill, to enquire whether there were groups who went to the dock area to alleviate some of the suffering of many of its inhabitants. One and all looked at us in amazement.

"But it is their destiny," they said. "It is all they deserve. Our work of keeping our homes free from demons, joining in the daily rituals and playing with the human children are important tasks. To be on Earth in itself is a penance; we have no desire to acquire extra burdens."

Sulic and I were dismayed. If there were not already groups, we had hoped to interest our fellow fairies in starting one. I had planned to offer to teach its members the basics of thought formation making, and so continue, in a modest way, our work at Onward. We visited every house in the area, but the answer was always the same. All the fairies were stereotypes, following the same pattern of work every day, with no thought for others apart from the family to whose households they were attached.

Later, when we went to live in the area, we realized that their ideas were not entirely their fault. They were but reflecting those of the humans living on the hill, who were mostly rich, proud and uncaring of the poverty and misery that were prevalent at sea-level. But we were more fortunate; the scholar's wife was kind, and Sulic and I often accompanied her and one or two of the children, who helped to carry the baskets laden with food for some of the most needy families, who lived on the waterfront in hovels and boats.

We quickly learned that the atmosphere of Earth is less stifling than that of the underworld, although suffering dwells there also. But whereas 'servers' are ready to help in the dark places, on Earth it is not so, and the people must rely on their own kind for consolation and acts of compassion.

For several months we alternated between our work at Onward and visits to Earth, in order to become acclimatized to its conditions. We lost our flowing bodies for more static ones, and when on Earth our minds were bereft of their ability to make flights to higher planes to visit our friends.

Earth is a school where freedom is exchanged for stability. But because our bodies are made of etheric rather than solid matter, we were still able to travel by thinking deeply of the place we wished to visit, and in a flash we were there. It was not necessary for us to walk or go in trains or cars, unless we wished to do so for the experience.

As the day of our departure drew near, the full realisation dawned that for many years we would be unable to visit or call upon our friends for help or power, as Augustine, Tepi and I had done during the battle of the Hatreds' domain.

Augustine has a large group of humans, angels and fairies, with whom telepathic links were formed on higher planes to assist him in his work in the underworld. They provide thoughts and power when necessary because, until they become acclimatized, the mental faculties of his helpers, when they are working in the dark places, are at a low ebb, and they would be unable to perform their tasks efficiently without this aid.

When humans and fairies work in the lower regions they are primarily there to help those in distress. Their sacrifice of Light entitles them to specific rewards when their work is over, and they live for a while on a higher plane than that of their normal residence. But when a fairy takes etheric form for an Earth-span of many years, whether he works with plants or man, he does so in order to experience life on a lower level than that to which he is used, in order to quicken his evolution. He gradually learns to deal with situations without prompting or advice from above; and those who have constant contact with man by living in his home, endure, through reflection, his pain and sorrows which in our land they know only to a minor degree.

This absence of communication with those on higher planes is one of the reasons why fairies come to Earth to live: to learn to perform their duties regularly with love, without receiving anything in return – no praise, no affection, no encouragement. It is not surprising that some of the younger ones fail to do their work properly, particularly when they are attached to an unhappy household.

Sulic and I were to live in this world, not as emissaries of the angels or our Teacher-Lord, but to test ourselves; to use our ingenuity to solve each problem as it presented itself, and to use our own will, rather than rely, even partially, on that of other people.

But we were not daunted. We had both received good training. We knew the effects that many of the forces could achieve, either alone or when blended together. We were also aware that all of them are present in the Earth's atmosphere and that we could harness them for whatever purpose they might be required; their actual efficacy on solid matter would be revealed only when we used them.

When our friends first heard our news, they had commiserated with us, but we insisted that to go to Earth was a great adventure, during which we would learn much about life unfamiliar to us in our own realm. But when the day of our departure came, I confess that, in spite of our protestations, there were tears in our eyes as we bade our beloved companions farewell.

* * *

Our first task on arrival was to build a home for ourselves in the garden, to which we could retire when our day's work was finished, in order to recover from the effects of so many human vibrations, the noise of the children and the perpetual movement of a busy household.

Man's vibrations are different from ours, being denser in substance and slower in action. When we first came into contact with them, it was similar to a human-being walking into a brick wall. We quickly learned to lower the speed at which our vibrations were functioning to bring them within the ratio of compatibility because, if we had failed to do so, we could have been severely injured.

The task of house fairies in a human habitation is to direct power towards and into all its contents, to tend fires, condition the air and water supplies and care for all the plants, of which there were happily many in our new home. Perhaps most important of all is contributing to the well-being of all the inhabitants, from master to lowliest servant.

Many of the scrolls hanging on the walls contained philosophical or ethical concepts, which emitted uplifting vibrations; and to these we added our own thoughts, and garlanded them with flowers from our garden. Sulic and I happily joined in the prayers and rituals, which were performed each day, the entire household taking part. Much power was generated, and enobling thoughts based on age-old principles, were made manifest. These we were able to use in the dark areas near the docks once we had adjusted ourselves to the conditions on Earth.

The two of us were not able to generate sufficient power to help many, so we decided to concentrate on the most deprived, among whom it was normal for several families to live in close proximity on boats and in hovels. Children swarmed, screaming or laughing; domestic birds pecked and animals, squeaking and grunting, searched the floors for morsels of food; street-hawkers extolled the virtues of their various wares with piercing cries; captains of ships barked at their crews; car horns honked; whistles blew; loading gear creaked; porters cursed. The noise continued relentlessly day and night; with music blaring from the open doors of dance halls or underground drinking dens. Everything seemed to happen at once. The sole manifestation conspicuous by its absence, was silence.

After a period of time we were able to lighten a little the atmosphere of the homes of our chosen families, soothe the sick and the bereaved and leave thoughts of a better world to comfort them. I began to teach Sulic to make the thought formations which we wrapped round the ailing children or weeping women. These contained not only suitable ideas, but also the appropriate force for the case in hand. Sulic has none of Tepi's spontaneous brilliance, but his gift of fun and love of laughter were added as embellishments to ease the serious conditions of those in distress.

We were always busy, but we were also happy, being in love, living and working together.

"Sulic, look at me," I said to him one day.

"My eyes rarely leave your face except when we are asleep or working," he grinned.

"Now be serious, Sulic," I said. "Do you discern anything about me that is unusual?"

"I see only that you are beautiful – and that can scarcely be called unusual," he said.

"Look at my eyes." His own widened.

"They are – yes, they are less round than they were," he said excitedly.

"And so are yours." We hugged each other, and after a closer examination we said simultaneously, "We are becoming Chinese."

Up to that time we had given little thought to our appearance because we had been occupied with the novelty of life on Earth. Of course we had given our bodies their normal attention – allowing the breeze to blow through them, splashing each other with water from the miniature lake in the garden, and each dawn we turned our faces towards the Sun to receive His blessing. But now the Chinese race was beginning to mirror its image on our features, and different aspects were being added to the long list of colours and ethnic characteristics that had provided the frames for our inner being in past form-lives.

As we studied one another each morning, Sulic noted that the curve of my eyebrows was changing and my lips were becoming smaller; and I was sure that Sulic's nose was rounder. And then one day, in answer to my query, he said, "Your eyes..." he paused. "Your eyes are like carnation buds waiting to open and find a new world."

Can you wonder that I love him?

We then decided to change our clothes to match our features, and we copied those of the scholar, his wife and their friends. At first we laughed at the novelty of our new appearance, but we soon became used to occupying and seeing our Chinese bodies, and we no longer thought about those in which we had lived before our transformation.

We spent many happy years, tending the possessions of the scholar and his wife, and helping the poor people who lived in the dock area of the town. We were indeed fortunate to have such an affectionate household in which to live; apart from those used to discipline the children in a gentle way, few severe words were ever passed between the members of the family or their servants, although sometimes the latter quarreled in their own quarters.

The scholar, as well as being a teacher and writer, was also a landowner with an estate in the country, which the family visited several times a year. These were especially enjoyable periods when we wandered in their large garden and through the fields and woods beyond. Watching the children ride their ponies, and accompanying the family when they had picnics with friends, delighted us too. We also welcomed the opportunity of studying the peasants in their own environment. Although they were poor, there was neither the squalor nor near-starvation that we had found in the towns. Their lives were simple, and they still followed the code of conduct of the old tradition by showing respect for their master and mistress. Visits from the children were always welcome, not only because they took presents with them; it was considered an honour for any member of the family to enter their homes.

∽ CHAPTER 32 ∼
THE ADVENT OF CHANGE

When we were resident at the town house, Sulic and I used to visit the harbours up and down the coast. We enjoyed exploring the modern cities, their transport facilities varying between bicycles, miniature man-drawn carriages and up-to-date power-propelled public and private vehicles. The shops, both large and small, with their variety of goods, intrigued us, but best of all we loved the beautiful temples, and when religious services were taking place with sacred songs intoned or chanted, we blended our love and praise with that of those assembled there.

But as the years passed, changes occurred – to us, unpleasant ones. Tension agitated the atmosphere among the crowds in bazaars and market squares. Previously they had been cheerful places, with vendors wooing customers, and buyers wandering from stall to stall seeking the best bargains. But now speakers harangued the shoppers, waving their arms as they yelled acrimoniously in harsh, bitter voices. Most paid scant attention to them, although a few gathered round, asked questions and encouraged them.

There were also student demonstrations with much flaunting of banners and shouting of slogans. At first the marchers were good-humoured, as though they were enjoying airing their objections to whatever had earned their disapproval; but as time went on, the crowds became unruly; they broke ranks and hurled stones and abuse when conflicting factions made their opposition to their views clear.

In the larger towns it was not only the students who demonstrated; masses of workers met, indulged in tirades and ran wild in the streets. Red flags were waved by some, the national colours by others; there were also groups who wore uniforms and carried different banners or emblems.

Visits by the family to our own small town for pleasure became barred. The three older children went to school, and the servants who escorted them came home with tales of violence they had witnessed, too often to be ignored. Serious discussions took place between the scholar and his wife to decide what they should do.

Although it was not holiday time, trunks and suitcases were hurriedly packed, not only with clothes and the usual necessities, but with jewellery and some of the smaller, more fragile pieces, such as jade, china and silver. In a short time the family, including some of the servants, moved to the country estate, leaving the scholar at the town house to continue his teaching.

The children were delighted at this unexpected change in routine; particularly those who were at school. After they had settled down, they protested when a tutor and governess were engaged to give them lessons; and they received an unusually stern admonishment from their mother – this was not a holiday, and the move had only taken place because of unrest in the town.

Sulic and I could detect no apparent difference in the attitude of the peasants towards the family. The scholar was a good landowner and left the running of the estate to a manager, who had once been a labourer. His master had educated him, not only because of his special love for the land, but also because he showed an aptitude for improvisation and ability to get on well with his fellow men.

All went well for about three years; then strangers appeared on the village streets. They called regular meetings, at which much shouting and shaking of fists took place. Naturally, there had frequently been arguments between the peasants concerning the behaviour of their respective masters, and the different methods employed to run the farms, but these had been on a minor scale; now the quarrels were long and bitter.

Not all the landowners were as considerate as the scholar, nor as efficient as his manager, and there had been a certain amount of jealousy because of the comparatively good living standard of our peasants. Gradually, the troublemakers gathered round them an ever-increasing audience, whose discontent was skilfully fostered. Fields of corn were set on fire and out-buildings were burned. Many of the landlords were insulted or attacked with sticks and stones; and one was murdered.

Dismay swept over us. We could understand that rebellion should take place in the towns where there was so much over-crowding, squalor and poverty, but here, where the sun shone on the bountiful countryside, and nature revealed her many, enchanting aspects through the ever-changing seasons, it seemed impossible.

In the past, other landowners and their families had often visited our house for good conversation, meals, music and general entertainment.

They continued to come but for a different reason – to plan revenge on those who had injured or reviled them.

The local militia was called in; they roamed the streets and fields with little supervision, and many people were killed. Our own peasants were warned by the manager to work only within easy reach of their homes. He organised a force of scouts, which took turns to scan the countryside, and at the first sign of soldiers in the area a warning was passed to the other peasants, and they either went home or hid until the danger had passed.

One day the scholar returned unexpectedly and after a long, earnest discussion with his wife, the packing began once more. This time, not only clothes, valuables and possessions especially precious to the children, were gathered together, but furniture and all the scrolls from both the town and country houses were prepared for what was obviously a long journey. A fleet of motorised transport arrived, and the family, servants, and of course Sulic and I, set off in vans and trains.

During the journey, we moved between those traveling by rail and their property by road, making sure that all was well. An air of sadness descended on the scholar and his wife, who had been forced by fate to leave both their homes in which their children had been born and much happiness enjoyed.

In contrast, the children were filled with excitement at the prospect of living in a different part of their vast country. But after two days the ever-changing landscape passing by the windows lost its magic, and they became bored and quarrelsome. It was therefore a relief to us all when we arrived, weary and disheveled – and apart from Sulic and me, with somewhat frayed tempers – at the hotel where we were to stay until the furniture arrived.

Once we had settled in, life became much as it had been when Sulic and I had first come to Earth. A prayer room was lovingly decked with some of the many scrolls, and the ritual accessories were displayed. Soon we were able to establish an atmosphere of felicity, peace and spiritual devotion.

The scholar had been allotted another teaching post and the children once more attended schools. With the family routine following its normal course, Sulic and I began to revisit the coastal towns in the East, which we had so much enjoyed exploring. But now the happiness of the past was erased by incessant battles, both physical and mental, taking place between opposing political parties intent on gaining supremacy over the population.

One day we became aware of a different and possibly greater peril as we gazed out to sea from one of the large harbours. Warships appeared on the horizon, and as they came slowly but inexorably nearer, we recognised the rising sun on the flags. We, who loved this symbol of enlightenment and often welcomed the reality as the herald of a new day, now knew it also as the harbinger of death by fire. We watched their arrival in fearful fascination, not for ourselves, but for the people among whom we lived and had come to love, in spite of our inability to understand their belligerence towards each other, leading to the slaughter of thousands of their own race.

Hoards of troops landed in small, swift boats, stormed the beaches and climbed the harbour walls. Guns roared and rifles cracked from besiegers and besieged, and after a vicious battle, part of the town fell to the enemy, who only withdrew after the Chinese had inflicted heavy casualties.

It was as though we ourselves had been invaded; sorrow filled our hearts and almost overcame us. Despite our knowledge of the higher forces, on Earth they were potent only when applied to individuals or small groups; the masses remained impervious to our constant endeavours to stem the flood of hatred continually released throughout the country.

At least part of our reason for coming to Earth was being unfulfilled; we were learning about human nature, its inconsistencies, its sudden passions, its overwhelming desire to possess and its ill-advised determination to liberate itself from the past by spurning not only the bad, but also the good.

The inspiration received by countless people from the religious and philosophical teachings, its often–admirable codes of conduct and its production of works of art of great merit and beauty, were being rejected along with the illiteracy, overwork and poverty of the masses.

In spite of our disillusionment concerning the minds of men, we were still drawn to the East in order to witness with sadness the disintegration of moral and civil law. By this time the food queues had become longer and the population thinner, and a haunted look of near-despair stared apathetically from many eyes.

On one of our visits, we noticed great activity taking place in one of the universities and its precincts. Thousands of students were packing their meagre belongings, and they began to walk towards the north in order to escape from both the invaders and their own countrymen, loyal to the nationalist cause.

We paid intermittent visits to the slowly-moving mass of struggling humanity on this desperate journey to find freedom of thought. Many died of starvation and exhaustion on the way, and years rolled by before they reached their destination – another university, which harboured sympathisers with similar ideals.

ᘙ᠎ CHAPTER 33 ᘙ᠎
HAPPINESS, DISCORD, HORROR

A t home we were enjoying a period of great happiness. The elder
daughter was in love with a fellow student; it was beautiful to
watch them as they embraced and planned their future, filled with
delight in each other, and oblivious of the strife afflicting much of their
stricken land. Sulic and I rejoiced with them for youth needs time to dream
before reality takes the reins and drives towards the pitfalls, frustrations
and sorrows inexorably lying in wait for travelers on life's road.

At about the same time the eldest son reached the age when he would
soon be called to serve as a conscript. After many discussions with their
respective parents, he and two fellow students decided to become full-time
soldiers. Everyone was pleased with this decision because the regulars were
likely to receive better treatment than the conscripts, who often had to
fight on insufficient food and be led by ill-trained officers.

The marriage was arranged to take place shortly before the three young
men would be leaving to join their units, and the sadness of their departure
would thus be tempered by the excitement of the wedding. In the past, the
period between the engagement of the young couple and their marriage,
would have been much longer. But who knew what might happen during
the following month, or even next week?

Preparation took place in an atmosphere of happiness and sorrow
combined for the parents, who were to lose both a son and a daughter
from the close-knit family circle. The day itself proved to be as festive as the
dwindling food supplies and general austerity permitted. Teachers, new
friends and fellow students of all the children came to watch the ceremony
and enjoy the music, dancing and refreshments that followed. For a few
hours everyone was happy; then on the following day the three young men
departed, their spirits high at the prospect of this new adventure.

Although we understood the likelihood of becoming involved in strikes,
skirmishes, or worse, Sulic and I still periodically travelled eastwards to
share the suffering of the people.

As we roamed round the town from which we had watched the warships' approach, followed by the entry and final dispatch of the enemy troops, we once more felt the vibrations warning us of yet another battle. We sent out seeker-rays to discover the direction from which the danger was coming; this time it was from the land and not the sea. Planes screamed overhead, and the air crackled around us until our auras quivered with shock and strain. As the enemy swarmed into the outskirts of the town like soldier-ants on one of their ruthless marches, we fled before our bodies succumbed to the blast of the guns.

When we had partially recovered, we felt ourselves being inexplicably drawn back to the doom-stricken city, as though by a magnet too potent for our rational minds to resist. We knew that we were powerless to prevent the slaughter or lessen the terror of the civilian population, but for some reason unknown to ourselves, we had to experience this moment of indiscriminate pillage, rape and carnage in our country's history.

As we gazed in horror at the sight of corpses sprawled in grotesque attitudes in tangled heaps on the ground, my extra vision opened and I saw the etheric bodies of those who had died. These ghostly forms were weeping as they clung to one another, some in relief, others in fear. Among them were the shining rescue team, talking, comforting and giving their power to soothe their state of shock. After a while, they began to lead them away on the journey from Earth to the plane of adjustment where, in due course, the 'dead' are divided into categories, depending on the success or failure with which they have fulfilled their allotted tasks during their recent incarnations; all circumstances are taken into account, including that of premature death, so that the scales of justice are equably poised.

My extra-vision then revealed something which seemed to be hidden from the guides. Some of those killed had been blown to pieces by bombs or big guns; not only had their bodies of flesh and blood been destroyed, but the etheric sheath, the link between Earth and the next plane of existence, had also been demolished. But, scattered about the town were their divine sparks; some were buried under fallen masonry, others were poised on branches of trees, or floating on the sea.

"Stop!" I called, but the helpers were so intent on their tasks of comforting the 'dead' that they were leaving behind countless precious sources of life.

We lifted our arms towards the blackened, smoke-masked sky, and for the first time since our descent to Earth, we called on our Teacher-Lord. A beam of light enveloped us, and, illumined by its radiance, we ran after the retreating figures.

"Stop!" I called again but, although some of the rescuers paused, they still could not see us. Then one stepped forward. "What is it that distresses you, little ones; these people are safe in our care."

"You have left many behind," I said. "They have lost their etheric bodies; only the divine sparks remain. Some are buried under the rubble; others are submerged in the sea."

She smiled. "Thank you for telling us. We are not yet able to discern those whose bodies are not mainly whole, but others will come who have this vision and they will gather the sparks, I promise you."

With relief we returned home, and this time we decided that, as all the dead were being lovingly cared for, we would be better employed trying to brighten the lives of those whom we had come to Earth to serve.

Memories lingered for months, but our love for one another healed the wounds inflicted on our minds and spirits as we became reabsorbed in our simple household tasks. We also continued our study of healing rays, and constructed simple thought forms with which we helped the young ones at school.

After a short period of comparative peace, another blow fell. Many of the original marchers, whose progress Sulic and I had followed from the east to the north, and other more recently-enrolled students, were forced by the presence of the enemy to leave their university, and after another journey, they began to filter into our relatively quiet town. As their numbers grew, thousands of them settled and a new university was founded there.

They were all revolutionaries and their ideas infiltrated the schools as well as the colleges. Our own children demanded that prayers should cease and the scrolls be removed from the walls, otherwise the whole family would be reported to the authorities as insurgents. The scholar patiently pointed out that it was the newcomers who were the dissidents. He was a nationalist and a traditionalist.

Sad days followed. When their student friends visited the young ones, instead of gathering in the sitting-room, as they used to do, to play card games, listen to the phonograph, make jokes or debate salient points in their studies, they retired to their own rooms. Their faces were grim as they discoursed on the uselessness of religion; the old customs, including the beautiful rituals, were all considered decadent and had no place in the new China, which was for the masses and not the elite. All must conform, or take the consequences. Youth was the key to the new order which would be formed with China's example inflaming the peoples of the world to rebellion and victory.

We did our best to calm frayed tempers when arguments took place between the second son and his father. The two younger children still loved their parents and at this time supported them, although they were also captivated by the image of a new China rising from the ashes of the past through an incongruous alliance of bloodshed and high ideals.

Life continued far from smoothly, but somehow their troubles strengthened our love for all members of the family, whatever their views. Then suddenly the atmosphere changed; packing started again and the disgraced scrolls were once more tenderly wrapped and placed in crates.

Arguments became rife and tears were shed as we stood by, helpless to influence the inflexible opposition of unbending wills in this family contest. The second son was now joined by the younger daughter in determination to stay at the university, live with fellow students and if necessary, earn money to do so by performing menial jobs in their spare time.

When the day of departure came, only the youngest son travelled with us, the other two, now with tears in their eyes, looked very immature and vulnerable as they waved us goodbye. Our destination proved to be a large town, teeming with foreign troops. Yet another flag, this time with stars and stripes, was added to the many that we had seen, waving in the breeze like gaily-coloured flowers that always bore in their centre the seeds of death.

The scholar had now forsaken his profession as teacher to become an interpreter. A pleasant house was allotted to us, and all the old treasures again displayed their beauty boldly in the light of day. Prayers were held openly, instead of clandestinely, and laughter was heard once more. The scholar and his wife were inwardly sad at the loss through love, duty, or political beliefs, of four of their five children, but their devotion for one another comforted them and outwardly they were calm.

Provisions were plentiful once more; the foreigners were entertained in the Chinese fashion, and hospitality was returned with mountains of strange food and alcoholic drinks. The scholar and his wife partook of the latter but moderately, and were good-humouredly chided by their hosts for their abstemiousness, but they remained firm and their wishes were respected. Many new friendships were formed with the foreigners, who were eager for knowledge of "your quaint old customs," and naturally the other Chinese interpreters and their families gathered together on many occasions.

Sulic and I frequently visited the two young people now living their own lives at the university and their married sister close by. Revolutionary songs were an essential part of college life, and slogans were shouted in high-pitched voices with near-frantic fervour on every possible occasion. Some of the students were more interested in joining the frequent demonstrations rather than pursuing their education, as our two were. They and a few of the more conservative teachers were constantly bullied and derided for their lack of enthusiasm for the new order.

The countryside often beckoned us and we floated dreamily over sweet-smelling grass and trees, our arms entwined. Soft warm breezes caressed us as we soared above woods and fruit-laden orchards, bestowing upon us a fleeting joy before our reluctant return to the tall, rigid buildings and hard surfaced streets where we lived.

Sometimes we watched the peasants at work, reminding us of happy days spent on the estate during school holidays. In sharp contrast to their comparatively peaceful occupations, we also saw batches of conscripts chained together preventing their escape. So great was their reluctance to leave their villages that many of them had to be dragged along at gunpoint until they dropped from exhaustion.

CHAPTER 34
THE TWO-FOLD
OBLITERATIONS

One day Sulic and I were sitting quietly at home, reminiscing on our many form lives together, and alternately planning our future when our present Earth-span was over. Onward lived ever in our hearts, and we dreamed of reunion with our many friends there, and of resuming once more our training and work with our Teacher-Lord and Augustine. How we missed them both.

The air vibrated violently. So great was the agitation we feared the house would collapse around us, but unbelievably it continued to stand. A tumultuous noise assailed our being, as though opposing armies of the thunder gods were locked in immortal combat, with the underworld exploding to incite them. Petrified, we clung together for a split second before fragmenting through chaos, into negation.

A single thought flashed then fled. Others darted hither and thither like dragon-flies on the wing.

One hovered and remained "I exist."

"Who am I?"

My mind sobbed, "Where am I?"

Darkness imprisoned me. I was blind and deaf. A latent faculty revised, and I experienced a pale spectre of the blast that had torn my mind and body to shreds.

A minuscule movement flickered … my divine spark was with me… I was Perima! Like a tiny intake of breath, I felt the spark draw towards it atoms, with which to clothe itself. The life force suffused my being and intelligence slowly returned. Stroking the rug on which I lay, I was vaguely aware of servants' voices in the adjoining room.

Terror seized me like a demon's fist.

"Sulic," my voice emerged as the faintest whisper.

"Sulic… Sulic…. Sulic," I called in a rising crescendo, as desperation transformed the whisper into a piercing scream. There was no answer.

I ran, weeping, from room to room, searching behind and under any object that could hide him. Eventually, my eyes were drawn to the top shelf of a cabinet, and there among the priceless porcelain and carved jade, I saw it. Rising to its level, I tenderly poured my love on the shining spark. The core began to pulse and, with a tiny sigh, it became Sulic-in-embryo. I enfolded him in my arms like a mother her child, and his form slowly returned.

He opened his eyes and gazed at me blankly; as his torpid memory returned, I felt him stiffen.

"What happened? What was it?" he asked in a quavering voice.

"I do not know; it cannot have been the end of the world, because the house still stands and I heard the servants talking."

H-I-R-O-S-H-I-M-A. The sound reached me as a prolonged and angonised groan. What did it mean?

Sulic and I remained in a semi-daze for we knew not how long, before the effects of the horror began to recede. We considered traveling to the centre of the turbulence in order to solve the enigma of what had erased us both, yet had left the people of the town unscathed.

We began to shake. Stark fear clutched us as we gazed at each other in disbelief. Then, as a deliberate act of will, we dissolved our bodies but retained our consciousness. As two sentient entities clothed in light we clung together, indivisible as cosmic twins. Gargantuan waves of devastation struck us, but were powerless against immortal reality – the eternal fragment of life possessed by every single being.

We experienced a massive shock, but our awareness remained intact. Instead of death the liberator releasing souls from bondage after their allotted span on Earth, with my extra vision I witnessed from afar, science, in the role of a heinous tyrant, assigning extinction to the body of young and old, innocent and guilty, strewing the ground with debris from collapsed buildings and scattering the scorched earth with the jagged remnants of human and animal flesh. But amid this apparent holocaust, I could also see thousands of sparks triumphantly shining as they lay unscathed amidst total ruin.

We waited until the convulsions abated and once again we re-formed our bodies, to find the house intact and the servants performing their usual tasks.

CHAPTER 35
THE FINAL DISSOLUTION

These dual horrors led to an increase in troop movements not only in the town and its surroundings but all over the country. The Rising Sun had set and we were no longer at war with aliens, but the battle in men's hearts was still raging.

Sulic and I again visited the married daughter and two young ones at the university in the west. We watched the inevitable uprisings and demonstrations against the influx of government troops and officials in the area, during which students were brutally attacked and fired upon, but the three dear to our hearts were still safe, as was the eldest son far away in the east.

With armed riots taking place all over the country, we yearned for peace but could find it nowhere. Insurrection had spread from the towns to the countryside and now, there seemed no ditch or hole in the ground where the nefarious vibrations of hatred, fear and power-infatuation could not find us. No-one could feel safe as the different political parties struggled for power.

We listened to the scholar and his wife as they talked endlessly together. Finally they decided to leave the military base where they had been comparatively happy and return to their country estate in the east in order to protect what remained of their land, and to find out how their peasants had fared in their absence. Once again packing commenced and another journey was undertaken.

On arrival, they found, to their relief, that the house had been well cared for, and the manager had performed his duties faithfully. Much of the land had been given to the peasants by the government, and most of them seemed satisfied with their new-found "wealth." But others, all over the country, were not so easily appeased. Many of them had worked for overbearing and even cruel landlords, and once divided among many, even the big estates failed to yield more than a modest living for the new owners. Constant visits from outside revolutionaries, who urged the peasants not only to demonstrate but to seek revenge on any landlord who still owned a house, ensured that many were humiliated and a number of them killed.

The scholar seemed satisfied with what, up to that time, were his legal rights, and he remained at home; writing, painting and attending to the needs of his peasants, whether they still worked for him or not.

To their sadness, the youngest son, who had come east with them and was now attending the university where his father had once taught, was rapidly absorbing the revolutionary dogma, taking part in demonstrations and waving the red flag with enthusiasm. But he still loved his parents, although when be was at home he refused to join them in the prayers and rituals which took place once again in secret.

News of another form of disruption in the village soon reached us. This time, the peasants were not being urged to attack the landlords; the target was the landowners themselves. We were all filled with apprehension because these trouble-makers were not rabble-rousers but officials.

When they came to the house, they entered brusquely, without permission and demanded to see the scholar. Although a traditionalist, he had never actively supported any of the rival political parties; but this was not the crime of which he was now accused: he had worked for a foreign country.

He pointed out to them that the foreigners had been on Chinese soil not only with the approval but at the invitation of the government in power.

"They are no longer in power," was the curt retort, and without giving him a chance to defend his actions, they dragged him into the garden. Then they shot him. We all screamed and his wife tried to break away from those who held her, but she was denied even the solace of weeping over her husband's blood-stained corpse. She was roughly pushed into the house and locked in a room while the peasants, who had gathered round, were ordered to dig a hole and bury him.

Sulic and I were stunned. He whom we had come to Earth, to serve and whom we had learned to love was no longer in the flesh. He could not comfort his distraught wife, although we could see him in his etheric body trying to do so; and she was unable to hear the words of encouragement that he spoke before being led away by those who came to fetch him.

We were not allowed to mourn for long. Officials were in and out of the house all day, listing its contents; articles that to us were beautiful were considered decadent, and were taken outside and either smashed or burned.

The house was soon taken over by other administrators and used as a headquarters for the division of the remaining land among the peasants drafted from poorer districts. The scholar's wife was allotted one of the smallest dwellings on the and she was also permitted to keep a patch of the land she had once owned. Some of the peasants' wives and their children, remembering her past kindness, helped her to remove the rubbish left by the previous tenants. They then scrubbed and cleaned the two rooms, while their husbands carried out modest repairs, making them at least habitable. She now had a roof over her head but only bare necessities, such as a mattress and a few pieces of rough hewn furniture remained as her sole possessions.

As she had always supervised her servants, she knew how to sweep and clean, but she had no experience of tending the soil. Once again the peasants came to her aid and not only dug and planted her plot of earth, but provided her with fruit and vegetables until it was ready to yield.

News travelled slowly, and it was several weeks before her soldier son came to see her. He stood in the doorway, horrified at the sight that met his eyes. "Mother, oh Mother, what have they done to you? You are so thin. And this wretched hovel. Where is all our beautiful furniture?"

"Your father was a traitor," she said – ironic for the first time in her life. "Much was burned or otherwise destroyed: the rest was confiscated. I am a pauper."

He took her in his arms. "You must come and live with us."

She began to weep; "Everything I had and loved has gone. Only the land remains; even though it is no longer mine, if I leave I have nothing."

"You have two grandchildren," he said.

Her eyes softened. "Two saplings with their roots embedded in the new China. They will blossom and bear fruit pertinent to this present age. My roots are deep in the past. This old tree will soon wither and return to the soil which was ours, and which I still love."

"Mother, you mustn't talk like that."

"I would have it so, my son," she said simply.

"What of your friends?" he asked. "Do they no longer come to see you now that your position in the community has changed?"

"They are afraid. I am the widow of an 'enemy of the people'. Sometimes they come at night, but if they were caught, it could cause their downfall."

Circumstances improved a little after his visit; he provided furniture and food and he insisted on giving his mother sufficient money at regular intervals for her to live on. She would accept no more than bare necessities. "If I do, you will be robbing your children," she said.

He also gave money to his brother to visit her periodically, which helped to relieve her loneliness.

She had managed to hide two of the precious scrolls with the aid of a faithful servant; and each evening she took them from their hiding place and gazed at them with love as she wept for the man with whom she had shared her life for so many years.

❖ ❖ ❖

Sulic and I had no heart to travel any more; we could no longer face the experiences that we knew we would have to suffer, so our world became very small.

The wars, both internal and external, were over, but still the contest for power was rampant. We yearned for peace, but could find it only when we journeyed to a clearing in a distant wood and performed our rituals with flowers and leaves instead of the gold and jeweled symbols to which we had become accustomed. And every time we fervently prayed that our future life should be revealed. We could not leave the scholar's wife as she struggled with her grief and the tasks that were alien to her. We yearned to use our talents as we had at Onward, or alternatively to serve, if necessary, in the sub-Earth, where we could help many instead of only one.

We examined ourselves and each other and saw two bedraggled fairies, battered by years of turmoil, with bodies and minds that still bore the scars of disintegration from the two greatest man-made explosions the world had ever known. We were weary beyond measure; all we had was our compassion for the scholar's wife and our love for each other.

We had completed our daily spiritual discipline and were sitting in the wood, dreaming of Onward and the happy years we had spent there before starting out on what we had then described as "Our great adventure," when both of us gasped. Before us stood our beloved Augustine. He knelt down and gathered us in his arms. We both wept uncontrollably and yet, at the same time, a hint of joy stirred within our leaden hearts.

After a while he tilted our faces towards his, and we realized he was more beautiful than we remembered. "Dry your tears, precious ones," he said, and we sat on the ground close to him, so that we could gaze at him and frequently touch him to assure ourselves that his presence was not a dream.

"It is over," he said simply.

"Are we really going back to Onward to work with you again?" I asked, my spirits rising.

He shook his head. "Your Earth-span is not yet finished." Hope wilted and tears gathered in our eyes. "But we will be very close," he added quickly.

He smiled. "Do you remember when I used to tell you about my 'special people' whom, although often unaware of the fact, I guide and protect during their incarnation?"

Yes, we remembered well.

"There is one who needs you," he said softly. We both wondered whether we were capable of fulfilling anyone's needs in our present state of exhaustion.

"She can talk to fairies," he added as though relating a conversational fact such as "She has a garden and likes flowers." We waited.

"She already has a group of fairies round her."

"If that is so, why does she need us?" I asked.

"It would perhaps be more accurate if I said that some of her fairies need you. Those that dwell in her home are beginners in the art of making thought formations." We brightened. He continued, "One among them is potentially brilliant, but there is a dark shadow which prevents his sun from rising, and at times, he is driven to despair."

"Like Tepi?" My heart began to stir in compassion for another who had slipped from the starlit path, or perhaps had not yet begun to tread it.

"Yes, just like your beloved Tepi. We feel that if you can channel his talents into this art at which you yourself are so brilliant, his sun will climb into the sky and his dark side will slink away."

My whole being was taking wing and Sulic's eyes were shining. "When will this be, Augustine, oh when?" we asked breathlessly.

He rose to his feet. "Now," he said. "Your replacements are already at the cottage. Come with me."

And at that fateful moment, Sulic and I, each clinging to one of Augustine's hands, left strife-torn China and came to England, where we have lived to this day with Daphne and her fairies.

HISTORY OF THE FAIRY & HUMAN RELATIONS CONGRESS

By Michael Pilarski, April 20, 2025

The Fairy & Human Relations Congress has a rich and illustrious history, both in the fairy realm and in the human realm. The very first Congress was in the fairy realm and was the idea of the nature fairies who worked with Daphne Charters. It was described in detail in Daphne Charter's 1956 book A True Fairy Tale. The purpose of the Congress was to bring together nature fairies from around the world to discuss the "human problem" and to brainstorm ways of improving the situation on Earth. Daphne was the only incarnate human who attended. The Congress was organized by and for the fairies. Around 1,000 fairies attended and it was so successful that they were held annually in the fairy realm up to at least 1985, which was the last one described in Daphne's writings. They grew in size until hundreds of thousands of fairies attended. It was a big deal in the fairy realm! Daphne's writing on this phase of the Fairy Congress are contained in the book *Forty Years with the Fairies*. We do not know the developments of this fairy phase after 1985.

I was inspired by Daphne's description of the Fairy & Human Relations Congress to organize something similar on the physical plane. It would include participation of physical humans as well as nature fairies and devas (the Devic realm). After a few years of gestation I organized the first physical Fairy & Human Relations Congress in 2001. It was held at the Skalitude Retreat Center in the Methow valley, a remote location in the eastern North Cascade mountains. Skalitude was the perfect place to hold the Congress being an inholding surrounded by National Forest in a fully-functioning, beautiful ecosystem with no other human habitation for miles. Skalitude was owned at the time by Lindsey Swope who had dedicated the property to human and nature spirit cooperation. Lindsey has been an important part of the organizing team up till this 2025 writing.

The 2001 Fairy & Human Relations Congress was superb and full of magic and heart. 125 physical human attended and thousands of fairies.

It was so successful that it has continued annually up to this time. It brings together humans who wish to communicate and cooperate with the fairy realms. It has always been the goal of the Fairy Congress to invite the most experienced fairy communicators in the world to share with us. We have had over 120 presenters over the years including some of the world's most famous. Robert J. Stewart presented at most of our first ten Congresses. David Spangler has presented five times, Dorothy McLean of Findhorn fame presented 4 times. Peter Tompkins, author of the pivotal book *The Secret Life of Plants* attended in 2005 and we presented him with an award. Many of our presenters have written books about their fairy work. Our presenters combined have written over 300 books on the topic and they constitute a repository of rich knowledge on fairy knowledge. Our website www.fairycongress.com has a chart of presenters at the Fairy Congress over the years.

The numbers of humans who attend the Fairy Congress has varied between 125 and 300 people over the years (with the exception of 2020, the year of the COVID lockdown when we had to publicly cancel the event and only 60 of the inner circle attended). We are told that the numbers of fairies and fairy realm beings has increased over the years and they number in the many thousands. They far outnumber the humans in attendance.

What started as an event for humans and nature spirits (fairies and devas of the Devic realm) has expanded over the years to include other types of beings. Dragons started showing up, then sasquatches, star-beings from off-planet. A notable addition has been the Sidhe, sometimes referred to as faeries, who are not nature spirits, who reside in another frequency of Earth. Add in other beings who might be referred to as gods, goddesses and muses and the Fairy & Human Relations Congress now hosts a wide diversity of beings from many realms. Truly a melting pot and a place of negotiation between many earth realms and beyond. There is nothing else quite like it in the world. The humans who attend are delegates and ambassadors. Together we are working for a more harmonious and healed world. Sort of a high-level United Nations. We are doing important work for humanity and all beings of the Earth. Plants, animals, the oceans, the atmosphere, the climate, etc.

Education is a big focus of the event and we generally have 12 to 20 presenters each year who give workshops and experiential journeys. Almost everyone attends these workshops where those who are the most experienced in working with the fairy realms share their insights and how-to with the rest of us.

Besides the serious nature of our fairy work, the Fairy Congress is a lot of fun! We do a lot of singing and dancing. Music and concerts. We hold ceremonies and rituals. We build deep friendships, There are a lot of hugs and laughter. A lot of people wear colorful, gay clothing. We especially dress up for our Saturday evening ritual and fairy parade. The participation and energy from the fairy realms are palpable during this time. Digital cameras capture thousands of orbs in photos. The fairy parade culminates in the Fairy Charge where we line up in long lines and charge across the field as two opposing lines. When we meet in the middle we do lots of hugs. An amazing and exhilarating experience!

Our rituals, ceremonies and fairy work reaches across the planet and affects all people and all realms. We are a force for good on the Earth.

The physical plane Fairy & Human Relations Congress has been held at 3 different venues so far and in 2025 will be held at a 4th and new location. The 2001 through 2003 Congresses were held at Skalitude in Eastern Washington; 2004 and 2005 were held on Hood River at the Riversong Sanctuary. 2006 thru 2020 were back at Skalitude and 2021 thru 2024 were at an Old-Growth Canyon outside of Salem, Oregon. 2025 will be at Twana Springs, near Quilcene, Washington on the Olympic Peninsula. 2025 will be the 25th anniversary in the physical realm and the 60th anniversary in the fairy realm!

To find out more about the physical plane Fairy & Human Relations Congress visit https://www.fairycongress.com

Everyone who has ever attended a Fairy Congress is invited to the 2025 reunion as well as interested new people. Come experience the Magic! Contribute to Healing the Earth!

HOW MICHAEL PILARSKI
MET DAPHNE CHARTERS

Michael Pilarski's (Skeeter) early connection with Daphne Charters was through her book *A True Fairy Tale*. Skeeter, a young man living in the Okanogan Highlands in 1976, had a deep love for nature, which led him to explore metaphysical and occult subjects.

His life was transformed when a woman gave him a book by Daphne Charters, which introduced him to a world of fairies and nature spirits. This book, despite its plain exterior, offered the most elaborate and fascinating accounts of the fairy realms Skeeter had ever encountered.

He was so moved by the book that he attempted to find a way to share it with others, but his search for the author was met with obstacles. The book lacked a publisher or contact details, and after a year of searching, Skeeter finally met someone who knew of Daphne Charters.

This led to a long-awaited correspondence with her which lasted over 32 years. Before Daphne's passing, she gave him permission to reprint the book in the United States. Skeeter's journey to publish A True Fairy Tale was filled with challenges, including a lack of funds, but his persistence paid off, and he eventually managed to print and distribute the book, which became popular among his friends and a wider audience.

NOTE: Those wishing a longer version of How Skeeter met Daphne Charters should refer to the preface in Volume I of the manuscripts – *Forty Years with the Fairies*.

A Biography Of
Daphne Charters

by Gay Burdett
[Gay Burdett was Daphne's niece and one of her closest friends in England. - MP}

Born February 24, 1910 in Berkshire, England.

The youngest of 3. Father: retired army officer.

She had 'the brains of the family' and could successfully, either have continued her studies after leaving school, or have had a career. But in those days, neither option was open to a young girl whose parents were of independent means. Unmarried daughters simply stayed at home with their parents and participated in social life locally.

However, hobbies were accepted. Daphne was interested in painting; and during the pre-war years, attended classes at Cedric Morris' art school in Dedham, Essex. At that time, her parents lived not far from there, near Colchester.

During the war she successfully ran the food office in Colchester (Food offices were responsible for ration books which were issued to everyone when food supplies were restricted.)

Also during the war, she married Jack Charters who was serving as a captain in the army. After the war, they went to Canada where Jack died tragically as a result of being caught in a snowstorm. No doubt it was Jack's death which prompted Daphne's interest in spiritualism.

In the late 1940's, shortly after Jack's death, Daphne returned to England and lived in Colchester with her widowed mother. It was during this period that she wrote her book *A True Fairy Tale*. She also became a vegetarian, which led to her joining 'Beauty Without Cruelty' - at that time a pioneer organisation in the field of cosmetics free of animal substances, and therefore manufactured without causing the suffering of any animals.

After her mother's death in 1962, Daphne moved to London. This gave her the opportunity to participate actively in 'Beauty Without Cruelty.' She became manageress of their shop in central London, and on their behalf, promoted good quality simulation fur coats, by organizing dress shows not only in England, but also abroad.

For the greater part of her life, Daphne was not a physically robust person, and during her latter years she did not have much respite from problems caused by poor health. However, in spite of this, she continued to record, in writing, her experiences inspired by fairies. Unfortunately the last nine months of her life had to be spent in a nursing home where she died on July 7, 1991.

She was wonderfully brave, was always good company and interested in other people, right up until the end.

She once said: "There is only one thing I regret in my life, and that is not to have had a career, because I know I would have made a success of it." And she would.

Daphne was more than a charity worker: She helped many people personally, but always discreetly, 'by stealth.'

- Gay Burdett

Some Biographical Notes on Daphne Charters

by Michael Pilarski

Although I never met Daphne Charters in person, here are a few things I would like to add to the Biography written by her niece and good friend, Gay Burdett. My relationship with Daphne was built through voluminous correspondence, primarily conducted through handwritten letters from Daphne and typed replies on a manual typewriter. Sadly, most of the correspondence was lost in several fires, though no humans were harmed in the incidents.

Daphne, who lived thousands of miles away, became a close friend of mine. She was always excited and grateful for my efforts to share her works with the world. Daphne was an exceptionally kind and gentle person, someone with a natural ability to connect with others and with nature. Daphne had a deep affinity for fairies, which became a central aspect of her life's work. She was also involved in the Beauty Without Cruelty movement, which promoted cruelty-free beauty products and alternatives to fur clothing, a cause she felt passionately about.

Daphne's relationship with her husband, Jack, was profound. After emigrating to Canada post-World War II, they lived on the Great Plains. Tragically, Jack died young after becoming caught in a blizzard. Daphne, however, continued to communicate with him from the "astral plane," a term she used to describe an otherworldly realm where Jack and other deceased humans resided. Over time, Daphne's connection with Jack deepened, and she also began to interact with fairies, leading her to develop a unique ability to bridge communication between the human and fairy realms. This connection is explored in depth in her manuscripts.

Daphne's work was also recognized by prominent individuals, such as Lord Chief Air Marshall Dowding, a high-ranking British officer during WWII, who believed in fairies. Dowding was impressed by Daphne's ability to communicate with fairies and encouraged her to publish her writings. He wrote the foreword for her first publication in 1951, *The Origin, Life and Evolution of the Fairies,* and later revised it for her self-published book in 1956, *A True Fairy Tale.*

Throughout her life, Daphne lived in several flats in London, particularly at Delaware Mansions. She had a garden where she spent time with friends and fairies, and she often sought solace from her favorite trees in the area. As Daphne aged, she faced numerous health challenges but maintained her sharp mind until her passing at the age of 82. Despite her illness, she never let it diminish her spiritual commitment or connection to the natural world.

Daphne never achieved the recognition she deserved during her lifetime, but her work continues to inspire people through the publications of her manuscripts. Daphne had worked tirelessly to document her experiences and knowledge, and not long before her death, she requested me to see to it that all her unpublished manuscripts would eventually get published and shared with the world, she said to me. "Now Michael, I don't think they would have had me go to all this work for nothing."